Readers love the THIRDS series by CHARLIE COCHET

Rack & Ruin

D1520394

"A roller-coaster ride of epic proportions, *Rack & Ruin* is a dream... ...g and emotional journey that you simply mustn't miss."

—Carly's Book Reviews

Rise & Fall

"…one of the best books I've read in a long time."

—It's About The Book

Against the Grain

"Every time I read a new THIRDS book I think it can't get any better… But it does!"

—Prism Book Alliance

Catch a Tiger by the Tail

"I love the THIRDS series. It's fun, action-packed, and hella sexy."

—Just Love: Romance Novel Reviews

Smoke & Mirrors

"If you aren't reading this series, well, you absolutely should be. And I, for one, have no qualms about recommending it to you."

—Joyfully Jay

Thick & Thin

"This series has always amazed me and the amazement continued when reading this one…"

—Three Books Over the Rainbow

By CHARLIE COCHET

Between the Devil and the Pacific Blue
Beware of Geeks Bearing Gifts
Healing Hunter's Heart
A Rose by Any Other Name
The Soldati Prince

THE AUSPICIOUS TROUBLES OF LOVE
The Auspicious Troubles of Chance
The Impetuous Afflictions of Jonathan Wolfe

DREAMSPUN DESIRES
#7 – Forgive and Forget

NORTH POLE CITY TALES
Mending Noel
The Heart of Frost
Vixen's Valor
Loving Blitz
Disarming Donner

THIRDS
Hell & High Water
Blood & Thunder
Rack & Ruin
Rise & Fall
Against the Grain
Catch a Tiger by the Tail
Smoke & Mirrors
Thick & Thin
Darkest Hour Before Dawn
THIRDS Beyond the Books Volume 1
THIRDS Beyond the Books Volume 2

Published by DREAMSPINNER PRESS
www.dreamspinnerpress.com

CHARLIE
COCHET

DARKEST
HOUR BEFORE
DAWN

Published by

DREAMSPINNER PRESS

5032 Capital Circle SW, Suite 2, PMB# 279, Tallahassee, FL 32305-7886 USA
www.dreamspinnerpress.com

ISBN: 978-1-63533-608-5
Digital ISBN: 978-1-63533-609-2
Library of Congress Control Number: 2017901549
Published April 2017
v. 1.0

Printed in the United States of America
∞
This paper meets the requirements of
ANSI/NISO Z39.48-1992 (Permanence of Paper).

ACKNOWLEDGMENTS

THANK YOU to everyone who's supported me on my journey. To Dreamspinner Press, my amazing friends, my family, my fabulous beta readers, the THIRDS Nerds, my fantastic narrator Mark Westfield, and everyone who's joined the THIRDS crew on their adventures. Thank you.

CAST MEMBERS IN THE THIRDS SERIES

(YOU'LL FIND these cast members throughout the THIRDS series, some being introduced in different books. This list will continue to grow.)

DESTRUCTIVE DELTA
Sloane Brodie—Defense agent. Team leader. Jaguar Therian.
Dexter J. Daley "Dex"—Defense agent. Former homicide detective for the Human Police Force. Older brother to Cael Maddock. Adopted by Anthony Maddock. Human-Therian Hybrid.
Ash Keeler—Defense agent. Entry tactics and Close Quarter Combat expert. Lion Therian.
Julietta Guerrera "Letty"—Defense agent. Weapons expert. Human.
Calvin Summers—Defense agent. Sniper. Human.
Ethan Hobbs—Defense agent. Demolitions expert and Public Safety Bomb Technician. Has two older brothers: Rafe and Sebastian Hobbs. Tabby Tiger Therian.
Cael Maddock—Recon agent. Tech expert. Dex's younger brother. Adopted by Anthony Maddock. Cheetah Therian.
Rosa Santiago—Recon agent. Crisis negotiator and medic. Human.

COMMANDING OFFICERS
Lieutenant Sonya Sparks—Lieutenant for Unit Alpha. Cougar Therian. Undercover operative for TIN (Therian Intelligence Network).
Sergeant Anthony Maddock "Tony"—Sergeant for Destructive Delta. Dex and Cael's adoptive father. Human.

MEDICAL EXAMINERS
Dr. Hudson Colbourn—Chief medical examiner. Wolf Therian.
Dr. Nina Bishop—Medical examiner. Human.

AGENTS FROM OTHER SQUADS
Ellis Taylor—Team leader for Beta Ambush. Leopard Therian.
Rafe Hobbs—Team Leader for Alpha Ambush. The oldest Hobbs brother. Tiger Therian.

Sebastian Hobbs—Team Leader for Theta Destructive. Was once on Destructive Delta but was transferred after his relationship with Hudson ended in a breach of protocol and civilian loss. Middle Hobbs brother. Tiger Therian.

Dominic Palladino—Defense agent. Close Quarter Combat expert for Theta Destructive. Human.

Angel Herrera—Defense agent. Pilot and BearCat driver for Theta Destructive. Human.

Osmond Zachary "Zach"—Agent for Alpha Sleuth in Unit Beta. Has six brothers working for the THIRDS. Brown bear Therian.

OTHER IMPORTANT CAST MEMBERS

Louis Huerta "Lou"—Dex's ex-boyfriend. Human.

Bradley Darcy—Bartender and owner of Bar Dekatria. Jaguar Therian.

Austen Payne—Squadron Specialist Agent (SSA) for Destructive Delta. Freelance operative for TIN. Cheetah Therian.

Dr. Abraham Shultzon—Head doctor during the First Gen Recruitment Program who was personally responsible for the well-being of the THIRDS' First Gen recruits. Was also responsible for the tests that were run on the Therian children at the First Gen Research Facility. Recently apprehended by TIN for creating an unsanctioned Therian mind-control drug and for kidnapping THIRDS Therian agents for an unauthorized project.

Wolf—AKA Fang, Reaper. Former TIN operative turned rogue. Wolf became a freelance agent for hire after feeling he was betrayed by TIN, the organization that caused the death of his partner. Wolf Therian.

John Daley—Dexter J. Daley's biological father. Anthony Maddock's best friend and partner at the HPF. Killed during a shootout in a movie theater during the riots. Human.

Gina Daley—Dexter J. Daley's biological mother. Worked for the CDC in NYC. First to volunteer to work with Therians. Killed along with her husband during a shootout in a movie theater during the riots. Human.

Darla Summers—Calvin Summer's mother. Human.

Thomas Hobbs—Ethan, Sebastian, and Rafe Hobbs's father. Suffers from Therian Acheron Syndrome. Tiger Therian.

Julia Hobbs—Thomas Hobbs's wife, and mother to Ethan, Sebastian, and Rafe Hobbs. Human.

Benedict Winters—THIRDS-appointed psychologist.

Admiral Abbott Moros—Chief of Therian Defense. Tiger Therian.

Arlo Keeler—Ash's twin brother killed during the riots in the 1980s.

Gabe Pearce—Sloane's ex-partner and ex-lover on Destructive Delta. Killed on duty by his brother Isaac. Human.

Isaac Pearce—Gabe's older brother. Was a detective for the Human Police Force who became leader of the Order of Adrasteia. Was killed by Destructive Delta during a hostage situation. Human.

Beck Hogan—Leader of the Ikelos Coalition. Killed during confrontation with THIRDS agents. Tiger Therian.

Drew Collins—Beck Hogan's second in command. Cougar Therian.

Felipe Bautista—Drew Collins's boyfriend. Wolf Therian.

Milena Stanek—Antiques acquisitions. Rosa's girlfriend. Leopard Therian.

GLOSSARY

Melanoe Virus—A virus released during the Vietnam War through the use of biological warfare, infecting millions worldwide and killing hundreds of thousands.

Eppione.8—A vaccine created using strains from animals immune to the virus. It awakened a dormant mutation within the virus, resulting in the altering of Human DNA, and giving birth to Therians.

Therians—Shifters brought about through the mutation of Human DNA as a result of the Eppione.8 vaccine.

Postshift Trauma Care (PSTC)—The effects of Therian Postshift Trauma are similar to the aftereffects of an epileptic seizure, only on a smaller scale, including muscle soreness, bruising, brief disorientation, and hunger. Eating after a shift is extremely important, as not eating could lead to the Therian collapsing and a host of other health issues. PSTC is the care given to Therians after they shift back to Human form.

THIRDS (Therian-Human Intelligence Recon Defense Squadron)—An elite, military-funded agency comprised of an equal number of Human and Therian agents and intended to uphold the law for all citizens without prejudice.

Themis—A powerful, multimillion-dollar government interface used by the THIRDS. It's linked to numerous intelligence agencies across the globe and runs a series of highly advanced algorithms to scan surveillance submitted by agents.

First Gen—First Generation Therians born with a perfected version of the mutation.

Pre–First Gens—Any Therian before First Gen Therians. Known to have unstable versions of the mutation, resulting in a number of health issues.

BearCat—THIRDS tactical vehicle.

Human Police Force (HPF)—A branch of law enforcement consisting of Humans officials dealing only with crimes committed by Humans.

Sparta—Nickname for THIRDS agent training facility at the Manhattan THIRDS headquarters.

TIN—Therian Intelligence Network. Therian equivalent to the Human CIA.
   TINMAN—TIN operative. Nicknamed after the Tin Man in *The Wizard of Oz* as TIN operatives are rumored to have no heart.
Anti-Therianism—Prejudice, discrimination, or antagonism directed against Therians.
Therian Classification—Tattoo marking on a Therian's neck displaying the Therian's classification, including family, genus, and species.

CHAPTER 1

"SPREAD OUT, and watch your backs."

Seb motioned for his partner, Dom, to follow him as the rest of Theta Destructive split off into pairs, with Peyton, Brianna, Lee, and Zoey in their Therian forms. They spread out through the trees, and Seb was grateful for the sunny day despite the biting chill in the air. In a couple of days, March would give way to April, which accounted for the temperature rising from polar ice caps to just above meat locker. In Seb's opinion, spring couldn't come quickly enough. Winter wreaked havoc on his joints, especially his bad knee.

"What did you get your boy for his birthday?" Dom asked from behind his raised tranq rifle as he scanned the woods around them.

"I still have two weeks." Seb held his rifle at the ready as they approached the pagoda where the four tiger Therians had last been spotted. "Sort of. I'll find something this weekend."

They were getting closer. Seb could feel it. They needed to round up these assholes before anyone else got hurt, especially since the perps were running out of places to hide. THIRDS agents managed to shrink the original perimeter around Prospect Park down to the boathouse, the pagoda, and Binnen Bridge. Cornering Felid Therians never went well.

"You're the only guy I know who buys presents for his ex," Dom said, stopping in his tracks. "Did you hear that?"

Seb didn't tear his gaze away from the path ahead as he tipped his head toward a tree to his left. "Squirrel."

Dom nodded, then moved forward, muttering something about furry pains in the ass.

Theta Destructive along with several other teams had been called after a shooting outside an auto club on Empire Boulevard led to one death, two injured, and four tiger Therians leading THIRDS agents on a chase through Prospect Park. Human agents cleared the park while Therian agents in their Therian forms sniffed out the perps, formed a perimeter, and hastily began to close in to reduce the square footage. Everyone knew parks provided the best cover to hide in. Unfortunately, parks were filled with citizens, tourists, pets, and wildlife. It was a security nightmare.

"Dex buys presents for his ex," Seb pointed out, smiling at Dom's snort.

"Are you seriously using Dexter J. Daley as an example of rational behavior?"

"Right." Seb chuckled. "What was I thinking. Anyway, you know Hudson is more than an ex-boyfriend." Dom knew a hell of a lot more than that. He was one of two people Seb had bared his soul to in his lifetime. Hudson was the first, and as of three months ago, Dom became the second.

"Cutting it kind of close, aren't you? What did you get him last year?"

Seb peered into a thick brush of shrubbery, but nothing stirred. He needed to be careful, making sure to sniff out their fellow agents so he didn't accidentally shoot a tranq into one. Of course, that would only happen if the Therian attacked, pretty much assuring him it wasn't one of their own.

"I got him this really nice, soft, blue robe that matched a pair of TARDIS boxer shorts he loves, and some fuzzy slippers."

Dom snickered. "The doc is such a nerd."

Seb couldn't help his dopey grin. "Yeah."

"Did he like it?"

"Are you kidding? He practically lives in it. He's a wolf Therian, remember? They love fluffy, cozy stuff." Unlike Seb, Hudson's favorite seasons were fall and winter. During the cold weather, Hudson wasn't content to simply sit or lie on the couch under a blanket. Nope. He'd draw his legs onto the couch and wrap up like he was cocooning himself, with only his face exposed, and even then he'd pull the blanket over his nose so it wouldn't get cold. Hudson hated having a cold nose. Fuzzy blankets brought out his Therian side like nothing else. It was the most adorable thing Seb had ever seen. Movie nights always included a host of snacks and a nest of blankets.

The air changed, and Seb stilled. Dom followed his lead, coming to a halt beside him. Seb tapped his nose and motioned ahead to the woods behind the pagoda. He was picking up two very distinct tiger Therian scents—neither THIRDS agents. Dom motioned to the right, and Seb gave him a curt nod. Seb would take the left.

Silently he stalked through the trees, listening for sounds not meant to be there. Wind rustled the leaves, water trickled somewhere in the distance, and birds chirped. A squirrel bounded from one tree to another. Seb's pulse picked up, and his muscles tensed as he hunted. The scent drew closer, and he followed it to a thick patch of shrubs. Finger on the trigger, Seb approached as the hairs on the back of his neck stood on end. He spun on his heel, and a near three-hundred-pound tiger Therian barreled into his knee head-on.

Motherfucker!

Pain exploded through Seb's body as he slammed onto the ground, his helmet cracking against a cluster of rocks, momentarily stunning him. The blow to his head was nothing compared to the electrifying burst of sheer agony shooting through his leg. He blinked away the tears and sucked in a sharp breath. His lungs burned from the gulps of air he rapidly dragged in. He couldn't black out. Not now. A feral growl got him moving, and his adrenaline spiked. If he stayed on the ground, he was dead. The tiger Therian shook himself before charging again, and Seb was still down.

Three tranq darts to the neck and a punch across the muzzle, and the tiger Therian was out. Good thing, considering Seb was still seeing stars. His muscles rippled with spasms, and he gritted his teeth. He felt as though his ligaments and tendons were being torn from his bone. As though someone had taken a hammer to his kneecap. He cursed his genetics for the thousandth time—not that it helped.

Seb was always careful in the field, as careful as someone in his position could be, and although he'd suffered plenty of injuries, it was the first time some asshole had head-butted his knee. If Seb had been a Human, something would have shattered. Instead, it only *felt* as if it had. The pain was blinding, and he was faintly aware of Dom hauling ass in his direction. *Damn it, what now?*

"Seb!"

A roar had him rolling onto his side, plowing through the pain and pushing up onto his good leg, putting all his weight on it. He needed a second to get his bearings, but the tiger Therian speeding toward him wasn't going to give him that chance. Two darts stuck out of its neck, but adrenaline was helping it push through, and with Dom being chased by a third tiger Therian, Seb was left to deal with this bastard. One wrong move, and it was over.

Seb readied his rifle, cursing under his breath when the last tiger Therian showed up, barely missing Dom as it leaped from the shrubbery.

"Fucking fuck!" Dom pulled a move worthy of any NFL running back, turning sharply and throwing his gloved hand to the ground to keep from keeling over face-first. He regained his balance and took off toward Seb just as a round of hair-raising roars resounded through the trees. Seb grinned.

Lee was the first through the trees, his mane providing protection when one of the perps tried to snap at his neck and got nothing but a mouthful of fuzzy mane. A second bite was thwarted by Brianna, her slender cougar Therian frame landing on the larger tiger Therian, claws outstretched. The perp's pained roar shook the trees around them.

Peyton and Zoey leaped from the greenery, fangs bared as they each faced off against a perp. Zoey was slightly smaller than the three male tiger Therians around her, but she was by no means the least fierce. In fact, Seb was glad he wasn't on the receiving end of her fury. Zoey could take down a Therian twice her size, no matter what form they were in, and she wouldn't even break a sweat.

Peyton eclipsed everyone, a gentle giant who stood at seven and a half feet tall and weighed three hundred and twenty pounds. He was the largest Felid Therian in Unit Alpha. Of course, right now, Peyton was anything but gentle. Not when defending his team.

"Get on the ground!" Dom demanded over the roars and hisses, his rifle aimed at one of the tiger Therians circling Peyton. The guy was hesitant to attack Peyton—so not a total idiot.

Realizing they were outmuscled, the three tiger Therian perps submitted, mewing and backing away to flop on the grass. Dom radioed for backup, and two BearCats pulled up onto the path to their right. Their back doors opened, and Human agents flooded out. Seb left them to round up their perps and get them into the cages. He turned to his Therian teammates.

"Collect your partners and get PSTC."

Lee trotted off, his mane swishing majestically, while Brianna bounced behind him, playfully swatting at his tail. Lee didn't pay her any mind. Zoey whizzed by them, and Lee grunted. He took off after Zoey, unwilling to be left in her dust, and Brianna was quick on their heels. Peyton, as usual, wasn't interested in his teammates' shenanigans. He released a huff and leisurely sauntered after them. Dom stayed behind, and Seb braced himself. He knew what was coming.

"You okay?"

"I'm fine," Seb assured him. "Just knocked the wind out of me."

Dom pressed his lips together in a thin line. He wasn't buying it, but Seb was in too much pain to care. With teeth gritted and jaw set, Seb headed in the direction his team had gone. Thankfully, Angel hadn't parked the BearCat very far. Instead of fighting the pain, Seb let it wash over him. He'd lived with physical discomfort and pain the majority of his life. It went with being a Pre–First Gen Therian. Granted, this was a hell of a lot worse than his usual bad days, but he wouldn't let his team know the extent of it. He straightened to his full height and squared his shoulders as he walked.

They all knew about the nerve and tissue damage to his leg. He was hardly the only Pre–First Gen at the THIRDS with health issues, but if his leg gave up the ghost, he'd be pulled off Defense, and he'd worked too damned hard to make Team Leader to give it up now.

"You okay, boss?" Cat asked, studying Seb as he approached.

Seb smiled and gave her shoulder a pat. "I'm good. Wasn't expecting to be used for a bowling pin."

"Must have learned it from Lee," Zoey said with a delicate snort. Having received PSTC and not eaten anything substantial yet, Zoey was in rare form, and as usual, Lee was the target.

Oh boy. Here we go.

"Fuck off," Lee grumbled before taking another swig of his Gatorade. "Not all lion Therians do that."

"What? Use their heads?" Zoey arched an eyebrow at Lee. "Ain't that the truth."

"Screw you, Z," Lee snarled.

Screw was what those two needed to do before they drove everyone nuts. The only ones who seemed oblivious to the attraction were Zoey and Lee. They were always giving each other a hard time. Seb hoped his team wasn't going the route of Destructive Delta. He loved Sloane like a brother, but if he had to deal with all the relationship drama Sloane did, he might start thinking about early retirement.

Zoey rolled her eyes. "In your dreams."

"All right, everyone in the truck," Seb grumbled. He needed to sit his ass down. Of course, he wouldn't be doing that until he reached his office, because once he sat down, getting up would require help, and weakness was something his team didn't need to see in him.

As soon as they reached HQ, his team escorted the perps into their holding cells, where they'd be ordered to shift back into Human form. They'd receive Postshift Trauma Care, then get processed. Seb dropped his equipment off at his locker in the armory before heading upstairs to his office, greeting fellow agents along the way.

Beside him, Dom was quiet. Not a good sign. As the youngest of four sons born to a Cuban mother and Italian father, Dom joked he only had three volume settings—"loud," "louder," and "make sure they heard you over in Jersey." When someone told him to bring it down, he just laughed in their face.

Finally they reached the office, and Seb gritted his teeth as he attempted to sit behind his desk. It required gripping the desk hard enough to turn his knuckles white and his good leg to ache in protest. Once his ass was in his chair, he felt marginally better.

"Let's see it."

"Dominic, we've discussed this," Seb replied gently, schooling his expression. "I like you, but I don't, like, *like* you."

Dom was not impressed, judging by his expression. "Don't be an ass. I know that's going to be a real stretch for you, but just give it a try. Now let me see." He reached for Seb's knee, and Seb smacked his hand away with a growl.

Next to Hudson, Seb trusted no one more than Dominic Palladino, and no one was a bigger pain in his ass. Dom was a mother hen. He fussed over the team, treated them like his baby birds, even Peyton who could easily crush Dom's skull with his bare hands. At some point, the team had lost the will to fight him on his mothering and accepted him as their surrogate father, some more begrudgingly than others.

"I said I'm fine. Stop fussing. What're you, my husband?"

Dom let out a snort. "Fuck no. I wouldn't marry you if you were the last dick left on the planet. I'd end up smothering you in your sleep."

"Like you haven't tried that already," Seb said with a grunt, amused when Dom threw up his arms, cursing in Spanish, then Italian—meaning Seb was *really* trying his patience. Seb tried not to look so happy about it.

"Seriously, bro?" Dom's face flushed a deep red, and he folded his arms over his expansive chest. "How many times do I have to tell you it was an accident? I knew I shouldn't have bunked with you. Is it my fault you take up so much fucking space? I could've bunked with Peyton and still had more damn room in that bed than I did with you."

"So now it's *my* fault you pushed a pillow into my face while I slept?" Seb kept his features stoic, even if he was laughing his ass off on the inside.

During one particularly bad snowstorm, Theta Destructive and several teams in Unit Alpha were forced to sleep at HQ in the sleeper bays. The agents outnumbered the bays, so teams had to share. Seb got the bed, not because he had senior status on his team, but because of his leg and lower back. Dom decided to bunk with him because, well, it was Dom and he wasn't "sleeping on the damn floor if there's a bed"—he didn't care who was in it.

Seb held back a smile. "I don't know anyone who moves that much in their sleep *and* takes their pillow with them," he managed with a straight face.

"So what? You're the one who kept trying to spoon me."

Seb shrugged. "I'm a cuddler."

"Fine. Whatever." With a huff, Dom marched over to his desk and dropped down in his chair. Seb grinned. Winding Dom up was too much fun. Of course, Dom gave as good as he got. Seb pulled up the file of today's incident and added his account of events. An hour later and it was time for his team's afternoon coffee run, this week being Angel's turn. The man popped his head in with a smile.

"Hey, boss. The usual?"

"Yeah, thanks, Angel."

Angel nodded. He turned his attention to Dom. "Dom Corleone?"

"No matter how many times you say it, Herrera, it still ain't funny," Dom griped. "If anything, I'm Clemenza."

Seb and Angel looked at each other before having a good laugh.

"What? Seb's obviously the Don, which makes me his oldest and dearest friend."

"We haven't known each other that long," Seb reminded him, holding back a smile, "but continue."

Dom flipped him off. "Unfortunately, I feel like I've known you for fucking eternity. Anyway, I'm also a great judge of character, have a keen eye for talent, and possess an unparalleled training record."

"Nope." Angel shook his head.

"I don't see it," Seb teased.

Angel snapped his fingers. "I know. Sonny."

"You know what? Fuck the both of you. Go get me my cappuccino, and tell Dex if he hogs all the powdered chocolate, I'm going to tell Sloane how his midafternoon coffee runs include scarfing down a frosted donut bigger than his head. Seriously. How is that dude still alive with what he eats? I've never seen a Human polish off a whole Therian-sized burger, fries, and still have room for a milkshake."

Angel nodded his agreement. "I think whoever put him together got the parts all mixed up and gave him a Therian stomach."

Or he got mutated by his jaguar Therian boyfriend and is no longer Human. Of course, Seb wasn't about to mention that.

Angel went off to get the rest of the team's orders, and on his return, he was accompanied by a scowling Dex.

"How dare you try to come between me and my afternoon donut?" Dex placed his hands on Dom's desk and leaned in to peer at him. "That powdered chocolate is mine, Palladino," Dex rasped. "Debbie brings it for me as a thank-you. I practically delivered that woman's child."

"You stepped in as a Lamaze coach, like twice," Dom drawled.

Dex straightened with a sniff. "That's why I said *practically*. You're not listening."

"Oh, I'm listening all right. Listening to all the reasons I should call Sloane this second. Today was triple chocolate frosting with bacon bits, wasn't it?" Dom put a finger to his earpiece, and Dex all but launched across the desk to grab Dom's wrist.

"Wait!"

"Yes?" Dom smiled sweetly.

Dex let his head hang in defeat. "I may have been a little hasty." He straightened and wrinkled his nose. "Fine. I'll tell Debbie I'm willing to share." With a grunt, he walked out the door, then spun on his heel to glare at Dom, a finger pointed at him menacingly. "But this isn't over, pal. I'm watching you."

Dom waved a hand in dismissal. "Yeah, yeah. Less watching, more sprinkling chocolate powder on my cappuccino."

Dex let out a snort of disgust before turning his attention to Seb. "Your partner's a jerkface."

Seb chuckled. "It must be my shower gel. I think it attracts them." He thanked Angel for his coffee and told Dex to get lost.

"I know you love me," Dex said in a singsong voice as he skipped off—literally skipped—to make mischief elsewhere. How Sloane kept up with that man was beyond Seb. He was already exhausted from the interaction.

Ignoring the crazy around him, Seb got back to work on his report and enjoyed his latte. He'd just signed off on the first set of documents when he looked up at Dom. He narrowed his eyes. Why was Dom grinning? Dom leaned back in his chair, his hands behind his head. *Shit.*

"What did you do?"

Dom waggled his eyebrows, and Seb's frown deepened. This wasn't good. What the hell had his *asshole* partner done now? Seb loved the guy, but sometimes he wanted to strangle him.

"Sebastian Hobbs!" a familiar voice demanded.

Seb's jaw went slack. "You didn't."

Dom's grin got bigger.

"You did! You narced on me?"

"Aw, are you mad?" Dom put a hand to his heart. "Well, tough shit. You brought this on yourself." Dom jumped from his chair, smiling widely as he patted Hudson's back. "Give 'im hell, Doc." He moseyed off, leaving Seb to face one very pissed-off Brit.

Hudson planted his hands on his hips. He had that narrow-eyed, thin-lipped glare on his face. Seb was very familiar with it. There was a time Seb could coax that stern frown away with a few strategically placed kisses. The good doctor wasn't easily deterred, but neither was Seb. He could be just as stubborn as his spirited little wolf. Especially when it concerned Hudson's happiness. Unfortunately, happy was *not* what Hudson was at the moment.

"I have half a mind to give you a right earbashing. Get in my office. *Now.*"

Seb groaned. He waited for Hudson to turn around, but as Seb expected, Hudson didn't budge. He studied Seb, waiting. The man was too smart for his own good. Unwilling to show Hudson how right he was, Seb clenched his jaw, put his weight on his good knee, and stood. The only Therian more pigheaded than Hudson was Seb, and Hudson was well aware of it. Hudson turned, cursing under his breath, and Seb did his best not to limp as he followed him out into the bull pen.

The agents didn't bother pretending not to notice what was going on, and the majority of them looked on in amusement. Seb had a reputation for being a hardass, albeit a fair one. His fellow agents respected him for a variety of reasons. No one would dare challenge him, disrespect him, or fuck with him. Which was why they found this situation so damned entertaining. There was only one man in this building Sebastian Hobbs didn't stand a chance against. One sole little wolf Therian who could make him quake in his boots.

Hudson Colbourn.

The best part? After all this time, Hudson still had no clue the power he had over Seb. His *Lobito* simply was who he was, and in Hudson's eyes, Seb wasn't a tiger Therian who had one hundred and thirty pounds on him or stood a foot taller than he did. Hudson was the only Therian Seb knew who didn't tremble at Seb's roar. He wagged his tail.

"What are you smiling at?" Hudson scolded. "I'm very cross with you."

"I was just thinking about you wagging your tail." *Crap.* He probably shouldn't have said that.

Hudson stopped to gape at him. The few agents who'd heard Seb snickered. Poor bastards. Hudson turned his glare on them. It was pretty spectacular as far as glares went.

"Something you'd like to share, Agents?"

The huge Felid Therian agents stumbled and practically mowed each other down in their haste to get away. Seb pressed his lips firmly together to keep from laughing. For a sweet wolf Therian, Hudson could be pretty scary.

The elevator ride down to the forensics department was a silent one. Seb knew better than to make things worse by speaking. Once they arrived, he followed Hudson out and greeted the medical examiners and agents he passed. Most noticed Hudson first before giving Seb a sympathetic look, though he was pretty sure a few of those looks meant "better you than me."

As Chief Medical Examiner, Hudson's lab and office were the largest on the floor, taking up the whole end of the corridor. Although Hudson was part of Destructive Delta, his title and status meant he could oversee and take over any case in Unit Alpha. Sparks often had him working on several cases at once for various teams. They finally reached the last room on the right, Hudson's private office. Once inside, Hudson hit the security panel, and the door swished closed behind them. He turned to face Seb and folded his arms over his chest, one eyebrow arched before he spoke.

"Drop your trousers."

CHAPTER 2

SEB'S EYEBROWS shot up near his hairline. "Uh… okay."

This was starting to sound a lot like one of his fantasies, except in those Hudson didn't scowl at him. Seb unfastened his belt before pushing his pants down as far as he could—which turned out to be not very far—before he sucked in a sharp breath and straightened, catching Hudson's narrowed gaze. Seb's shirt allowed him some modesty by covering his groin and ass, leaving only the ends of his gray boxer briefs peeking out from under the hem.

Hudson stepped up to him and tapped his shoulder. "Put some of your weight on me."

Seb nodded, doing as asked, gritting his teeth as he sat down. The moment his ass hit the padded leather chair, the relief was instant. At least until Hudson kneeled in front of him and took hold of his pants. He carefully pulled them the rest of the way down, unaware of what he was doing to Seb. Hudson was in doctor mode. He gently but clinically undid the straps of Seb's industrial, Therian-strength knee brace. The familiarity of it, the intimacy, was almost too much. It took Seb back to a time when Hudson had fussed over him, rubbing ointment over Seb's knee when it was sore and swollen.

The brace came off, and Seb winced at the fire that filled Hudson's bright blue eyes. It was less sexy heat and more "you're lucky you're hurt right now because I seriously want to kick your arse."

"Oh, for the love of—look at your knee! And you're walking around like it's a minor inconvenience?"

"It *is* a minor inconvenience."

Hudson's head shot up, his expression grim. "Don't you dare, Sebastian. Or do you forget who you're talking to?"

"Never." How could he? Even when Hudson was indignant, he was beautiful.

"Then you damn well know better than this, don't you? Have you taken anything for the swelling?"

Seb cringed.

"I could throttle you right now." Hudson stood, then headed to one of the many secured cabinets around the room.

Seb could think of plenty of things he'd like Hudson to do to him right now, but knowing what was good for him, he kept his mouth shut. Hudson returned with a familiar-looking black tactical bag and a bottle of water. He handed the water to Seb before kneeling to rummage through the bag. He found the right drugs, popped the top, and tapped it against his hand until two pills tumbled into his palm. After sealing the bottle and tossing it back into the bag, he held up the pills.

"Take these. For the pain and the inflammation."

"Thank you." Seb smiled at him as he took the pills, then tossed them in his mouth, followed by a swig of water.

Hudson wasn't impressed. "Don't thank me yet. I haven't decided whether to strangle you or not. The moment I felt it, I told myself, 'He's sensible. He'll look after himself.' And then Dom called, and look at you. Sensible my arse. I have DBs in my lab with more sense."

Seb didn't know what to say to that. As Hudson removed supplies from the bag, Seb couldn't help his dopy grin.

"Why are you looking at me like that?"

Their bond meant they felt the other's pain if it was significant enough. The love they shared made it so Hudson didn't have to look at Seb to know Seb was smiling at him. He could sense Seb's gaze on him, just like Seb could sense Hudson's. Always. Despite the days, the distance, they were every bit as connected now as they'd been back then, which made being apart so painful. Not calling Hudson every time Seb felt him hurting was torture.

"You still have it," Seb said softly.

Hudson blinked down at the black bag as if noticing it for the first time. Anyone else might have been able to hide their reaction, but Hudson's fair skin betrayed him, his cheeks blushing furiously.

"I, um, yes."

"Why?" Seb cocked his head as he studied Hudson. Not that he hadn't mapped out the man's features years ago. How was it possible to need someone more than air itself?

"Because I can't very well trust you to look after yourself, now can I?" Hudson's lips quirked on one side as he motioned to Seb's knee.

Seb leaned forward. "That's only half the truth, Doctor."

Hudson arched a thick black eyebrow at him. "Believe what you will."

With a grin, Seb sat back. All the medication in that bag was prescription. Hudson had to order them specifically. He kept them stocked in case Seb needed them. When they'd been together, Hudson had kept a kit at home and another in his office. Years after they'd broken up, he maintained the kit.

"Don't look so smug," Hudson muttered, removing the cap from the ointment.

Seb wrinkled his nose. "That stuff is rank."

Hudson chuckled. "You seem to forget that summer the cooling system and the backup generator at the morgue malfunctioned."

"Oh God." Seb gagged just thinking about it. "You're right. That was worse. Much worse." He closed his eyes and put a fist to his mouth. He'd gone in to meet Hudson for lunch and ended up bolting out. Lunch, or any food, didn't happen for a whole day. The smell had been so potent it burned. He hadn't been able to ingest anything stronger than vegetable broth, which meant he hadn't been able to shift into his Therian form because PSTC was impossible. He let out a bark of laughter, making Hudson laugh.

"What?"

"Remember when Sloane thought I was fucking with him, so he dragged me and Maddock down there to see for himself?"

Hudson gasped before laughing again. "That's right! He threw up on Sergeant Maddock's boots."

"Yes!" Seb held on to his side, he was laughing so hard. He could still see Maddock's horrified expression. If Seb hadn't been in danger of losing what little contents he'd had in his stomach as well, he would have snapped a picture with his phone.

"Poor Sloane." Hudson shook his head as he squeezed ointment into his hand. "He was mortified. Couldn't stop apologizing."

"Maddock avoided standing next to him for weeks." Seb wondered if Dex was privy to that little tidbit of information about his future husband. Hmm. He might just keep that ace up his sleeve.

Seb still couldn't believe Sloane was engaged. Had someone asked him years ago which member of his team was least likely to end up married, Seb would have said Sloane. His friend and former Team Leader believed himself too messed-up to make anyone happy for long. Seb understood where Sloane was coming from. When Seb had found out Dex and Sloane were involved, he'd been knocked for a loop. The two couldn't be more different.

Seb was happy for them. On the job, public displays of affection between them were understated, but anyone who knew them could see how in love they were. The way they looked at each other, the subtle way Sloane reassured himself and others that Dex was his by keeping physical contact with Dex, whether by placing his hand on Dex's lower back or shoulder. The way they murmured to each other or whispered in the other's ear spoke of a tender intimacy and fierce love that was at times too painful for Seb to witness.

Hudson's warm hands on him sobered Seb up in a heartbeat. He swallowed hard as heat spread through him. A heat that had nothing to do with the ointment seeping into his skin and everything to do with the man's searing touch. Hudson worked deftly as he massaged the medicine into Seb's knee and the muscles around it. It hurt like hell, always did, but Seb was too mesmerized by Hudson to pay attention to the pain.

Hudson's beautiful face was a picture of focus as he took care of Seb's knee. When they'd been together, Hudson had done this for Seb every day at work and at home. No one looked after Seb like Hudson. His care was unexpected, and had it come from anyone else, Seb would have thanked them and continued to do everything for himself, like he always did. But he'd never forget the warm smile or the affection in Hudson's eyes the first time he'd gone to massage Seb's knee. Seb would never forget his words either.

"Let me take care of you, love. I want to do that for you. Will you let me?"

Seb hadn't simply let Hudson take care of him—he'd relished it, thrived on it. He'd put himself, his trust, everything he was in Hudson's hands. Vulnerability was something he could never afford, and he found it hard to give up control, to let down his guard. He missed Hudson so goddamn much it choked him up inside.

"Have you been sticking to your routine?" Hudson asked.

"Yeah." Seb's voice came out rough, and Hudson turned his gaze up. He never missed a beat, an intake of breath, a look. "It's not the same," Seb admitted. "Not like when you do it."

"Well, I *am* a doctor." Hudson turned his attention back to Seb's knee.

"That's not why." Seb leaned forward to touch him, and Hudson stilled, his breath hitching. He swallowed visibly before slowly removing a roll of bandages from the kit. Seb's gut clenched, and he sat back, returning his hand to his knee. He no longer held the right to touch Hudson when the urge struck him. Hudson might bear his mark, but he wasn't Seb's.

Seb averted his gaze while Hudson wrapped his knee. Damn, he hated this. Their relationship had been far from perfect, and they'd argued like any couple, but it never lasted. Seb couldn't stand having Hudson mad at him, and he couldn't bear to be away from him for long. All Seb had to do was look into those bright pools of blue, and he was lost, drowning in the love he had in his heart, so he gave in. He was a pushover where Hudson was concerned. Giving in was better than fighting. He couldn't stand the fighting. It tore at his insides. The subject of their worst arguments never changed—Seb was too protective.

Seb had given in to Hudson from the beginning, allowing him to take care of Seb like he wanted to, but when Seb tried to do the same with Hudson, he came up against a wall. It was engrained in Hudson. Stiff upper lip and all that. He prided himself on his steadfast composure, his ability to guard against any vulnerability he might feel, and his self-reliance. Just because he let Seb in, allowed Seb to *see* him like no one else did, did not mean he was vulnerable. He did *not* need sheltering. However, Seb couldn't help himself, especially after he'd marked Hudson. He *needed* to protect what was his. The urge had grown with every passing day until one day he'd fucked it all up.

Hudson's hands on his calf had him drawing a sharp breath and brought him back to the present. Despite the anguish in his heart, having Hudson in the same room made him smile. Very few understood Seb's inability to move on. There was no moving on from Hudson Colbourn.

In their years apart, Seb had several sexual encounters, but he wasn't interested in moving beyond a few nights of sex with any of those guys. None of them was Hudson. Cael had been the first to change things. Seb had let down his guard with the young cheetah Therian, and the two had become good friends since, but in his heart of hearts, Seb had known it wouldn't work, and not just because Cael was in love with someone else. No one could come close to the man before him.

With a smile, Seb leaned forward, and this time, he put his fingers under Hudson's chin. He lifted his face, and their eyes met.

"Hey."

Hudson gave him a bashful smile. "Hey."

"Thanks for helping me out."

Hudson's expression softened, and he relaxed. "Of course. Promise me you'll be more careful."

"I promise." Seb gave him a wink and sat back. He looked down at himself. "Guess I should pull my pants back up, huh?" He waggled his eyebrows. "Unless you don't want me to."

"You cheeky bugger." Hudson smacked Seb's flank playfully. "Stop it." He strapped Seb back into his leg brace before standing up.

"Admit it, you love that about me."

"I do," Hudson said with a sigh before catching himself. His face flushed, and Seb couldn't help but tease.

"Better get dressed, then. Don't want you distracted for the rest of the day."

Hudson's eyebrows shot up, and he laughed. "Oh, it's like that, ay?"

Man, he loved that laugh. Seb pushed to his feet with Hudson's help, then pulled up his pants, his grin wide. "Yeah. What is it Dex says?" Seb snapped his fingers. "That's right." He turned around and lifted his shirt. "Who's got the booty? *I* got the booty."

Hudson let out a bark of laughter. "Oh good Lord. You've been spending far too much time around that man. Next thing you know, you'll be leaving a trail of gummy bears in your wake."

"Hardly. Doesn't make my statement less true, though," Seb said, fastening his belt.

Hudson snickered and shooed him. "Get out of my office, you scoundrel. And no more flashing your arse at me."

Seb headed for the door. He looked at Hudson over his shoulder. "If you change your mind, you know where to find me."

"Get out," Hudson ordered, the gravity lost when he chuckled. A thought seemed to occur to him, and he hurried over. "Wait. How's Julia?"

Seb was touched by Hudson's concern, but not at all surprised. Hudson was always asking about his parents, even if he didn't ask Seb specifically. Usually Hudson sent his love through Ethan, who then passed the message on to Seb to give to his parents. "She's okay. It's been a bit of a tough week."

"Thomas?"

Seb nodded. His dad had his good days, not so good days, and days where his mom cried herself to sleep. Those were the hardest for Seb. She tried her best to hide it from him, but he could tell when he spoke to her on the phone or came by to check on her. Most people assumed the Hobbs boys got their strength from their father, and although Thomas Hobbs was stronger than most and had obviously passed the trait on to his tiger Therian sons, they'd inherited their strength of heart from their mother. No matter the hardship or heartache she encountered over the years thanks to her husband's condition, she never gave up on him, never turned her back on him, and never stopped loving him.

"Do you think…?" Hudson worried his bottom lip with his teeth. "Do you think it might be all right if I called her?"

Seb blinked at him. He quickly snapped out of it. "Yeah, I think she'd love that."

Hudson's smile was radiant. "I will, then. Thank you."

"Okay." Seb gave him a wink. "Have a good day, *Lobito*."

Hudson shook his head as he walked back inside. "Be safe, Sebastian."

Well, at least Hudson hadn't asked him not to call him that. His knee was still killing him, but it felt less awful. Seb couldn't keep from grinning as he walked down the hall.

Back in Unit Alpha, his fellow agents busied themselves as he walked by, doing everything to avoid eye contact in case he had something to say to them.

When he reached his office, it was his turn to avoid eye contact. He took a seat behind his desk and logged into Themis. Seb didn't have to see Dom to know he was grinning like a dope. Dom was the kind of guy people noticed when he walked into a room, either because they heard him or because his presence demanded attention. At over six foot two and almost two hundred pounds, Dom had a square jaw, full lips, and hooded, hazel eyes with long, thick lashes. His eyebrows were dark and his brown hair short and tousled, adding to his roguish look, his expression always one of boyish mischief.

"You're welcome."

Seb grunted. "You're asking to get that smug look knocked off your face."

"Whatever," Dom said with a snort. "It went well. You were smiling like an idiot."

"Only idiot here is the one sitting across from me."

Dom gasped in mock hurt. "Ooh, ouch. You wound me, bro."

"If only," Seb muttered, but then his earpiece beeped, and Spark's voice came over the line.

"Seb?"

"Yes, Lieutenant."

"Would you come to my office, please?"

"Of course." The line went quiet, and he stood. "I need to go see the lieutenant. Could you check on the team? Lee hasn't submitted his report yet, and I want to make sure Zoey hasn't convinced Brianna to lock him out of his desk. Again."

Dom gave him a salute, and Seb headed out into the bull pen. Why couldn't Sparks have called him before he'd made it to his office? All the sitting and standing was doing nothing for his knee. At the end of Unit Alpha, he took a left and found Sparks's office open. He walked in, surprised when she put the room into privacy mode.

"That's new." Sparks's office had always been secure with no need for additional security measures. This didn't bode well.

"Yes, well, the world was a different place a year ago." She motioned for Seb to sit in the empty chair across from her desk, and he did. Whatever she wanted to talk to him about, he had a feeling it had nothing to do with his job at the THIRDS.

"Thank you for coming."

"Of course."

Sparks took a seat behind her desk, her intense gaze fixed on him. "Can I assume a speech on discretion is unnecessary?"

"Got it." Definitely not about the THIRDS.

"We need to discuss you appointing yourself Dr. Colbourn's personal security."

At the mention of Hudson and his safety, Seb tensed. "Have you heard from Wolf?"

Six months ago, what they had thought was a routine callout for Destructive Delta regarding a gang execution, turned out to be much more. Wolf had tried contacting Sloane and Dex about something, but the messenger he'd used was killed before he could deliver the message, forcing Wolf to come out of hiding to deliver it himself. No one understood why Wolf would insist they protect Hudson, but no one was taking the warning lightly. Hudson had promised he'd be more careful, but he wasn't about to go into hiding or allow his life to be interrupted, especially since they had no idea who they were protecting him from. If Hudson's life was in danger, Seb wasn't about to let Hudson out of his sight.

"We'll get to that, but first, I need you to understand the severity of the situation and what you're signing up for. Despite several attempts to appoint Dex with one of the very best doctors TIN has to offer, he refuses. The only doctor Dex trusts is Dr. Colbourn. As the first surviving Human-Therian hybrid, Dex is invaluable to TIN."

"So because Dex is invaluable and only trusts Hudson, that makes Hudson invaluable." As messed-up as that was, Seb had been a THIRDS agent long enough not to be surprised. Organizations like TIN were all about intel and how valuable an asset was. He didn't have to be a covert operative to know how it worked. Maybe he didn't know the ins and outs, and it was probably better that way, but the implications of her words weren't lost on him.

"There's still so much we don't know about Dex and his mutation, other than the fact he shares Sloane's DNA and is exhibiting Therian traits. We've been monitoring his activity, as has Dr. Colbourn. So far Dex has developed our strength, healing capability, speed, and metabolism. Only time will tell what jaguar Therian traits he may possess as well."

Seb nodded his understanding. "Do you think he'll shift?"

"We can't say for certain, but it's unlikely, as Dex was born Human."

"So were a lot of Pre-First Gens," Seb reminded her. "My dad was Human before he became infected with the Melanoe virus. Now he's a Therian."

"That's true. I suppose all we can do is wait. We're also monitoring the select number of First Gens who possess the same anomalies in their blood that Sloane does. Let's get to the reason I called you in here, shall we? Admiral Moros was a member of a cabal known as the Makhai—Therians intent on keeping Therians the dominant species. For decades they've been killing off Humans like Dex, who were infected by their First Gen partners. Dex is the only one of his kind that we know of. His quick thinking in seeking out Dr. Colbourn for medical attention rather than going to the hospital has kept him off their radar."

So it was possible there were more Humans like Dex. "And this organization is still out there?" Great, just what they needed. Another, scarier, more secretive group of nutcases.

"Although Moros was one of its founders, we have reason to believe the Makhai is still in operation. They've retreated into the shadows, most likely to regroup. However, we believe the two gang members killed by Wolf six months ago, Juarez and Turner, were working for the Makhai. It's possible they're gathering intelligence and will soon resurface." She tapped away at her desk, and the screen on the wall behind and above her head flickered to life. Surveillance images of Dowling, Juarez, and Turner popped up on the screen. "Dowling was paid by Wolf to warn Sloane and Dex that they needed to protect Dr. Colbourn. Juarez and Turner killed Dowling so he couldn't deliver the message. Wolf then killed them. As Juarez and Turner were working for the Makhai, we believe the Makhai not only arranged Dowling's murder but sent Juarez and Turner to Greenpoint."

"Why?"

"Intel. Moros's death is classified. According to those documents, he died by my claws."

Seb stared at her. "Does Dex know?"

Sparks nodded. "He wasn't happy about it but agreed that we need to keep what he is a secret as long as possible. Unfortunately, I believe the Makhai have their suspicions."

"How do you know?"

"As I said, Juarez and Turner were sent to Greenpoint. After debriefing Destructive Delta, it became clear that the two had targeted Cael. No matter who they were up against, they kept trying to get to Cael. I believe they were trying to get Dex to out himself."

"Shit." Seb shook his head. If there was a surefire way to make Dexter J. Daley lose his shit, it was to fuck with his family. "Let me guess, he went all Human-Therian hybrid on their asses."

"So to speak. Juarez and Turner may have been killed before they could relay the information to their superiors, but there's no telling if any of the other Therians in Greenpoint were plants. It's been six months, and we haven't picked up any chatter regarding Dex or his abilities. However, if Wolf felt the need to warn us, then the Makhai must know something. None of this is a coincidence. Even if they discover what Dex is, between him, his newfound traits, and Sloane, I'm confident they'll manage. Dr. Colbourn is a different matter. In the very near future, Dex and Sloane may not be available to offer their protection. Steps are being taken to assure the utmost discretion. Dr. Colbourn has no association with TIN, but at this time, we can't confirm the Makhai hasn't taken an interest in him."

Shit. "It's his association with Dex, isn't it?"

"Yes. Dr. Colbourn is Dex's personal physician. If they can't get to Dex...."

"Hudson's the next best thing." Seb ran a hand over his face. Fuck, this was worse than he thought. He knew it. The moment Dex walked into Hudson's house, he'd made Hudson a target. As pissed off as Seb was with Dex, he had to respect Hudson's decision, no matter how much he hated it.

"This is where you come in," Sparks informed him.

"Or where Hudson steps out."

She didn't so much as blink. "Dex and Dr. Colbourn have formed a bond due to the marks they carry from their mates."

Seb couldn't help but flinch at the word *mates*. She was fully aware of their situation. Seb might be Hudson's mate, but unless Hudson took him back, they remained two halves of a whole. Incomplete.

"Dr. Colbourn has taken Dex under his care. Do you really believe he'll walk away now?"

Seb clenched his jaw. They both knew the answer to that. Hudson would never turn down someone who needed him, much less a friend he cared for dearly. Seb wasn't sure what to think about the two bonding over their marks. Was that why Dex was playing matchmaker? The guy wasn't nearly as subtle as he thought he was. His heart was in the right place, but he had some real unorthodox methods. Not to mention unpredictable ones.

"Okay. I get it. Hudson might be in danger if this cabal knows what Dex is or Hudson's association with him and TIN. That just means you're going to be seeing a whole lot more of me."

Sparks didn't skip a beat. "How does Dr. Colbourn feel about seeing a whole lot more of you? How are you going to deal with seeing him?"

"I've made it clear to him that I'm not going anywhere."

"Easier said than done."

Tell me about it. "His safety is my priority." As much as it might crush him being around Hudson, knowing Hudson was safe was all that mattered.

"I have plenty of good operatives I can assign—"

Seb held up a hand to stop her. "If you want to have operatives keep an eye on him from a distance, that's fine. I would appreciate someone looking out for him when I can't be around, but I'm not walking away. It'll be a cold day in hell before I leave him out there on his own to face God knows what. I'm in this, whether he likes it or not. Whether *I* like it or not." He wasn't unreasonable. He couldn't very well shadow Hudson every moment of the day. They had jobs to do, cases to work, callouts. Seb could hardly follow him home.

"Very well. Dom will assume the role of Team Leader on Theta Destructive if you're called away. I'll arrange your cover." She tapped away at her desk's interface. An icon appeared on the screen. It was a pair of silver shoes. Okay. That was… weird.

"When you see that symbol appear on any of your communications devices, you tap it. It means you have a secure, incoming message from TIN." Her grin sent a chill through him. "Congratulations. Sebastian Hobbs, you are now part of the TIN Associate Program. Your training commences next week. Austen is your liaison."

Seb blinked at her. "I'm sorry, what?" What just happened? TIN Associate? Training? *What?* "Wait. Are you telling me Austen is TIN?"

"Yes. You want to protect Dr. Colbourn? You need training. He does too, for that matter."

"I *have* training." Training he continued every day, even when his knee was giving him hell. Sparks gave him a nod, and he frowned. What the hell was going on?

"Hey, Sebby."

"Shit!" Seb sprang from his chair so fast he almost fell face-first onto the carpet. He spun around, his heart in his throat as he stared at Austen. "Where the hell did you come from?" He looked from Austen to Sparks and back. "The room's still in privacy mode." Seb hadn't heard him, smelled him, or even felt Austen approach.

Austen waggled his eyebrows and dropped into the chair Seb had just vacated. "Training. And my general awesomeness."

"You'll be a stronger agent for it," Sparks assured Seb. "It's done wonders for Destructive Delta."

Seb peered at her. "Are you telling me Destructive Delta are TIN Associates?"

"They've been put through the TIN Associate Training Program." Some kind of unspoken exchange happened between her and Austen. Seb wanted nothing to do with it.

"So you want to make Destructive Delta TIN?"

Sparks shook her head. "Only Therians can be TIN operatives, or in Dex's case a Human-Therian hybrid. As good as Ash, Cael, and Hobbs are, they're better suited for the THIRDS, but with their skill set and TIN Associates training, they make valuable assets."

It took a second for her words to sink in, and he gaped at her. "Dex is a TIN operative?"

"He and Sloane will be sworn in after they return from their honeymoon. As TIN operatives, it's imperative they have a trustworthy network of assets."

Seb couldn't believe what he was hearing. Dex and Sloane, TIN? He was having trouble processing this. "Does Destructive Delta know?"

"Yes. Dex and Sloane will continue to work at the THIRDS under new roles. It's important they still have access to their team, which is why there will be some structural changes to Destructive Delta.

"TIN operatives are required to bring on their own assets and contacts upon swearing in. No operatives are recruited without a team already in place. Dex and Sloane will work undercover, with Destructive Delta on hand to provide support if and when necessary. As TIN associates, you and Dr. Colbourn will become part of Dex and Sloane's assets."

If Destructive Delta was ready to become an asset, it meant they'd been training for some time. Sparks cocked her head as she studied him.

"You look thoughtful."

"You've been preparing them for this." He still couldn't figure out why, though. She couldn't have predicted what Sloane's blood would do to Dex. "What if Dex hadn't become what he is? He couldn't be TIN, right? What then? Why train Destructive Delta?"

"I would have taken them on as my personal assets."

Seb was willing to bet his tiger Therian stripes that Destructive Delta wouldn't have accepted were it not for Dex and Sloane. Regardless. Whatever his friends' decisions, it had nothing to do with him. He didn't know TIN, and quite frankly, he didn't trust Sparks.

"I'm not getting into bed with TIN."

"You're an exceptional agent, Seb. Think of what you could accomplish as a TIN associate with the right training and the right… medical enhancements."

"Medical enhancements?" Seb stared at her. "What the hell are you talking about?"

Sparks dropped her gaze to Seb's knee before lifting her eyes back to his. "TIN could help you."

"But only if I join you?" He shook his head in disgust. "You people are unbelievable." He wasn't sure what he found more astounding, that TIN had the medical capabilities to help him or the fact they would only do so if it benefited them. The thought infuriated him. "I'd rather live with the pain than work for TIN."

"Seb—"

"Keep your training, your associates program, your goddamn *enhancements*," he ground out through his teeth. "I want nothing to do with it. Protecting Hudson is my priority, and I'll do that my way. Now if you don't mind, I have a job to do."

Sparks took the room off security mode. By the time the door opened behind him, Austen was gone. Seb hadn't even seen him leave.

"Am I interrupting?" A handsome leopard Therian in a THIRDS uniform stood in the doorway.

"Ah, Agent Carson. Perfect timing. Seb, this is Team Leader Trent Carson on loan from Unit Alpha over at Philadelphia HQ. Agent Carson, this is Agent Sebastian Hobbs, Team Leader for Theta Destructive."

Seb held out his hand. "Hey, welcome."

"Thanks. It's great to meet you."

"Agent Carson is interested in transferring to our office. Seeing as how Agent Taylor is on leave for an unknown period of time, it would be a good opportunity for Agent Carson to show us what he's made of. He'll be in charge of Beta Ambush until further notice."

Agent Carson gave her a curt nod. "I really appreciate this opportunity, ma'am. I won't let you down."

"I expect not. Seb, please give Agent Carson a quick tour of Unit Alpha, then take him to Conference Room A. Sergeant Maddock will join him there with the rest of Beta Ambush."

Seb nodded. He left the office with Carson at his side. Taylor hadn't been the easiest to get along with, and he could be a major pain in the ass, but he was a good guy and a hell of a Team Leader. Seb hoped he returned soon. Beta Ambush and Theta Destructive had a long history together. When either team was called out, they were usually backed up by the other, and they were the first on call to provide backup to Destructive Delta. Not having Taylor around was strange.

"I'm going to assume you've been briefed, Agent Carson?" Seb asked, making his way through Unit Alpha.

"Call me Trent. And yes, I have. Whatever you need, Agent Hobbs, just let me know."

"Call me Seb or everyone will think you're talking about my brother Ethan. Everyone calls him Hobbs. It's more of a nickname."

"His surname is his nickname?" Trent looked confused.

Seb couldn't help his chuckle. "His partner's name is Calvin. He's short and blond."

Understanding crossed Trent's face, and he laughed. "That's hilarious."

"If you value your life, you won't tell Cal that. He's small, but he will bust your shit up. He's also a sniper."

"Right. Don't piss off the sniper. Got it. So you've got a brother working in the same unit? That's great."

"I've got two, actually. My older brother, Rafe, is Team Leader for Alpha Ambush, and Ethan's a Public Safety Bomb Technician for Destructive Delta."

"Destructive Delta?" Trent let out a whistle. "I heard they've got a track record for kicking ass and taking names."

"Yeah, just don't get too close, or you'll get *your* ass kicked. Those guys don't mess around. Well, one of them does, but that's a whole other story." They walked through the bull pen, and Seb pointed to the office behind his. "That's Taylor's office, so you'll be working with your partner from there."

"Is that Sloane Brodie?"

Seb followed Trent's gaze to the end of the hall where Sloane leaned against the wall next to his office talking to Dex. Seb nodded. "That's him."

"I can't believe the guy got blown up and lived."

"Sloane's a survivor." Seb admired that. Sloane had been dealt a shitty hand from the start, and over the years, it seemed like bad luck had a hard-on for him, yet Sloane kept fighting. He put one foot in front of the other and kept wading through the shit, grief, and darkness determined to bury him until he made it through to the other side. "Want me to introduce you?"

"Yeah, wow, thanks, man. So, uh, what does it take to lead a Team like Destructive Delta?"

"Besides a nifty little piece of paper confirming you're certifiably insane? Retirement." It took a special kind of crazy to lead Destructive Delta. Seb loved his job, loved being a Team Leader, but lead Destructive Delta? Hell no. Being their driver had been a tough gig, and that was before Dex, before all the relationship drama or the nutjobs crawling out of the woodwork. Seb missed his teammates, working with his baby brother, and his BearCat, but they were all where they were supposed to be now. Plus, Ethan had quickly stepped in, taking over the BearCat's care. He loved that damn truck as much as Seb had.

Trent looked confused. "I don't get it."

"Destructive Delta has only ever had one Team Leader." Seb motioned to Sloane, who laughed at something Dex said. "They're also his family, so anyone looking for an in not only has to earn his trust and approval, but prove they'd be a good fit for his family."

Trent shrugged. "All teams are tight."

"No, I mean they're actually his family." Seb stopped walking and nodded over to Dex. If Trent was going to survive backing up Destructive Delta, he needed to know. "See that guy he's talking to?"

Trent nodded. "He looks kind of familiar. I think he's been on the news. Shit, he's pretty."

"Yeah, keep that to yourself. That's Dexter J. Daley. Remember that name, because if you fuck with him, you're finished. He's Sloane's partner, fiancé, and mate."

Trent's eyes went wide as saucers. "Fuck."

"Yeah. Dex's little brother is Cael Maddock."

"Wait. Maddock? As in Sergeant Maddock?"

Seb chuckled at the horrified look that crossed Trent's face. "Yep. He's their dad. And Cael's boyfriend is Ash Keeler, Sloane's best friend. They're more like brothers, actually. Grew up together. Letty is Ash's partner. Rosa is Letty's best friend and Cael's partner. Then there's my brother Ethan, who Dex is a little protective over. Even if he wasn't my brother, you'd have Ethan's boyfriend, Calvin, to deal with."

Trent braced a hand against the wall. "Shit. They told me I'd be providing backup, but…. Shit."

Clearly no one had told Trent what he was getting into with Destructive Delta. Seb clapped him on the shoulder.

"You'll be fine. Just don't piss Sloane off. Or Ash. Or the girls." He went thoughtful. "Don't piss anyone off. They're pretty laid-back and get on with most everyone, so you shouldn't have a problem."

Trent breathed in deeply. "Right."

Seb headed toward Sloane and Dex, with a somewhat pale Trent following along.

"Hey, guys." Seb smiled when the pair turned in his direction. "This is Agent Trent Carson. He's stepping in for Taylor while he's on leave."

Trent's smile couldn't get any wider as he shook Sloane's hand. The guy obviously had a little hero worship going on, despite his newfound terror. "It's an honor to meet you, Agent Brodie. I've heard so many great things about you and your team. You're a real inspiration. Please, call me Trent."

"Thanks, Trent. Just doing our jobs," Sloane replied with a smile. "This is my partner, Dexter J. Daley."

"Call me Dex," Dex replied with a bright smile, taking Trent's hand.

"Nice to meet you. Uh, wow." Trent stared into Dex's eyes and took a step closer. "You're…. Wow."

Seb groaned internally. What part of *mate* did Trent not understand? *Come on, pal, you gotta be stronger than this.* The rest of their unit had had time to adjust to Dex's mark, plus everyone loved the guy. Whether they were pulled in by his charm, amused by his antics, or preferred his company in small doses, everyone had his back. Also, not one agent in Unit Alpha was stupid enough to challenge Sloane Brodie or the backup that came with him. Everyone respected Dex and Sloane, and they were more than aware Dex was off-limits, no matter how much Dex's scent and mark tried to screw with their Therian halves. It took discipline but wasn't unachievable. Trent was obviously finding it hard to resist. Seb wondered if the guy was even trying, considering the way he began to stroke Dex's hand with his thumb.

Dex cleared his throat and politely tried to pull his hand out of Trent's grasp. Trent held on.

Let go. Now.

Trent continued to hold on to Dex's hand, and Sloane straightened to his full height, his pupils dilating.

Let. Go.

Sloane took a step forward, and Seb grabbed Trent's shoulder, jerking him back. "Hey, look at the time. Maddock's expecting Trent. Excuse us." Seb dragged Trent along with him, whispering hoarsely at him, "Are you out of your fucking mind? What did I say?"

"Oh God, I'm sorry. I'm so sorry. He… he just smelled so damned good. His eyes, and, Jesus, that mouth. Did you see those lips? Fuck, he's hot."

Seb turned the corner and brought Trent up against the wall. "Listen and listen good. You are not off to a good start. You're talking about another guy's *mate*."

"It's not my fault," Trent huffed. "Come on, man." He smirked and playfully smacked Seb on the chest. "You understand that kind of pull, right? Besides, those guys know what they're in for. I think some of them secretly like the attention."

Seb straightened. "What?"

"Those guys that let themselves get marked. They know what they're in for, know other Therians are gonna want to, you know." He shrugged, his lips curling into a wicked grin. "They're practically begging for it. Am I right, buddy?"

Seb shoved Trent hard, slamming him into the wall. He ignored the man's pained grunt and fisted a handful of Trent's shirt, pinning the smaller Therian to the spot. When he spoke, there was no mistaking the threat in his low growl.

"Now you listen here. I'm not your friend or your buddy. I hear you say shit like that again, and not only will I make sure you're on the first flight back to Philly, I will personally drag your ass over to Sloane Brodie, and you can look him in the eye and tell him his mate is begging for it."

Trent threw up his arms. "All right, I'm sorry. Shit, man. I had no idea that was such a touchy subject for you."

"Touchy subject?" Seb thrust a finger at the end of the hall. "Conference room is that way. You better fucking impress me out in the field, because right now, I am *not* impressed." He released Trent and turned to leave but not before growling over his shoulder, "Nice to fucking meet you, Trent. Stay the fuck out of my way."

Seb shook his head as he stalked back to his office. If there was one thing he didn't tolerate, it was talk like that, and not just because of Hudson or Dex. That mentality that Humans and Therians invited trouble because they were marked pissed Seb off—though not as much as those who believed a marked mate getting sexually assaulted was the victim's fault, because it was "in their nature." It was disgusting.

"Whoa, who pissed in your Cheerios?" Dom asked, looking concerned.

"Just met Taylor's replacement. Agent Trent Carson."

"That good, huh?"

Seb didn't keep anything from Dom, and Dom didn't keep anything from him. They were partners and, more importantly, friends. His first instinct was to confide in Dom. However, Seb knew him well, and when something or someone pissed Dom off, there was no hiding it. Dom's passions ran hot, and his temper, if not controlled, was explosive.

Seb pressed his lips together and sat without saying a word.

Dom groaned. "It's going to piss me off, isn't it? What? Is he a douche?"

Seb sighed as he took a seat at his desk. "I'll tell you if you promise to be an adult about it."

"I'm always an adult," Dom protested, his frown deep. "But now that I know what you're gonna say is gonna piss me off, you expect me to be nice to this asshole?"

"No, just—"

"Fucking tell me already."

Seb did.

Dom's expression darkened, a silent fury washing over him. The only hints he was royally pissed off were the set of his jaw and the steel in his eyes.

"Yeah, definitely an asshole," he ground out.

Seb grunted. Even if he hadn't been keeping an eye on Hudson, he would be now. The last thing he wanted was to have Trent sniffing around him. The thought alone was enough to get his blood boiling. Again. Trent Carson better watch himself, because if Seb got even the smallest hint the guy was up to no good, Seb wouldn't hesitate to teach him some manners.

CHAPTER 3

THIS WAS a terrible idea, but also the most obvious choice.

Hudson paced the concrete room, his wolf unhappy with the enclosed space. The small room made him anxious. He could only imagine what Sloane must be feeling. Felid Therians abhorred tight spaces. "Are you certain you want to do this?" Hudson asked for the umpteenth time.

"Positive, but Sloane has to stay here," Dex replied, cringing at Sloane's glower.

"Are you out of your mind? You want me to stay in here while you face a Therian stuck in feral form?" Sloane shook his head. "Absolutely fucking not."

"It's not just any Therian. It's Taylor," Dex reminded them.

"Exactly! Taylor who tried to kill us!"

Dex appeared to give that some thought. "He wasn't trying to kill *me*. Only you. I think."

Sloane threw up his hands. "Oh, well, I feel so much better now." He folded his arms over his chest, his lips pressed in a thin line.

Hudson couldn't blame Sloane for his concern. Taylor was far more lethal in this state, but Dex also had a point. If Sloane was present, Taylor's hostility would increase exponentially, and any chance Dex might have to reach Taylor would become nonexistent.

"Babe." Dex tugged at Sloane's arm, and Hudson held back a smile at the way Sloane's anger melted away.

Sloane pulled Dex into his embrace, his words laced with tenderness. "What if he hurts you? It's been weeks since Moros injected him with that fucked-up version of Shultzon's drug. We have to consider that maybe… maybe Taylor's gone."

Hudson swallowed hard, his stomach lurching at the thought. For weeks TIN scientists and medical experts had worked furiously to determine what concoction Moros injected Taylor with to force his humanity to become dormant. Mere hours ago, they were informed Moros had pumped extremely high doses of Thelxinomine into Taylor's system. Hudson was horrified to discover it was the same drug Shultzon managed to get into Sloane, Ash, and Ethan before they were kidnapped, in hopes of turning them into mindless soldiers. With enough doses, Thelxinomine would short-circuit the Therian brain, leaving the feral half in control and susceptible to Peitharchia7, which would allow the Therian to be controlled in their Human form. The thought of what Moros had done to Taylor made Hudson sick to his stomach. He turned to Sloane.

"We need to do what we can to help him, Sloane. What Moros did was barbaric. It's a miracle Taylor isn't dead."

Dex nodded his agreement. "If seeing me helps him in any way, I have to do it. Yeah, he's pulled some real dick moves, but he'd gotten his act together, and he sure as hell doesn't deserve this. Moros used him to get to us. We can't do nothing. Besides...." Dex sucked in a sharp breath, his expression pained as he held up his hand. Hudson stared at the claws piercing Dex's skin as he drew them out. "Things are different now."

Hudson couldn't stop from taking Dex's hand to examine it. "Extraordinary."

Dex chuckled. "Weird, huh? It's taking some getting used to." Something occurred to him, and he gasped, his wide eyes on Sloane. "Dude, I was right. X-Men."

Sloane rolled his eyes. "You are not an X-Men."

Dex looked unimpressed. He waved his clawed hand in front of Sloane.

"Yeah, okay, Wolverine. Go do whatever it is you gotta do, and try not to give me any heart palpitations today. You might be strong, but your bones aren't made of Adamantium."

With a big smile, Dex kissed Sloane. "I love that you're as big a nerd as I am."

"No one's as big a nerd as you are. Except maybe your brother." Sloane gave Hudson a pointed look. "Make sure he doesn't do anything reckless."

Hudson's expression was deadpan. "Oh? Mastered the feat yourself, have you?"

"You know what, Doc? You're starting to sound like him. Stop it."

Hudson laughed before knocking on the steel door. It was immediately opened by a very large bear Therian in a black suit and auburn tie. He towered well over seven feet tall, was as wide as the doorframe, and looked as though he was carved from granite. Hudson pondered how a man that size could be a spy.

Seeming to read his thoughts, Dex leaned in to murmur, "I'm guessing they send him to places with a lot of mountains. Blends right in."

Hudson snickered, following Dex and the giant bear Therian down a somber-looking corridor. Where were they? Dex had picked Hudson up at his office, and with Sloane, they'd walked to the THIRDS garage, where a black Suburban with opaque tinted windows waited for them. Inside, a partition ensured they couldn't see the front of the vehicle or who drove it, and the windows were as black on the inside as they were on the outside. Hudson attempted to listen to his surroundings but was met with nothing but silence, and all his sense of smell picked up was Dex and Sloane. It was impossible to discern where they were being taken, other than to a secure TIN facility.

A large iron door slid open at the far end of the gray concrete corridor. Two uniformed soldiers with frightful-looking tranq rifles emerged and took positions outside the room. Hudson swallowed hard. He certainly didn't want to come up against those men in a dark alley, or anywhere for that matter.

The vast room was bare, with nothing but what Hudson suspected was a two-way mirror high on one wall. At the end of the room was a steel cage, and inside, Taylor paced in his leopard Therian form, hissing and spitting. Hudson stopped cold with a gasp. He knew of feral Therians, had even come across several in his time at the THIRDS, but seeing someone he knew, one of his colleagues, in that state was difficult. Dex put a hand to Hudson's shoulder, and Hudson nodded.

"I'm all right."

They approached the cage, and Hudson's heart squeezed. *Poor bloke.* Taylor might have been brash, rude, and often inappropriate, but he didn't deserve to be locked up in a cage like a rabid beast. Inside that ferocious leopard beat the heart of a man, a good man despite his many flaws and past indiscretions. Taylor's change over the last few months had come as a surprise to everyone in Unit Alpha. At some point, the inappropriate comments had ceased. He no longer spoke incessantly of sex or his conquests. Where he'd once flirted with anything and everything that had a pulse, he had become thoughtful and at times playful. Hudson had overheard him reprimanding a fellow agent for boasting in lurid detail of his night spent with another agent. Hudson had no idea what had brought on such a change in Taylor, but it suited the man.

Dex slowly approached the cage but stopped far enough away that if Taylor were to swipe his paw through the bars, he wouldn't reach Dex.

"Hey, buddy, it's me."

Taylor continued to pace, fangs bared as he hissed. He was agitated and frustrated by his confinement. Canid Therians despised being locked up, but they could cope far better than Felid Therians. A trapped Canid Therian would lose heart, whereas a trapped Felid Therian would lose its mind.

"Taylor, listen to my voice. It's Dex. You remember me, right? I know you can smell me." Dex edged closer, gingerly approaching the bars. Hudson remained still. If Dex should need him, he'd have to move quickly. Dex crouched in front of the bars just a foot away, and Hudson stifled a gasp when Taylor roared and made a swipe at Dex through the bars. To Hudson's astonishment, Dex smacked Taylor's paw away before he could get slashed. He'd never seen a Human move that fast.

"Knock it off," Dex scolded. "Don't be a jerk. I'm here to help you." Taylor hissed, and Dex moved closer. "Hey, what did I say? I'm here to help you, you ass. I *want* to help you. I know you're in there. Come on." Dex moved his hand closer to the bars, and Hudson had to refrain from asking him what the bloody hell he thought he was doing. If Dex lost a hand, Sloane was going to kill them both.

Hudson waited with bated breath as Dex slipped his hand between the bars. "Come here," he said softly. "It's me. You like me. I like you too."

Taylor flattened his ears. He lifted his head and sniffed. When he opened his mouth, Hudson thought they were doomed. Instead of biting, Taylor stuck out his tongue. He was sniffing the air, trying to get a better idea of who Dex was.

"Yeah, that's it, buddy. It's me. Come on." Dex held his palm up, and Hudson stared, stunned as Taylor edged closer. He stretched out his thick neck and sniffed at Dex's hand.

"Yeah, that's it. You remember me, don't you? It's okay. I'm not mad."

Taylor rubbed his head against Dex's hand, and the very distinct motor-like sound of purring filled the room. *Oh, thank bloody goodness.* Hudson released a shaky breath.

"Yeah, you remember. I'm here. It's okay. Everything's gonna be okay."

Taylor lowered his head, releasing a grieving wail that broke Hudson's heart. He padded to the corner of the cage, where he curled up in a tight ball, his back to them.

"Hey, don't do that. I know you didn't mean to. You probably don't even remember most of it, and that's okay. It wasn't your fault. Someone messed with you. Why don't you shift so we can talk about it?"

Another low wail followed by a mewl came from Taylor. Hudson was familiar with the sound of a heartbroken Felid. Curious. Taylor no doubt felt remorse for his actions, but why did he sound so... despairing?

"We've been worried about you. You need to come back to us."

Nothing.

Dex took a deep breath before speaking, his voice gentle. "Ellis Taylor, you listen to me."

Taylor's ears perked up, and he looked at Dex over his shoulder.

"It's okay. I promise. Please. I'm not going anywhere. I'm going to be right here. For you."

Taylor stared at Dex for a minute before getting up. He walked to the center of the cage and released a huff. After several failed attempts, an anguished cry left Taylor's mouth as his muscles flexed and shifted beneath his fur. Hudson shut his eyes tight as the roars gave way to harrowing screams. Taylor was clearly in great pain. It was to be expected after how long he'd been in his Therian form. When the screams ebbed, Hudson opened his eyes. Taylor's transformation was nearly complete.

Hudson turned to one of the guards. "Bring us a blanket, please."

"Someone open this door," Dex ordered, standing aside while one of the guards crossed the room, then opened the cage door just as Taylor finished shifting. He was so weak he lay curled up on his side, shivering violently. Hudson took the blanket from the guard and handed it to Dex, who quickly laid it over a stark-naked Taylor.

The door opened, and several medical officers rushed into the room. Taylor flinched and curled up even tighter, shaking his head vehemently.

"Hey, it's okay," Dex assured him gently, running a hand over Taylor's head. "They're going to give you PSTC and take good care of you. I promise. Then we'll talk, okay?"

Taylor opened his mouth to speak, but only a hoarse sound escaped. He cleared his throat and tried again, his voice low and rough. "Don't go."

"I'll be right here," Dex promised.

They stood to one side as the medical officers administered PSTC. They dressed Taylor in a pair of sweatpants and a white T-shirt, a hoodie, and white crew socks. He looked like he'd been dragged through hell, deep dark circles around his bloodshot hazel eyes. Once Dex coaxed Taylor into eating some protein, they helped Taylor out of the room and into the room next door. It was as sparse as the one they'd vacated, but instead of a cage, it was filled with medical equipment, including a state-of-the-art hospital bed. They helped Taylor sit on the bed, and then Dex pulled up a chair next to him. Hudson took a seat beside Dex.

"Tell me what happened?" Dex asked gently.

Taylor stared down at his hands. "I... I'm so sorry." He winced, as if it hurt to talk.

Whatever tremulous hold Taylor had on his emotions shattered, and Dex was there to catch him, holding him as Taylor quietly sobbed against Dex's shoulder. Taylor clutched Dex's arms, as if Dex was the only thing holding him up. Several minutes later, Taylor pulled back with a sniff. He rubbed his eyes and averted his gaze, embarrassed it would seem. His face was flushed, his nose and eyes red.

"I think you need to rest," Dex said gently. "We'll come back."

Hudson agreed with Dex. Taylor didn't look well. He'd been in a feral state for so long, who knew if there was any internal damage after his shift? The room flooded with TIN medical staff, and a tall, elegant-looking cougar Therian with bright green eyes stopped at the end of the bed. Her smile was warm.

"Agents," she greeted. "I understand Agent Taylor has important information you need. However, I must insist we be allowed to take all the necessary measures to ensure his health—both physically and psychologically—has not suffered irreparable damage due to the ordeal. I would suggest returning in two days."

Taylor's eyes widened, and he grabbed Dex's hand, the fear in his eyes tugging at Hudson's heartstrings. Dex covered Taylor's hand with his.

"It's going to be fine. She's right. You're more important. We'll talk about what happened when we return. I promise you I'll be back. Do you trust me?"

Taylor nodded, his shoulders slumping in resignation.

"Hey, you can do this," Dex assured him, squeezing Taylor's bicep. "You're a THIRDS agent, remember? We're made to kick ass, right?"

Taylor's lips curled up on one side. He wrinkled his nose and nodded.

They stayed a few minutes longer as the doctor in charge explained to Hudson what they'd be doing for Taylor, the tests they would be running, along with any medication he might be given. Dex spent some time reassuring Taylor, as well as making certain the doctor knew to contact him immediately if anything changed.

"I'm leaving him in your hands," Dex told her.

Despite his smile, Hudson didn't miss the intensity in Dex's eyes. He was certain the doctor hadn't missed it either. If anything happened to Taylor under her watch, she'd be dealing with Dex. What startled Hudson was how much sway Dex seemed to have around here. Not as surprising, however, was the confident manner in which Dex seemed to embrace that power.

BACK AT the office, everything continued as if they hadn't left. Being involved with an organization as powerful as TIN was definitely odd. So much went on behind closed doors with not even a hint as to their existence. Of course they existed, and everyone knew they did, but on the surface, it appeared as if they didn't. No one spoke of TIN. What was there to speak of? Operatives were out there, but it wasn't as if they announced themselves or listed their employment as "Operative for the Therian Intelligence Network."

As Hudson walked to his office, he surmised it was likely TIN had more operatives working at the THIRDS. Hudson's phone buzzed, and he received a text from Nina stating she was in the canteen grabbing some lunch and would be back soon. Hudson had just taken a seat behind his desk and powered up his desk interface when someone stood in his doorway. Rafe hovered by the door, and Hudson wondered if Rafe had been waiting for him. Odd. He couldn't remember the last time Rafe had been to his office.

"Nina's not here," Hudson informed him. "She's gone to the canteen for some lunch."

"Actually, I'm here to talk to you." Rafe motioned to the chair in front of Hudson's desk. "May I?"

"Of course." What on earth could Rafe Hobbs have to talk to him about? Having Rafe in front of him was difficult. He stirred up too many painful memories of a time when Hudson had once again found himself losing what he cared for most. For some time, Hudson had feared he might lose his career as well. His life had been placed under a microscope. Every case he'd ever worked on, every testimony, every signature had been called into question, all of it gone over with a fine-tooth comb. Even though Hudson knew his work was beyond reproach, he feared for his position, feared losing the only thing he had left. It had taken years to repair his reputation. Few blamed Seb, believing he had no choice but to protect his mate, while most placed the blame on Hudson, even if they didn't say as much. As the one who was marked, his "pull" on his mate—as if he had any control over the actions of others—was always brought up. It wasn't fair, by any means, but it was the way it had always been. Hudson lay the blame at both his and Seb's feet. Together they had failed, and a little boy died because of it.

"How are you doing today?" Hudson tried to summon a smile. The least he could do was be civil, for Seb's sake. The brothers were closer than ever, and Hudson wasn't about to come between them. Rafe squinted at him, and Hudson let out a soft sigh. "I'm not being snide. I'm genuinely interested."

Rafe still had a way to go to redeem himself in Hudson's eyes, but Hudson felt for him. Having known the Hobbs family for years, being present for some of Thomas's worst days, Hudson wouldn't wish the condition on anyone. The knowledge that Rafe would one day end up in a wheelchair like his father, at the mercy of agonizing pain, hurt Hudson. Rafe was Seb and Ethan's big brother. A huge tiger Therian, built of what seemed like solid muscle. At seven foot two and over three hundred pounds, he eclipsed Hudson's smaller wolf Therian frame. As big as Seb was, Rafe was just that tiny bit bigger, certainly broader. It saddened Hudson. Rafe hadn't always hated him. Once upon a time, Rafe had been kind to him, even smiled.

"I'm okay," Rafe replied. He cleared his throat, looking larger than life as he sat across from Hudson. "Thank you for asking."

Hudson nodded. "What can I do for you?"

"I wanted to talk to you about Nina. I know things are still strained between the two of you, and it's my fault. She did it to protect me. Please, don't be mad at her. She loves you, Hudson. If you could only see how much pain she's in, how much she misses you."

The last six months had been rather awkward. Although Hudson was on speaking terms with Nina, their relationship had suffered greatly. How could they get back to the way things were after she'd purposefully kept him in the dark? For months, day after day, she'd looked him in the eye, going on as if nothing had happened, and all the while sharing Rafe's bed.

"I would have thought you'd be happy to be rid of me once and for all. She's the only connection left between me and your family." There was no bitterness in Hudson's voice, only sadness.

Rafe straightened, looking affronted. "How can you say that? You're connected to my brother in the most significant way possible, which, by the way, I don't get you. You took three bullets for him, are obviously still as much in love with him now as you were then, and he worships you, yet you keep pushing him away. Why won't you come home?"

Hudson inhaled sharply. Rafe's words hit him harder than expected. "Why… why would you say such a thing?"

"That you two should be together?"

"No. That I should come home."

Rafe raked a hand through his hair and let out a heavy sigh. He appeared to give a lot of thought to the question, as if trying to find the right words.

"Fuck it." Rafe met Hudson's gaze, his eyes intense. "Because you're a part of our family, always were. You're his home, Hudson. He's been lost since you left, and I don't want to see him in pain anymore. He deserves to be happy, and that'll never happen without you. He needs you. My family needs you. My mom misses the hell out of you. She's always asking about you. Ethan misses you, my dad—"

"Don't," Hudson pleaded, blinking back the tears in his eyes. "Please don't use Thomas."

"It's the truth. You may not want to hear it, but that's the way it is. We are your pack, Hudson. You walked away from us, and yes, I hated you for a long time for what I believed you were doing to my brother, but I think I also resented you."

Hudson was stunned. "For what?"

"For leaving. No one blamed you. Okay, *I* blamed you, but I was an asshole. My mom, dad, Ethan, Seb, none of them blamed you. They just wanted you home."

Hudson didn't know what to say. The Hobbs family had taken him in, a lone wolf without a pack in dire need of a family, of love. They'd embraced him from the moment they met him. Unlike his own family, who had looked down their noses at Seb, the Hobbs family had welcomed Hudson with open arms, despite knowing his family had cast him out. If anything, it made Julia more determined to show him how much he was loved. How could he have thought they'd not miss him?

Hudson studied Rafe, a man who for so long had been a source of grief for him. Unlike Seb and Ethan who looked so much like each other, sharing their father's pitch-black hair and bright green eyes, Rafe had his mother's chestnut hair and hazel-green eyes. His edges were harder, his expression stoic. Seb and Ethan had kind eyes, and despite their size, appeared gentle. Everything about Rafe radiated fierceness, which was why Hudson was caught off guard when Rafe reached across the desk, his palm up and his eyes filled with unshed tears.

"I'm sorry for what I did to you. Even if you never forgive me, don't turn your back on Nina. Please."

Hudson had opened his mouth to reply when a knock at the door startled him.

"I'm so sorry. I didn't mean to interrupt. I'm looking for Dr. Colbourn."

"Yes?" Hudson asked. An agent he'd never seen before stood in his doorway. A handsome leopard Therian. Curious. The patch on his uniform stated Beta Ambush. "Can I help you?"

Rafe turned in his chair to look at their guest, his expression darkening. Hudson could only fathom that Rafe's walls were once again rising firmly into place. Why else would he scowl so deeply at the poor man?

"You're Dr. Colbourn?" The agent approached with caution, his gaze flickering to Rafe's name tape before he swallowed. He moved his gaze quickly back to Hudson and gave Rafe a wide berth as he approached Hudson's desk. Hudson smiled warmly at him.

"Last time I checked." Hudson stood and held out his hand. "And you are…?"

Rafe stood, and the agent almost jumped out of his skin. With a smile that could only be categorized as frightening, Rafe slapped a hand down on the agent's shoulder. "Agent Trent Carson on loan from Philly," Rafe answered, his voice a deep growl. "He's stepping in for Taylor." He leaned into Carson, his voice slightly lowered but still loud enough for Hudson to hear. "You made some first impression."

"Yeah, um, your brother Seb's quite the guy," Carson said, then cleared his throat. He winced when Rafe gave his shoulder a squeeze, then released him. Carson held out his hand to Hudson. "It's nice to meet you."

Hudson shook his hand. "Good to meet you, Agent Carson."

"Trent. Please. Call me Trent," Carson said with a smile, earning a scoff from Rafe.

What on earth was going on? Rafe shook his head. He turned to Hudson, his expression softening for a slip of a moment.

"I'll talk to you later, Doc." Rafe turned and gave Trent a hearty pat on the back before heading to the door, calling out behind him, "See you around, Carson."

Hudson blinked after Rafe, wondering what that was all about. He turned a questioning gaze to Trent, who simply shrugged, a lopsided grin on his handsome face.

"New-guy syndrome. You know how it is."

Hudson chuckled. "Welcome to Unit Alpha." He resumed his seat and motioned to the chair in front of him. Trent shook his head.

"I just wanted to stop by and introduce myself since we'll be working together. I've heard a lot about you."

"Oh?" Hudson's smile faltered, an old habit he had trouble breaking after years of hearing his name whispered around the office. He braced for a pitying look.

"Yeah, heard you're one of the smartest guys around here."

Hudson let out an indelicate snort. "Someone's been filling your head with nonsense. I'm extremely good at my job, but I'm hardly one of the smartest around here."

"You seem to have done pretty damn good for yourself."

There was no mistaking the implication, and Hudson had grown weary of these games years ago. "You mean for a marked Therian lacking his mate?"

Trent had the courtesy to look abashed. "I didn't mean to imply you wouldn't have, uh, or I mean... shit." Trent laughed. "I'm sorry. I'm really shitty at first impressions." He smiled wide, and it reached his eyes. "I don't care that you're marked, and I don't think anyone else should either. I just meant that despite what obstacles you clearly faced, you rose above all that shit. I admire you."

Hudson peered at him. "You really don't care?"

Trent shook his head. "Why should I? It's none of my business. All I see before me is a very successful, smart, beautiful man."

Hudson opened his mouth, then closed it, uncertain of how to respond. His cheeks felt warm, and he bit his bottom lip. *Bollocks!* He was blushing.

"Anyway, I just came by to introduce myself, and make an ass of myself apparently." He laughed, embarrassed. "I'm sorry. I'll, uh, leave you to more important things." He turned, and Hudson called out to him.

"Wait, Trent."

Trent paused, then turned back, smiling at him. "Yeah?"

"You didn't make an arse out of yourself. Thank you for stopping by."

Trent nodded. "Thanks. I better go, or I'll just stand here all day listening to that accent of yours. What part of England are you from?"

"Kent," Hudson replied.

Trent smiled, and with a wave, he walked out. Hudson sat, unable to help his smile. His cheeks were still somewhat flushed, which was a strange sensation—mostly because someone other than Seb had put it there. At times he wondered if anyone else in his unit felt the same as Trent and simply didn't approach him out of respect for Seb, which was silly, considering Hudson was no longer with Seb and had no obligation to him.

"Who was that?" Nina walked into his office, holding a cup of coffee in one hand and a cup of tea in the other. The familiar tag at the end of the tiny white string dangling from beneath the lid gave it away. She placed it on his desk before depositing herself in the chair Rafe had vacated.

"Thank you. And that was Agent Trent Carson from Philadelphia HQ. He's filling in for Taylor while he's on leave." He removed the lid from the steaming-hot cup of tea, unable to help his contented sigh. This was just what he needed. Now that Trent was gone and Nina was here, it brought him back to Rafe's visit. He took a sip of his tea and closed his eyes for a moment. Nothing soothed him like a good cup of black tea with a little milk and sugar.

Nina took a sip of her coffee, and Hudson could tell she was trying hard to make it appear as if nothing was wrong. They'd been playing this little game for months now, skirting each other, being polite, cracking the occasional smile. Nina would sit with him in his office, much like now, and they'd have their tea or coffee, but whereas before it was filled with lighthearted banter, gossip, and teasing, now there was a heavy silence, a thick fog of hurt between them. Hudson missed his friend. One thing was for certain; they couldn't continue like this. Rafe's visit gave him a lot to think about.

TWO DAYS later, as promised, Hudson once again accompanied Dex and Sloane to the TIN facility holding Taylor. Sloane waited in a separate room as he had the first time, only now he was a little more at ease since he no longer feared Dex would lose a limb. He'd been relieved the first encounter had gone without incident, until Dex recounted what happened, and Sloane all but had a bloody aneurism after he learned Dex had stuck his hand inside the cage while Taylor had been feral. Sloane's blustering left him red-faced and winded, and Hudson couldn't help but pat Sloane's shoulder in sympathy. A few sweet kisses and a little purring from Dex helped soothe Sloane and his bristled jaguar Therian half.

Hudson and Dex were led to an infirmary of sorts, and inside they found Taylor resting. The back of the bed was inclined, so they smiled when Taylor opened his eyes. He smiled in return.

"You came back." Taylor's voice was still rough, and he clearly had quite a bit of recovery to do, but he certainly looked better than he had two days ago.

"Of course," Dex replied, coming to stand by Taylor. "Let me get you some water. I'll be right back." Dex patted Taylor's shoulder and walked to the door. Hudson studied Taylor as he followed Dex's every move. The yearning in his eyes was unmistakable.

"I'm sorry," Hudson said quietly. "I didn't realize."

Taylor gave a start, as if he'd only just remembered Hudson was there. "You care for him."

Taylor shook his head, his frown deep before he let out a shuddering sigh. "I don't know when it happened, when it went from just wanting to… sleep with him, to thinking about him all the time. It's not like we get to talk on callouts, or any other time, really, but when I'm around him, he just… he takes my breath away, and that's never happened to me before. I know I can't have him, ever, but a part of me keeps hoping, and I hate myself for it because he's happy. If Sloane left him tomorrow, I wouldn't care that he's marked."

"You wouldn't?" Hudson blinked at him, stunned by the intensity in Taylor's gaze.

"No." Taylor let out a heart-wrenching sigh. "I don't know what to do. I need to forget about him. To move on. How do I do that?"

"He's getting married," Hudson offered gently.

Taylor scrunched up his nose, the gesture clearly more to keep his emotions at bay than anything else. He pressed his lips together in a thin line and nodded. "Yeah." His voice broke, and he cleared his throat. "That'll do it, then. Thanks, Doc."

Hudson nodded. He knew what it felt like to love someone and want nothing more than to move on with your life, yet find yourself unable to do anything but wish to be in that person's arms. If he could provide Taylor with any solace, help him leave behind the torture of pining for a man he couldn't have, then Hudson would do what he could.

Dex returned with a pitcher of water and a stack of paper cups. He placed them on the small tray table beside the bed before taking a cup to pour Taylor some water. Hudson declined the offer. While Dex and Taylor made small talk, Hudson removed his tablet from his messenger bag and swiftly typed away, taking notes of everything that had occurred up to this moment. Hudson wasn't merely here as Dex's personal physician. He was here to witness and document everything for Dex, and for reasons Hudson had yet to uncover, TIN was allowing it. Hudson had every intention of getting answers from Dex once they were in private, away from TIN.

"Can you tell me what you remember?" Dex asked, leaning forward, his hand on Taylor's arm.

Taylor released a steady breath. "I was in the armory, double-checking the inventory on my team's equipment when Moros walked in. I can't remember why he said he was there, but something felt... off. I figured it was just my general dislike of the guy. I'd always thought he was an asshole. I love my job and what we do, but I hate those fucking pricks. They sit behind their desks, breathing down our necks for every little thing we do, while we're the ones risking our lives out on the streets. I know we signed up for it, but they're supposed to help us, not throw us under the bus to save their own asses. Besides, he might have been a soldier once, but he betrayed that part of himself a long fucking time ago.

"Anyway, he asked me to accompany him to his car, said he wanted to talk to me." The muscles in Taylor's jaw clenched before he continued. "There was no reason for me not to trust him. As much as I disliked him, he was the Chief of Therian Defense. If the man tells you to jump, you say, 'Yes, sir,' and fucking jump. When we got to his car, he patted my cheek, and then everything went black." Taylor closed his eyes, and Dex leaned in to put a hand on Taylor's shoulder.

"Take your time. There's no rush."

Taylor nodded. He opened his eyes, his smile tremulous at best. "Thanks." He continued, his voice unsteady, "When I woke up, I was so out of it. I had no idea where the hell I was. I couldn't see anything. There was this blinding white light in my face. I... I remember not being able to move, and I thought my heart was going to explode with how fast it was beating. The smell was rank. I thought I was dying. My body was on fire. Like my muscles were being torn from their bones, and my head felt like it was being crushed. I think I might have been sick at one point, but I blacked out soon after." Tears welled in his eyes, and he rubbed his eyes with the base of his palms.

"You're doing great," Dex said, smiling at Taylor.

Taylor breathed in deeply through his nose, then released it slowly through his mouth. He nodded. "I heard voices. Moros and some other guys, but I didn't recognize them. I think I had a seizure or something, heard shouting. Someone said I was going to die." Taylor frowned in thought. "When I next woke up, I was at work, in one of the sleeper bays. I was a little sore, but fine, so I figured I'd just had a really fucked-up dream.

We were called out, and I remember shifting in the back of the BearCat. I jumped out and helped round up those frat boys. I…." He worried his bottom lip with his teeth before dropping his gaze to his hands.

"Taylor?" Dex ducked his head so he could get Taylor's attention. "Tell me."

"Everything was fine, and then… I caught your scent. I saw you running, and this overwhelming need to catch you came over me. I took off after you, and suddenly I realized I wasn't in control. I was fading. I screamed, and then everything went black." Taylor started shivering, and he wrapped his arms around himself. "I'd never been more scared than I was at that moment. I was clawing to stay, but something was dragging me into the darkness." The tears spilled over, and Taylor gulped for breath. "Everything went black, and I couldn't see, but I could hear you screaming at me, and fuck…." Taylor doubled over, his body racked with sobs. "I was hurting you, and I couldn't stop. I screamed and screamed, but something took hold, pulling…. I was on the verge of disappearing into nothingness."

"It's okay." Dex stood, leaned in, and brought Taylor into his embrace. Taylor held on for dear life, the trauma of what happened to him turning his face ashen.

Hudson's hands trembled, and keeping his tears at bay took effort. He couldn't imagine a worse fate than feeling himself fade away within his Therian form, to lose himself completely to his feral half. His inner wolf was a part of him, offered comfort, protection, and the unfaltering truth that Hudson was always present, in control. At times it was an incredible freedom, shifting into his wolf Therian form, running with the wind in his fur, his paws on the dirt, and his senses heightened. But to lose himself? To be forced into the farthest recesses of his own mind without the assurance he'd return? It was the stuff of nightmares.

Forcing past the emotions, Hudson resumed his typing. Taylor would require extensive help recovering from this event, but Hudson was grateful Taylor hadn't ended up on his examining table, the tragic victim of a deranged man.

Dex was gentle with Taylor, and Hudson's heart broke a little at Taylor's wobbly smile. Poor Taylor had it bad. He'd been very good at hiding his feelings for Dex. Hudson was aware of the aggression between Taylor and Sloane, but Hudson, like most of their unit, had assumed Taylor's interest in Dex was purely sexual. The fact Dex was marked by Sloane, an Alpha who'd ruffled Taylor's fur from the beginning, aided in the assumption Taylor simply wanted what was Sloane's.

When Taylor had calmed, Dex motioned to the door. "Sloane's here. Do you mind if he joins us?"

Hudson looked from Dex to Taylor and back. Was that a good idea?

"Sloane? Shit, he probably wants to kick my ass."

"He knows it wasn't your fault," Dex assured him.

Taylor nodded with some reluctance, and Dex stood. He pounded twice on the door, and it opened. Sloane stepped into the room, his expression softening when he saw Taylor. Clearing his throat, Sloane took a seat on the other side of Taylor. He held his hand out, and Taylor stared down at it before taking it.

"I'm glad you're okay." Taylor's voice was rough when he spoke. "I'm sorry for what happened."

"It wasn't you." Sloane released Taylor's hand and sat back. He didn't look angry or upset, and Hudson was relieved.

Taylor was having trouble meeting Sloane's gaze. "Do you believe that? After everything I've said and done?"

Sloane nodded. "I do."

"Thanks." Taylor shifted uncomfortably. "Congratulations, on, um, your engagement."

Sloane smiled, a genuine one that reached his amber eyes. He put a hand on Taylor's shoulder and gave it a gentle squeeze. "Thank you. You need to get better, okay? Your team needs you, and Herrera's been driving everyone nuts."

"Why?" Taylor look puzzled.

"He's been worried about you. Whenever we see him, it's 'Do you think Taylor's okay? When do you think Taylor will be back? Why isn't Taylor back? Have you heard anything about Taylor?'"

This piece of information seemed to have thrown Taylor for a loop. His mouth opened, but no words were forthcoming. He closed his mouth and looked up at Dex for confirmation. Dex shrugged and chuckled.

"It's true. You should see him. It's like he's lost without you."

Taylor blinked at him. "Herrera? Angel Herrera?"

"You guys have been friends for like, ever, right?" Dex asked.

"Yeah. We were at the THIRDS Training Academy together. Graduated in the same class." Taylor squinted. "That was about ten years ago, I think, maybe a little longer." He appeared to be processing what Dex and Sloane told him, a frown on his face. Brows furrowed, he looked up at Dex. "He was really worried about me?"

Dex nodded. "I think he misses you too, so, you know, when you get back, maybe let him fuss over you, huh?"

Taylor's eyes went wide. He nodded. "When do you think I'll be back?"

"That depends," Sloane said thoughtfully. "They need to run some tests and monitor your health for a while, but if you agree to some checkups, scheduled sessions with Dr. Winters, and you're willing to ride a desk for a while, Sparks will reinstate you. A month or two. As for how long it'll take before you're cleared to go out in the field, that I can't say."

Taylor thought about it before extending his hand to Sloane. "Deal. To be honest, I'll just be happy to get my life back."

Sloane took Taylor's hand and smiled wide. He patted Taylor's shoulder and stood. "I'll let her know. If you need anything, you have Dex's number."

Taylor smiled. "Thank you, Sloane." He turned to Dex and held out his hand. "Thank you. For everything."

Dex gave him a wink. "That's what friends are for, right?"

Taylor looked stupefied. "Friends?" He shifted his gaze to Sloane, who nodded. "I don't know what to say."

"Just get better," Sloane said, heading for the door.

Hudson put away his tablet and stood. Taylor grabbed Dex's arm, stopping him from leaving.

"Could you, uh, do me a favor?"

"Sure."

Taylor cleared his throat, his face somewhat flushed. "Do you think they'll let me talk to Angel?"

Dex's smile was dazzling. "I think I can make that happen."

Taylor's smile mirrored Dex's, his relief instant. "Thanks."

Hudson patted Taylor's shoulder before he followed Dex and Sloane out of the room. The door was closed behind them, and they walked down the corridor. Hudson couldn't help his smile. He cast a sideways glance at Dex.

"Lost without him, ay?"

Dex shrugged, his smile sly. "I may have embellished a bit."

"Right."

"Herrera's definitely missing Taylor, and if you ask me, he's a little in love with the guy. He just hides it well. Really well."

"And you know this how?"

Dex sobered up, and he elbowed Sloane gently. Sloane cleared his throat.

"He kind of lost it a little bit when Ash took Taylor's name off the roster. Herrera cursed at Ash and shoved him."

Hudson stared at Sloane. "Herrera shoved Ash? The same man who fears retribution for the infamous fern incident?"

Sloane nodded, amusement in his eyes. "The very same. He told Ash what he could do with his fern."

"Oh dear Lord. What was Ash's response?" Hudson was stunned that Herrera, who was not only a cheerful, even-tempered man, but spent a good portion of his time avoiding Ash Keeler, would not only have a few choice words for the fierce lion Therian, but shove him.

Sloane cocked his head. "After the initial shock wore off, Ash just stood there quietly until Herrera was done. Then Herrera stormed off."

"And Ash let him go? Pardon me, but did you say Ash stood there and let Herrera curse at him?" Hudson shook his head. Was he missing something? Ash Keeler had let another person—one whom he threatened with imminent demise on an almost daily basis—be aggressive toward him?

"Ash is more perceptive than he gets credit for," Sloane replied. "Herrera's not one to fly off the handle like that. And he did. About Taylor. Seeing his name removed from the roster hurt him somewhere deep. Ash saw that."

Hudson agreed Ash was a very perceptive man. He was far more intelligent than most believed him to be. Sadly, it was one of many ridiculous assumptions made about lion Therians. That they were lazy, thick-skulled hotheads. Ash might have quite the temper, but he possessed a greater range of emotions than simply anger. His relationship with Cael exhibited as much. The young cheetah Therian seemed to bring out Ash's gentler side, one few believed he possessed. Hudson's thoughts wandered off to his relationship with Seb, and how much Hudson had changed from the man he'd been when he first arrived in New York City. He'd been so closed off from the world, from everything around him.

Two TIN operatives appeared out of nowhere, startling Hudson from his thoughts. He let out a very—in his opinion—rugged squeak before glaring up at one of them, a sleek-looking jaguar Therian.

"Blooming hell! Honestly," Hudson huffed, "must you pop out of the shadows like some bleeding vampire? We're in *your* facility. There's no one else here!"

Sloane had some manners and put a fist to his mouth to keep from laughing. Dex on the other hand had been raised in a bloody barn and didn't bother, laughing without reserve.

"Oh, quiet, you." Hudson pointed a menacing finger at Dex. "If you ever sneak up on me like that, I will kick your arse."

"No, you won't," Dex said with a chuckle.

Hudson pursed his lips, his eyes narrowed. "Well, I'll be miffed at you, that's for certain."

"That, I don't doubt," Dex said, throwing an arm around Hudson's shoulders, his boyish grin wide.

Hudson grunted his displeasure at being so blasted predictable. Maybe he wouldn't kick Dex's arse, but he'd certainly want to.

They were escorted out into an empty garage, where an SUV like the one that brought them waited to transport them back to HQ. The doors had closed behind them when Dex surprised Hudson by taking a seat beside him instead of across from him where Sloane was sitting.

"Everything all right?" Hudson asked.

"Yeah. So, you know how TIN let you come along with us and take notes?"

"I was curious about that," Hudson admitted. "Why were they so… agreeable? Whatever you asked for, they jumped to it, as if you were—" Realization slammed into him, and he gasped. He moved his gaze from Dex's concerned expression to Sloane's somber one and back. "You…? Both of you…?"

Dex nodded, but Hudson couldn't seem to grasp the situation. Dex and Sloane… TIN?

"But… how? *Why?*"

Dex explained all the good he wanted to do with TIN, and the more Hudson listened, the more it made sense. Dex was a passionate man, with a strong sense of righteousness the likes of which he'd never seen. Family was as vital to Dex as breathing. After everything he had suffered with the loss of his parents at the hands of Moros and his cohorts, it was no surprise he wanted to do everything in his power to protect the family he had now. Hudson understood. For Sloane, his passion was akin to that of his future husband.

"I know I've put you in danger by bringing you into this, but it's not too late to back out," Dex said, placing his hand on Hudson's shoulder. "If anything happened to you because I pushed you—"

Hudson put his hand up to stop Dex. "You didn't push, Dex. You came to me in need, and I agreed to help. Since that day you walked into my home, you've made no secret of the dangers I could be facing. You've given me ample opportunities to walk away, and have continued to voice your concern since Wolf's warning. I appreciate it. I truly do, but I *want* to do this." He smiled warmly at Dex. "You're not the only one who wants to make a difference. I've spent a long time dealing with victims who've met their ends too soon. If I can do something to help prevent them from ending up on my examiner's table, then please, let me do that. Let me help you."

Dex nodded. "Okay. But if you ever want out, you tell me."

"You have my word."

Hudson loved his job, but sometimes he wished he could do more. This was his chance. It had been rather frightful knowing a lethal killer had been observing him closely enough to have photographic evidence of events in Hudson's life. Why Wolf decided Hudson needed protecting was beyond him. Then again, no one could explain why Wolf did anything. The man was an enigma. It could all be an elaborate setup. For now, Hudson would continue to exercise caution.

With Hudson's assurances, Dex changed the subject to a more jovial topic, including the party taking place this evening at Dekatria. Dex and Sloane would be announcing their wedding date, which they refused to share with Hudson despite his poking.

"Very well," Hudson said with a sigh. "Any thoughts on the stag nights?"

Dex eyed him. "The what now?"

"Stag night. The, um…." What the hell did Americans call it? "Oh." He snapped his fingers. "The bachelor party."

"Ah, stag. Right. Makes sense." Dex shrugged. "I have no idea, to be honest. Cael's my best man, so he's been put in charge of that."

"Ash will be putting mine together since he's my best man," Sloane said, smiling.

Dex shook his head, his eyes wide. "I don't know whether to laugh or be absolutely terrified at the idea of Ash putting together a bachelor party. I can't even picture it. The dude hates everything. A gun-range theme maybe? Bobbing for grenades?"

Sloane rolled his eyes. "I'm sure it'll be fine."

"Just as long as he brings you back in one piece," Dex replied sweetly, patting Sloane's knee.

Hudson looked between Dex and Sloane. "Two stag nights during which both of you will be without the other. This should be interesting."

Sloane sat up suddenly. "Shit, that's right." He stared at Dex. "I won't be there for your bachelor party."

"That's sort of how it works, babe," Dex said, laughing softly.

"You'll be at a bachelor party, where there's lots of alcohol, and then let loose on the city. All night. Without me." Sloane looked like he was on the verge of hyperventilating. "Please don't blow anything up."

Dex arched an eyebrow. "Being a tad dramatic, aren't we?"

"Who's going to keep an eye on you?"

Hudson pressed his lips together to keep from laughing. Poor Sloane.

"Babe, it's fine," Dex cooed, running his hand through Sloane's hair to soothe him. "I won't be alone. Lots of people will be there."

Sloane scoffed. "Yeah, none of whom are equipped to handle a Threat Level Fuchsia." He gasped and clamped a hand over his mouth.

"A code what?" Dex peered at him, and Sloane groaned. He let his head fall into his hands.

"What's a Threat Level Fuchsia?" Hudson asked. Whatever it was, clearly Dex didn't know either.

Dex crossed his arms over his chest, his eyes narrowed. "I'm waiting, oh love of my life. Husband-to-be. Holder of the sexy pants. Snuggle muffin who is five seconds away from sleeping on the couch tonight."

"All right. It's a code Ash and I came up with when you first joined." He put his hands up, his expression pleading. "It was before we were dating. I'm so sorry. It was immature."

"And when was this code used?" Dex asked, his expression unreadable.

"When we came across a situation that might possibly lead to you going a little, um, nuts, and where maybe it would be necessary to keep the situation contained."

Dex studied him. "So, let me get this straight. You and Ash came up with a threat level code for me and my crazy, and when said threat level code was used, it meant you and/or Ash would need to contain the situation."

Sloane winced. "Yeah, something like that."

"And who would be the one in charge of containing my crazy?"

"Well, me obviously. You're my partner. Ash helped. Sometimes. Not often."

Hudson had no idea what to think of that, other than it was genius. Not that he was about to mention it.

"Sloane," Dex growled, and Sloane pouted before Dex threw himself into Sloane's arms. "That's the sweetest thing I ever heard! You were crazy about me from the start even if you didn't know it." He trailed kisses all over Sloane's face.

"You're not mad?" Sloane asked, laughing at Dex's enthusiasm.

"Mad? Even if I was your partner and nothing more, you didn't have to care. You could have just looked the other way, or reported me, but you didn't. You cared, and you kept an eye on me, and you and Simba cared enough to give me my own code. Whatever he says, I know Ash loves me too. This confirms it."

"Yeah, I think maybe we should keep this between us. You're really not mad?"

Dex chuckled. "Are you kidding? I have my own threat level. How awesome is that? Let me guess, Ash picked the color."

Sloane nodded.

"Of course he did. The big dork."

"So we're good?" Sloane eyed him.

"Yes," Dex promised. "And don't worry about my bachelor party. Hudson will keep an eye on me." Dex turned his 1,000-watt smile at Hudson. "Right, Hudson?"

Bollocks.

CHAPTER 4

HUDSON ARRIVED at Dekatria a little earlier than the time indicated on his invite, as per Dex's request. Destructive Delta was already there, save for Sergeant Maddock, who preferred intimate family get-togethers over boisterous parties filled with "boozed-up, karaoke-singing shenanigans." Hudson couldn't blame him. Maddock had, after all, raised Dex and Cael on his own. He deserved some peace and quiet.

As per usual, Destructive Delta had commandeered the entire second floor of Dekatria, and later in the evening, they would move up to the roof garden as well. Bradley was very generous, graciously closing the bar for their private events. Dex had tried to pay Bradley once, and very handsomely, but Bradley had refused to take his money, stating he didn't need it. He much preferred the company.

Ethan smiled brightly when he saw Hudson and came over to pull him into a huge bearlike embrace, making Hudson chuckle. Ethan was an exceptional hugger.

"Hello, love." Hudson pulled away, noticing Calvin was over by the bar with Dex, helping him pour snacks into giant colorful bowls. "How are things between you and Cal?"

Ethan beamed at him and put his thumbs up.

"I'm so glad." Hudson cleared his throat, his face growing warm. "Is, um, your brother here?"

Ethan shook his head. He tapped his watch and put up both hands, fingers splayed.

"Ten minutes?"

Ethan nodded. He patted Hudson's shoulder before Calvin called him over to help, warning him not to eat more than he put out, then handed Ethan a large bag of some unnaturally orange curled cheese snack. Hudson

was tasked with moving the biscuit trays over to the long table at the end
of the room, seeing as he was the least likely to eat what he was putting
out. Silly buggers. Hudson pilfered a couple of chocolate-and-caramel
biscuits when no one was looking. Ooh, the double chocolate biscuits
with cherries looked heavenly! He took one of those too, as payment for
services rendered. Did they think he'd work for free? He had a biscuit in
each hand, and one between his teeth, when he turned and almost ran into
someone.

"Shooz me," he mumbled around a mouthful of chocolatey goodness.
A low grumble of a chuckle stilled him, and he looked up, eyes going wide.

"Caught red-handed, Lobito." Seb peered at him, amusement lighting
his eyes. "Does Dex know he's put the Cookie Monster in charge of his
cookies?"

Hudson wrinkled his nose since he couldn't scoff. *I don't know what
you're talking about.*

"I think you need to back away from the table, Dr. Colbourn. Back
away slowly," Seb teased, taking hold of the chocolate biscuit poking out of
Hudson's mouth. Hudson refused to release it, a low growl rising from his
throat. This was *his* tasty treat. Seb tugged at it, and Hudson narrowed his
eyes. Was Seb seriously attempting to take a delicious morsel of food from
him? He knew better.

Seb laughed. He snapped the biscuit, then popped it into his mouth.
Hudson gasped around his remaining half of biscuit. The fiend! He cursed at
Seb, who waggled his eyebrows as he chewed, then let out a decadent moan.

"That was so good."

Hudson put his biscuits on the table and removed the one from his
mouth to curse at Seb, but Seb snatched the remaining piece from his hand.

"Oh, you bastard!" Hudson made a grab for the biscuit, but Seb raised
his arm high above his head. "You give me that back, you thief!"

"Technically, you thieved it first."

Hudson latched on to Seb's T-shirt with one hand to hold him in place,
while stretching to reach his biscuit, except not even standing on his toes
could he reach Seb's palm.

"Why are you so blasted tall?" Hudson griped.

Laughing, Seb threw an arm around Hudson's waist and tucked him at
his side to make getting the biscuit even harder.

"I don't know. Why are you so adorable?"

"Flattery will get you nowhere," Hudson said with a huff as he pushed
at Seb's arm. "Give me my biscuit!"

"Your what?"

"Piss off, Sebastian. It's a biscuit."

"It's a cookie, and there's a whole tray of them," Seb said, motioning to the table, as if he didn't already know Hudson's reply.

"None of them are my biscuit." It was ridiculous, but wolf Therians were very particular about what was theirs, and they did not like having their food thieved. Anyone who attempted to take food from his plate did so at their own risk.

"It's not like I borrowed one of your DVDs and never gave it back."

Hudson gasped in horror. "Don't joke about such things."

Seb threw his head back and laughed. At that moment, Ethan walked by, plucked the biscuit from Seb's fingers, and tossed it into his mouth. Seb and Hudson protested simultaneously.

"Hey!"

Ethan waved a hand cheerfully before returning to the bar.

Hudson pouted miserably. "He ate my biscuit."

"Half of it," Seb corrected, patting his stomach. "I ate the other half."

Hudson folded his arms over his chest and glared up at Seb accusingly. "He gets that from you, you know. Bloody biscuit thieves, the lot of you."

Seb laughed, releasing Hudson when he poked Seb's side. He noticed Seb glance at the table where Hudson's remaining biscuits sat. Seb's grin turned wicked.

"Don't even think about it," Hudson warned, backing up against the table and placing his hands to his sides to cup his biscuits. "Get your own."

Seb's lips curled up, a sinful tug of his mouth that sent Hudson's pulse racing. How was it possible the man grew even more beautiful with age? Several additional silver strands had appeared in his pitch-black hair in the years since they'd met, and a few more laugh lines joined the others at the corners of his eyes. He dressed in a stylish faded green T-shirt that made his eyes stand out even more and emphasized the expanse of his broad chest and shoulders before tapering down to his waist. His black jeans encased powerful thighs and legs, and what Hudson personally knew was an incredible arse. The heavy, black biker boots on Seb's feet probably weighed more than Hudson. Seb exuded strength, yet his heart was capable of a gentleness that could bring Hudson to tears.

Seb stepped up to Hudson, widening his stance so he could get in closer, Hudson's feet between Seb's. Hudson could smell his shower gel—a fruity, minty concoction—mixed with his own masculine scent. Butterflies appeared in Hudson's stomach, fluttering wildly as Seb took hold of

Hudson's right hand and tenderly pulled it away from the table, his eyes never leaving Hudson's.

"Such a messy little wolf," Seb purred, turning Hudson's hand over. Hudson dropped his gaze to his now-chocolate-covered palm. Bugger. He'd melted the chocolate off his biscuit. Seb lifted Hudson's hand, and Hudson's breath hitched. He wouldn't....

Seb smiled sweetly before running a finger across Hudson's palm. He brought his finger to his mouth and closed his lips around his chocolaty digit before sucking on it. A tremor ran through Hudson, and a small whine escaped him before he could stop it. Seb chuckled. He winked at Hudson before walking away. Swallowing hard, Hudson quickly straightened, relieved no one had been paying them any attention. He grabbed a napkin and cleaned his palm before tossing the napkin in the trash bin at the end of the table. Inhaling deeply, he straightened his cardigan, then let his breath out slowly through his mouth. He was fine. He could do this.

Boisterous cheering and catcalling resounded from the stairs, and Hudson smiled as fellow agents from Unit Alpha arrived, all of whom Hudson knew. Dom and the rest of Seb's team soon followed, along with Beta Ambush, including Trent Carson. Trent looked around the room and smiled at Hudson when he spotted him. Hudson returned his smile.

"Thank you, everyone, for coming tonight."

Dex's announcement caught the room's attention, and everyone quieted, gathering around Dex and Sloane, who stood in front of the bar facing them.

"What's going on?" Ash asked with a wicked grin. "Sloane knock you up already?"

"Ain't you cute," Dex drawled. "No. Next September, on the twenty-third, it'll mark four years since Sloane and I first met. We've decided to make that our wedding day."

The room erupted into cheers, and Hudson joined his friends as they rushed Dex and Sloane. When it was his turn, he gave Dex a big hug. He couldn't help but get all teary-eyed. He was such a sucker when it came to weddings.

"I'm so happy for you both," Hudson said as he pulled away. Dex wiped a tear from his eye before playfully punching him in the shoulder.

"Stop it. You're going to shatter the illusion of what is otherwise an exceptionally cool and composed agent of awesomeness."

Hudson gave him a sly grin. "This from the man who just the other day screamed like a small child over a spider."

"Your memory seems to be failing you, Doctor. It wasn't a spider. It was a hairy, eight-legged mutant beast out to steal my soul right before it sucked my brain out through my nose. It was undoubtedly a minion of that goat hell-beast that attacked me last week."

Hudson looked to Cael for verification of this hell-beast.

"It was a pygmy goat, and it was adorable," Cael said, laughing at his brother's stricken expression.

"It tried to kill me!"

"Kill you, huh?" Cael pulled out his mobile, tapped the screen, then scrolled through his photos until he found what he was looking for. He handed his mobile to Hudson, who let out a bark of laughter. There stood Dex in full tactical gear, holding his tranq rifle, his expression one of horror as a tiny goat in a pink knitted jumper chewed on his shoelace.

Dex put a hand on his chest. "I can't believe you took a picture of me in the midst of such a traumatizing experience."

"You're exaggerating," Cael said, rolling his eyes.

Hudson returned Cael's mobile before studying Dex. "Do you really have a goat phobia?"

"It's not a phobia," Cael informed him. "He just doesn't like them."

"No, not dislike." Dex narrowed his eyes, his voice coming out low and gravelly. "Loathe. I loathe them."

Cael shook his head. "You're such a drama queen."

Ash appeared at Cael's side. He held his hand out to Dex. "Congratulations, man."

"Are you... are you getting misty-eyed?" Dex peered at Ash, and Hudson tried his best not to laugh. Ash did look a little flushed, and his eyes were glassy.

"Screw you, Justice." Ash turned away only to have Dex tug on his sleeve.

"Aw, come on, big guy. Bring it here." Dex held his arms open wide, receiving a glare in response. "Dude, I'm entitled to two hugs from you in my lifetime. Now, and my wedding day, so suck it up like a big boy and bring it here."

Ash hung his head in defeat. He shuffled over to Dex, who wrapped his arms tight around him and closed his eyes.

"Mm, yeah, just like that. So good."

Ash pushed Dex away from him, ignoring his laughter. "You had to make it weird."

"I think we all need to cut loose." Dex clapped his hands together before declaring, "Shots all around!"

Everyone cheered, and Bradley began lining up shots at the bar. Dex grabbed Hudson's arm. "That includes you, Doc."

Hudson's eyes went wide. "Oh, no. Dexter, no." Unlike most of his brethren, Hudson could not hold his liquor. It was sad, really. Ash was always teasing him that he was a disappointment to Brits everywhere.

"Dexter, yes." A wicked gleam came into Dex's pale blue eyes, and he led Hudson over to the bar. Down the length of it was a row of colorful shots. "We're celebrating my engagement, and we are going to get shitfaced."

Ash gave Dex a hearty pat on the back that knocked him into Hudson. "Hurry up and pick your one shot that'll get you shitfaced, and leave the rest for us grown-ups. That goes for you too, Doc. You're as bad as he is."

"Piss off," Hudson muttered, his eyes narrowed at Ash.

"Ooh, look at that. The Doc can get snippy. Who'da thought? So you boys gonna drink something or just look at the pretty colors all night?"

Hudson and Dex exchanged glances before they picked up a shot glass in each hand. Hudson held his up.

"Cheers."

A mischievous smile came onto Dex's face as the blue of his eyes melted into amber. *Absolutely fascinating.* Equally interesting was the fact Dex was now on his fourth shot and didn't appear the least bit fazed. Realization seemed to hit Ash, and with a low growl, he turned and punched Sloane in the arm.

"Hey, what the hell, man?" Sloane rubbed his arm with a frown. "This is my party. Why are you hitting me?"

Ash thrust a finger in Dex's direction, and Hudson chuckled as Dex waggled his eyebrows and threw back another shot.

"That's his sixth one, and he's not shitfaced." Ash poked Sloane in the shoulder. "That's your doing."

"Oh." Sloane pursed his lips, looking thoughtful. "Did I forget to mention he can drink you under the table now?" Sloane laughed at Ash's horrified expression before punching him in the arm. "That's for hitting me."

"Dick," Ash grumbled.

Dex grabbed Hudson's arm, turning him to give him another shot. He really shouldn't, but it was a special occasion.

"Why not." Hudson took the shot glass and tapped it against Dex's before they threw back the burning liquid. Hudson was feeling wonderfully tipsy. He needed this. It was good to let go for a while. A pink shot glass materialized in his hand, and Hudson didn't hesitate. He tossed it back as well. "Oh, goodness." That tasted phenomenal! Like pink lemonade. Frankie Valli's "Grease" burst from the speakers, and Dex grabbed Hudson's arm.

"Come on. Time to boogie."

"Dex, I appreciate the gesture, but it's not necessary. I—" He caught Seb's eyes on him then. Bloody hell, Seb was handsome. Hudson smiled, but Seb looked away, his attention seized first by Dom joining him at the table, then by a very pretty young man. Hudson recognized the agent.

West Delray was a king cheetah Therian who worked Recon for Theta Destructive. Not only was he a very rare classification of Therian, he was stunning. Petite, slender, with sandy-blond hair interspersed with black streaks, West possessed a heart-shaped face, a dazzling smile, and the golden-amber of his eyes stood out against the dark kohl around them. He looked more like a rock star than a THIRDS agent. The winning combination of good looks and cheeky personality made it so West had a steady stream of admirers vying for his attention, all eager to become the object of his affections.

Dom flexed his arm, and West laughed. He squeezed Dom's bicep before turning to give Seb's bicep a squeeze. He leaned in close to Seb to say something. Whatever it was, it made Seb laugh. Not a polite laugh, but a genuine laugh that reached his green eyes and formed little creases at the corners. What could West have to say that could possibly be so entertaining? Seeming to take Seb's laughter as an invitation to join him, West grabbed an empty chair from the table behind him and placed it between Dom and Seb before dropping down into it. He looped his arm through Seb's as he laughed with Cael. The two cheetah Therians had become good friends since Seb had taken over Theta Destructive. Hudson frowned. Why hadn't Seb pulled his arm out of West's hold?

Not that Hudson could fault West. Seb was ruggedly handsome, and despite his large size, muscular build, and lethal tiger Therian classification, he had a kind face and gentle eyes. He was a protector. A nurturer. It was no surprise Humans and Therians alike sought the comfort and safety his fierce tiger Therian frame offered. Cheetah Therians especially craved affection and possessed an inherent need to feel safe. They tended to gravitate toward those who could fill those needs, something not easily found in some larger Felid Therians.

"Hudson?"

Hudson gave a start. For a moment, he'd forgotten all about Dex. "Terribly sorry. You go ahead. I think I'll have another one of those lovely shots."

"Okay. See you on the dance floor." Dex gave him a wink and headed off, dancing his way to Sloane.

"Hey, Doc."

Turning, Hudson found Trent smiling brightly at him. "Oh, hello, Trent."

"Listen, um, I was wondering if you'd dance with me?"

Hudson was going to politely decline when he heard West laughing and asking Seb to protect him. He turned in time to catch West all but climbing onto Seb's lap in an attempt to avoid Dom's playful assault. Instead of extricating West from his person, Seb simply laughed. He threw an arm around West's back, catching him before West could topple out of his chair. Hudson's inner wolf bristled as Seb pretended to drop him, making West flail and laugh. He threw his arms around Seb's neck as Seb pulled him up.

The hell with it. Seb clearly wasn't giving Hudson a second thought. Besides, they weren't attached. Seb could flirt with West all he wanted, and Hudson could dance with the handsome Trent Carson. Time he stopped pining after Seb like a lovesick pup. Trent didn't care Hudson was marked, and he was clearly interested in him. Why shouldn't Hudson give the man a chance? He'd been telling himself for years that he should see other people. Perhaps it was time he stopped being such a coward.

Sod it. Hudson turned and took Trent's hand. He smiled brightly.

"I would love to dance with you."

"STOP POKING me," West said through his laughter. "You're so pokey." He rolled and jumped to his feet. "Wanna dance?"

"Thanks, but I'm good." Seb gave him another poke in his side just for good measure. He pulled his hand away before West could swat it. With a big smile, West grabbed Cael's arm and tugged. "Come on, Chirpy. Let's bust some moves."

"Oh my God, you did not just call me that, you turd!"

"Ha!" West darted off with Cael on his heels.

"Those two are adorable," Dom said with a chuckle.

Seb agreed. West was a great addition to the team. He'd originally been recruited by Intel for his IQ and talent, but unlike the rest of the agents who made up Unit Alpha's Intel Department, West was not content to sit behind a desk. It went against his very cheetah Therian nature. West needed action. He needed to be out on the streets.

Putting in a transfer and pleading his case to Sparks herself had gotten West transferred to Recon for Theta Destructive. He and Cael hit it off right away after a callout placed them both behind the same security console in Destructive Delta's BearCat. Dex had taken one look at the two excitedly "talking nerd," as Dex put it, and officially adopted West, much to everyone's amusement. Ash didn't seem to mind that his boyfriend had found a new best friend.

Ash's smile had Seb groaning. "West's single, you know."

"We're just friends," Seb assured him, then took a sip of his beer. Why was everyone always playing matchmaker? Was his love life in that bad a state that even Ash felt the need to get involved? Shit. It really was.

Dom let out an indelicate snort. "Yeah, I always sit in my friends' laps."

"He wasn't sitting in my lap. Come on, man. He's like Cael. He's affectionate and very hands-on. It doesn't mean anything."

Ash shook his head. "Cael's playful, but he doesn't flop all over other guys. You can't be that blind, bro."

"Whatever, Keeler."

"What? He's a good guy, and he obviously likes you."

"I like him too. As friends." Cheers and catcalls caught Seb's ear, and he moved his gaze to the source of the ruckus, his jaw muscles clenching. Beside him, Dom cursed under his breath, and Ash leaned in to Seb, his voice low.

"You maybe wanna reevaluate that?"

Trent Carson was wrapped around Hudson from behind, his front plastered to Hudson's back as Trent all but dry-humped Hudson on the dance floor. Hudson had his fingers in Trent's hair, his free hand over Trent's where it rested on Hudson's inner thigh. It was provocative, sinful, and boiled Seb's blood. Not because Hudson was dancing like that with another guy—though he wasn't over the moon about that either—but because Hudson was looking at Seb while he was doing it. *Son of a bitch.* Keeping an eye on Hudson was going to be the death of him. Mostly because he couldn't seem to keep his eyes *off* Hudson.

"Christ, man. Just watching you watching him is fucking torture. Why do you do this to yourself? I would have hightailed it outta here years ago. Transferred out of state or something."

"Yeah, 'cause you did such a bang-up job staying away from Cael." Seb met Hudson's blue gaze, the slow smirk all the confirmation Seb needed. Hudson knew exactly what he was doing. Well, this was a new development.

"Completely different. I was the dick screwing things up. He was waiting for me. Hudson's told you time and time again that it's not happening."

Seb couldn't tear his gaze away from Hudson, or the way he moved his lean, sculpted body against Trent's. "So what you're saying is I should abandon my team, my family, my life, and then what? Start over?"

"I'm saying you can't keep doing this to yourself."

"On that we agree," Dom muttered.

Right now he wasn't doing anything to himself. Hudson was the one baiting him, and he didn't appreciate it. Had it been anyone else, he might have given them a pass, but no one knew him like Hudson, and right now his ex-lover was using that knowledge to light a fire under his tail. What reaction was Hudson hoping for?

"Excuse me." Seb stood, and Dom's iron grip on his wrist made him pause.

"Come on, Seb. Just leave it."

Seb turned to meet Dom's hazel eyes, and the concern he found there. "You see what he's doing, right?"

"Yeah, and it's fucked-up, but you gotta keep your shit together. Not here. Not now."

Ash nodded, his expression stern. "It's Sloane's engagement party, man."

His friends were right. He let out a heavy sigh. This was a happy occasion. It would be shitty of him to drag his friends into his drama and ruin their evening.

"I won't let it get out of hand. I promise."

After some hesitation, Dom nodded and released him. "I'm here if you need me, okay?"

Seb patted Dom's shoulder before he made his way over to the crowded dance floor. He stopped in front of Hudson, his voice just loud enough for Hudson to hear.

"I need to talk to you. In private."

"Perhaps later, Sebastian," Hudson cooed, his head falling back against Trent's shoulder.

"Now," Seb demanded, grabbing hold of Hudson's wrist and jerking him away from Trent, who took hold of Hudson's arm.

"Hey, what—"

"Back the fuck off," Seb snarled, putting his hand to Trent's chest, stopping him in his tracks. "This is your only warning." Trent peered at Seb, his jaw muscles working. He released Hudson but didn't move away.

Hudson chuckled. "Well, this is a bit of a pickle, isn't it?" He put a hand to Seb's chest. "Trent, you know Sebastian. He's my old mate. I'm sure you've heard all about him. He's something, isn't he? So strong. The boys *love* him. Like a moth to a flame. Can you blame them? Look at him. Sebastian, I believe you know Trent." Hudson moved his hand to Trent's jaw. "He's a very good dancer, and I suspect he's very good at other things. We were getting to know each other."

Christ almighty. Really?

"That's enough." Seb dragged Hudson along with him, ignoring his protests and his attempt to get out of Seb's grip. The music was loud, and with so many people crushed together on the dance floor, no one paid them any attention. Their friends were too far away to know what was going on. Thankfully Trent didn't follow Seb as he pushed Hudson through the door leading to the back of the club. Seb brought Hudson up against the wall, crowding him so he couldn't walk away.

"What are you doing?"

Hudson pushed his glasses up the bridge of his nose, his eyes slightly wide. He poked his tongue out to lick his bottom lip.

Christ, how could one man have such an effect on him? Seb put a hand to his heart, the other against the wall to the side of Hudson's head. "You're killing me here, Lobito."

"Don't call me that."

"No."

Hudson eyed him. "No? What do you mean 'no'?"

"I'm not going to stop calling you that." Just like he'd never stop loving Hudson, or missing him, needing him, wanting him. He'd had enough of giving in to Hudson's every whim simply because Hudson asked. It was what he'd always done, and look how well that turned out. Time to do things a little different.

Hudson blinked up at him. "But… I asked you not to."

"Well, we don't always get everything we want, do we, sweetheart?"

"Why are you being so difficult?"

"Why are *you* determined to drive me out of my fucking mind?" Seb growled.

"I'm doing no such thing."

"Really? So you weren't letting Trent dry-hump you to make me jealous?"

Hudson's jaw dropped. "Of all the bloody cheek!" When he next spoke, it was through his teeth. "I was dancing."

"And watching me."

"Because *you* were watching *me*. Or do you think I can't feel it when your eyes are on me?"

Seb grunted. "Hard not to when you're making a spectacle of yourself."

Hudson's cheeks flushed a deep crimson, fire burning behind his eyes. "Piss off, Sebastian. I can dance with whomever I damn well please. What you choose to believe is your concern. How dare you judge me? Why don't you go find West? He couldn't keep his hands off you, and you obviously enjoyed it." Hudson was indignant, a pain in the ass, and the most beautiful thing Seb had ever seen. Since when did Hudson get jealous? Not even when they'd been together had Hudson ever become jealous. If he had, Seb never saw it. Hudson was always calm and in control, rational and sensible.

Seb placed his fingers under Hudson's chin and lifted his face so he could look into his eyes. "You've ruined me, you know. I can't love anyone else."

"You need to move on, Sebastian."

"Then give me back the heart you stole from me." Seb ran his thumb over Hudson's bottom lip. "You're a very beautiful thief. Stealing hearts, just to break them and leave them irreparable."

"If West isn't enough, I wouldn't fret. There's no shortage of cheetah Therians in Recon to fill your bed."

"Jesus, the mouth on you," Seb growled, feeling his anger rising. Hudson knew which buttons to push, and he was pushing them all mercilessly. "When are you going to grow up and stop being such a spoiled brat?"

Hudson gaped at him. "I beg your pardon?"

"You're a spoiled rich boy used to getting everything he wants. Your parents, your brothers and sisters, they all bent over backward to make you happy, but you never were. The more they gave you, the more you rebelled. Their precious little Colbourn prince. That's why you went out with me in the first place, wasn't it? One last 'fuck you' to the old man just before he disowned you. That's what your sister Evelyn told me when she had her husband's lackey track me down. What a pleasant phone conversation that was, by the way. Oh, how disappointed Mummy and Daddy were when you took up with a poor American nobody. Then your big brother had me investigated. His telling your folks I lived in a car at one point with my mother, big brother, unemployed disabled father, and spaz little brother was a nice touch. That's what George called Ethan, remember? A spaz."

"Stop it! Why are you bringing this up now? And you bloody well know that wasn't why I said yes to you."

"The only one who didn't put up with your bullshit, with your family's bullshit, was Alfie, and where did that get him? Six feet under."

The sting left behind by Hudson's hand to Seb's cheek was both startling and well deserved. What the hell was wrong with him? Seb drew in a deep breath, then let it out slowly. "I'm sorry. That was uncalled for."

"Is that why you brought me back here?" Hudson seethed, tears in his eyes. "To hurt me? I don't need you to remind me why my brother's dead, Sebastian. I know why he's dead."

"I didn't mean that."

"You did. You wanted to hurt me, and you have, in spectacular fashion. How could you? You know how much he meant to me. He was the only one who understood me. The only one who *saw* me. Before you, he was *everything*. He was all I had." Hudson's breath hitched, and Seb put his hand to Hudson's cheek.

"You're right. I was hurting, so I wanted to make you hurt. That was really shitty what I said. I'm so sorry. Please believe me." He meant every word. It was a low blow. Next to Seb, Hudson loved no one more than his brother Alfie. The guilt ate away at Hudson to this day. "Forgive me," Seb pleaded softly.

Hudson nodded, and he flattened his hands against the wall to his sides, his fingers splayed, as if the wall was the only thing holding him up. His eyes were hooded, his dilated pupils leaving only a sliver of pale blue rims. His lips were pink and slightly parted, his cheeks flushed, and hair tousled. Gingerly, Seb drew closer and slipped his leg between Hudson's. Their bodies were almost pressed together, the heat coming off Hudson almost choking him. Hudson's anger melted away, leaving him vulnerable and trembling in front of Seb. Hudson might make excuses, even lie, but his body would always betray him. All Seb had to do was nudge Hudson, the way he was doing with his knee against the bulge in Hudson's slacks. The way he shivered almost undid Seb.

Seb placed his hand to Hudson's cheek, his heart skipping a beat when Hudson closed his eyes and leaned into the touch ever so slightly. His skin was so soft and smooth. Images of them in bed flashed through Seb's mind. Tangled limbs, the sound of soft laughter, and the beauty of Hudson's face as Seb brought him to release. Making love to Hudson had been nothing short of a divine experience for Seb, a display of worship, of his undying adoration. Seb brushed his lips against Hudson's temple, leaving a feathery kiss behind before turning his face. God, he smelled so damned good.

Hudson tentatively moved one hand onto Seb's abdomen, drawing a quiet gasp from him. He thought Hudson might push him away, but instead Hudson slid his hand slowly up, his touch burning through Seb's T-shirt.

Seb lowered his head, their faces so close he could feel Hudson's breath on his skin. "You make me crazy," Seb murmured, brushing his lips over Hudson's in a butterfly kiss. Hudson parted his lips and angled his face up. He trailed his fingers down to Seb's belt, tucking them between it and Seb's skin, the touch scorching. Was he trying to keep Seb close? Seb leaned in for a kiss as Hudson moved his eyes to meet Seb's. They were glazed, and the tip of his nose rosy. Seb realized he could have Hudson inside the utility closet with his pants around his ankles with very little persuasion. The alcohol would make sure of it. The idea sent a surge of anger through him. He slammed his fist against the wall, startling Hudson.

"I'm sorry," Seb said gruffly, hating that he'd scared Hudson. He tore himself away and thundered out. Dex and Sloane were at the bar. Seb gave Dex a look of warning when Dex opened his mouth. "Hudson's out back. Make sure he gets home. Alone."

Dex didn't ask questions or argue. He quickly headed off toward the back while Seb grabbed his leather jacket from the coatrack by the stairs. He wanted Hudson. Wanted him more than anything, but not like that. Not while he was shitfaced and his defenses were down. If Hudson wanted him, he could damn well do it while he was sober. The last thing either of them needed was more guilt. As it was, Seb couldn't believe he'd dragged Alfie into this. He cursed himself for his stupidity, for lashing out at the man he loved more each day.

"Fuck." He hurried out of Dekatria, into the cool night air, his heart aching. This wasn't how it was supposed to go. What happened to time healing all wounds? It was bullshit, that's what it was. Seb clenched his fists at his sides as he walked. He needed to calm down. A horn blared, and Seb was jerked back as a car flew by. "Shit." What the fuck was wrong with him? He'd walked right into the middle of the road.

"Dude, are you okay?" A guy jogged over. "If that guy hadn't pulled you back...." He shook his head, and Seb raked his fingers through his hair, his heart beating in his ears. He looked around. Aside from the few pedestrians staring with either concern or like he was crazy, the sidewalk was empty.

"Did you see where he went?"

The guy looked around, scratching his head. "He was here like a second ago, and just... disappeared."

Seb didn't blame the guy for not sticking around. Probably thought Seb was some kind of nutcase. "Thanks," Seb said, checking the street this time before crossing. At least someone was looking out for him. He needed to pull himself together and not rely on a guardian angel to save his sorry ass, or he might not be so lucky next time.

HUDSON SLID down the length of the wall, his heartache forming a lump in his throat.

Not a day went by that he didn't think about or miss his brother. Alfie had only been a year older than Hudson, but he'd always been the big brother. He was the only one who looked out for Hudson, took care of him, taught him how to tie his shoes, how not to be scared of his Therian form. Alfie taught him how to be confident in who and what he was. They'd been two peas in a pod. When they were little, they pretended to be Sherlock Holmes and Dr. Watson, searching for clues and chasing villains. As soon as they turned eighteen, they set off on real adventures, traipsing around Europe until their father's lackeys brought them home. Years later, Alfie still teased Hudson, calling him Watson. Hudson had wanted to be Holmes, but Alfie refused, joking that if anyone was to end up dabbling in questionable substances, it would be him, while Hudson was more likely to end up the respectable doctor.

Their oldest brother, George, busied himself being the perfect heir, and although Theo had been kind, he was the second oldest, with a never-ending list of responsibilities that kept him away. Lewis and Evelyn spent their time going from one posh party to another. They were too concerned with their high-society friends, getting photographed with the right people, and adding to the Colbourn wealth to worry about their little brothers. Their mother, Emilia, spent her time managing Colbourn Cottage, a gothic-style manor built on twenty acres of land in Sevenoaks, Kent, where Hudson and his siblings had been born. It had a very modest seven bedrooms, five reception rooms, four bathrooms, a conservatory, tennis court, and swimming pool. The large staff, steady flow of visitors, and grand parties kept Colbourn Cottage in a constant flurry of activity. Hudson had never felt more alone than he did in his family home. His home had been Alfie, and one day his home was gone.

"Hudson?" Dex knelt beside him, a hand to his shoulder. "Hey, buddy. What happened?"

"It's my fault he's gone," Hudson said quietly, his hands on his drawn-up knees.

"Who? Seb?"

Hudson shook his head. "Alfie."

Dex sat down, his body pressed up against Hudson's, offering comfort. Hudson's inner wolf settled, feeling the warmth coming from his friend.

"Who's Alfie?"

"My brother. You would have liked him." Hudson couldn't help his smile. "He was a cheeky bugger. Always up to some mischief. Quick-witted, so confident and smart. He was charming and handsome too. Wherever he went, he left a trail of admirers. Everyone wanted to be where he was."

"Sounds like quite the guy."

Hudson nodded, tears welling in his eyes once more. "We were inseparable."

"Want to tell me about it?"

Hudson closed his eyes and let his head fall back against the wall. It had been so long since he'd talked about Alfie. Seb was the only one who knew the truth. "I'm afraid you might think less of me."

"Hey. You're my friend. Nothing you say will change that. I know you, Hudson. You're a good man. Whatever it is, you can tell me, but only if you want to." Dex put his hand on Hudson's arm, and Hudson opened his eyes. He rolled his head to look at Dex. The concern and affection in Dex's bright blue eyes eased Hudson's uncertainty.

Hudson pulled in a deep breath and let it out slowly. "My family comes from wealth. Old money passed down through generations. My great-grandfather was an earl or some such nonsense. I was never interested. Our name and wealth ensured my father never lost his place in society after he and my mother were infected with the virus. Unlike many, they embraced becoming Therian. My father used it to his advantage, boasting how his family had been gifted with an even greater strength. He'd always been an intimidating man, and after becoming Therian, no one dared speak against him.

"I'm the youngest, before me came Alfie, then Millie, Evelyn, Lewis, Theo, and George. All of us born wolf Therians. We became a pack, one my father sought to mold in his image. He wanted our family to become one of the most influential Therian families in England. He believes Therians are superior to Humans. How can they not be? He's one of them after all." Hudson shook his head in disgust. "My father, Dr. Felix Colbourn, was, and still is, a strict man, very set in his ways. No matter what we were, he had certain expectations for all his children, paths he'd chosen for all of us. There was no question of who would do what. Our entire lives were mapped out, from what schools we would attend, to what age we would marry, and who we would marry. Therian of course."

Dex frowned. "That sounds… harsh."

Hudson shrugged. "It was expected. My brothers and sisters fell into line, eager to please my parents and make them proud. They wanted the money and prestige. Alfie and I, we didn't want our lives dictated. We couldn't understand why it was so important to them. Everything had to be perfect. As the youngest, I was spoiled. Given everything I asked for. It was easier to placate me than spend the effort required to understand me. Whatever my siblings wanted, Alfie and I wanted the opposite, at times simply out of spite. We rebelled all through our youth. In our teens, we were always getting into trouble. We wanted to see how far we could push everyone.

"My father decided Alfie and I would pursue a career in cardiology, but from a young age, we'd been fascinated by forensic science, the way puzzle pieces are discovered and examined to form a bigger picture. We wanted to help those no longer capable of helping themselves, and perhaps bring peace to those left behind. The THIRDS caught our interest, and when I brought it up at dinner one evening, my father was absolutely livid."

"Why? The THIRDS is an elite worldwide organization that does great things."

"It's, to quote my father, 'a lowly position for men who desire power but are too poor to rise to much else.' Plus the idea of having any of his children working toward equality when Humans were so very much beneath us was simply too appalling for words."

Dex let out a scoff. "Charming."

"Quite. The arguments were never-ending, growing worse every time. They usually resulted in Alfie and I storming out and going on the piss."

"What's that again?" Dex asked, pursing his lips in thought. "That's different from taking the piss, right?"

"It means binge drinking."

"Ah. Right."

Hudson let out a shuddering breath and closed his eyes. He let his head hang as the familiar anguish washed over him.

"It was after we'd finished our residency. Evelyn was pregnant, and our family was throwing her a big bridal shower at a very grand seaside hotel in Cornwall. It was outdoors. Alfie and I decided we were going to tell our parents we'd applied to the THIRDS. It went as well as you can imagine. My father slapped me. Alfie and I got completely drunk off our arses. It was shambolic. Evelyn's husband and my brothers confronted us, and when George pushed me, Alfie punched him. We took off, and they followed. They caught up to us round the back of the hotel near the overhang...."

Hudson swallowed past the lump in his throat. A chill swept through him, and he shivered.

"George grabbed my arm, and I swung at him. I was so drunk I could barely see straight. Unbalanced. Alfie caught me before I fell and pushed me back, but he was nearly as drunk as I was. He lost his balance and stumbled back. I scrambled to my feet in time to watch him fall off the side of the cliff."

Dex gasped, his hand tightening over Hudson's arm, but Hudson barely felt it. He was numb, chilled to the bone. In front of him, he could see nothing but an expanse of dark ocean under a gray sky. The icy wind whipped at his tearstained face as he screamed, the sound drowned out by waves crashing against the cliff's side.

"I was there the next evening when my family went to identify... him." Hudson murmured, staring out into nothingness. "Quite frankly, everyone was astonished by the pristine state Alfie was in and how quickly he'd been found. Within minutes of calling emergency services. It was astounding, really.

"I won't ever forget his face, so handsome, looking as if he was asleep. The medical examiner had been startled by the death. Alfie had somehow missed the rocks at the base of the cliff. He hit his head, but that wasn't what killed him. The icy water, and the current... the shock... he never stood a chance. We'd been shown mercy, and Alfie had been washed up near the cliff's edge, so he didn't sink down to the bottom of the ocean. God knows when he would have resurfaced and in what condition. I wanted to touch him, assure myself it was really him on that table, that he was really... gone, but I couldn't bring myself to move. I was frozen to the spot, afraid if I did, I would shatter.

"My family blamed me. If I hadn't been so spoiled, if I'd listened, done as they asked.... The reasons were endless. When I was accepted to the THIRDS, a position suddenly opened up at HQ in Manhattan. I didn't hesitate. I needed to leave. My father cut me off. I sold what was mine, bought a plane ticket to New York City, and never looked back.

"They tried contacting me. It seemed as if the phone calls would never cease. At first I thought perhaps they wanted me back, but all they did was tell me how foolish I was. How I would never amount to anything on my own in America. My brother hired an investigator to keep an eye on me, which is how he discovered my relationship with Seb. George told my father all about the Hobbs family. My father demanded I leave Seb, and I told him to go to hell. He disowned me that very day, and I haven't spoken to him since."

Dex cursed under his breath. He handed Hudson a napkin, and Hudson smiled as he took it. He blew his nose and frowned. "Seb is cross with me."

"Why?"

Hudson explained, waiting for Dex to reassure him. Instead, Dex shook his head, his disapproval evident on his handsome face.

"You know I love you, man, but that was a dick move."

Hudson frowned. That wasn't what he'd been expecting. "Oh?"

"You were trying to make him jealous."

Hudson opened his mouth to refute the accusation, but Dex held up a hand to stop him.

"We both know Seb. He's not the kind of guy to play games. From what you said, it sounds like you wanted his attention, he didn't give it to you, and you got pissy. Trent was in the right place at the right time. You can't get mad because Seb called you out on your behavior. You either want to be with him or you don't, Hudson. You can't push him away, and then when he does what you want him to, get mad." Dex got up and held a hand out to him. "Come on. Let's get you home."

Hudson nodded. "Perhaps a shower and cup of tea is in order." He found it difficult to look Dex in the eye. "Forgive me. This is a happy occasion, and I'm being an arsehole."

Dex threw an arm around Hudson as he led him out into Dekatria. "All is forgiven, and if you need anything, you call me, okay?"

Hudson nodded, allowing Dex to help him into his jacket before escorting him downstairs and outside. Dex called him a cab, made certain he was settled in the backseat, and instructed the driver where to take him. Hudson thanked Dex and let his head rest against the window so he could look out into the streets. He pulled his keys from his pocket so he'd have them ready when he got there. His head was fuzzy, and he dozed off before the cab driver roused him awake with a gentle shake to the shoulder.

"Oh, terribly sorry." He thanked the man and made a mental note to treat Dex to lunch for paying his cab fare and tip. Outside his home, he was digging through his pockets for his keys when he felt odd. Like he was being watched. Peering down one end of the softly lit residential street, he found it empty. Same with the other end. It was most likely his alcohol-riddled brain. Where the hell were his keys? He groaned when he remembered he'd taken them out of his pocket. They'd most likely fallen somewhere in the cab. He turned, and a silver gleam caught his eyes.

"Thank bloody goodness." They were right there on the pavement. He picked them up, frowning down at them. They must have fallen on his person somewhere, then onto the ground without him realizing. With a sigh, he headed for his front steps. The back of his eyes stung, and he turned to sit on his stoop. He gazed up at the sky, feeling miserable.

"I miss you," he murmured.

His brother would have known what to do. He always did. Maybe then he wouldn't feel so alone. "How did I manage to lose *two* families, Alfie? That has to be some kind of record." He shook his head before running a hand through his hair. "I suppose I should be grateful you're not here to see how pathetic I've become. But then if you were here, I wouldn't be so alone." His mobile rang, and he tapped the screen before putting it to his ear. He hadn't bothered looking at who it was.

"Hudson?"

The soft voice brought a smile to his face, and the ache in his chest eased. "Julia?"

"Hello, sweetheart. I hope you don't mind me calling. I was making myself a cup of tea, and when I sat down on the couch to watch TV, one of the photo albums was there. I must have left it out when I was dusting the bookcase. Anyway, I went to return it to the shelf, and a photograph of you fell out. I missed your voice."

Hudson swallowed past the lump in his throat. "I missed your voice too. I'm so glad you called." Warmth spread through him, and he couldn't help his smile as he stood to head inside, Julia's sweet voice lifting his spirits. Her timing couldn't have been more perfect, and as he walked into his house, he said a silent little thank-you to his brother, wherever he was.

CHAPTER 5

"DON'T LOOK at me like that."

Hudson popped a couple of Tylenol into his mouth and took a long swig of his bottled water. Nina was giving him *that* look. The "I can't believe you did that" look. Apparently his work day was going to be as shite as the pounding in his head, but then he should have suspected as much, considering he'd started his day with a particularly gruesome autopsy. It was soon followed by phone calls and e-mails from a number of Therian solicitors who all believed their case was the most important case in the history of New York City and specifically wanted him to testify in court as their expert witness, not to mention were under the illusion Hudson was their personal circus poodle ready to jump through hoops on their command, because really, how long could a DNA analysis take? And surely cause of death could be easily determined by simply staring at a body long enough, and how dare he declare that piece of evidence contaminated—it had only been trampled on by four HPF officers, minimum.

He was waiting on a toxicology report, a ballistic report, had two subpoenas to sign off on—pending an inquest he had yet to do—an in-box filled with inquiries from dozens of agents from Unit Alpha, and was scheduled for two court appearances this week, one involving a defense attorney who wouldn't piss on Hudson if he were on fire, all because Hudson dared turn him down for a date. It wasn't even lunchtime.

What he needed was another cup of tea and a bed he could crawl back into. What he *didn't* need was a lecture from Nina. Last night he'd spent several hours catching up with Julia, and it had been wonderful, a ray of sunshine to his drab and cold existence. *All right, that's enough of that.* He was done feeling sorry for himself. Too bad he wasn't done with this blasted hangover. He'd been so swept up in his conversation with Julia, he'd forgotten to hydrate, and was paying dearly for it this morning.

"What were you thinking?"

Hudson groaned as he took a seat behind his desk. He glanced at his tablet and the blinking blue light denoting freshly arrived e-mails, then promptly turned it over. Last time he checked his in-box, he'd wanted to howl mournfully and curl up on himself. "I was thinking, 'Here's a good-looking bloke who wants to dance with me. I'm pissed. Why not?'"

"You know that's not what I'm talking about."

Hudson cursed under his breath. "First Dex, now you. I don't see what was so blasted terrible. Seb and I are not together, Nina." He was clearly not going to get any work done until she said her piece.

"And who's the one stopping that from happening?"

Hudson removed his glasses and pinched the bridge of his nose. "I'm not having this conversation."

"You never want to have this conversation." Nina flopped down into the chair across from him.

"Because it's none of your bloody business," he snapped. "Not anymore."

"That's not true." Her voice softened. "You're my closest friend. You can't pretend like the last ten years didn't happen."

Hudson scoffed.

"Don't be petulant," she ground out.

Hudson peered at her. "You lied to me, Nina. For months."

"You know why I did. I said I was sorry, and I am."

Hudson reclined back in his plush chair, his arms crossed. "Well, that's not good enough."

"What do you want from me? What more can I do to show you how sorry I am? Please, Hudson. You and him, you're the most important men in my life. Don't make me choose. I love him."

Hudson stilled. He looked up at her and saw tears in her deep brown eyes. "You… really love him?"

"Yes." She took his hand, a tear rolling down her flushed cheek. "It tore me up inside, not being able to tell you, but I never expected to…. I never thought I would fall for him. The more I got to know him, the more I realized what he put out there for everyone to see wasn't the man he was. He needed me, Hudson. He was all alone, in so much pain, terrified. How could I turn my back on him?"

Hudson had never seen her like this. Nina was sweet, but she was also an incredibly strong woman, one who could have easily been out there in the field with any of Unit Alpha's Defense agents, facing down threats. But she preferred the quiet of the lab, studying, dissecting, evaluating, investigating, reconstructing events, scenarios, causes of death. She was meticulous, and her sense of humor meshed perfectly with his. They kept each other and the other examiners from getting lost in the horrors they faced on the job. She was lighthearted, always smiling, laughing, playful, and the last person Hudson would have imagined could fall for a man like Rafe Hobbs.

"Do you love him or pity him?"

Nina's glare was indignant. "I do *not* pity him. Do you pity Seb?"

"Seb and Rafe are nothing alike."

"Really? You, me, the Hobbs family, we're the only ones who know how much pain Seb endures every day just walking, because if he didn't push through it, he'd have a permanent limp. He goes to physical therapy every week, and the only reason he doesn't take the needed level of pain pills is because he wants to stay in the field and not have it affect his job. So he suffers through it."

Hudson's jaw clenched, but he remained silent.

"When he'd come to your office, almost on a daily basis, I teased you that you two couldn't keep your hands off each other, but I'm not stupid, Hudson. You think I didn't see his eyes when he left here? I pretended not to know the real reason he was in here was because with you he felt safe enough to cry his fucking eyes out because his body hurt so goddamned much."

"That's enough," Hudson said quietly, the back of his eyes stinging. He didn't need a reminder of the pain the man he loved suffered, or of how much Hudson wished he could take that pain from him.

Nina leaned forward, gripping his desk's edge tightly. "What you feel right now is what I feel every time I see Rafe wince. It kills me that I can't do more. All I can do is be there and show him how much I love him. I didn't tell you because, as much as I adore you, Hudson, you can be spoiled and selfish sometimes."

Hudson stared at her. "I beg your pardon?"

"You reacted like I thought you would. It's all about you and how *you* feel. Rafe is going to end up like Thomas, and you're upset I chose to protect him. He didn't want to bring his family any more heartache. He didn't want his brothers treating him different or patching things up just because they pitied him. I did what you would have done for Seb."

"I—"

Nina put up her hand to stop him and stood. "Don't. Don't treat me like an idiot."

"I would never," he protested angrily, standing.

"Then don't act like you've always told me everything. I'm not saying I needed to know everything, because I didn't. What went on between you and Seb was none of my business. As long as you were happy, I was happy. But you always did things your way, no matter what anyone said. You listened, but you still went ahead and did whatever the hell you wanted. Always."

"That's bollocks. How can you say that?"

"Really? Can you name one time you argued with Seb where you didn't get your way?"

Hudson frowned deeply. "There were plenty of times."

"Like?"

"I can't remember every disagreement we had. If he thought I was so bloody wrong, why did he give in?"

"Because he's crazy about you! The man was so damn head over heels in love with you that he'd give in, even if he didn't agree, just to make you happy. That's not a sustainable relationship, Hudson, and I think deep down you know that." Her gaze was unwavering as she leaned her hands on the desk. "That's the real reason you won't give him another chance, because if you fuck it up this time, that's it. There's no going back."

Hudson's temper flared, and he slammed his hands on the desk. "That's enough! I don't know where you've gotten that ridiculous notion, but it couldn't be any further from the truth, and I am done explaining myself to you. I hope you and Rafe are bloody happy together, because you deserve each other."

Nina flinched. She straightened to her full height. "I know you meant that as an insult, but it's not to me. He's a good man, who deserves to be loved. He treats me as his equal. We're a partnership. He's not a self-righteous asshole."

Her words stung, and he opened his mouth for a rebuttal but instead only a choked sound escaped. His vision blurred, and he dropped down in his chair, turning away from her in the hopes of gaining some control over his emotions. He was so damn tired. This wasn't like him at all. Last night at Dekatria, Seb's words, hearing from Julia again, Alfie's death replaying itself in his nightmares over and over…. He'd barely slept. It was all catching up to him. A soft touch to his cheek startled him, and he was taken aback to find Nina kneeling beside his chair, her beautiful face void of anger or disdain. She cupped his face, wiping a tear from his cheek with her thumb.

"I'm sorry," he whispered. "You're right. Everything you said…." For years he'd been telling Seb what they'd had was broken, unfixable, and somewhere inside him he feared that had been the case, even before the incident that tore them apart. They loved each other fiercely, of that he had no doubt, but Nina was right. Hudson had always pushed, and Seb gave in. What a fool he was, believing he'd changed. That coming to the States would give him a new life, a different one, but he hadn't changed at all. He and Seb had been happy, but how long would it have lasted with Hudson's incessant need to push, to be right, to be so bloody perfect? And Seb gave in every time. Was that really what he wanted from Seb?

Tears clung to the thick black lashes of Nina's hooded, almond-shaped eyes. How could Rafe's heart not melt? She was beautiful inside and out, kind, and selfless, unlike Hudson. Nina never hesitated in putting someone else's needs before her own. She wanted to take care of everyone. She deserved to be happy, and if she'd found that with Rafe, Hudson should be excited for her. Who the hell was he to judge? In fact he should be the last person to judge anyone's relationship. God, when had he become such a mess?

"I'm sorry I pushed you away. I missed you." Hudson sniffed, and his heart swelled when she threw her arms around his neck, squeezing the breath out of him. How could he have been so petty? So pigheaded? It hit him how terribly he'd missed her, missed them, their friendship. He'd been walking around with a Nina-shaped hole in his heart, wallowing in his own self-imposed misery, and he hadn't even realized what an arse he was being.

"I love you," Nina said between sniffs before kissing his cheek.

"I love you too." He wiped at his face and smiled up at her when she stood. "Do you forgive me for being such a pillock?"

She chuckled and nodded, leaning against his desk, her delicate, long fingers gripping his hand firmly. "You know I do." She worried her bottom lip, and he gave her hand a gentle tug.

"You can tell me."

"How long are you two going to keep dancing around each other?"

It was a perfectly valid question. One Hudson didn't know the answer to. Actually, he did. "I'm afraid to let him go, Nina, but I'm even more afraid of… of having him. You're right. We were broken, and not just because of what happened. Even if we somehow moved past the guilt of that day, we can't go back to how things were. We'd never last, and knowing it's over for good would kill me. At least now I have hope. What will I have if things don't work out? If neither of us has changed? *I* haven't changed. You've said so yourself." His heart ached, and the mark on the back of his shoulder blade burned. He'd spent so long refusing to think about what had been and what could never be that the very real possibility of not having Seb in his life terrified him. His inner wolf stirred, whining softly.

"It doesn't mean things can't change," Nina suggested softly. "But you need to decide, Hudson. This can't go on. He gets close, and you let him, only to push him away when you get scared." She leaned in to cup his face. "Honey, you're living half a life. You deserve more."

Hudson nodded. What else could he say? More importantly, what could he do?

"Come on, I know something that will cheer you up." She grabbed his hand, pulled him to his feet, and led him to the door.

"It's all right, love. I—"

"Dex has leftover cookies from last night's party."

"Oh." Hudson smiled. "Well, in that case, he really should share." They strolled down the corridor arm in arm, and for the first time in months, he could breathe again. Maybe there was hope for him after all.

THE REST of the day had gone better than expected and was a vast improvement on his morning. After confiscating several of Dex's biscuits—a result of Hudson and Nina making big puppy eyes at him—they returned to the lab with their tasty treats. They'd been rushed off their feet the rest of the day, but having Nina chatting and laughing with him again made all the difference.

Hudson was in high spirits, and it was still light out when he left work. He dropped by the market on his way home and picked up some vegetables and beef. The rest of the ingredients he needed, he had at home. He hadn't made Cornish pasties in a while.

Thomas and his boys loved Hudson's homemade pasties. Of course, when he used to make them, it was usually over at the Hobbs house, because the number of ingredients and pasties required to feed four tiger Therians was staggering and certainly not something he could do without help. Julia and Seb always pitched in, though Hudson spent a good portion of his time threatening the brothers with imminent bodily harm if they continued to eat his ingredients.

For now, he made enough for Thomas and a few extras in case one of the boys dropped by. His pasties were secured in a large insulated container he'd slipped into a sturdy rectangular carrier bag that he held on his lap as the cab headed for the Hobbs residence. The butterflies in his stomach fluttered wildly, and he took a deep breath when they arrived. Hudson paid the driver and thanked him before getting out with the large bag. It had been so long since he'd been here.

Fortifying his nerves, he walked up the pavement to the front steps. The door opened before he reached it, and Julia stood with her hand to her mouth and tears in her big hazel-green eyes. He reached the top step and smiled.

"Hello, Julia." His voice cracked, but he managed to keep from bubbling like a baby. She took the bag he handed her, placed it on the table next to the door, then flung herself at Hudson. He caught her with a chuckle and held her as she squeezed him tight. When she pulled back, her wobbly smile made his chest hurt.

"Oh, sweetie, it's so good to see you." She cupped his face. "Just as handsome as the last time I saw you."

Hudson swallowed hard. "I wanted to see you and Thomas. I brought him some pasties."

"Julia, is that a crazy new air freshener, or do I smell Cornish pasties?"

Julia laughed. She stepped aside, and Hudson walked in, his heart squeezing at the way Thomas's smile lit up his handsome face when he saw Hudson. It was hard not to get teary-eyed. His own father had never looked at him the way Thomas Hobbs did. As if nothing made him happier than seeing his son home, because to Thomas, Hudson had been another son. He liked to remind Hudson often, as if knowing Hudson needed to be reassured he was wanted.

Thomas drove his electric wheelchair forward and stopped in front of Hudson. He looked up at him, the same emerald-green eyes he'd gifted his sons bright with unshed tears.

"It's good to see you, son."

Hudson pressed his lips into a thin line to keep himself together, but that was made difficult when Thomas lifted the armrests of his electric wheelchair and held his arms out. Hudson didn't hesitate. He crouched next to Thomas and threw his arms around him, burying his face against Thomas's broad chest. Thomas's arms were strong, and being hugged by him was like being enveloped in a protective bubble, like nothing could touch Hudson because Thomas was there to chase away the monsters lying in wait under his bed.

Thomas petted Hudson's hair before releasing him, his smile wide when Hudson stood. He took Hudson's hand and gave it a squeeze. His smile fell away.

"We wanted to come see you when you were in the hospital, but Seb…. He thought it would be best if we didn't."

Hudson nodded. He shoved his hands into his pockets, regret filling him. "He was right. It would have been too difficult. It was hard enough having him there." Hudson cleared his throat. "He wouldn't leave my side."

Thomas nodded his understanding. "I expected no less of him. Thank you for saving his life. I don't know what we would have done without either of you."

Unable to stand the heartache in Thomas's face, Hudson pointed to the bag behind him. "I made you my Cornish pasties."

Thomas's eyes sparkled, and he grinned like a little boy. He put the armrest with the controller down and moved to the table to take the bag and place it on his lap. With a deadpan expression, he met his wife's gaze.

"If the boys ask, these were never here."

Hudson laughed, watching as Thomas headed for the kitchen, calling out over his shoulder, "Especially Ethan. That boy eats more than the other two combined. I swear he has a black hole where his stomach should be."

"He's a growing boy," Julia cooed, following Thomas into the expansive country-style kitchen. She took the bag from him and placed it on the island counter.

Thomas let out a snort. "Growing boy my butt. Darling, he's thirty-six and almost as big as Seb." He wrapped an arm around her waist and tugged, lifting his face for a kiss, which his wife happily gave. Hudson all but melted, leaning against the counter and wondering how Julia and Thomas did it. They'd been through so much—losing everything, watching their boys have to work before they were of age, working through Ethan's selective mutism and social anxiety, through Thomas's condition. How had Julia and Thomas Hobbs survived all that and still looked at each other as if they were falling in love for the first time?

At the first crisis that hit them, Hudson and Seb had crumbled under the weight. Hudson cleared his throat, fidgeting from one foot to the other.

"How do you do that?" he asked softly. Propriety scolded him for being so intrusive and brash, but he was desperate to know.

They turned to him, Julia's hand on Thomas's shoulder and her expression tender.

"How do you forge ahead, never losing yourselves or the love you have for each other, after… everything?"

No question what Seb would look like when he got older—Seb and Ethan were both the spitting image of Thomas Hobbs. At sixty-five years old, Thomas was a handsome man, with a square jaw and green eyes that sparkled with life and mischief. His once-black hair was now salt-and-pepper, and although some of his leg muscles had deteriorated over the years due to his condition, he was still a tiger Therian, strong-bodied and strong-willed. Much like Ethan refused to allow his condition to define him, Thomas refused to be defined by his Therian Acheron Syndrome. Life had never been easy for the Hobbs family, but they endured, always together.

"Son, love is a precious gift, but love alone isn't enough to weather the storms in life. You know as well as I do that life can be hard, messy, infuriating, terrifying, and unfair, and love will certainly help ease the pain," Thomas said, taking Julia's hand in his. "But unless you use that love as a foundation to build on, you'll get swept away in the maelstrom."

Hudson nodded his understanding. He smiled warmly at Thomas before motioning to the Cornish pasties. "Your secret's safe with me."

Julia placed several pasties on a plate and handed them to Thomas with a kiss. Thomas thanked Hudson for the pasties, then declared he'd be upstairs watching his favorite TV show and instructed Julia on hiding the remaining pasties. Then he looked up at Hudson with those big green eyes filled with hope.

"Stay for dinner?"

Hudson caved so quickly it was pitiful. "Of course."

With a wink, Thomas took his plate of pasties and was off.

Hudson turned to Julia, arching an eyebrow at her. "Oh, he's good."

"Honey, that look is how we ended up with three boys. By the time Ethan was born, I made sure I was immune to it."

Hudson waggled his eyebrows. "Not completely immune, I'm sure."

Julia gasped and playfully swatted his arm with a laugh. "Hush, you." She pointed to one of the chairs at the large oak dinner table. "Sit your pretty little butt down. We have a lot of catching up to do. Tea?"

"Yes, thank you." Hudson took a seat, watching as Julia moved around the kitchen. Everything looked just how it did the last time he was here. He loved her kitchen. It was the biggest, warmest part of the large brownstone, with varnished wooden floors, white cupboards, silver-marble countertops, and state-of-the-art stainless-steel appliances. The Hobbs boys spared no expense where their family home was concerned. They might have moved out years ago, but this was still home. Even Thomas's electric wheelchair was high-end. Thomas had been reluctant at first, especially when he discovered how much it cost, but his sons refused to budge. If Thomas was going to be in a wheelchair, his boys were going to make damned sure it was the best out there.

The large brownstone had cost a mint. Seb and Rafe made the purchase after joining the THIRDS, and once Ethan had joined the organization, he chipped in to help his brothers. By the time Rafe had made it to Team Leader, the house was paid off. Thomas struggled with his pride for some time after having gone from being the sole breadwinner to having his sons take care of everything. With his family's help, Thomas learned that depending on a family who loved him and wanted to help didn't make him weak. Years later, with Therian aid, social security, and the support of their boys, Julia and Thomas lived comfortably without the fear of losing their home a second time.

The kettle boiled as a classic tune floated up from the digital radio on the counter. Hudson smiled, recalling a time when he'd spent hours at this very table in this same seat with Julia talking and laughing. Often Darla Summers would join them. That reminded him.

"How's Darla? I asked Cal about her this afternoon, and he just grunted that she was fine."

Julia chuckled as she placed Hudson's cup of tea in front of him. It was exactly the way he liked it. With a wicked smile that told Hudson some juicy gossip was forthcoming, Julia took a seat across from him with her own tea.

"Oh, honey, Darla's got herself a new man."

Hudson almost choked on his tea. He dabbed his mouth with a napkin Julia passed him before gaping at her. He leaned in. "When was this?"

"About three months now. Darla's crazy about him. He's a bear Therian. Used to coach college football. He's retired now. You should see the way he looks at her."

"And how does Cal look at him?" Hudson took a sip of his tea. As if he didn't know the answer.

"Like he wants to put him on the first ship heading into the Bermuda Triangle."

They both laughed. It was hard not to picture Calvin's face glaring daggers at his mother's new beau. Calvin was as protective of Darla as he was of Ethan. Hudson couldn't blame him. Darla was the only family Calvin had next to the Hobbs clan. It had been just the two of them for so long, making one sacrifice after another, trying their hardest to be a family, to make ends meet and survive.

"Cal's such a good boy. You know he wants her to be happy, so he's trying very hard, but trust doesn't come easy to him. He might be a grown man, but deep down, where Darla is concerned, he's still a little boy afraid of seeing his mother get hurt again. After what that bastard father of his did to them, who can blame him?"

Hudson nodded. "I wouldn't worry, love. If Cal catches so much as a hint that Darla is in distress, he will put the fear of God in that man, bear Therian or not. Cal's small, but he can be intimidating as hell."

"Are you kidding?" Julia leaned in and tapped her nail against the table. "If anyone lays a finger on Darla, my boys will be over there so fast the man won't know what hit him. Well, he will. It'll likely be Seb's fist. My boys know violence isn't the answer, especially with them being tiger Therians, but you push their buttons, and you deserve what you get. Seb has no tolerance for abuse of any kind, and you know how protective he is of his family."

Hudson took another sip of his tea. Boy, did he know it. They continued to chat and gossip, drinking copious amounts of tea and then nibbling on biscuits Julia put on the table.

"I'm so glad you came by," Julia said, smiling warmly. She placed a hand on his. "I missed this."

"I missed you," Hudson admitted. He took his teacup to the sink and rinsed it off when "Shake Your Groove Thing" by Peaches & Herb came on the radio. Julia had told him stories of when she and Thomas dated, how much they loved to get their groove on at the discos. She'd shared pictures with Hudson, images of a twentysomething couple in love, Julia looking fabulous with her Farrah Fawcett hair and bell-bottom jeans, and Thomas with his skintight T-shirt, his feathery hair reaching his ears. They made a stunning couple. Hudson quickly dried his hands on the dish towel before rounding the counter. He took Julia's hand, walked her away from the table, then twirled her, loving the sound of her laughter.

"I haven't danced to this in years." Julia's smile was radiant. She was a beautiful woman who hadn't lost her glow despite the trials and tribulations she'd faced over the years. Hudson clapped his hands in time to the music, bumping his hips into hers. She threw her arms in the air, dancing her way back to Hudson to bump her hips to his. Hudson laughed, giving it all he had as he shimmied around the kitchen before ending in front of her again. She took his hands and turned him, right into something hard.

Hudson gave a start. "Good Lord." He put a hand to his chest and let out a shaky laugh. "For heaven's sake, Sebastian. You scared the life out of me." *Blasted Felids and their stalking.*

Seb chuckled, little wrinkles forming at the corners of his eyes. "Don't stop on my account. Has Mom shown you her funky chicken yet?"

Julia giggled as she danced over to Seb. She pulled him into the kitchen, and he laughed, shaking his head. "Whatever dance genes you and Dad have were not passed down to me. You both know this."

"Nonsense." She pulled him up to the left of her and held out her other hand to Hudson, who didn't hesitate in taking it, allowing her to pull him to her right. "Come on, boys. Just like I taught you."

They lined up and did the hustle, stepping forward and back in unison. They clapped before pulling a John Travolta in *Saturday Night Fever*, followed by the roll. Hudson couldn't believe he remembered. Julia had taught him and Seb several moves for a disco-themed wedding they'd attended years ago. Hudson laughed as they started again, keeping in time with the music.

The first time he'd seen Seb dance, he'd been amazed by the fluidity of his movements. He'd been a little surprised, and a hell of a lot turned on. Tiger Therians were large, bulky, and muscular, but Seb was far better at controlling his body than he gave himself credit for. As for dancing, all he had to do was observe and follow along. He picked up the steps quickly, then adjusted them to fit his frame. The movement of Seb's hips gave Hudson terribly naughty thoughts.

Soon Thomas wandered downstairs to see what the commotion was all about. Julia shimmied to him, and he laughed, the adoration in his eyes unmistakable. She danced around him, and he joined in, clapping along, doing the roll and pointing. Julia murmured something at him, and he grabbed her by the waist. She let out a girlish squeal as he pulled her onto his lap. He whispered in her ear, and she blushed, batting him playfully.

Seb took Hudson's hand and twirled him before dipping him, making him laugh.

"Don't you dare let me go." Hudson was going for serious reprimand, but it was cancelled out by the half laugh, half yelp he let out when Seb pretended to drop him. "Sebastian!" Hudson clutched at him, unable to help his giggles. Good Lord, he was giggling. Fine, so he could see why West had reacted the way he had. It was hard not to when Sebastian Hobbs was holding you in his strong arms. His roguish smile should be considered a lethal weapon.

"Never, Lobito," Seb promised, his voice low and husky as he brought Hudson back up.

Realization of what he'd said and Seb's reply had Hudson's cheeks growing warm. He pretended nothing had happened.

"Son, could you bring the laundry up for your mom?" Thomas asked, his arms around Julia as he kissed her cheek.

"Sure thing." Seb kissed the top of her head before giving his dad a hug. "You two behave yourselves. We have company."

Julia batted her lashes innocently. "Us? We're not the reason the basement had to be soundproofed." She and Thomas both turned their knowing gazes to Hudson.

Hudson gasped, his face going up in flames. "Oh my God!"

Thomas grinned. "Yeah, we heard a lot of that coming from downstairs."

"Oh my God!" Hudson clamped a hand over his mouth, mortified. The two broke into laughs and giggles while Seb was of no help at all, cackling his head off. Hudson smacked Seb's arm. "Why didn't you tell me?"

"Ouch! I didn't want you to feel embarrassed."

"Well, that was a failure of epic proportions. I'm going to strangle you!"

Seb took off around the counter and out of the kitchen with Hudson darting after him.

"Get back here so I can wring your neck!"

"You want me to kneel so you can reach it?"

"Oh! You… you scoundrel!" Hudson chased him across the living room to the door leading down to the basement/game room. Downstairs, Seb ran around the pool table, putting it between him and Hudson. "You told me it was soundproofed so the sound system wouldn't disturb Thomas."

"True, but mostly it's because everyone could hear you…." Seb let out a low, guttural moan that went straight to Hudson's cock. Seb gripped the edge of the pool table, his face an expression of pained ecstasy. "Oh God, Seb, yes, please, oh God, yes, right there, do it again, love."

Hudson gaped at him, his face all but ready to spontaneously combust. "That's not…." He sputtered, trying to find the right words. "Your accent is terrible," he huffed, crossing his arms over his chest.

Seb laughed, rounding the pool table to pull Hudson close. Hudson growled but allowed himself to be pulled into Seb's embrace. Seb kissed his cheek, his breath tickling Hudson's ear when he spoke.

"You made the most beautiful noises when you were under me."

Hudson cleared his throat and pointed off behind him. "You should, um, see to the laundry." He ignored Seb's chuckle, following him to the large cupboard set in the wall housing the washer and tumble dryer.

Hudson knew this room well. How many hours had he spent down here with Seb, playing games, laughing, making out like a couple of teenagers, and apparently treating the whole of the household to the sound of live porn?

When Thomas was having a rough week or needed extra care, Seb and Hudson would stay at the house to help Julia and offer support. He and Seb would play table tennis, snuggle together to watch a movie, or just lie together on the incredibly comfortable L-shaped couch, murmuring tender endearments while drifting off to pleasant dreams.

The Hobbs brothers had fixed up the basement not long after Ethan started at the THIRDS. It had quickly become a favorite, filled with high-tech gadgets, a pool table, an air hockey table, dartboard and darts, a big-screen TV, Blu-ray player, sound system, a bar, several video game consoles, and a couch Hudson wanted to live in. It was plush perfection. The boys had a chairlift installed so Thomas could join them during get-togethers or when he just fancied using the room.

Hudson leaned against the wall as Seb opened the tumble dryer, his shirtsleeves stretching over his biceps when he reached in to remove clothes and place them in an empty laundry basket.

"Thank you for coming. I really appreciate it. It made them both so happy," Seb said, his smile bright as he filled the basket.

Hudson swallowed past the lump in his throat and turned his gaze to the room. He hadn't expected this house to still feel like home after all this time. "I missed them," he admitted.

Julia and Thomas had been the parents he never had, which was a sad statement considering his own parents were alive and well. So much of Julia and Thomas's behavior had baffled him at first. When one of the boys broke something by accident, Julia would wave it off, her only concern that they hadn't hurt themselves. No reprimands or talk of how much something cost were forthcoming. Julia never told Ethan he was clumsy or Seb that he should pay more attention to what he was doing.

The first time Julia hugged Hudson and kissed his cheek, Hudson had frozen to the spot. When Seb asked him what was wrong, Hudson whispered that his parents never hugged or kissed him. Seb had been shocked, then saddened. Hudson hadn't understood the reaction. He could hardly miss something he never had. Seb asked Hudson if he was okay with it, and Hudson nodded. It would take some getting used to, but it was nice. It was nice how Thomas patted him on the back, a smile on his face as he wheeled by just because he was happy Hudson was there. It wasn't that Hudson's parents didn't love him, because they did, in their own way. They simply never showed affection. It wasn't who they were. Love was shown in other ways, usually involving money or boasting of achievements to other prominent figures.

"Lobito? You okay?"

"I didn't think it would feel like this. Like I never left," Hudson replied, sighing before he could stop himself. So many happy memories in this room, a safe den filled with love and laughter. In this room, Hudson had dreamed of one day being married to Sebastian Hobbs, of being husband to a man who was everything Hudson had ever wanted.

"I know."

Seb's soft-spoken admission snapped Hudson from his thoughts, and he dared to look at Seb, surprised by the love in his stunning green eyes. Why did the man have to be so beautiful, so warm, kind, and damned patient?

"We had a lot of firsts down here." Seb pointed in the direction of the TV. "That's where you kicked my ass at Mario Kart for the first time." He moved his finger to the air hockey table. "That's where you kicked my ass at air hockey." When he moved his finger again, Hudson chuckled. "That's where you kicked my ass at table tennis. What kind of nerd are you? You're not supposed to beat the jock at sports."

Hudson shrugged. "I was always rather good at sports."

Seb pointed to the pool table. "At least I kicked your butt at pool."

"Only because you cheated," Hudson reminded him, arching an eyebrow.

Seb gasped, a hand going to his chest. "Me? Cheat?" He shook his head. "I won that game fair and square."

"Pardon? Fair my arse." Hudson walked over to the pool table to stand at the end of it. He leaned in to tap a spot on the table. "Right here. I remember quite clearly. I was one perfect shot away from obliterating you, and you—"

Seb stepped up behind him and placed his hands to Hudson's hips, his groin all but pressed up to Hudson's arse. The power of speech eluded Hudson.

"That's right," Seb said, his voice a husky drawl, folding himself over Hudson's back, his warm breath against Hudson's temple. "I remember now. You were bent over, ready to take the shot, and I came up behind you just like this, and you hit the ball so hard it flew off the table and made a big dent in the wall."

Hudson swallowed hard. Slowly he drew himself up, Seb following his movement, and Hudson's body ended up pressed against Seb's. A shiver racked through Hudson, and he closed his eyes. Being in Seb's arms brought a flood of want through him.

How many nights had he spent awake in bed, yearning for the man, wishing Seb was at his side, holding him, kissing him? How long would they be paying for their sins? Had it even been a sin? It was a tragedy, one Hudson wished with all his heart hadn't occurred, but he'd sacrificed his mate, his happiness, the other half of him in penance. Almost seven years. Seven years barely living, going through the motions, attempting to have a semblance of a life, pretending he wasn't dying a little inside with every passing day. Maybe if they hadn't bonded, if Seb hadn't reached into Hudson's soul and claimed it as his own, then maybe Hudson could have moved on, but simply being around Seb, seeing his smile, had been enough to hold him over, to keep him hoping that one day things would be different. Yet no matter the pain, not once did Hudson regret falling in love with Seb or being marked by him.

Seb gently turned Hudson to face him, their lives together reflected in his captivating eyes. Hudson put his fingers to Seb's jaw and the permanent stubble Hudson loved to feel against his bare skin. Seb had a strong nose, square jaw, and thick black eyebrows. His eyes were hooded, and his smile crooked. When he laughed, really laughed, a dimple appeared, and he put his heart into his laughter, filling with glee like a little boy. At seven feet tall and three hundred pounds, built of solid muscle, with a fierce tiger Therian lurking inside him, Sebastian Hobbs should have been frightening, and for some he was. Hudson had never felt safer than he did in Seb's embrace. He'd never felt more loved or cherished.

"I don't come down here so much anymore," Seb murmured, his hands still on Hudson's waist. His voice was gravelly, a sexy roll of sounds that formed words and promises of worship, and that's what it felt like to be loved by Sebastian Hobbs. Seb didn't love halfheartedly. He didn't hold back or hide a part of himself. He bared his soul, left himself vulnerable to those given the gift of his love.

"Why?"

Seb put his hand to Hudson's cheek, his thumb stroking softly. "Hurts too much."

Hudson gingerly put his hands on Seb's chest, splaying his fingers over the hard pectoral muscles beneath the fabric of Seb's cotton T-shirt. His mind was awash with memories of Seb's sculpted body over Hudson's, pressing him down into the mattress, strong hands caressing Hudson's neck, Hudson's legs wrapped around powerful thighs beneath a perfect arse. Hudson's pleasure was paramount to Seb. He always thought of Hudson before himself, and Hudson had accepted. Nina was right. He'd been selfish, always taking what he needed from Seb, believing he gave enough, that Seb had everything he needed from Hudson, but how could he have everything when Hudson held so much back?

"I'm sorry," Hudson said, the words caught in his throat. "I'm so sorry."

"For what?"

"For the other night at Dekatria." *For not appreciating you like I should have.*

Seb shook his head. "Don't worry about it."

"No. What I did was shameful. Seeking your attention like some scorned juvenile." Pushing Seb away only to get upset when the man did as asked. It was deplorable.

Seb blinked at him. "You wanted my attention?"

Hudson hesitated before nodding, his cheeks burning when Seb lifted Hudson's face so their eyes could meet. Seb's voice when he spoke was low and throaty.

"Baby, you always have my attention. Always. There's never a time when you don't have it, even when you're not around."

Hudson sighed heavily. "Why do you have to be so blasted wonderful?"

"I think Dom would call me something else," Seb said with a chuckle.

"You never did know what to do with compliments." Hudson inhaled Seb's scent, a mixture of heady male, shower gel, and aftershave. He smelled so damned good it almost had Hudson whimpering. It was unfair. Seb was more than a temptation; he was a walking wet dream of sensual tastes and touches, which Hudson had been blessed to experience.

"Not when they come from you."

Hudson studied him. "What do you mean?"

Seb covered Hudson's hands with his, his gaze never faltering. "Because I know you. I know when you're just being polite and when you're speaking from your heart. Knowing what you think of me, having you look at me the way you do… it's breathtaking." Slowly he bent his head forward, and Hudson dropped his eyes to Seb's full lips. He remembered how soft they were, how good they tasted. Seb's tongue exploring his mouth, his body thrumming with desire, radiating heat all because of Hudson. His trousers grew tight, and Hudson closed his hands into fists against Seb's chest. He'd never wanted anything so badly.

Hudson's eyes drifted closed as Seb's lips brushed over his in a feathery kiss, and Hudson gasped, feeling as though his heart had been electroshocked, beating with life after years of dormancy. Seb dropped his hands, his smile sheepish as he began to pull away.

"I'm sorry, I shouldn't have—"

Panic struck Hudson. He grabbed the back of Seb's neck, and fisted his other hand in Seb's T-shirt as he stood on his toes to press his lips to Seb's. Seb's sharp intake of breath left him open to Hudson's tongue, and he dove in without hesitation, kissing Seb as if Seb were the only source of breath in Hudson's body. If he didn't kiss Seb, didn't taste him, feel Seb's tongue entwined with his own, he would break. He was so weary of dreaming, yearning for his mate's touch. It was time he did something about it.

CHAPTER 6

SEB WRAPPED his arms around Hudson, pulling Hudson up hard against him, their bodies crushed together so tight, as if trying to become one. Hudson melted against Seb, allowing Seb to hold him up. He didn't trust his own legs at the moment, not when he was filled with the sensation of Seb kissing him. He couldn't hold back his moan as Seb's gentle, heated kiss led to Hudson's mouth being ravished, the hunger and heat threatening to make him combust. Closer. Hudson needed to be closer. He tugged at Seb's T-shirt like he used to, and Seb reached down, grabbed his arse, and lifted him with ease. He sat Hudson on the pool table's edge and stepped between his legs so their erections pressed together. Hudson wrapped his legs around Seb's thighs, in case he had any ideas about moving away.

Hudson gasped as he was forced to come up for air, and Seb took advantage, moving his lips to Hudson's neck to suck and nibble. Had Hudson wanted to say something, anything, the power of speech had abandoned him. He tangled his fingers in Seb's short hair, his breath panting, and his cock straining against his trousers. Seb slipped one hand under Hudson's shirt, the other cupping Hudson's left arse cheek. Hudson arched his back, a whimper escaping him as he writhed in Seb's hold.

"My beautiful Lobito." Seb's voice was husky, and Hudson all but came in his pants.

"Darling," Hudson pleaded, uncertain what he was asking—begging—for. Forget tomorrow. Only right now mattered, and he needed Seb so badly it was painful.

"We should—"

Hudson cut Seb off with his mouth. He shook his head, reaching between them to cup Seb through his jeans. Seb moaned into Hudson's mouth, and Hudson pushed him hard. Startled, Seb stepped back, his lips swollen from kissing, his cheeks pink, and his hair sticking up. He'd opened his mouth to speak, when Hudson hopped down, took hold of Seb's waistband, and undid the buttons of his fly.

"Lobito...."

Hudson tugged down Seb's jeans and boxer briefs to midthigh, moaning as Seb's beautiful, thick cock sprang free, jutting up toward his stomach. If Hudson didn't taste Seb, he was going to lose his bloody mind. He wrapped his hand around the base of Seb's already leaking cock, loving the tremor he felt go through Seb. Hudson licked up the length of Seb's erection. He drew the rosy-hued knob into his mouth and sucked at the salty pearls before pressing his tongue to the slit.

"Oh, fuck." Seb slipped his fingers into Hudson's hair, kneading his scalp as Hudson took Seb deep down his throat, relishing the guttural moan Seb released. As much as Hudson wished he could swallow Seb down, he was far too big. Hudson's mouth was only so wide, and his throat only so deep. Regardless, Hudson devoured Seb, sucking, licking, and nipping at Seb's tender skin, every taste fueling Hudson's hunger. Hudson moved a hand to Seb's arse cheek and dug his fingers into the firm, rounded globe.

"Baby, I'm not gonna last," Seb said through a gasp. "The last test came back negative, so you know."

Hudson expected no less from Seb. He hummed an acknowledgment around Seb's cock, doubling his efforts, his body all but trembling with the anticipation of having Seb come down his throat. He moved his hand from the base of Seb's cock to his balls, slipping his other finger between Seb's arse cheeks. Seb bucked in his mouth, releasing a litany of curses as Hudson sucked hard, fondling Seb's balls and circling his puckered hole with his other finger, teasing, pressing, driving Seb mad with his touch.

Seb's hold on Hudson's hair tightened, and he sucked in a sharp breath. "Baby...."

With a moan, Hudson pushed a finger inside Seb, and salty come shot into his mouth. Seb's body went rigid, and Hudson looked up at him, shivering at the molten heat in his near-black eyes, only a sliver of green remaining. Hudson sucked the last remaining drop from Seb before letting Seb's cock slip from between his lips. Seb reached down and grabbed his arm, then jerked Hudson to his feet and against him, their mouths crashing together in a breathless fervor of sucking, biting, and kissing.

Seb pushed Hudson back against the pool table, took him and turned him roughly, then pressed up against Hudson's back. He fumbled with

Hudson's trouser buttons before finally managing to get them undone, then slipped his hand inside Hudson's pants to grab his hard cock.

"Oh God," Hudson said through his gasp, his hands flat against the pool table's surface as Seb squeezed his painfully hard erection. He released Hudson and brought his hand up.

"Spit," Seb growled, and Hudson shivered again at the feral command. He did as Seb demanded, spitting into Seb's hand. When Seb took hold of his cock again, now slick with Hudson's spit and precome, Hudson feared he might lose it right then. Seb had other plans for him.

Seb tugged and twisted, moving his hand up and down Hudson's cock, as his free hand yanked down Hudson's trousers until they were under his arse. Hudson's gasp at the feel of Seb's hard cock pressed against his crease.

"Darling," Hudson murmured, his head falling forward as he widened his stance. Seb pushed his cock between Hudson's cheeks, and Hudson trembled at Seb rutting against him. He stroked Hudson mercilessly with one hand, his other hand going to Hudson's shoulder to hold him in place as he intensified the friction, his chest pressing to Hudson's back.

Seb nipped at Hudson's jaw. "You're so fucking beautiful, my heart can't take it."

The pressure inside Hudson increased, and he bucked his hips. Unable to stop, he drove himself in and out of Seb's strong hand.

"That's it, sweetheart. Pretend it's my ass you're fucking."

Hudson whimpered. "I can't." Having Seb's cock between his cheeks, rubbing, pressing against his hole, it was too much. "Sebastian, love, please…."

"Fuck me, Hudson." Seb squeezed Hudson's cock, and Hudson cried out Seb's name before thrusting into his hand over and over, his movements growing erratic as he threw his head back and to the side, seeking Seb's mouth. He was rewarded with Seb's tongue slipping between his lips, plundering, demanding, reducing Hudson to a whimpering, keening mess.

"Oh God, Seb!" Hudson's orgasm plowed through him, and Seb's growl joined Hudson's cry, hot come dripping between Hudson's arse cheeks as Hudson coated Seb's hands. His body shook, and Hudson doubled over as his release continued to course through him. Seb folded over him, and Hudson heard his heart pounding in his ears, his cock twitching in Seb's grasp.

Hudson closed his eyes, smiling at Seb's gentle kiss. They remained unmoving for the longest time before Seb pulled away, and Hudson groaned at the chill hitting his bare arse, but the feel of Seb's come running down his thigh brought his smile back. A heartbeat later, Seb returned and cleaned up Hudson with a damp washcloth. Hudson would have fallen asleep on the pool table if

Seb let him. Instead, Seb tenderly pulled Hudson's trousers up, turned him, and kissed him. He fastened Hudson's buttons, his own clothes set to rights. Hudson hummed, smiling stupidly as Seb pulled him into a warm embrace. Hudson snuggled close, his bones feeling like jelly. A contented sigh escaped him, and Seb chuckled. He ran a hand over Hudson's hair and kissed the top of his head.

"I know it's tomorrow, but happy birthday, Lobito."

Hudson blinked up at him. "Good Lord. It *is* my birthday tomorrow, isn't it?"

Seb laughed softly. "How is it you remember everyone else's birthday but not your own?"

Hudson shrugged. "I suppose it doesn't feel very important."

"Oh, sweetheart, it is important. It's important to me." Seb nuzzled Hudson's temple, his lips brushing against Hudson's skin. He took Hudson's hand and led him to the couch. "I have something for you. I'll be right back. Don't move."

Hudson wasn't surprised, but he was no less touched. Seb always remembered his birthday, and he always had a gift for Hudson, despite Hudson telling him countless times it was unnecessary. Hudson had a terrible habit of forgetting his own birthday, but Seb was always there to remind him, and the bashful smile on Seb's face when he gave Hudson his gift made Hudson's heart flutter every time. He sat back, his heart happy. Had he really just thrown himself at Seb? His lips curled into a smile, and he couldn't help the heat that rose in his face when he thought of Seb's body against him, his rough, firm hands on Hudson's bare skin.

Easy there, fella. If he didn't stop thinking about it, Hudson was going to have a very different sort of surprise for Seb.

Seb returned and took a seat beside Hudson on the couch, their legs pressed against each other. He had a medium-sized box wrapped in silver and white with a frosty, blue ribbon around it. "I was going to give it to you tomorrow, but when I spoke to Nina and found out you were going to drop by to see Mom, I knew I had to bring it to you here. It's kind of personal, so I didn't really want to give it to you at work."

"Thank you." Hudson smiled warmly at Seb. "You really didn't have to."

"I know." Seb kissed his cheek. "But I wanted to. It took me a while to figure out. I hope I did okay."

"Whatever it is, Sebastian, I'm certain it'll be wonderful." Hudson pulled at the ends of the ribbon, slipped it off the box, and placed it to his left. He carefully removed the giftwrap, finding a slim square box beneath. What on earth could it possibly be? Opening the box, Hudson cocked his head. A photo album?

Curious, Hudson lifted it from the box, moved the box aside, and placed the album on his lap. He opened to the first page, and his heart leaped into his throat. Tears filled his eyes, and he snapped his head up to stare at Seb. When he spoke, his words were almost a whisper.

"Where…? How did you get this?"

Seb's eyes became glassy, and he moved his gaze to his fingers, his smile shy. "I sort of broke a few rules and enlisted Dex's help, got him to use his charms to contact THIRDS HQ in London to get Millie's cell phone number. I called her up and begged her to sneak into your parents' house and steal it for me."

Hudson was speechless. When he finally found his voice, it was rough and laced with emotion. "You spoke to my sister?" Millie and Theo were the only ones who hadn't blamed Hudson for Alfie's death. They hadn't wanted him to leave for America, but Hudson couldn't stay, and they understood. Unfortunately, their father kept them under his thumb, holding their children's educations over their heads, threatening to cut them off if they had any contact with Hudson. Hudson had promised them he wasn't cross with them. How could he blame them for taking care of their children? He would never do anything to hurt his nieces and nephews.

Seb nodded. "She was so happy to hear you were okay. I told her to make sure she didn't get into any trouble. I gave her my address, and a week later it arrived."

Hudson still couldn't believe it. He ran his fingers reverently over the old photo of him and Alfie as children hugging each other tight, big smiles on their cherub faces.

Seb handed Hudson a tissue, and Hudson laughed softly as he wiped his eyes. "Thank you, Sebastian. You don't know how much this means to me."

"I think I do," Seb said quietly.

Hudson closed the book, overcome with emotion. He didn't want to stain the pages with his tears. Seb had found a way to contact his sister and somehow got her to retrieve the album containing his and Alfie's pictures. It had been so long since Hudson had seen it. He gently placed it to one side, turned, and threw his arms around Seb, hugging him tight.

"You're an amazing man, Sebastian Hobbs."

Seb ran a hand tenderly over Hudson's hair. "You're pretty amazing yourself, Dr. Colbourn."

Hudson shook his head, unable to reply. He closed his eyes as Seb held him, stroking his hair and murmuring sweet words. When Hudson was certain he wouldn't turn into a blubbering mess, he pulled back, blew his nose on a clean tissue, and returned the album to his lap. The leather was pristine and sturdy, looking as though it had been purchased yesterday and not decades ago. He inhaled deeply and released a steady breath through his mouth before opening the cover.

"If it wasn't for your expressions, you'd look like twins," Seb said with a smile. He pointed to the small boy on the left with the shy smile. "That's definitely you."

Hudson studied the photo, his heart squeezing. "We looked very much alike when we were children. Both with the same thick, pitch-black hair and eyebrows, same blue eyes. We even smiled the same. When we hit our teenage years, I was still gangly and awkward, while Alfie grew into his body, sleek and muscular. I looked very much the science nerd I was, and Alfie looked as if he'd stepped off the cover of a magazine. Left a trail of broken hearts wherever he went." Hudson turned the page and laughed at the picture of them on a pony, Alfie with one hand tucked inside his waistcoat, the other pointing forward and his mouth open as if leading a charge. They'd been about ten years old at the time.

"Is your brother pretending to be Napoleon?" Seb asked.

Hudson nodded. "My father was livid. He'd brought in a ridiculously expensive photographer to take a picture of us for some society column, and every time the man tried to photograph us, Alfie would strike the most ridiculous pose. None of the photos were any use for the column. This was our nanny's favorite, which is why it made it into the album. She was the one who started this album for us."

Their parents couldn't be bothered with such a menial task. Having pictures taken and put into albums was the job of the house staff. In a way, Hudson was glad, because it meant the albums were filled with fun, very real moments rather than staged portraits intent on displaying their family's false perfection.

Hudson went through every picture with Seb, telling him stories of his and Alfie's shenanigans just before that particular photo was taken. Alfie and Hudson pulled funny faces, dressed up as pirates, as Sherlock Holmes and John Watson, as bobbies, and knights, always acting out a scene for the camera. Hudson stilled at one picture he had completely forgotten about.

"Wow." Seb's voice was hoarse, and when Hudson looked up at him, he was surprised to see tears in Seb's eyes.

"Seb?"

"Sorry." Seb wiped at his eyes and laughed at himself. "It's just, you can really see how much he loves you. The way he's looking at you."

Hudson smiled warmly. "It was at some posh banquet. I can't even remember what for. One of my father's associates was receiving another award or some such thing. I do remember Alfie had turned nineteen that day, so I was eighteen at the time. My father and I had a bloody great row the night before. He believed the banquet was far more important than his son's birthday, and I disagreed. I decided we'd celebrate Alfie's birthday at the banquet. We had so much fun ignoring everyone, dancing and being a couple of nuisances. We drank, ate nothing but cake. By the end of the evening, I was exhausted."

The photo was one of Hudson's favorites. He couldn't even remember who'd taken it. The two of them sat together on a bench, Hudson slumped against Alfie, his tuxedo tie undone, hair rumpled, and glasses sitting crooked on his nose. Alfie had his arm around Hudson's shoulders, holding him close as he smiled down at him. The adoration in his blue eyes was unmistakable.

"I miss him so much." Hudson blinked away his tears.

"I'm sorry, I didn't mean for this to bring you any pain."

Hudson closed the album, then put it to one side before launching at Seb and knocking him onto his back, kissing him. Seb didn't hesitate. He wrapped Hudson in his embrace and returned his kiss. Hudson slowed his kissing, taking his time in exploring Seb's mouth, showing him how much this gift meant to him, how much he adored Seb for his thoughtfulness, for just being him. When they came up for breath, Seb searched Hudson's gaze.

"Lobito—"

A smoke alarm went off somewhere upstairs, and they both started. Seb looked to the stairs before turning his attention back to Hudson, his expression torn.

"Go," Hudson said, his voice breathy. "I'm right behind you."

Seb gave him a quick, heated kiss before gently moving Hudson off him. He jumped off the couch, then ran for the stairs and took them two at a time.

With a shaky breath, Hudson straightened his clothes and raked his fingers through his hair. His glasses were somewhat fogged up, and he chuckled. Cleaning them on his shirt, he hurried upstairs. Smoke was coming from the kitchen, and Hudson ran in just as Seb placed a blackened roasting pan in the sink. It appeared to contain the charred remains of some kind of beef, possibly. He ran water on it before grabbing a dish towel and fanning the smoke alarm. Julia was on the verge of tears.

"I'm so sorry, honey. Your dad needed me, and it took longer than I thought, and now dinner is ruined."

Hudson gathered up Julia in his arms and kissed the top of her head. "There, there, darling. Nothing to fret over. It's still early. Seb and I will go to the market and pick something up. Then we can cook together. How does that sound?"

Julia wiped a tear from her eye. "I was going to surprise you with your favorite roast since it's your birthday, but...."

"Oh, Julia." Hudson squeezed her tight. "My being here with you means more to me than anything. Please don't fret."

"Mom, it's okay," Seb assured her, then gave the top of her head a kiss. "Promise."

She pressed her lips together, putting one hand to Seb's cheek and the other to Hudson's. "Such good boys."

"We'll be back in no time," Seb promised.

Hudson gave her cheek a kiss before following Seb to the front door, where Seb picked up his keys and wallet. He took Hudson's jacket from the coatrack and held it out to him with a wink.

"Such a gentleman," Hudson cooed, slipping his arms into the sleeves before turning to kiss Seb's lips. The most wonderful sigh escaped Seb, and when Hudson made to move away, Seb took hold of his chin and kissed him again. Hudson chuckled against his lips. "Your mother is waiting for us, Sebastian."

"Right," Seb said with a breathy laugh. He put on his jacket and opened the door for Hudson, followed him out, and locked the door behind them. They took Seb's red-and-black Dodge Ram Rebel. Hudson thanked Seb for opening the passenger-side door for him, and he took Seb's hand when he offered to help Hudson up. It was a beast of a machine, but then Seb had always driven large trucks, Destructive Delta's BearCat being one of them. Seb had loved the damn thing. The Hobbs brothers had a natural talent for maneuvering starship-sized vehicles, and they had a habit of driving said vehicles as if they were competing in the Daytona 500.

Seb's favorite supermarket was on West 37th Street. It had the feel of an old-fashioned grocer but sold organic fresh foods along with gourmet options. It offered Therian-sized cuts of meat, with a deli that made Hudson's mouth water. Plants hung from the awning, and fresh flowers in an array of colors and bouquets were on offer to the right of the entrance, while fresh fruits were displayed to the left. Hudson couldn't help his smile. It had been so long since he'd been here, he forgot how much he enjoyed his trips with Seb.

They received a cheerful greeting from several of the employees when they walked in. The store was as bustling and filled with customers as Hudson remembered. As they headed for the deli, Seb bumped him playfully.

"Hey, you want me to grab some chips and that organic salsa you love? You're going to be hungry like an hour after dinner."

Hudson arched an eyebrow at him. "Are you insinuating that I eat a lot?"

"Not insinuating. Next to Dex and Cael, you have the biggest appetite I've ever seen in a guy your size. It's all those smarts you got up there," Seb said with a wink, tapping Hudson's head. "Burns a lot of calories."

Hudson wrinkled his nose. "You're lucky you're pretty to look at, Sebastian."

Seb gasped in mock horror. "Are you saying you only love me for my body?"

"Well…." Hudson pretended to give it some thought, laughing when Seb poked Hudson's side right where he was ticklish.

"Dr. Colbourn?"

Hudson's heart stopped. He knew that voice. How could he forget it? It haunted his nightmares.

"Mrs. Palmer?" Instinctively Hudson straightened, and he felt Seb stiffen beside him. "How are you?" The words were out of his mouth before he could stop them. Her jaw muscles clenched, and her gaze dropped to Hudson's hand in Seb's before moving on to Seb. Tears welled in her big blue eyes. Anger soon followed.

"As well as you can imagine. Kurt would have started high school this week."

"I'm sorry," Hudson said, his voice rough. "I'm so sorry."

"Your apology means as much now as it did then. It won't bring my son back, Dr. Colbourn."

"Mrs. Palmer," Seb began gently, only to have her put a finger up.

"Don't you dare. There is *nothing* left for you to say to me. Had you done your job, my son would still be alive." She shook her head, tears spilling over to roll down her cheeks, her bottom lip trembling. Hudson took a step forward only to have her recoil from him. "Stay away from me," she snapped. The anguish and loathing in her eyes made Hudson wince. What could he do? What could he possibly say to ease her pain? Her son's blood was on his hands, just as it had been the day he was killed.

HUDSON COULD recall the incident in detail, from what he had for breakfast to everything that happened after. He remembered the conversation he had with Nina that morning in his office over tea and coffee before they were called out. Nina had driven since it was the van and not the mobile command center. She hated driving the massive vehicle. He recalled the scene clearly. Recalled crouching beside Nina, inspecting the body of a man gunned down in a residential neighborhood not far from Central Park. The area was sealed off before their arrival, no traffic coming in or out, while THIRDS agents maintained the perimeter, keeping watch.

Hudson inspected the man's wounds with his gloved hands while Nina checked the man's pockets for identification. "Three gunshot wounds to the chest." He had carefully rolled the deceased onto his side when a familiar scent hit his nose. Hudson smiled.

"Good morning, Sebastian."

Seb crouched down beside him, his smile wide and his voice low. "Morning, sunshine. Tell me you're as sore as I am."

Hudson shushed him. "You're going to give Nina the wrong impression of me."

"Please, like I buy this whole prim-and-proper act of yours," Nina teased. She elbowed Seb playfully. "I bet he's all wild and freaky in bed."

"Nina," Hudson hissed. "Honestly." He motioned down to the body on the ground.

"What?" Nina blinked innocently. "He's not going to tell anyone."

"You're incorrigible," Hudson said, shaking his head.

Nina laughed and stood. "I'm going to let Sloane know we're ready to take the body."

"You do that." Hudson ignored her poking her tongue out at him, along with Seb's rumble of a chuckle.

"I was thinking we might have dinner at that cute little Korean place over on East 31st Street, the one where we had our first date."

Hudson beamed up at him. "Really?"

"Yeah, there's something I want to talk to you about, and I know how much you love that place." Seb's cheeks flushed, and Hudson's heart skipped a beat. He had opened his mouth to reply when a fellow agent called Seb over. "Hold that thought."

Hudson watched Seb go, admiring the breadth of his shoulders, the way his body moved beneath the layers of his uniform. It took everything he had not to release a breathy sigh, and he reminded himself a crime scene was certainly not the place to leer at his hot boyfriend.

Movement from the corner of his eye caught Hudson's attention. A man emerged from behind one of the BearCats.

It all happened in a blur. The man aimed a gun at Hudson's chest just as Hudson hit the pavement, Seb shielding Hudson with his body.

Shots rang out a heartbeat before a barrage of gunfire exploded through the air. The world seemed to slow to a crawl, and Hudson was engulfed in silence, hearing nothing but his ragged breath. The quiet was shattered by a bloodcurdling scream. Hudson lifted his head, his heart leaping in his throat.

"No," he whispered, pushing at Seb. Seb rolled off him, and Hudson scrambled to his feet, tears blurring his vision as he sped over to the woman holding a small lifeless boy in her arms. Hudson dropped to his knees, bile rising in his throat and threatening to choke him at the sight of the gaping wound in the tiny body. *No, oh God, no.* Frantically, he felt for the boy's pulse, refusing to listen to his brain as it told him the boy was gone. The woman screamed, each shriek like a knife to Hudson's ears. She held her baby to her, rocking him, her hands and clothes covered in blood. Looking down, Hudson inhaled sharply at the blood on his trembling hands.

"I... I'm so sorry." Hudson's words were a broken whisper. Tears rolled down his cheeks as agents and EMTs darted around them, trying to assess the situation, get to the boy, and calm the mother. She had gone ashen, her body racking with shivers. What if he was wrong? He had to check again. Maybe the little boy was all right, maybe if he checked again.... Someone grabbed Hudson under his arms, and Hudson fought against them.

"No, I need to check again. I'm wrong. I have to be. He has to be—he can't—please." Hudson was dragged back and pulled to his feet away from the hysterical mother. His knees buckled, and he would have crumpled to the ground if Seb hadn't held him up. Hudson gazed up into the tearful eyes of the man he loved, the heartache and guilt a reflection of Hudson's own. It should have been Hudson. The bullet had been meant for him. Maybe it would have killed him, maybe he would have survived, but either way, the child would be alive. Because of their bond, their first instinct had been to protect each other when it should have been to protect the public.

"What have we done?" Hudson's words were barely a whisper.

"YOU TORE my family apart, and here you are like nothing happened." Mrs. Palmer's voice snapped Hudson from his trance, and Hudson thought he might be sick.

"Is that what you think?" Seb asked in disbelief. "That we picked up where we left off? I know I can't possibly fathom the extent of the loss you've suffered, but we didn't just carry on with our lives. It ripped us apart.

I might not have lost my mate to a bullet that day, Mrs. Palmer, but make no mistake, I lost him."

"Your bond made you both unfit to serve, and you proved as much with your actions that day. My son lost his life due to your animal instincts. The courts may have ruled in your favor, but they were wrong. Marked mates have no place in law enforcement, much less in the same department. You're no better than animals, unable to control your impulses."

"Forgive me." Hudson ran from the supermarket, ignoring Seb calling his name. He took off toward 10th Avenue, grateful for the head start. Seb wouldn't just take off and leave a distraught Mrs. Palmer standing in the middle of the grocery store in tears. If Seb decided to go after him, Hudson would never make it to the 7 train station on 11th Street. For all his bulk, Seb was a tiger Therian. If he pushed enough, he could easily catch up to Hudson.

By the time Hudson reached the escalators down to the train, he was out of breath, but the lack of air and burn in his lungs was nothing compared to the pain in his heart. How could he have been so foolish, believing he and Seb could have a life together? Mrs. Palmer was right. Their bond made them unpredictable. They'd sworn an oath to protect the citizens of New York City, yet when they were together, their instincts fought against that promise. Hudson was often called out to Theta Destructive's crime scenes. Seb was fiercely protective of him as it was. How much worse would it be if they were together again? Hudson couldn't take the risk of history repeating itself.

He wiped at his eyes, refusing to fall apart in the middle of the damned train station in front of strangers, but as he crowded into the corner of the car, he couldn't hold back the crushing grief that washed over him. There was no going back to Seb.

Ever.

"HEY."

Seb was faintly aware of someone hovering over him, carefully removing the beer bottle from his hand. What time was it? How long had he been sitting here on the couch staring at nothing? The last half of the evening was a blur, a jumble of images and events. He pinched the bridge of his nose, trying to remember.

Mrs. Palmer.

Seb had apologized again and again. Not that it would do any good. He spewed word vomit at her, pleading for her to listen, to understand. He doubted she had, and he didn't blame her. Why should she care? How the fuck was she supposed to move on from losing a child? The area should have been secured. They'd been informed it was secure. Why did she choose *that* exact moment to leave her home? Seb let out a snort of disgust. How many times was he going to ask himself the same questions?

When the gunman emerged, gun pointed at Hudson, Seb reacted to Hudson being in immediate danger, all the while believing the mother and child weren't targets. In court, it was argued that he'd breached protocol by not preserving the life of the mother and child, but the defense argued that since the intended target had been Hudson and the gunman had aimed solely at Hudson, Seb had done his duty in preserving life. It never occurred to Seb that the mother and child would end up in the linc of fire or that the gunman would get another shot off before being neutralized. The court had ruled in Seb and Hudson's favor, and the agent who'd given the all clear took the fall, but the damage had been done. Seconds. That was all it took to shatter two families.

Once Mrs. Palmer left the grocery store, Seb did the same. He called his mom, and calm as could be, lied, telling her he was sorry, that work had called and they wouldn't make dinner. He couldn't bring himself to tell her the truth. No doubt she saw right through him; she always did. But he just… couldn't. He arranged for dinner to be delivered to his parents from a local restaurant. Then he picked up *a lot* of alcohol from… fuck, he couldn't even remember where. Someplace.

The room was blurry, and his head felt fuzzy, thick. His limbs uncooperative. At some point he'd gotten rid of his shirt, too hot and uncomfortable in his own skin. Someone tilted his head back and waved a hand in front of his face. Seb swatted at the shadows with a grunt, or at least he thought he did.

"Shit. Look at you. How much did you drink?"

Curses followed the sound of clinking bottles.

"Not enough," Seb muttered, scoffing at himself. He patted the cushion next to him. Where the fuck was that bottle? He frowned and squinted at the face in front of him. "Dom? What you doin' 'ere?"

"You butt-dialed me."

"I did?" Seb felt his jean pockets. Wouldn't his phone need to be near his butt to butt-dial someone? Where the hell was his phone? With a frown, he scanned the living room. His phone lay on the coffee table across from him. How did it get over there? Then again he'd kind of tossed things wherever as soon as he got home, intent on drowning his sorrows.

"When you didn't answer, I got worried."

"I'm fine," Seb grumbled, letting his head fall back against the couch cushion. He squinted up at the ceiling. Was it his eyes, or was a square patch of ceiling slightly discolored. Like it had a translucent sheen to it.

With a scoff, Dom took a seat beside Seb. "Yeah, nothing says 'fine' like alcohol poisoning Therian style."

"Go 'way." Seb tried to get up. He needed more booze. Maybe then his heart would stop fucking hurting so much. Maybe then it would... stop... just stop. He didn't want to *feel*.

"Don't say that."

Seb stilled. Shit, had he said that out loud?

"Yeah, you're fucking using your outside voice, genius." Dom sounded mad. Why the fuck was Dom mad? Seb rubbed at his eyes and sucked in a sharp breath. They burned. When had he taken off his shoes?

"How long you been here?" Seb squinted at Dom, leaning toward him to point a menacing finger at him. "Stop moving my shit."

Dom shook his head at him. "I just got here, and I don't know what you're talking about."

"You took my shoes," Seb accused. He lifted his socked feet. "See."

"You took off your own shoes, asshat. They're right there."

"I did?" No, he didn't. Did he? God, he was drunk. He must have. Seb lolled his head to where Dom was pointing and there were his boots, neatly tucked under the side table. With a shrug, he searched the couch. "Fucking fuck. Where is it?" He grabbed at Dom. "What did... what you did with it?"

"Okay. I see we're going to have to do this the hard way."

Seb flipped him off. Maybe. He moved his hand. It got quiet, and he forced himself to sit forward, elbows on his knees and fingers in his hair. Man, he felt like shit. Water ran somewhere behind him.

"Hey, I found your booze stash. It's over here."

"Yeah?" Seb waved a hand. "Bring it."

"Nah, bro. It's too heavy. You need to come get it."

Seb let out a sound of disgust, peering at Dom when Dom wrapped an arm around his back, grunting as he tried to lift Seb.

"You wanna maybe help me out here? It's like moving a fucking cement truck."

"You need to bench-press more," Seb grunted, his face pushed away from Dom's.

"And you need to fucking talk downwind and not in my face. Your breath smells like something fucking died."

"That's just my heart."

Dom paused. "What?"

"That died. My heart died."

"Jesus. Okay, come on, big guy. One step at a time."

Seb followed Dom into the kitchen, scowling at the lights. Everything was so damn bright, like it was trying to set him on fire. Maybe that was the alcohol. Why were they in the kitchen? Seb wasn't hungry. Thinking about food made him want to puke.

A thought occurred to him. "You curse a lot," he grumbled. "Don't roll your eyes at me, Dom—Dominic."

"Your observation skills are outstanding, and don't call me that. Who are you, my mother?" Dom turned him to face the kitchen cabinet. He took hold of the back of Seb's neck, his thumb stroking his skin. "Hey, look at me," Dom said softly.

Seb did. Or tried to.

"This is for your own good, okay? Just remember, I love you."

"I love you too." Dom was a good guy. He was always looking out for Seb.

One minute Seb was smiling at Dom, the next he was drowning in icy water. He scrambled for purchase on the counter, but the water made his hands slip. The ice chilled his body, and his face was frozen, or so it felt. He slapped at the back of his head where Dom's hand was as he held Seb's head underwater. Seconds later, Seb gasped and sputtered, drawing in a lungful of air before he was plunged back down into the water. It took Seb three dunks before he was pushing Dom away. Seb reeled back, away from Dom and the sink, shivering from the cold.

"Fuck. Asshole! What the… what the fuck are you doing? Are you trying to kill me?"

"No," Dom spat out, tossing him a towel. "You were doing a pretty good job of that yourself, dumbass."

"What?"

Dom motioned to the island counter littered with empty beer bottles.

Shit. Okay. "That was stupid," Seb admitted, drying himself, then his hair.

"No shit." Dom's expression softened as he studied Seb. "Why don't you tell me what happened?"

Seb shook his head, his lips pressed together to keep it all in. He didn't want to think about it, but all he could do was fucking think about it. For hours he'd tried calling Hudson, leaving voice mails, texting him, pleading, and then it all sank in. Numb was good, but he wasn't numb anymore.

Every scar he had was torn open, a gaping wound of putrid flesh spreading sickness through him. His body shook, and the back of his shoulder burned. It wasn't just his pain he was feeling; it was Hudson's. It was excruciating, like his insides were trying to tear him apart. His inner Felid woke with a roar, threatening to come to the surface. It paced furiously, hissing and clawing. Seb groaned and forced himself to walk. He ran for the door, Dom chasing after him.

"Where the hell are you going?"

Seb threw open the front door and listened. It was faint, barely there, and if it hadn't been so late at night, he wouldn't have heard it. The mournful howl shook him down to his soul, and there was nothing he could do about it. Inside him, his Felid half answered his mate's call with a roar of its own, one so fierce and raw that it tore through Seb's mouth, an unhuman cry echoing through the empty street. Throat raw, Seb slumped against the door, tears blurring his vision.

"Come on, buddy. Let's get you inside." Dom gently tugged at Seb's arm, and Seb followed.

"Seven years," Seb whispered, dropping down onto the couch beside Dom. "Seven. Fucking. Years. He kissed me. *He* kissed me. We…. He… he let me feel him, touch him…. It was so damn good, just like it used to be. He felt so good, and for a second, I believed….

"He kissed me, Dom. He let me hold him, let me…. Fuck. It was beautiful. He was beautiful, vulnerable, giving himself to me. He held my hand at the supermarket. He was happy, and he laughed and smiled, and the walls were crumbling."

"What happened?"

"We ran into Mrs. Palmer at the supermarket. She was so…. It didn't go well."

"Fuck." Dom raked a hand through his hair, his own eyes glassy when he met Seb's gaze.

The heartache in Dom's eyes was too much for Seb, and a sob racked his body. "It's over. This time, it's really over."

Dom pulled him into his arms, and Seb buried his face against his best friend's shoulder, soaking in all the comfort he could get. He didn't think it was possible, but damn if it didn't hurt even more than the first time. His inner Felid slinked off to lick its wounds and mourn the loss in peace. There would be no such peace for Seb.

CHAPTER 7

NINA BLINKED at him. "Say that again?"

"I have a date," Hudson replied, smiling widely as he packed up his messenger bag. He was leaving an hour early to get ready—mostly so he had time to calm his nerves.

"Really?" Nina clapped her hands gleefully. "When?"

"Tonight. Trent's picking me up at seven."

Nina stilled. "Wait, Trent?" She planted her hands on her slim hips and narrowed her eyes at him. "Trent, the guy you were dancing with to make Seb jealous?"

Hudson rolled his eyes. "Trent, the very nice fellow who wants to take me to dinner and doesn't care that I'm marked." He tapped his security clearance into his desktop interface to place it into overnight mode.

"Is this what you really want?" Nina asked, her tone gentle.

Of course it wasn't what he wanted. What he wanted wasn't possible. Not anymore. A week had gone by since Hudson's world had come crashing down for the third time in his life. Thankfully, Seb was staying away from him, only stopping by the office once—while Hudson was out—to drop off the photo album Hudson had left at Julia's. It had taken everything Hudson had not to give in to his grief yet again when Nina asked him what it was. He'd lied to his dearest friend, unable to get into it at the time. He would tell her eventually. Right now everything was too raw, too… painful. But it was for the best. Dom was sweet, pleading Seb's case, despite knowing Seb would be cross with him if he found out. After the fourth day, Dom simply smiled sadly at Hudson and told him if he needed anything to call him.

"I'm moving on, Nina. I know I've said that before, but this time I mean it. My Therian half will simply have to stop being such a tosser and get on with it. Seb and I are over. For good. Perhaps if I finally move on as

I intended to do years ago, Seb will too. He deserves to be happy." Every word was a fresh wound to his heart, but it was the only way. How much longer would they have gone on the way they were? Living off lingering glances, feathery touches, or the brush of a hand. Hudson couldn't go back to that slow death. Maybe he should nudge West in Seb's direction, and then Hudson would no longer have a choice in the matter.

"What about you, hon? You deserve to be happy too."

Hudson nodded. One day, if he was lucky, he'd find love again. "This will do for now." Who knew? Maybe Trent would surprise him. "I'm off, then." Hudson tried his best to be excited. Trent deserved a chance. Hudson kissed Nina's cheek and promised he'd tell her all about his date in the morning.

Traffic was awful, as usual, but he'd left work an hour early. He still had plenty of time to shower and figure out what to wear.

Once he faced his wardrobe, he started to feel nervous and a little nauseous. His inner wolf was not happy about this.

"Behave yourself," Hudson scolded, determined to have a good time tonight. It had been months since he'd so much as attempted going on a date, and even longer since he…. Hudson's cheeks burned. Thinking about sex was certainly not helping matters. Should he… be prepared? What would it say about him if he brought supplies on a first date? Still, better safe than sorry. THIRDS agents were tested regularly, and Trent would have undoubtedly been tested this quarter, the same as everyone else, but that hardly mattered without seeing the results.

"All right, I think that's enough of that. One fret at a time." He chose a pair of dark blue jeans, a brown leather belt, and a blue-black-and-white-checkered shirt, which he tucked into his waistband before neatly folding the sleeves to his elbows. His hair required a little more product than usual. It was probably time to cut his fringe. Perhaps then it would stop incessantly falling over his eyes. Should he wear his contacts? Sod it. He despised those things.

Standing before the mirror, he looked himself over. The outfit was casual but neat, accentuating his body in all the right places. A horn honked, and Hudson let out a slow, steady breath. He could do this. If he didn't, Seb might go on believing there was hope for them, and Hudson couldn't allow that. He should have done this sooner. If he hadn't been such a coward, they both might have been spared the heartache. He'd been so foolish, kissing Seb, letting things go as far as they had at Julia's house. If he didn't do something, the memory would drive him out of his mind—Seb's hands on him, the feel of his hard body pressed against Hudson's….

"Bollocks." Hudson turned off the lights in his bedroom and quickly headed downstairs to the front door. He opened it, smiling brightly at Trent, who looked so handsome in his black turtleneck and slacks. So sophisticated.

"Hi, Trent."

"Hey." Trent raked his gaze over Hudson and let out a low whistle. "Wow, Doc, you look amazing."

Hudson waved a hand in dismissal. He grabbed his jacket and locked up after them before following Trent down to the street. Hudson stopped short.

"Is that your car?"

Trent turned the alarm off with a beep and opened the passenger-side door of the flashy, red convertible, a wide grin on his face.

"Yep. Are you impressed yet?"

Hudson smiled coyly. "Well, it's not a terrible start."

Trent laughed, closing the door after Hudson climbed in. It would seem Trent Carson was quite fond of the finer things. Having been surrounded by wealth all his life, they had never been important to Hudson.

Trent slipped in behind the wheel, and the engine roared to life. The tires squealed as Trent peeled away, and Hudson was thankful he'd thought to put on his seat belt before they'd taken off. He had no idea where they were going, and the butterflies in his stomach were out in full force.

"Thanks for saying yes," Trent said gently. "I wasn't sure you would. I know you're still, um…." He cleared his throat. "Heard maybe you still had a thing for Sebastian Hobbs."

Hudson shook his head. "That's over." He summoned up a bright smile. "Let's not talk about Seb. Tell me about yourself."

"What would you like to know?"

"Why Manhattan HQ?"

Trent smiled. "Well, if you're a THIRDS agent, it's kind of where you want to be, right? I mean, you guys have the best equipment, the biggest budgets, see the most action. I don't think a week goes by without one of your teams showing up on the news. You guys are treated like heroes."

That was certainly news to Hudson. "I believe it's a matter of perspective and how the press is feeling that day. I'm quite certain you heard about the incident with Agent Summers not long ago."

Trent frowned. "Yeah, I remember that. He did his job, saved those other civilians, and they wanted to paint him a Therian killer. Can't believe that agent was so stupid, giving intel to that reporter. Doesn't matter that they were sleeping together. They shouldn't have been waiting for Summers after he returned from taking that shot. The guy had already killed someone. He had several more hostages and was going off the deep end. What happened was messed-up, but we weren't the ones who put the gun in his hand and told him to take hostages."

"Yes, well, there are two sides to every story, but they're rarely reported. The truth is no longer enough. Scandal sells." Hudson shook his head sadly. "They perpetuate anger and hate. As if civility between Therians and Humans isn't strained enough. It's frightful, and the bigger the city, the more challenging it is. Therian crime has grown bolder, more lethal."

"Ain't that the truth. I remember when Therian perps used to wet themselves at the mention of the THIRDS. Now we're getting perps who think confronting us is some kind of show of how tough they are. Like if they can kick our asses, then it proves something. I don't know."

Hudson nodded. It was rather frightening, some of the stories being spread by those who believed Therians were the superior race. How if the THIRDS didn't exist, Therians would be running the world. How Therian agents were traitors.

"I actually jumped at the chance to be here, because some friends of mine from college moved to New York City a couple of years ago, and they keep trying to convince me to transfer," Trent said with a big smile.

On the ride to the restaurant Trent had picked, he told Hudson about his life in Philly, about his parents and sisters. Trent was enthusiastic, energetic.

"I love socializing, clubbing, good food, and…." He put his hand on Hudson's briefly. "Good company."

Hudson couldn't help his blush as he returned Trent's smile.

Trent had made reservations at a chic French bistro on W 44th Street. The décor was modern, with framed artwork of bicycles matching the red, black, and white hues. The wood-paneled walls and glowing orb chandeliers gave it a warm feel. They were asked for their jackets, and Hudson promptly removed his and handed it to the lovely attendant, who checked them in before an elegantly dressed cougar Therian showed them to their table. Hudson was pleasantly surprised when Trent pulled Hudson's chair out for him.

"Thank you."

The waiter arrived with their drink menus, and Trent looked up at Hudson from behind his menu. "Do you drink wine?"

"A little. I'm afraid I'm not very wine savvy."

"Lucky for you, I am." Trent gave him a wink. He smiled his dazzling white smile at the waiter and put in an order for a wine Hudson had never heard of and doubted he could pronounce. The waiter seemed very pleased.

He bowed before taking off. They were soon brought some delicious-looking appetizers, at least until Hudson realized they were stuffed mushrooms.

"I hope you don't mind," Trent said, looking sheepish, "but I took the liberty of ordering us an appetizer. These are to die for." Something on Hudson's face must have given him away, because Trent winced. "You don't like mushrooms?"

Hudson shook his head. "No, it's not that. They look amazing. It's just… I'm allergic to mushrooms. I'm sorry. I should have said something."

Trent waved a hand in dismissal. "Totally my fault. I should have asked first. I'm sorry. I got a little carried away. I'll have them take it back."

"Nonsense. They look delicious. You should enjoy them."

Trent's brow furrowed. "Are you sure?"

"Of course." The waiter appeared just in time with a basket of sliced bread and some butter. "This is perfect."

"It's not too late to order something else."

Hudson waved a hand and smiled. "Believe me. I love freshly baked bread. Too much, actually." The sliced baguette was crunchy and warm and tasted fantastic with the imported butter; Hudson couldn't help but moan. "God, this is so good."

"Never thought I'd be jealous of bread."

Hudson blinked at him, half a bread slice in his mouth. "Hmm?"

Trent leaned forward, his voice lowered and a wicked gleam in his eyes. "I'm jealous it's the bread causing you to make that sound and not me."

Hudson almost choked. He finished swallowing and drank down almost an entire glass of water.

"You okay?" Trent asked, looking amused.

Hudson nodded. He didn't trust himself to speak. The wine arrived, and the waiter poured them each a glass, then left the bottle at the table. They put in their orders and continued to chat and eat after the waiter left. Well, Trent talked. Hudson ate his weight in delicious bread. He was going to have to put in twice the workout this week, but sod it. He was on a date. Bleeding hell, he was on a date! *Calm down. People do this all the time. It's no big deal.*

"Can I be honest?"

Hudson took a sip of his wine first. "Of course."

"I thought you were going to be kind of stuck-up."

"Oh?" Hudson cocked his head. "Why's that?"

Trent hesitated. He looked adorably embarrassed. "Well, I heard you come from this big, wealthy family. I kind of figured you wouldn't give me the time of day. I mean, you're this smart, handsome, rich doctor, and I'm some nobody from Philly." He met Hudson's gaze, his smile apologetic. "I kind of judged you before I knew you."

"It's all right," Hudson assured him. "Honestly it is. I left that life behind a long time ago. I was a poor fit from the start."

Trent studied him. "Wealth really doesn't matter to you, does it?"

"I admire those who work hard for what they have, no matter how much or how little. From a very young age, I was aware of the privilege I'd been born into. I simply couldn't understand my family's response to those who had less than we did. It was even more apparent when my grandparents took me on trips to London. During one particular outing to Covent Garden, I saw a little boy about my age, at the time, huddled by a trash bin, shivering from the cold. I pulled my hand out of my grandmother's and ran over to him. I took off my cap and gave it to the boy. He gave me the most wonderful smile. I remember how good it felt to see him so happy. I returned his smile just before I was yanked away and scolded by my grandfather. I was confused by his anger. It was only a hat, and I had so many at home. Why couldn't I give it to someone who didn't have any? I thought about it on the train ride home, and I decided the reprimand wasn't going to stop me from doing it again. And I did. Again and again. Gloves, scarves, hats, money for sweets." Hudson laughed at the memory. "I'd come up with the most outlandish tales for how I lost them." His smile fell away, and he dropped his gaze to his fingers.

"They didn't take it well, huh?"

Hudson shrugged. "I was different. Stubborn and difficult. Some things never change."

"Hey." Trent covered Hudson's hand with his. "Look at me."

Hudson did, surprised by the warmth in Trent's eyes. "You're amazing. If they couldn't see that, it's their loss."

"Thank you."

Hudson was having a lovely time. He ignored his inner wolf's growls. It was not happy with Hudson in the slightest. In fact, the sweeter Trent was, the more furious and unsettled his inner wolf became. Pacing, growling, spitting, refusing to behave itself or take a bloody nap.

Calm your fucking tits, all right? Piss off.

The coq au vin was delicious, and Hudson appreciated how Trent had informed the waiter to exclude the mushrooms as Hudson had completely forgotten. He was feeling a little warm from the second large glass of red wine Trent insisted he have. Hudson wasn't much of a wine drinker, but he didn't wish to be rude. It was delightful, of course, but far more than Hudson usually drank. After one glass of wine, Trent stuck with nonalcoholic drinks, since he was driving, a detail he admitted to having overlooked in his eagerness to impress Hudson.

After their sumptuous meal, where they talked about everything from work to the weather, they walked next door to Glaukos, a posh martini bar awash in blue lighting, with comfortable chairs and a pleasant atmosphere. Hudson's blueberry lemonade was fabulous. He'd have to tell Dex about this place. Dex loved a good cocktail.

"I don't get it."

"What's that?" Hudson asked, before taking another sip of his cocktail.

"How someone so gorgeous hasn't been swept off his feet." Trent leaned against the bar, facing Hudson. It was a little disconcerting being the focus of Trent's intense gaze, but that was likely due to the fact Hudson hadn't been looked at in such a way in a long time, at least not by someone who wasn't Seb. Trent took Hudson's hand, his thumb stroking Hudson's wrist, making Hudson's cheeks flush.

"Yes, well, being marked tends to put a damper on things for some."

"Good thing I'm nothing like those idiots. Some people can be so narrow-minded. I admit, I didn't really get it at first, the whole being marked or marking someone, but it makes sense. I mean, you fall hard for someone, think they're going to be with you forever, and one day they're not. Why shouldn't you find happiness again?"

Hudson's heart skipped a beat when Trent slowly straightened. He put his hand to Hudson's cheek, his smile stunning. "You deserve to be happy, Hudson."

Before Hudson could respond, Trent kissed him. Hudson stiffened, the taste, scent, and feel of Trent foreign to him. This was not his mate, and his inner wolf was livid. Hudson quickly shook himself out of it. He leaned into the kiss and placed his hands on Trent's shoulders, slanting his mouth and parting his lips in response. It was a sweet kiss, their tongues exploring languidly, tasting, caressing. Trent was in no hurry, and Hudson relaxed. When they came up for air, Hudson felt his face flush at Trent's incredible smile.

"Wow."

Hudson laughed softly. He averted his gaze, but Trent gently turned his head back to him.

"I really, *really* don't want to say good night. Not yet. I thought maybe, since I missed your birthday, you'd let me make it up to you?"

"Oh?" Hudson blinked at him, surprised Trent had known about Hudson's birthday.

"Yeah, I got you a little something. It's back at my place. You can say no. I'll just bring it in to work tomorrow, and it's all good." Trent laughed and shook his head. "My God, that sounded like the cheesiest pickup line ever."

"You bought me something for my birthday?"

"Yeah."

Hudson was touched. He really was having a good time. What would it hurt to extend the evening a little longer? It wasn't late by any means, and they were just getting to know each other. They didn't get to speak much at work, and it wasn't as if Hudson was committed. Besides, Trent wasn't some stranger he'd met at a bar or club. He was a colleague. This was the perfect opportunity to see where things could go with Trent. A chance at a new beginning.

"All right."

"Great!" Trent got up and offered his arm to Hudson, who took it with a bright smile. It started to rain, and Hudson laughed as they ran down the street to the garage where the car was parked. By the time they reached the front door of Trent's ground-floor flat, Hudson's hair was a mess. They were both a bit of a mess, actually.

HUDSON TOOK a seat on the couch in Trent's living room as Trent fetched them each a towel. Hudson dried his hair and ran a hand through it before wiping his glasses. They'd fogged up from the run, forcing him to take Trent's hand.

"Thank you," Hudson said, handing the towel to Trent. The flat was sparse but neat. A few boxes remained unpacked in one corner, but the living room was set up, for the most part. The leather couch Hudson sat on was comfortable, matching the sleek black-and-silver coffee table in front of it. A furry white rug lay elegantly beneath the coffee table, and a large flat-screen TV was nestled in a black entertainment center, its shelves occupied by video equipment, movies, and books. Everything was high-end, but a little… impersonal. No photographs of family, friends, or even art hung on the walls or sat framed on shelves. Perhaps Trent simply hadn't decorated yet.

"Be right back." Trent left the room, and seconds later returned singing "Happy Birthday" and holding a blue-frosted cupcake with a lit candle in the center.

Hudson laughed softly, touched by the gesture. Trent sat beside him and held the cupcake out. "Make a wish."

Hudson thought about it. He smiled at Trent and made his wish, the only one he'd ever wanted to come true—to find happiness once again. Trent removed the candle and tossed it onto the napkin he placed on the coffee table. He held the cupcake out to Hudson, and when he went to take it, Trent tapped the frosted peak against Hudson's nose, making him laugh.

"I'm sorry," Trent said with a chuckle. "I couldn't help it. You're so damn adorable."

Hudson felt himself blushing as he took the cupcake. He peeled back the paper and split it in half. He bit down on his and handed the other to Trent. Instead of taking it, Trent took a bite while Hudson held it. Hudson watched Trent eat from his hand as he finished off his own cupcake. Two of Hudson's fingers were covered in frosting, and he gasped as Trent pulled them into his mouth and sucked the frosting off with a decadent hum.

"I wonder if the rest of you tastes this sweet." Trent waggled his eyebrows, and Hudson's laughter was cut short by Trent kissing him again. The shock quickly wore off, and Hudson closed his eyes, parting his lips to give Trent access to his mouth. Trent tasted sweet, and Hudson leaned into him, allowing Trent to slip his hand around Hudson's nape, drawing him closer and deepening the kiss. Hudson curled his fingers into Trent's shirt, heat building inside him as Trent pushed gently. Hudson followed Trent's lead, lowering onto his back as Trent continued to kiss him. Trent shifted, bringing Hudson's leg up off the floor and over his hip so Hudson lay stretched on the couch beneath him. It felt so good to be desired, to feel Trent's ragged breath against his skin, to know Trent didn't care that Hudson had another man's mark scarred into his skin.

"You're so beautiful," Trent said against Hudson's lips before he moved his mouth to Hudson's neck. Hudson's breath hitched as Trent ground his hard erection against Hudson's. It had been so bloody long....

The doorbell startled Hudson, and he put a hand to Trent's chest.

"Shit. Sorry." Trent stood, calling out over his shoulder as he walked to the door, "I hope you don't mind, but I invited a couple of friends over."

Hudson was confused. He sat up and ran a hand through his hair. "Oh. Um…. Okay." Was their date over? Perhaps the evening hadn't gone as well as Hudson had thought. Trent seemed to have been enjoying himself. Had he not expected things to go smoothly? Why else would Trent invite friends to join them?

"Guys, this is Hudson. I told you he was gorgeous, didn't I?"

Smiling, Hudson waved at the two Therians. He wasn't quite sure what to say. Or do. This felt… odd. Trent dropped down on the couch beside him again, and the two men took a seat to Hudson's left, far too close for comfort. The one closest to Hudson put his hand on Hudson's thigh. Hudson bolted to his feet.

"I should, um, I should go, Trent." Hudson smiled apologetically. "I had a wonderful time tonight, and thank you for the cupcake, but I have a very early start tomorrow." He lied. He had a half day tomorrow and wasn't due in until noon. "You know how it is." He headed for the door, but Trent caught his hand, turning Hudson to face him. He looked disappointed.

"Don't go. Please." Trent's pupils dilated as he stepped closer to Hudson. He ran his thumb across Hudson's knuckles, his other thumb brushing Hudson's bottom lip. "I think you'll enjoy yourself."

It took Hudson a moment to catch Trent's meaning. Suddenly he felt sick to his stomach, not to mention incredibly foolish. Was that why Trent had asked him out on a date?

"Oh, I, um, I thought you—" Hudson shook his head. "Never mind. I'm sorry, Trent, but I'm not interested. I hope you have a good night." He tried to leave, but Trent gripped his wrist tightly. Hudson's inner wolf stirred, his hackles going up.

"Come on, Doc. None of us care that you're tainted. It's just a bit of fun."

Tainted.

Hudson glared at Trent. He didn't know which insult he found more disturbing. "I see. I'm tainted, so therefore I must be desperate for a shag from anyone who's willing and able to put their dick inside me." Hudson jerked his arm away, his voice a low growl. "Well, thank you for your charitable offer, but I would rather go celibate the rest of my life than let one of you touch me. Excuse me."

"Come on. Don't be that way. We had such a good time at dinner, which wasn't cheap, by the way."

"And neither am I," Hudson snapped. Was Trent serious? "Had you made your intentions clear from the start, I would have declined your generous offer." He ignored Trent's pleas, grabbed his jacket, and left the flat as quickly as he could, slamming the door behind him. He threw open the front door to the building and ran down the steps, then took off down the street, not caring about the rain, not caring that he had no idea where he was or where he was going. He just needed to get as far away from here as possible.

Hudson hated himself for the sting in the back of his eyes. He'd been such a bloody idiot, believing someone might love him for who he was, mark and all. What a fool. Falling for Trent's charms, for his smile and sweet words, when all Trent wanted from him was a bit of fun. Hudson had nothing against a casual hookup. He wasn't such a prude, but to believe Hudson was so desperate for intimacy he would eagerly accept what Trent offered. Because he was *tainted*.

Hudson had been called many names in his life. It came with being a Therian in a world that at one point believed them to be an abomination, a scientific mistake. But to be looked down upon by his own kind? It hurt more than any slur ever flung at him.

Where the hell was he? He paused long enough to glance around, and found a closed thrift store to his left and warehouses to his right. The street was poorly lit, consisting of either residential buildings or businesses closed for the day. A blow to his lower back had him reeling forward, and he hit the pavement hard, his hands getting scraped on the concrete. His glasses landed several feet away. He pushed up to his knees, but he was dragged into the thrift store's empty parking lot and tossed to the ground behind a set of huge dumpsters. He hit the asphalt, the wind knocked out of him. With a groan, he rolled over and stared up at the three hooded men.

"You think you're better than me?"

Hudson's eyes widened. "Trent?"

"You tainted piece of shit."

Hudson scrambled to get up, but Trent kicked him in the stomach. The blow had him gasping for air. The kicks were fast and fierce, and Hudson did his best to protect his head. He grabbed one guy's leg and was kicked in the face. Coughing, Hudson tasted blood.

"Stop! Please." Hudson put out a hand. "I work for the THIRDS! You won't get away with this."

Trent crouched down and snatched Hudson's wrist so he wouldn't punch Trent in his stupid face. "Oh, you're not going to say a word. They never do."

"Fuck off, you miserable wanker piece of shit!" Hudson spat in his face, and Trent laughed.

"Ooh, I knew there was a wild wolf under all those sweater vests." Trent dragged Hudson to his feet and shoved him into the wall. He moved in, his fist raised, but Hudson managed to duck. He threw a right hook, catching Trent on his ribs and making him cry out. Hudson was going in for another hit when one of the other men grabbed a fistful of his hair and slammed him into the brick wall, his head smacking against it. He gasped for air, the world spinning around him. For a slip of a moment, he thought he was going to pass out.

Refusing to give in, Hudson fought with all his strength, keeping his fists up in front of him. He kicked out, bit, and scratched whoever came close enough as they took their hits. Trent fell over as Hudson got a good kick in and managed to stagger free of the group, only to get tackled. His hands and knuckles were bleeding, his body sore from being used as a punching bag. They kicked him, and someone punched him in the kidney. Hudson shielded his head, but a blow to the face stunned him, his vision growing blurry. Another kick to the stomach had him coughing and wheezing as he curled up on his side.

"You're a fucking tease, Colbourn," Trent spat. "You think you can strut around like you're better than everyone, getting guys to wine and dine you, and then when they get close, you pull the rug out from under them, acting all chaste, instead of the filth you are? Like that cocktease Daley."

"You stay the fuck away from him," Hudson snarled. He kicked out, catching one of the bastards in the knee, relishing the painful howl the cougar Therian released.

"You little shit."

If it had been just Trent, Hudson could have defended himself and perhaps even subdued him. Hudson was a trained agent, after all, but he wasn't trained like Trent. Defense agents were prepared for all manner of lethal situations—situations THIRDS medical examiners rarely expected to encounter. Against three Felid Therians much larger and stronger than him, Hudson didn't stand a chance.

The lights above the thrift store's side entrance flickered, and Hudson prayed it wasn't his vision, that he wasn't about to lose consciousness. Everything was plunged into darkness, and Hudson gasped, scrambling to get away. A white light burst around them, blinding him, and from the shouts behind him, the other men as well. A pungent odor Hudson couldn't pinpoint flooded the air around him, wreaking havoc with his sense of smell. He coughed, crawling carefully toward the parking lot exit. This was his chance to escape. He had no idea what the hell was going on, but if he didn't move now, Trent and his friends were going to put him in the hospital. If that's what they even intended. A firm grip on his arm startled him, and he clawed at the hand, finding it was gloved. Fear swept through Hudson, but before he could say a word, he was hauled to his feet.

"Get the hell out of here," the figure growled in a low voice before shoving him past the chain-link fence and out onto the pavement. Hudson flailed but managed to stay on his feet. He spotted his glasses on the ground and swiped them up, then put them back on. One of the lenses was cracked, but he could see well enough. The rain poured down, but he was free. He forced his legs to move and ran down the street. A cab sat idle in front of one of the buildings. Hudson ran over, surprised when the cabbie opened the window.

"You call a car? Geez, you okay, man?"

Hudson nodded. He hadn't called a car, but the cab driver didn't need to know that. He got in and gave the address of the only place he would be safe. As the cab pulled away, Hudson wrapped his arms around himself as he began to shiver uncontrollably. It would be okay. He'd be okay soon. He just needed to get home.

"COME ON. Answer your damn phone."

Seb paced his living room, trying not to lose his shit or put in an emergency call to headquarters. He prayed he was overreacting. That any minute now Hudson was going to call him back and tell him to fuck off.

His body was sore, his muscles ached, and his stomach was queasy. He hurt all over. Where the hell was Hudson, and why wasn't he answering? Even when Hudson didn't answer Seb's calls, he'd text to let Seb know he was being ignored. They hadn't talked in days, but Hudson wouldn't let him worry like this if he was okay. Hudson was out there somewhere, hurt.

The doorbell rang, and Seb stilled. A multitude of scenarios ran through his head, none of them setting his nerves at ease. What if it was one of their own agents come to let him know something terrible had happened to Hudson? That he was lying in a hospital somewhere. Seb shook his head and hurried over to the door, unlocked it, and threw it open. He was stunned silent by the sight before him.

Seb's heart warred with itself, struggling between the overwhelming need to comfort and the sheer rage threatening to consume him. He would have given anything to have been wrong. Hudson shivered violently as rivulets of water streamed down from his hair, over his bruised and bloodied face, to the torn, dirt-stained clothes plastered to his skin. The left lens in his glasses was cracked, and from behind the right lens, Seb could see the redness in Hudson's tear-filled eyes. His bottom lip was bloodied and trembled, much like Hudson's voice when he spoke.

"I... I'm sorry. I know I shouldn't have come... after... what I did, but I... I need.... You always make me feel safe."

Seb didn't hesitate. He held out his hand, and Hudson took it. Seb closed the door behind them and locked up before leading Hudson upstairs to the bedroom. He grabbed a big fluffy towel from the closet and began drying Hudson in the hopes of warming him up. Hudson tried to move away from him.

"You're soaked to the bone and freezing."

Hudson shook his head. "I ran out on you, and now you're taking care of me. Why?"

Seb cupped Hudson's face. "You know why."

Hudson nodded. He allowed Seb to take his hand and lead him into the bathroom. As Seb turned on the water and checked the temperature, Hudson stood silently, staring at the floor. It was likely shock was beginning to set in. What the hell happened to him? He had bruises, scrapes, and cuts all over. By the looks of his hands and knuckles, Hudson had fought fiercely. Seb didn't want to leave him, but Hudson didn't need him adding to his unease.

"I'll be just outside, okay?"

Hudson nodded. He looked up at Seb, his blue eyes filled with so much heartache and pain. Seb wanted nothing more than to take that hurt from him. If only Hudson would let him. Hudson opened his mouth as if to speak, then closed it again. He turned away from Seb and started unbuttoning his shirt. Seb quietly stepped into the bedroom and closed the bathroom door behind him. He walked to his dresser and pulled open the bottom drawer to remove a pair of soft pajama bottoms and a comfy T-shirt.

Seb couldn't help his smile. When Hudson walked out nearly seven years ago, he left some clothes behind, and Seb never had the heart to get rid of them, telling himself Hudson could have taken those too. It had given him hope. The clothes sat where Hudson had originally stored them in the dresser. The gray T-shirt had an atom symbol in the center, and beneath the drawing, it said: "Never trust an atom. They make everything up." Hudson was so fucking nerdy it was adorable.

Seb went to the bathroom door and cracked it open. "I'm just going to leave some clothes for you on the hook behind the door, okay?"

There was no reply. Seb stepped inside, mindful to give Hudson his privacy. He hung the clothes up and stood facing the door. "I need to know you're okay, sweetheart." More silence. He was about to turn around, when Hudson spoke up, his voice barely audible over the spraying water from the showerhead.

"I'm okay."

"I'll be outside, then. Take as long as you like." He left the door slightly ajar in case Hudson needed him. While Hudson showered, Seb turned down the bed. The water turned off quicker than expected, and a heartbeat later, Hudson was standing in the bathroom doorway, a frown on his face as he held his dirty clothes.

"I don't want these," he murmured, looking as if he were on the verge of tears. "Can you get rid of them? I don't want them."

Whatever the hell had happened, it had done a number on Hudson. Seb didn't make any sudden movements. He crossed the distance between them at a normal pace and carefully took the clothes from him, his voice gentle.

"You got it. Why don't you lie down and rest? I'll be right back."

Hudson nodded, and Seb left the room, hurried downstairs, and dropped Hudson's clothes off in the laundry room on the washing machine. He'd worry about them later, but at least this way they were out of sight. He made sure there was nothing Hudson might need in any of the pockets. Hudson's wallet, keys, and phone were still in his jeans. Seb removed them and brought them upstairs. Hudson hadn't moved from the spot where Seb left him. Seb's heart squeezed at Hudson's flushed cheeks and dazed expression. He looked like a lost little boy.

Seb placed Hudson's belongings on the nightstand, then returned to him. He didn't touch Hudson, afraid he might spook him.

"Sweetheart?"

Hudson didn't even blink.

"Lobito?"

A sharp intake of breath was followed by Hudson's bright blue eyes meeting his. "Seb?"

"Yeah, baby, I'm here. Why don't you come rest?" Hudson was a little unsteady on his feet, and Seb was afraid he wouldn't be standing much longer. He looked exhausted and in pain. Seb held out his hand. "Come on."

Hudson nodded. He took Seb's hand and followed him over to the bed, where he sat down on the edge. Several heartbeats later, he lay down on his side, turning away from Seb. He curled up on himself, and Seb's heart broke all over again. He yearned to comfort, to seek out the source of Hudson's pain and take it away, but this wasn't about what *he* wanted. It was about what *Hudson* needed. Seb pulled the blanket over Hudson and stroked his hair before he realized what he'd done.

He pulled back his hand. "If you need anything, just let me know. I'll be downstairs." He turned off the light and was about to leave when Hudson sat up.

"Don't leave me."

Seb turned, swallowing hard at Hudson's wide, glassy-eyed stare as he sat with the duvet pulled up to his chin. He looked so unlike himself, so… vulnerable.

"Please. Please don't go."

Seb climbed into bed under the covers. He lay on his side facing Hudson but didn't move. Hudson searched Seb's gaze. What was he looking for? Without a word, Hudson gingerly moved closer and shifted down, his head under Seb's chin as he snuggled as close to Seb as he could, as if he were trying to burrow inside Seb. He slipped an arm around Seb, his face buried against Seb's chest, and his right leg in between Seb's. His entire body was pressed against Seb's. When he was settled, he released a heart-wrenching sigh.

"I'm not going anywhere, Lobito," Seb murmured before kissing the top of Hudson's head as he wrapped an arm around him, holding him tight. "I promise."

Hudson nodded. He trembled in Seb's arms, his silent sobs tearing at Seb's heart. Closing his eyes, Seb pushed down his rising fury. Someone had hurt Hudson, and Seb wanted nothing more than to find whoever it was and return the favor. For now, he'd remain right where he was and be whatever Hudson needed him to be.

CHAPTER 8

HUDSON WOKE to the most wonderful smell.

The pain that coursed through his body when he rolled onto his side was certainly *not* wonderful. With a groan, he opened his eyes. Wait. This wasn't his bedroom. Slowly he sat up. Last night came rushing back to him with exceptional clarity. He'd been jumped by that arsehole Trent and his friends, and someone had stepped in. Hudson remembered the gloved hand, the strange scent, and some kind of smoke, which was odd, but then again, everything happened so quickly. He could have sworn the man had said something to him. Perhaps someone walking by who heard the commotion? Whoever it was, Hudson hoped they were all right. He hated to think someone might have been hurt attempting to help him. He would make a discreet inquiry.

Sitting on the edge of the huge Therian-sized bed, Hudson scanned the room. He was in Seb's house. In his bed. The room had barely changed since the last time he'd been in it. It looked somewhat different without his belongings littered about. Not that Hudson was messy; he simply had a habit of misplacing things and not realizing they were right in front of him. He had lost count of how many times he went mad looking for his glasses only to find them perched on his head. Speaking of…. He found his glasses on the nightstand and picked them up with a smile. They were his backup pair. Seb must have had them fetched from Hudson's desk drawer at work. Looking down at his clothes, he ran a hand over the soft cotton of the familiar T-shirt. He'd worn it often around the house. Their house. Had it really been so long ago that Hudson had called this home?

Home.

Last night when he climbed into that cab, he could have gone anywhere. He could have gone to Nina's or Dex and Sloane's house. Hell, he could have gone to any of his friends for help, but he didn't. He came here. To Seb. To the man he knew without any reservation would always be there to catch him, no matter what they were to each other. It wasn't Hudson's intent to hurt Seb. In fact, Seb was the last person on earth Hudson wished to hurt. He'd just never expected to be so weak. For so long, he believed staying away from Seb was for the best, but he'd never imagined it would get harder with time.

Hudson stood and winced. His body felt as though he'd been hit by a BearCat. As he left the bedroom, he recalled last night. He'd been so dazed, uncertain of what he needed. Seb had no such doubts. He hadn't poked or prodded for answers as Hudson had feared he might. In the past, he would have. He'd have demanded to know who hurt Hudson, and they would have likely argued over it. Instead, Seb left him to his thoughts. He cradled Hudson in his arms, held him close, and gave Hudson what he needed—time and space to work through what had happened. Hudson was still working through it, but Seb had been there for him, comforting him, his touch and words tender.

Downstairs, Hudson found Seb in the kitchen with Dom. Dom sat at the counter, drinking coffee as Seb stood at the stove cooking up something delicious. He turned off the heat and moved the pan to one side before turning and stilling when he saw Hudson. At Seb's reaction, Dom turned around. Dom's hazel eyes darkened, and his expression turned grim. Was Dom angry with him for being here? Hudson wouldn't blame him in the slightest. Dom had become very protective of Seb in the years since Seb joined Theta Destructive. The two were close friends, and Hudson was grateful for it, knowing Dom had Seb's back in all matters, not only on the job.

Dom stood, and Hudson remained where he was, rubbing his arm absently as Dom strode over. He stopped in front of Hudson, and Hudson braced himself. Whatever harsh words Dom had for him, he deserved them for showing up here after what he'd put Seb through, expecting Seb to take care of him after breaking the man's heart time and time again. Seb confided in Dom, and next to Hudson, Dom was the only one permitted to witness any vulnerability in Seb.

Dom's lips pressed into a thin line, and he reached up. Hudson couldn't help his flinch. He hadn't meant to. It wasn't as if he didn't trust Dom. He was a good man and a good friend. Dom frowned.

"It's just me, Doc," he murmured.

"I know. I'm sorry," Hudson replied quietly, holding still when Dom placed his fingers under Hudson's chin and turned his head first to the right, then the left.

"You okay?"

Hudson swallowed past the lump in his throat. He couldn't reply, so he simply nodded. Dom wasn't angry with him; he was concerned. Why? He should be angry. Hudson couldn't understand it. Dom resumed his seat at the counter, and Seb appeared in front of Hudson, his bright green eyes filled with worry. He stood so close, his big, solid frame offering shelter. He was still dressed in his pajama bottoms and a threadbare T-shirt Hudson yearned to slip his hands under. Being this close to Seb and not touching him was painful, but Hudson basked in Seb's warmth, in the sense of calm and safety only Seb could provide. It was incredible how the man inspired such a feeling of absolute security.

"I spoke to Nina and told her you weren't feeling well, and she said not to worry. She's got everything under control, so you've got the day off. You stay here as long as you need to. I left the spare key upstairs on my nightstand, and if you need anything at all, you call me, okay?"

"Thank you," Hudson replied, his voice hoarse. Seb was still taking care of him.

"You good to eat something?"

Hudson nodded. He joined Dom at the island counter and took a seat in one of the tall chairs. He thanked Seb when a plate filled with two fried eggs, crispy bacon, sausage links, hash browns, Heinz baked beans, and buttered toast was placed in front of him along with a cup of tea. He stared down at his plate before moving his gaze to Seb.

"You remembered the beans."

Seb winked at him. "Of course. What's a full English breakfast without the Heinz beans? No mushrooms of course."

The dish was one of Hudson's favorite comfort foods, but he was very particular about which beans he had with his full English. He'd shown Seb how to make the dish years ago, and on mornings after a particularly rough workday, Hudson would wake up to his favorite breakfast. Seb would bring it up to the bedroom on a tray with a cup of tea and a small vase with a rose in it. They'd have breakfast in bed together, cuddle, shower, then make love before having to shower again and head out to work. Seb wasn't one for grand gestures. He showed his love in countless other ways. He was exceptional at small details. When Hudson mentioned something he liked or would like, something he'd seen or something that made him smile, Seb remembered. If it concerned Hudson, Seb remembered every detail. He never tried to impress Hudson with flashy gifts, never presumed to know what Hudson was thinking or wanted, never made decisions for him. He was thoughtful. Always putting Hudson before himself.

Hudson was suddenly overcome with emotion, and he bit down on his bottom lip to keep it from trembling. "I'm sorry," he said with a sniff. "Bloody arse. Crying over beans."

Dom got up, his voice low when he spoke. "I'm, uh, just going upstairs to use the bathroom. Excuse me."

Seb stepped up beside Hudson and swiveled his chair around to face him. He placed his hand to Hudson's cheek, and Hudson leaned into the touch, a shuddered sigh escaping him as Seb brushed his fingers down Hudson's jaw, his touch tender.

"When you're ready to talk about what happened, I'm right here."

Hudson met Seb's gaze, his heart in his throat. "What if I'm never ready?"

The muscles in Seb's jaw flexed, and his eyes darkened on instinct. Hudson waited for an argument, surprised when it never came.

"Then I'll respect your decision." Seb brushed his thumb over Hudson's bottom lip, and Hudson let out an unsteady breath he hadn't even realized he'd been holding. "Whatever you need, I'm here."

"Seb, I—"

Seb put up a hand. "I mean it. I'll always be here for you." He motioned toward the counter. "You should eat something before it gets cold. I'm going to take a shower and get ready."

"Thank you for breakfast and for these." Hudson tapped the frames of his glasses. "I hope it wasn't too much trouble."

Seb smiled that beautiful boyish grin of his. "I had Dom pick them up from work this morning and bring them over." With a wink, he headed for the stairs just as Dom came down.

Hudson turned back to his breakfast. He was hungrier than expected and finished everything on his plate. Dom was silent beside him, which was very unlike him. As soon as Hudson washed up, he leaned on the counter across from Dom and studied him.

"Something on your mind?"

Dom released a heavy sigh. "It's killing him, you know. Not knowing who hurt you. You plan on telling him?"

Hudson leaned forward on his elbows, his gaze unwavering. "Three men jumped me last night and beat the hell out of me for being marked and having the audacity to walk away from a proposition. If a stranger hadn't come to my rescue, I would most likely be in the hospital now. I know one of the men who attacked me, and so does Seb. Now tell me, Dominic.

You're his best friend. What do you think would happen if I told Seb who did this to me and why?"

"Shit." Dom ran a hand through his hair and shook his head. "*Shit.* So you're just gonna let the son of a bitch get away with it?"

"I don't know what I'm going to do, but what I won't do is have Seb pay for my mistake." Hudson didn't bother telling Dom not to speak a word of this to Seb. Dom was many things, but most importantly, he was a good man. He wouldn't betray Hudson.

"And if he finds out?" Dom asked. "This is Seb we're talking about."

"He gave me his word."

Dom nodded. He released a heavy sigh. "Okay. You know if you need anything, all you have to do is ask."

Hudson smiled warmly. "Thank you. I really appreciate that."

Dom wasn't happy with Hudson's decision, but he accepted it. Most likely because he knew Hudson was right. If Hudson told Seb, there would be no stopping Seb. When it came to Hudson's safety, Seb listened to no one, not even Hudson. It had been the source of many an argument between them. Hudson didn't need codling. He could take care of himself. Granted, he hadn't done a very good job of it last night, but he'd made a mistake, one he'd have to live with. Having Seb be there for him instead of rushing off to avenge him was what Hudson needed, wanted. What he'd always needed.

Seb came downstairs, looking handsome as always, his hair wet and roguishly tousled. The man was breathtaking, and all he had on was a faded green T-shirt, the fabric pulling over his biceps and chest as he moved, while his jeans hugged his powerful legs and tantalizing arse. He had on his heavy biker boots, and he grabbed the beat-up leather jacket from the hook by the front door and slipped into it with ease and grace. Hudson stood in the kitchen, mesmerized by Seb's muscular frame as he moved around the house. Seb grabbed a bottle of water from the fridge and frowned.

"Shit, I forgot to empty the dryer."

"I can do it," Hudson offered as he came around the counter and stepped up beside him.

"It can wait until I get home." Seb shrugged and smiled. "Don't worry about it."

"It's fine, Sebastian. Honestly. I don't mind." Hudson reached up absently and straightened the collar of Seb's jacket.

"Okay. Thank you." Seb made to lean in, then caught himself. He cleared his throat and pulled back nonchalantly, motioning toward the door.

"I'll, um, talk to you later. Just maybe leave me a note or send me a text if you go, so I know you're okay."

Hudson nodded. He followed Seb to the front door, and Dom opened it for them.

"Have a good day at work," Hudson told them, standing in the doorway as Seb headed down the steps. He took hold of Dom's arm before he could get far. Dom turned, his brows furrowed in silent question. "Keep him safe, please."

Dom's smile reached his warm hazel eyes. "Always, Doc."

Hudson had turned to go inside, when he spotted Seb's wallet on the small table by the door. *Bollocks.* He snatched it and rushed out the door.

"Seb!"

Seb strode back from around his truck and hurried over. "Everything okay?"

Hudson held out his wallet to him, his smile wide. "You might need this."

"I think you might be right." Seb took it with a chuckle and pushed it into the back pocket of his jeans. "Thanks."

Hudson couldn't stop from tugging at the ends of Seb's jacket. "Take care out there."

"I will," Seb promised, his voice low and husky. "You should get inside. You're barefoot."

A sudden sense of possessiveness washed over Hudson, and he closed his fingers around Seb's sleeves, holding him there. He wanted Seb to stay. It was ridiculous, and he had no idea where the urge had come from. Hudson couldn't explain it. His thoughts were jumbled, and his pulse was erratic. His inner wolf stirred awake and whined. It wanted Seb here with him. Hudson flinched at the pull from his Therian half.

"Lobito?"

Hudson quickly released Seb. He stood on his toes and kissed Seb's cheek before turning and heading back into the house. He was breathless by the time he closed the door. Once it was locked, he slumped against it. The engine of Seb's truck roared to life, and a heartbeat later it pulled away. Hudson remained where he was until he was certain Seb was gone.

"What the bloody hell was that?" Hudson groused. He pushed away from the door, irritated. Had he actually kissed Sebastian Hobbs on the cheek and then run off? What was he, some chaste preteen at a school social? "I must be losing my bloody mind." He had to get it together before he truly lost it. "Trousers would be a start," he muttered. It would be best if he found something to wear and went home. Staying here was not a good idea. First, he would get Seb's clothes out of the dryer like he'd promised.

Past the kitchen, tucked away in a cupboard was the washer and tumble dryer, same as it had been. An empty basket sat on top of the washing machine, and Hudson began to move dry clothes into it. Once all the clothes were out, he carried the full basket upstairs, then placed it on the bed. He could hardly leave it there. It wasn't as if he were in any particular hurry, and Seb would likely have enough to do when he came home after a long day. Hudson picked up a pair of Seb's socks and hesitated. Would Seb be bothered by Hudson putting his clothes away? It would mean opening drawers and hanging items up in the closet. Perhaps he shouldn't. Then again, this was Seb. If he were to get upset at all, it would be due to Hudson troubling himself. As if putting a little laundry away was any trouble.

With that settled, Hudson busied himself removing items from the basket, folding them, and neatly putting them away. Everything was exactly where it had been years ago. Curious, Hudson opened the bottom drawer, and a lump formed in his throat. It still contained the clothes he'd left behind. A pair of jeans, tracksuit bottoms, black trousers, a couple of T-shirts, a shirt, jumper, and zip-up cardigan. The drawer above it had also been Hudson's, and he was surprised to find it lay empty. Hudson closed the empty drawer, then removed the jeans, shirt, and cardigan from the bottom drawer. He changed clothes, borrowed a pair of Seb's clean socks, and found his shoes by the bed. Once dressed, he folded up the pajamas and returned them to the bottom drawer.

As he put away Seb's socks and boxers, a sense of intimacy washed over him, and he stilled. What was he doing? He needed to finish up and leave. This was no longer his home, and he would be foolish to give in to the nostalgia. He couldn't get swept away in the emotions this place stirred up. There would be no curling up on the couch with a fuzzy blanket and hot cup of tea to watch telly until dinnertime. No welcoming Seb home with a kiss, no cuddling or teasing or Seb absently running his fingers through Hudson's hair as they lay on the couch together. No falling asleep in Seb's warm embrace.

Two shirts and a pair of slacks needed to be hung, so Hudson went to the closet to find hangers. After opening the right door, he glanced up and stared at the black bag. It was Seb's camera bag. It struck him then that what he'd believed was the lack of his belongings strewn about the place that made it look different, was actually the lack of photographs. When Hudson had lived here, the house had been filled with framed photos of them, their friends, and family. Seb loved taking photos, loved capturing life's little moments. He was also very talented, something few expected from the huge tiger Therian Defense agent. Seb had a keen eye for detail, as reflected in the snapshots he captured. Hudson had gifted him a camera when they'd been together. Seb had been hesitant to accept, due to how expensive it was, but Hudson had convinced him.

It saddened Hudson to think Seb had stopped taking photographs. He'd loved it. The camera bag sat on the shelf, and Hudson carefully took it down. He walked over to the bed with it and removed the camera from its case. It looked new, but then Seb had always been exceptionally careful with it. All the lenses were neatly and securely tucked in their cases. It was digital with high definition video capability. Hudson turned on the camera, and a gasp caught in his throat at the timestamp of the video, the very last moment captured by Seb. It was the morning of the shooting. Hudson's hand shook as his finger hovered over the Playback button. Unable to stop himself, he pressed Play, and his chest tightened at the glorious smile on Seb's face. Someone else was filming.

"I can't believe you're filming this," Seb said with a bashful laugh. He shook his head, his face somewhat flushed. A thumbs-up appeared in front of the camera, and Hudson smiled. Ethan. He held a hand out to Seb and made a "show me" motion.

"What if he says no?" Seb removed something from his pocket, and Hudson sank down onto the edge of the bed, his heart in his throat and his pulse soaring. It couldn't be….

Seb inhaled deeply through his nose and released the breath through his mouth. He looked straight at the camera, his green eyes sparkling and his smile forming creases at the corners of his eyes. He held out a black box and opened it.

Hudson covered his mouth to stifle his gasp.

"Lobito, by the time you see this, I really, *really* hope you've said yes. I hope you've said yes and made me the happiest guy in the world. I want you to always be at my side. Please be my husband."

The camera went shaky and was placed on the bed, capturing part of Ethan as he lunged at his brother to squeeze the life out of him. Seb laughed and returned his embrace. The video went on for several more seconds as the brothers hugged. There was some sniffling, and then Ethan smiled big into the camera and waved before turning it off.

Hudson stared down at the black screen and the tear that fell onto it. He wiped at his cheeks and then the screen before placing the camera in its case. Quickly he returned it to its bag and put the whole thing back where he'd found it. Had Seb watched it lately? Was that why the battery was fully charged? He hung up Seb's clothes, closed the closet door, then grabbed his wallet, phone, and keys. He hurried downstairs, turned off all the lights, and all but ran from the house after locking it behind him.

That's what Seb had wanted to talk to him about when he'd asked him to dinner. He was going to propose that evening. Hudson stopped, finding it difficult to breathe. He leaned against the iron railing in front of someone's garden. It took him a moment to realize he was out of breath because he'd been running. How far had he gone? It didn't matter. He needed to walk, to clear his mind.

For hours he wandered around the city, lost in thought. He went to the park, sat, and people-watched. It soothed him, sitting quietly, watching the city he lived in and loved go about its business. It reminded him of London in some ways. Always bustling, people walking with purpose while others lounged in parks, tourists strolling, the sound of traffic, of life. It felt like a lifetime ago that he'd moved here, but really it had only been roughly ten years or so. The longer he sat, the cooler the day became. He had no idea what time it was, only that he was no closer to sorting his thoughts than he had been when he left Seb's house. Seb….

Their bond should make them stronger, not weaker. Mrs. Palmer believed marked mates shouldn't be in law enforcement, much less on the same team. She made a good point. Protecting their mates was a fierce pull, and fighting that pull went against their nature. It was challenging, but not impossible. Hudson gasped, realizing the answer was right in front of him. Mrs. Palmer was wrong. Bonded mates could successfully work together. Hudson witnessed it every time he went out in the field with Destructive Delta. Dex, that cheesy-doodle-crunching nut, proved Mrs. Palmer wrong.

Dex and Sloane's relationship was far from perfect, and they'd fallen along the way, but they showed that marked mates could not only protect each other, but those around them. When it came to protecting Dex, Sloane was fierce and terrifying, yet he believed in his mate's capabilities. He trusted Dex to not only remain safe, but to do his duty. They worked together as a team and part of a team. They built each other up, leaned on one another, teaching, learning. Dex and Sloane were the reason the fraternization rule had been amended. They'd proved love wasn't a weakness, but a strength.

Hudson stood with a smile. Trust Dex to give him hope without even being there.

Hope.

It was a start.

THE HOUSE was empty.

Seb hadn't expected Hudson to be home when he arrived, and he chastised himself for feeling disappointed. He walked around, the sense of loss palpable. His laundry had been folded and put away, which was very sweet of Hudson to do. There was no reason for him to stay. Seb had taken care of Hudson because he'd wanted to, not because he expected anything in return, and he certainly didn't want Hudson staying out of guilt or a sense of duty. It was better this way. No false hopes. Waking up to Hudson in his bed, having the man in his arms, their bodies pressed together, had been a blessing, and he would cherish that memory, but it was time to stop wishing for something that would never be. Seb had meant what he'd said. He would always be there for Hudson, no matter what they were to each other. Hudson's absence made it clear they were only friends. Seb would learn to live with that.

After a shower, he made some dinner, then sat down to watch TV. He was mindlessly flicking through channels, lost in thought, when a knock startled him. He turned off the TV, went to the door, and was stunned to find Hudson there.

Seb swallowed hard. His instincts screamed at him to pull Hudson into his arms, but he remained motionless, waiting for Hudson to say what he obviously came to say. His face was flushed, his eyes red-rimmed, and his hair a mess, chest rising and falling with rapid breaths as if he'd been running.

"I would very much like to come home, Sebastian."

Home.

"If you'll have me." Hudson's face crumpled. "Please. I want to come home."

Seb crossed the threshold and scooped him up, then carried him inside before kicking the door closed behind him. Hudson buried his head against Seb's neck, his skin cold to the touch. How long had Hudson been outside without a jacket? Seb carried him upstairs into the bedroom and placed him gently on his feet.

"I can't... anymore," Hudson said quietly.

"Can't what, Lobito?"

"That," Hudson said with a sniff. He placed a hand to Seb's cheek, his blue eyes pleading. "I can't—I'm tired of living my life for someone else, for something I can't change. I'm tired of pretending I'm okay, of waking up without you by my side. I don't want to be without you anymore. I never, ever want to leave your side again. I know I've been a complete arsehole, and I was wrong, so wrong. Please say you'll keep me?"

Hudson shivered, and Seb covered Hudson's hands with his own, cursing under his breath. "You're freezing. Why the hell didn't you take a jacket?"

"Sebastian, please." Hudson was waiting for his reply.

"Of course I'll keep you. It's all I ever wanted. I—"

Hudson kissed him, the taste of him exploding through Seb's mouth, sending a tremor through him. He wrapped his arms around Hudson and brought Hudson up against him, intent on bringing his lover warmth. His mate wanted to come home. Seb could hardly believe it. After all this time, his sweet Lobito was coming home to him for good. It wasn't his words that told Seb as much—it was his body, his mouth, the way he clung to Seb. The wall was gone. Before him, Hudson stood, yearning to be taken care of, thrumming with vulnerability, his soul bare to Seb. Hudson shivered, and Seb reluctantly pulled back.

"Wait."

"We've waited long enough," Hudson breathed.

"I know, but you're hurt and freezing. We need to warm you up." Seb placed his fingers to Hudson's cheek. "Please. For my peace of mind. What's a few more minutes?" He sensed Hudson's hesitation and pushed forward. "For once, baby, let me in. Let me take care of you."

Hudson nodded and allowed Seb to lead him into the bathroom. As Seb turned on the shower and adjusted the temperature, Hudson wrapped his arms around Seb's waist from behind, his head pressed against Seb's back, his voice a quiet whisper Seb wouldn't have heard over the water had he not been a Therian.

"I need you."

Seb closed his eyes for a moment, his hands covering Hudson's. This was the first time since he'd known Hudson that his beautiful Lobito had made such a confession. It wasn't a need brought on by lust or desire, but a declaration of Hudson exposing a part of himself he'd never revealed to anyone.

"I'm here," Seb replied, turning to kiss Hudson's cheek. "Lean on me." He undid the buttons to Hudson's shirt one by one. With trembling hands, he pushed it off Hudson's milky-white shoulders, letting it drop to the floor. Hudson toed off his shoes as Seb unfastened the button on Hudson's jeans. He rained tender kisses around Hudson's face as he undressed him.

Seb would take care of Hudson, but he wouldn't assume Hudson wanted him in the shower with him. As if reading his thoughts, Hudson slipped his hands under Seb's T-shirt.

"You're always so thoughtful," Hudson murmured, helping Seb out of his clothes. When they were both naked, Seb helped Hudson into the expansive Therian-sized bathtub. He gently maneuvered Hudson under the hot water, smiling at Hudson's moan of pleasure as he closed his eyes and let the water run over him. Seb poured a generous amount of shower gel on the soft sponge, his heart skipping a beat when Hudson stepped out from under the showerhead and presented Seb with his back. He looked up at Seb over his shoulder, his beautiful blue eyes dark with lust, yet his smile was timid. Hudson's cheeks were flushed, and it spread over his skin down to his shoulders. Seb had missed that rosy hue.

He washed Hudson with deliberate care, mindful of the bruises still marring his beautiful body. Seb pushed aside his rising anger and concentrated on Hudson, taking his time to cover every patch of delicious skin, every freckle, and the very prominent scars over his Lobito's left shoulder blade. Seb traced his fingers reverently over the very distinct claw marks. His claw marks. He shuddered, and Hudson turned, his blue eyes filled with love and anticipation. Seb lathered up Hudson's chest, moving the sponge over one tempting pink nipple, then the other before tracing a line down Hudson's flat stomach to the dark patch between his legs and the beautiful cock nested there. He kneeled, loving the feel of Hudson's hands in his hair, softly stroking as Seb washed Hudson's legs, up in between and back to his ass. It was a sweet, slow torture, and he was loving every minute of it. He wanted nothing more than to press Hudson up against the tiled wall and fuck him senseless, but they'd waited so long, he wouldn't rush even if it killed him.

Seb stood, and Hudson took the sponge from him, rinsed it out, and added more shower gel. Seb remained still, his breath unsteady, as Hudson washed him, one hand moving the sponge over his body, the other exploring as he went along, fingers tracing every muscle, causing the heat between them to rise to a temperature Seb was certain surpassed the water coming out of the showerhead. He closed his eyes and let his head fall back as Hudson moved behind him, a hand running down Seb's spine, making him shiver. The sponge moved over his ass, a hand slipping between his asscheeks, and Seb congratulated himself on not bucking forward.

"You're going to drive me out of my fucking mind."

Hudson's chuckle resonated through Seb, his fingers brushing down Seb's arm as he placed a tender kiss between Seb's shoulder blades. Seb hummed with pleasure. Unable to take it anymore, he grabbed Hudson, moved him under the shower, and rinsed him off before he rinsed himself. Seb turned the shower off, got out, and helped Hudson out. They dried each other, and Hudson tossed the towel to one side so he could slide his hands up Seb's abdomen. He pressed his lips to Seb's chest over his heart. A sigh escaped Seb, and Hudson continued to trail scorching kisses across Seb's chest. Seb lifted Hudson's chin so he could see his mate's beautiful face.

"I can't believe you're here."

Hudson smiled, and it was radiant. He stood on his toes, cupped Seb's face, and pulled him down for a butterfly kiss. "Take me to bed, Sebastian."

Seb pulled Hudson along with him out into the bedroom before turning him and seizing his lips. Hudson parted his lips, and Seb brought their tongues together. The fire that lay dormant in his sweet mate flared to life. He returned Hudson's feverish onslaught, releasing a groan when Hudson sucked on Seb's bottom lip before Hudson returned to kissing him as if breath could only be obtained through Seb's lips.

When they were forced to come up for air again, Seb took the opportunity to bury his face against Hudson's neck. He inhaled Hudson's sweet scent. Unable to help himself, he nipped and sucked at the smooth, pale flesh before licking the pink spot he'd created. Hudson's fair skin flushed easily, and it drove Seb crazy. He couldn't get enough of the taste of him.

"Oh dear God. Sebastian, please."

In the rec room, Seb had all but come undone at having Hudson's bare skin against his, at the feel of those round globes pressing against Seb's rock-hard cock. It was a miracle he'd lasted as long as he had. Seb wanted to consume him, to become a part of him.

"Maybe… we should… go slow," Seb stated, breathless.

"Slow later," Hudson pleaded. "I need you inside me. I'm going to go mad if I don't feel you filling me up." Hudson reached down, making Seb jump when he closed his fingers around Seb's rock-hard shaft. "I need this gorgeous cock inside me right now, Sebastian."

Releasing a growl, Seb grabbed Hudson by the waist and hoisted him up against him, thrilled by the feel of Hudson wrapping his legs around Seb's middle, his arms tight around Seb's neck, and Hudson's erection digging into Seb's abdomen. They kissed feverishly, both shaking from sheer need. So many years of wanting, yearning, and now….

Seb fell onto the bed with Hudson, mindful of not crushing him, nestling between Hudson's thighs. His trailed kisses over Hudson's face, down his jaw and neck. He caressed Hudson's skin, brushing fingers down Hudson's torso and over his hip to his thigh. Unlike Seb, who was all hard muscle, Hudson was soft, his muscles defined but sleek and sinewy. Seb kissed Hudson's smooth chest, moving his lips over one nipple, suckling on it before flicking the taut, pink nub with the tip of his tongue. Hudson slipped his fingers into Seb's hair, arching his back and writhing beneath Seb as he moved on to the right nipple.

"My Lobito, so beautiful."

"Yours, always." Hudson's words were a breathless whisper, and Seb relished the way Hudson shivered, as if he were about to shatter into a million dazzling stars, all from Seb's touch. Seb wanted to devour him, to taste, touch, kiss every glorious inch of him. He licked at Hudson's naval before moving down to nibble at the inside of Hudson's thigh, making Hudson jerk with a laugh. Still a sensitive spot. Seb chuckled before leaving more kisses. He took hold of Hudson's long hard cock and kissed the rosy head before lapping up the precious pearls of precome.

"Sebastian," Hudson whispered his name like a prayer. "There's been no one since you."

Seb froze. "No one?" Hudson hadn't had sex in almost seven years?

Hudson's cheeks flushed furiously. "I… took care of things myself. I couldn't stand the thought of anyone but you inside me." He met Seb's gaze. "I never gave up hope."

Seb swallowed past the lump in his throat. There hadn't been many guys since Hudson, but he'd had sex. "I'm sorry, I—"

"No." Hudson put his fingers to Seb's lips and smiled warmly. "It was my decision. What felt right for me. I never expected you to do the same. No more guilt."

Seb smiled past the tears in his eyes. "No more guilt, baby." He took Hudson's fingers and placed them to his lips for a kiss. "I never bottomed for any of them. Only you." There was only one man Seb could give up complete control to, and that was Hudson. Seb enjoyed being fucked, but leaving himself open like that was reserved for his mate and no one else. Seb swallowed Hudson down to the root, and Hudson bucked under him, releasing a barrage of polite curses that made Seb chuckle around Hudson's shaft.

He held Hudson's hips down as he bobbed his head, sucking, licking, and nipping at the gorgeous cock in his mouth. The scent of his mate was driving him out of his mind. How had he survived this long without having Hudson in his bed, under him, in his arms?

Hudson gasped and moaned, pleas and promises escaping his lips as he threw his head back, one leg over Seb's shoulder as Seb deep throated him.

"Oh God!" Hudson writhed, his fingers curling around the bedsheets. "Sebastian." He reached down to fist Seb's hair and tugged. Seb obliged, releasing Hudson's cock and moving up his body to kiss him, or rather to have his lips ravished by Hudson. Coming up for air, Hudson looked up at him through lowered lashes, and Seb smiled wickedly. He remembered that look. It accompanied an innocent, demure exterior that quickly gave way to something extraordinary. "Sebastian?"

"Yes?" Seb's voice was low and husky with anticipation. Hudson ran his hands down Seb's biceps before he reached down between them to palm Seb's hard dick, drawing a gasp from him.

"I need you to put this stunning cock inside me. *Now*. I want it hard and deep. I want you to fuck me until I scream your name."

Seb cursed under his breath before covering Hudson's mouth with his. A violent fire roared from deep inside him, rushing through every nerve, every cell. He ground his hips against Hudson's, lacing their fingers together as he sucked on Hudson's tongue, then lower lip, their breaths hot and panting as Hudson arched up against Seb as if he were trying to merge them into one. Seb's skin burned, his blood ready to boil as he grabbed a pillow, his mouth still on Hudson's, and lifted his hips just enough for Hudson to do the same so Seb could shove the pillow under him.

Hudson's body trembled as if he might fall apart if Seb didn't fuck him this very instant. Seb replaced his lips with two of his fingers, moaning at the decadent sight of Hudson wantonly sucking Seb's fingers into his mouth, his tongue circling them, his penetrating blue eyes on Seb. He'd never seen anything more sinful.

Unable to hold back any longer, Seb pulled his fingers out and placed them to Hudson's hole, his eyes never leaving Hudson's face as he circled the rim before gently pushing in. Hudson gasped, and Seb carefully worked Hudson's tight muscles, groaning at the anticipation of what it would feel like to bury himself to the hilt.

Hudson trembled and moaned beneath him, his face flushed crimson and his luscious kiss-swollen lips parted as his head fell back. Seb had never seen anything so bewitching. Seb pushed his fingers in to the knuckle and changed his angle, smiling when Hudson cried out.

"Sebastian," Hudson pleaded, his fingers digging into Seb's biceps.

Seb kissed him hard, tongues wrestling, teeth scraping together as he removed his fingers and threw a hand out to the bed where he knew the lube was. He flicked a nail under the lip of the lid and popped the cap open. He turned the tube in his hand, squeezed, and took hold of his cock with his lubed hand. He stroked himself, spreading the thick lube over his cock before placing the head to Hudson's entrance.

"Tell me you're mine," Seb demanded, his brow beaded with sweat as he restrained from plunging in. Hudson squirmed beneath him, letting out a huff.

"Sebastian, please."

"Tell me," Seb growled, enjoying the way Hudson shivered beneath him.

"I'm yours. I've always been yours."

"And you always will be," Seb said before sucking in a sharp breath as he pushed inside Hudson. It had been so long for Hudson, and Seb refused to hurt him. "Oh fuck, baby, you're so tight."

"I didn't want anyone else inside me. Just you, darling."

"Just me. Only ever me," Seb said through his teeth, then released a growl as he breached the ring of muscle, sitting balls-deep inside Hudson. "Fuck."

"Please do," Hudson said with a breathless laugh.

Seb grinned wickedly. "You got it." He pulled out and plunged in deep, making Hudson cry out. God, how he loved that sound. It lit him up from the inside out, and he burned to hear it again and again. Seb snapped his hips, the room filled with the sounds of skin slapping skin, of Hudson's moans, curses, and pleas for more. Hudson dug his fingers into Seb's asscheeks as he pushed up with every thrust, meeting Seb's. So many nights dreaming of this, and now he had Hudson in his arms, begging, writhing, giving himself to Seb completely.

Hudson's nails scraped down Seb's back, and Seb relished the sting. He wrapped Hudson in his arms, ravishing his mouth as he pulled Hudson up with him. He turned and sat against the headboard. He murmured into Hudson's ear. "Show me how much you want my dick."

Seb reached up with both hands and took hold of the headboard. He might be bigger than Hudson, but Hudson was a Therian. He was stronger than most gave him credit for, evident by the sculpted body he hid behind his posh manner and geek-chic wardrobe. More importantly, his Lobito hid a tempestuous streak that burned molten, and it burned for Seb alone.

Hudson put his hands on Seb's shoulders, his pupils dilated to the point his blue eyes looked black. He pulled up, and impaled himself down on Seb's cock.

"Fuck!"

Hudson's smile was sinful as he drove down onto Seb over and over, his nails scraping down Seb's chest, leaving a sharp sting and red marks that would take days to subside. Hudson bounced and fucked himself on Seb's cock before he tweaked Seb's nipples, then leaned in to suckle on one, then the other. Seb cursed under his breath, holding on to the headboard like it was a lifeline. Hudson alternated between rotating his hips and impaling his body, his skin glistening with sweat, his hair falling over his brow. His lips were swollen and pink from being kissed, his skin flushed, and the sounds he was making as he fucked himself on Seb's dick and stroked his cock pushed Seb over the edge.

With a roar, Seb threw his arms around Hudson and jerked him back, thrusting his hips up into Hudson's tight heat, determined to make his little wolf lose the last of his sanity. Seb thrust up into him, slamming his groin against Hudson's ass, his cock hitting Hudson's prostate.

"Seb!" Hudson gasped, his fingers tugging on Seb's hair.

"That's it, Lobito. Feel me. It's my dick inside you. It'll be yours in my mouth later. I love the taste of your cock on my tongue, love the way you fuck my mouth, love taking that sweet dick down my throat."

"Oh fuck, fucking fuck. Fuck!" Hudson cried out, his orgasm rushing out of him, and in turn his ass squeezed Seb's cock. Seb's release rolled through him like a tsunami, and he threw back his head, his eyes closed as a feral roar tore from his lips, his come coating the inside of Hudson's tight channel. Seb gripped Hudson to him as the tremors worked through his body before his muscles relaxed, and he was grateful for Hudson's weight on him. He might just float away otherwise.

Hudson snuggled close, his head on Seb's shoulder as he traced shapes on Seb's skin. He kissed Seb's jaw. "So… you were saying something about bottoming?"

Seb laughed. He kissed Hudson before he had to come up for breath.

"Maybe, when I can move again," Hudson said through a sated sigh. He was quiet for a moment before speaking up, his words almost a whisper. "I'm sorry it took me so long." He pulled away enough to cup Seb's face. "I thought I was doing what was best for us, but I was wrong. This is what's best. What's always been best for us. I love you so much, Sebastian."

Realization of what was happening finally sank in, and Seb ran a hand over Hudson's head, unable to believe the man was here, in his bed. He made to place his fingers to Hudson's chin and paused.

"Fuck, my hands are shaking," Seb said with a throaty laugh.

Hudson took his hand and brought it to his lips, then kissed each digit before placing Seb's hand to his cheek and humming.

"This is where I'm meant to be."

Seb brushed his lips over Hudson's. "Where you'll always be. Please."

"Always," Hudson promised, parting his lips for Seb's gentle kiss.

They moved down on the bed, and Seb reached into the nightstand for a couple of wipes. He dropped the lube in, cleaned them up, and tossed the little sheets onto the floor by the bed. He'd pick them up later.

Snuggling close behind Hudson, he placed a kiss behind Hudson's ear. "I love you, Lobito." He buried his face in Hudson's hair and inhaled his scent. Unable to get enough of his mate, of the feel of him, the smell of him, the taste of him, Seb planted a kiss on Hudson's shoulder and let his hand roam tenderly over Hudson's body. Hudson hummed his pleasure, a soft sigh escaping him. Long after Hudson drifted off to sleep, Seb lay awake. He was afraid of closing his eyes. What if he woke up to find this was all a wonderful dream?

As if sensing his fears, Hudson rolled over, cuddling up to Seb, his arm around Seb's waist. He nuzzled Seb's neck, lifting his face to place a kiss on Seb's chin. Hudson's words were quiet and laced with sleep when he spoke.

"Go to sleep, darling. I'm not going anywhere."

Seb closed his eyes. He kissed the top of Hudson's head, a smile on his face, and for the first time in so very long, when he fell asleep, it was with Hudson in his arms and a heart overflowing with joy.

A BUZZING sound woke Seb up in the middle of the night. With a groan he sat up, then smiled down when he saw Hudson fast asleep, his pitch-black hair a sharp contrast to the white pillowcase, as was the bruising on his beautiful skin. Seb's jaw clenched, and he turned, searching for the source of the buzz. A cell phone sat on his nightstand, and he couldn't remember putting it there. He picked it up and found it was Hudson's. Seb was going to put it down when a preview of a text popped up on the screen. It was from Trent, and it was disgusting.

Seb would never intrude on anyone's privacy, much less Hudson's, but the vile words staring back at him were more than he could ignore. He tapped the security code into the phone's screen, his heart squeezing that Hudson hadn't changed it. It was still Seb's birthday.

The phone unlocked, and dozens of texts popped up, each one as hateful and threatening as the one before it. Seb read the texts calling Hudson a tainted piece of filth. A cocktease who tempted men with his ass only to deny them. He threatened to ruin Hudson if he told anyone about their date or what happened after, if he spoke up against him or his friends. *Friends? Jesus.* The texts went on and on, and the more Seb read, the more furious he became. Going into Hudson's contacts, he found Trent's number, along with his address.

Exiting the screen, he placed the phone back on the nightstand. He kissed Hudson's cheek, the back of his eyes stinging as he ran his fingers through Hudson's hair. *How can someone say such vile things about this wonderful man?* Trent had done more than spew hateful words. He'd dared to lay a hand on Hudson, and somehow involved his friends. Nausea hit Seb, and he closed his eyes, breathing slowly in through his nose and out through his mouth. It didn't take a genius to know what Trent had been insinuating. From Trent's anger-fueled texts and snippets of events, it was obvious Hudson had managed to escape somehow. Seb had promised he'd respect Hudson's decision, but Trent had just taken that choice away from them.

Hudson let out a soft sigh, but other than that didn't stir. His Lobito was exhausted, and not just from the sex. Seb placed a feathery kiss on Hudson's cheek.

"I'm sorry, baby. I love you."

Seb carefully got out of bed, his muscles tight, rage simmering under his skin, feeling as though he were on fire. He pulled on a pair of black jeans and a black T-shirt, grabbed his black gloves and boots. Downstairs, he put on his black leather jacket. He grabbed his keys, wallet, and the crowbar sitting in the corner by the hall closet. He'd meant to put it away with the rest of his tools in the basement. Good thing he hadn't.

TWENTY MINUTES later, Seb stood at Trent's front door, his heart pounding in his ears and his grip firm on the crowbar. The entire car ride here, all Seb could think about was what Trent had done, or almost done. It wasn't bad enough he'd lured Hudson into a date with the intention of fucking him—because why would Hudson turn him down? He was tainted, after all—but he'd also invited friends along for a little gang bang.

The door opened, and Seb's lip curled in disgust at the man sporting his own bruises. At least Hudson had gotten in a few good hits, by the looks of it.

"Hi."

"Fuck." Trent tried to slam the door in Seb's face, but Seb kicked at it, sending it slamming into the guy. Trent reeled back, nearly falling on his ass. Seb let himself in, closed the door behind him, and made sure he locked it.

"You're not a very good listener, are you, Trent?"

Trent put up a hand in front of him as he backed away into the living room, Seb following him. "Let's talk about this."

"It's a little late for talking."

Trent ran to the coffee table, pushing magazines, remote controls, and random objects out of the way. "Fuck, where is it?"

Seb grinned. "Lost your phone? Shame." He shrugged.

Trent peered at him. "It was you, wasn't it? What did you do to my friends?"

Seb had no idea what the hell Trent was talking about, and he didn't care. Trent let out a fierce growl as he stupidly charged Seb, a fist raised to punch him. Seb ducked and slammed his fist into Trent's stomach, forcing him to double over. Not waiting for Trent to recover, he brought his right fist in for a right hook, catching Trent's kidney. Trent gasped for air and wheezed, his face turning red and his eyes glassy as he tried to push away from Seb, but Seb was bigger. He was stronger. He was also far more pissed off.

"You're a disgrace to your badge, you piece of shit." Seb brought the crowbar down against Trent's back, sending him down onto the wooden floor. Trent coughed and gasped for air before he managed to push onto his hands and knees.

"He left you," Trent spat out, blood on his lips. "What the fuck do you care?"

Seb grabbed a fistful of Trent's hair, forcing his head up. "Don't mistake his not being with me with his leaving me. He's my mate. He never left me. Do you have any idea what it's like to feel your mate in pain? Why don't I demonstrate?" He dragged Trent up by his hair and kicked him, his boot striking Trent's chest and sending him flying against the couch. Trent landed with a bounce. He grabbed at his chest, his eyes squeezed shut before he sat up.

"For every bruise you and your friends gave him, I'm going to give you two." Seb punched Trent across the jaw, hard. Had Trent been Human, his jawbone would have broken. A few more strategically placed punches, and Trent was scrambling, desperate to get away, his training lost on him.

Too bad. Seb would have enjoyed the challenge. "How does that feel, Trent? I'm taking a little creative license here. Is my point getting across to you?"

"I didn't fuck him!"

"But you were going to, and so were your friends! You sick son of a bitch! The only reason you didn't was because he walked out on you, but you couldn't let him go, could you? You couldn't let a tainted dog embarrass you in front of your friends. That's what you called him in one of your texts, right? A dog?" Seb whacked the crowbar across Trent's thigh. The man cried out, grabbing his leg and falling onto his side, tears streaming down his face, nose full of snot as he blubbered and pleaded for his life.

"I don't know what texts you're fucking talking about. Don't kill me."

Seb leaned in, and Trent threw up his hands in front of his face. "I want the names and addresses of the other two."

"Please."

"Listen to me, asshole. Trust me when I say the only reason I'm not putting a bullet in you is because he wouldn't want that. The guy you beat to shit is the only thing keeping your repulsive carcass from being buried six feet under, because he's the kind of man you could never even hope to dream of being. Now tell me where they are, or I might just reconsider your whole being-alive situation."

"You wouldn't... do that."

"I've come this far, Trent. Do I look like I give a shit about what happens to me? He's all that matters."

Trent started to shiver. "I didn't know."

"You shouldn't have to. You don't need to know if he's got someone to avenge him. All you need to know is that you shouldn't treat people like shit or try to stick your dick where it's not wanted. You have five seconds. Five."

"Please," Trent cried, snatching hold of Seb's jacket. Seb pushed him away, placing a boot against Trent's balls and pressing down.

"Four." Seb grabbed Trent's index finger and cracked it back.

Trent howled in pain, his head lolling to one side as he clenched his teeth.

"Sorry, I forgot to mention. I'm going to break one finger for each second of my time you waste."

"Larry and Craig. The addresses are in my phone. It was on the coffee table!"

Seb twisted his body to look over his shoulder at the messy coffee table. He removed his boot from Trent's balls and swiped up the phone with a grin. "It's your lucky day."

Trent stared at the phone in Seb's hand. "But…. What the fuck? That wasn't there." Trent held on to his broken finger as he doubled over.

"Thanks for this." Seb copied the addresses into his phone and tossed Trent's phone at him. Trent jumped out of the way, a blubbering ball of blood, saliva, and body fluids.

Seb left the house and drove to the home of the first guy on his list. When he approached the door, he paused. Shit. The door was slightly ajar. After checking the neighborhood, Seb slipped inside. The house was dark, but he could see just fine. Quickly he searched the place. It was empty. There were no signs of a struggle. Maybe the guy had gone out and forgotten to lock up. Or maybe he wasn't a total idiot and skipped town.

That explanation seemed less likely after Seb reached the second guy's house. Same thing. Door slightly ajar, and no one home. Fuck. Maybe they'd gotten scared and taken off? It was probably a good thing they weren't around, because Seb was still fuming.

By the time he got home, his anger had faded into numbness. After washing the crowbar, he returned it to its spot by the hall closet. Then he hung up his jacket, removed his gloves, washed them, and tossed them in the trash. The house was silent and dark. Seb took a seat on his couch and waited.

He didn't know how long he sat there, feeling… nothing. No, not nothing. He felt anger and sadness for what happened to his Lobito, for what could have happened. That night he'd felt sick to his stomach, the helplessness overwhelming. It was the worst feeling in the world, knowing Hudson was hurt and Seb could do nothing about it. Well, he'd done something now.

Hudson kneeled in front of him and put his hand on Seb's cheek. "Darling, what's wrong?"

"I'm sorry," Seb whispered. The doorbell rang, and he flinched. At least it would be quick.

Hudson stood, and Seb followed him to the front door. Two THIRDS agents stood on the other side, one looking remorseful, the other angry.

Hudson greeted them politely. "Good evening, Stevens. Rodriguez. Is everything all right?"

Agent Rodriguez cursed under his breath as his partner spoke. "We're going to need Agent Hobbs to come with us."

Hudson stared at them before moving his gaze to Seb. "What's going on?"

"Sebastian Hobbs, you're under arrest," Rodriguez said, looking from Seb to Hudson and back. His resolve crumbled. "Man, please tell me you didn't do this. Tell me you didn't throw everything away over that asshole."

Seb swallowed hard. He kissed Hudson's cheek before meeting Rodriguez's gaze. "Not for him."

Hudson shook his head. "What is he being charged with?"

"Assault and battery," Stevens replied, motioning for Seb to turn around.

Hudson gasped, and Seb forced his gaze away. He couldn't stand to look Hudson in the eyes, couldn't face the pain he'd put there. Instead he turned and placed his wrists together so they could be restrained. Hudson stepped in front of him and cupped Seb's face, his eyes searching Seb's.

"Tell me you didn't. Please, darling."

"I'm sorry. I love you, Lobito. Always."

The agents read Seb his rights as they led him out of the house to the idling SUV parked in the middle of the street. The lights were off, sparing him the bright blue-and-red flares that would have drawn out his neighbors. Someone was looking out for him, trying to keep things from turning into a circus. Seb was grateful. Hudson didn't need that kind of attention on him. Hudson closed the door behind him and ran after them.

"Dr. Colbourn—" Stevens began when Hudson took hold of Stevens's sleeve.

"Please."

With a sigh, Stevens nodded, and Hudson climbed into the back of the Suburban before the two agents helped Seb in. It wasn't usual for a Therian suspect to be picked up in anything other than a BearCat with the rest of the team in attendance. It was all incredibly low-key.

"Sparks?" Seb asked, and Stevens nodded from the front seat. He should have known.

Hudson fastened his seat belt, then slipped his hand around Seb's bicep. He looked out the window, not saying a word as they drove down to HQ. Hudson wouldn't remain quiet for long. He was likely taking it all in. Seb closed his eyes and let his head hang. He'd had it all and lost it just as quickly. Again.

CHAPTER 9

"I CAN'T believe this."

Hudson paced the cell floor furiously as Seb stood staring down at his shaking hands. Seb had just thrown his career away, his life. A tear rolled down Seb's cheek, and he wiped it away absently. Oh God, this was it. They were going to crucify him, bury him so deep no one would ever find him again. Their family, Julia, Thomas, *Ethan*.... Fuck. *Fuck*.

"Damn it, Sebastian!" Hudson shoved Seb before moving away, his hands in his hair. "How could you?" The only reason they'd even allowed him near Seb's cell, much less inside, was because of who he was. And because Seb was a THIRDS Team Leader, they'd taken him to the private cellblock, the one reserved for high-profile cases or cases requiring discretion, such as this one.

"I don't regret it," Seb replied quietly as he sank down onto the steel bench bolted to the floor.

"Why?" Hudson dropped to his knees in front of him. He cupped Seb's face. "I just got you back. Why would you do this to us? I'm tired of losing you."

"The way he hurt you? They could have killed you. I lost it." Seb shook his head. "When I saw those filthy texts—"

Hudson straightened. "What texts?"

"Your phone woke me up, and I'm sorry, I know I shouldn't have pried, but when I saw those disgusting words, things he said... I couldn't stop myself. I read the texts. Then I found his address in your contacts, and—"

"How?" Hudson removed his mobile phone from his pocket. He scrolled through his texts and shook his head. "There are no texts here, Sebastian." Hudson showed Seb.

"What?" Seb grabbed the phone and stared at it. "No, that's not possible. They were there. Dozens of them." Seb tapped away at Hudson's phone, his eyes going wide. "The address was here. In your contacts." He looked up, pleading. "I'm not making it up."

Hudson took his phone and returned it to his pocket. "I believe you." He paced the cell, his heart breaking. "What are we going to do?"

"We?" Seb shook his head. "You're going home. This was my choice, and now I'll face the consequences of my actions. If I'm lucky, the judge will go easy on me. It would have been worse if Trent had been a regular citizen. Since we're both THIRDS agents, the fact I have training shouldn't be used against me. He could have fought back, but he didn't."

Hudson stopped pacing to face Seb. "Haven't we paid enough?" His voice broke, and he closed his eyes. He was so tired. All he wanted was to live a relatively normal life with his mate. Was that too much to ask? They were both quiet as they waited. And waited.

"Why haven't they booked me yet?" Seb asked, looking around.

The rest of the private cells were empty, and the usual agents on duty were absent. Hudson agreed it was odd. Seb should have been processed by now. The THIRDS had Seb's personal information along with his fingerprints, but agents would have taken a mug shot by now. His personal property should have been confiscated, recorded, and stored. Not that Hudson was in any hurry, but it was certainly not the usual. Of course, the usual would have meant a cellblock filled with detainees.

"You should have taken me up on my offer. This could have been avoided."

Hudson started at the familiar voice. The cell door opened, and Sparks stepped inside. *Bloody Felids. Wait....* He looked from Sparks to Seb and back. "What offer?"

Seb didn't reply, so Sparks answered for him. "To join TIN as an associate. He would have been trained, his knee given the best medical treatment available. He would have been protected from all this."

Hudson considered her words and read between the lines. With Sparks, one was often forced to really listen in order to hear what wasn't said. "If he joins you, would this situation be... cleared up?"

Sparks cocked her head, her piercing blue eyes studying him. "It's too late, Dr. Colbourn."

It couldn't be. Hudson wouldn't allow it. After years of heartache, of needing his mate, he wasn't going to lose him now. This was his mess too. Seb was here because of him.

"You can have me, and not as an associate. I'll join TIN as an operative."

Seb jumped to his feet. "Absolutely not."

"You have no say in this, Sebastian," Hudson snapped. "It's my decision." He was already in bed with TIN through Dex. Why not make it official? He couldn't let Seb lose everything because of him.

"The hell I have no say," Seb hissed, taking hold of Hudson's arm. His expression softened, fear and panic in his eyes. "You're my mate."

"And what good will that do us when you're in prison? I won't let them come between us. Not this time. Trent was the one who acted reprehensibly, and I'm supposed to sit back and watch them punish *you*? What you did was wrong, Sebastian, but what Trent did, what he was going to do, what he's gotten away with?" He pressed his lips together in an attempt to calm his rising ire. He'd allowed others to dictate his life, and what had it gotten him? He'd lost what was most important to him. He'd been bloody miserable. This was his life, their life. For years he'd fought against his family, refusing to have his path chosen for him, only to arrive in the States and end up in the same position, submitting to his guilt and the will of others. He'd had enough.

Sparks shook her head at him. "That's not how it works. You don't simply get to become a TIN operative because you feel like it."

"You asked Dex and Sloane."

"Yes, but I don't see what—"

"Then you can ask me," Hudson insisted. "I'm valuable, and not just because of Dex. I can be a trained operative, as well as one of your TIN medical examiners or medical specialists. I know I can be of value to you, to TIN." Whatever it took to have some semblance of a life with Seb, Hudson would take it. At least he wouldn't be on his own with TIN. He'd have Dex and Sloane. That would be enough for him. Sparks seemed to give it some thought.

"What if you get us both?" Seb asked.

Sparks arched an eyebrow at Seb. "I'm listening."

"If you make this go away, and you take Hudson… you get me too. But we're a partnership, just like Dex and Sloane. We come together or not at all."

Hudson swallowed hard, his nerves somewhat eased when Seb's hand slipped into his and gave it a squeeze. After what seemed like an eternity, Sparks turned away from them.

"Agent Jones. We're done here."

Apparently, Sparks wasn't the only TIN operative working undercover inside the THIRDS. Hudson had suspected as much. Were Stevens and

Rodriguez operatives as well? The huge tiger Therian approached, and Hudson took a step closer to Seb. *Please don't take him from me.* Agent Jones opened the cell door and waited. Sparks spoke quietly to him, but loud enough for Hudson and Seb to hear.

"Get Agent Hobbs cleaned up, and cut him loose. Protocol Poppy Fields."

"Both of them?" Agent Jones clarified.

Sparks nodded. She paused to look over her shoulder at them. "We'll be in touch, Agents. Welcome to TIN." She walked off without so much as a second glance. That was it? Hudson felt somewhat weak in the knees, and Seb walked him over to the bench, where Hudson took a seat. Could it be that easy? What the hell was he thinking? *Easy?* What they'd just done was as far from easy as they could get.

Agent Jones removed his phone from his pocket and tapped away at it. Once he was done, he returned the phone to his pocket and stood motionless. Hudson and Seb exchanged glances. *Now what?*

Several seconds later, another agent appeared. He handed Agent Jones a large bag through the bars. Receiving a nod from Agent Jones, the leopard Therian left. Were all TIN's operatives so deadly serious? Hudson thought of Dex, and he almost felt sorry for Sparks. Was she aware what she was about to unleash in her organization? She had to know. Agent Jones handed the bag to Seb, his stoic expression never faltering.

"Change. Take everything you have on and put it in the bag, including your phone."

"It's THIRDS issued," Seb reminded the operative. All THIRDS agents were issued secure cell phones to use while on and off duty. Just because they weren't on the job twenty-four hours a day didn't mean the THIRDS could take any chances with classified information.

"Regardless, you need to hand it over. We need to make sure nothing connects you to Trent Carson's friends. It'll be returned later."

Seb nodded. He took the bag, placed it on the bench, and started undressing just as Hudson's phone rang.

Hudson frowned, feeling certain he'd never had a ringtone of "Somewhere Over the Rainbow," much less applied it to any of his contacts. The caller was unknown. He answered quietly.

"Hello?"

"It's taken care of."

Austen. Blimey, that was quick.

"Did you change my ringtone? Never mind. What does that mean?" Hudson asked, afraid to hear the answer. What Trent did was unforgiveable, but that didn't mean Hudson wanted him dead. Oh God, what if TIN had… disposed of him? Would they do that? Trent was a THIRDS agent. Surely someone would notice Trent's sudden disappearance.

"It means it's taken care of. Sorry, Doc. You don't get to ask questions until you're sworn in and get a pretty new tie. I would recommend a blue hue to match your eyes."

"Are they…?"

Austen released a heavy sigh. "The arresting agents work for TIN, and douchebag Trent is being privately escorted back to Philly, where he'll face charges for three counts of assault and battery and six counts of sexual assault on marked Therians. Seems his victims suddenly feel safe enough to talk. Trent is going away for a very long time."

Hudson couldn't believe what he was hearing. It struck him then, how much worse it could have been the evening he'd been attacked. *That bloody wanker.* "What if he mentions me?"

"You? Trent's never met you. He has no idea who you are or that you exist. There is nothing that connects you to him, his home, or his friends."

Hudson was going to ask how that was possible, but then he remembered who he was speaking to. If TIN could make Dex forget about his seizure, why wouldn't they have the means to make Trent forget? It was… terrifying. "And the others? His friends?"

"We're not worried about them."

"But what if they go to the THIRDS?"

"That's not going to happen."

Austen sounded so sure. Hudson stood, unable to stop from pacing. "Did TIN…?"

"No, your guardian angel took care of them."

Hudson froze. "What?"

"Wolf got to them first."

A chill swept through Hudson, making him shiver. Oh heavens. Was that who had come to his rescue? He was grateful for Seb's strong arms around him, holding him up. Why had Wolf taken an interest in him? Why save him from those men? Far more frightening was Wolf dispatching those two men for what they'd done. It meant he felt something, whatever it was, but why would he? Hudson had never even seen the man, only heard of him. It was unsettling, having the attention of a trained psychopath.

"What are you talking about?"

"Neither men were in their homes when TIN arrived. An operative at each scene received an anonymous text telling them not to worry, that it was taken care of. There was also a nice little tip on where to find Trent. Your man, Seb, must have put the fear of God into him, because after he called in Seb's visit, he was on the way to the airport with a one-way ticket to LA."

"What does TIN know about Wolf? And why does he care what happens to me?"

"TIN operatives aren't the sharing type. Besides, when Wolf went off the grid, he destroyed any information TIN had on him. All we have to go on is what Sparks personally knows about him. There's something else, but you're not going to like it. I told Dex, and he almost had kittens. So to speak. Wouldn't that be something if he could?" Austen snorted out a laugh. "Sloane would lose his shit."

The man was off his trolley. "Austen," Hudson hissed. "Tell me."

"It looks like Wolf might have been keeping an eye on you longer than we thought. It's likely he stepped out of the shadows because someone forced his hand. Possibly the Makhai."

Sparks had told Hudson briefly about the Makhai, the group Moros had been associated with. Hudson walked back to the bench and sat down, Seb worriedly accompanying him, his eyes questioning. He held up a hand. He'd tell Seb everything in a minute; he just needed to process all of this.

"Why?"

"Your guess is as good as mine."

"So what happens now?"

"That's up to the boss lady. What I can say is she doesn't like cleaning up other people's messes, and this whole thing with Wolf has her all kinds of pissy. Anyway, consider this one a welcome gift. Next time, you'll owe her, and trust me, you don't want to owe her."

"Thank you."

"See you around."

Hudson returned his phone to his pocket, his thoughts going to Wolf. It just didn't make any sense.

Seb placed his fingers to Hudson's jaw. "Lobito, what's going on?"

"We'll discuss this when we get home."

Agent Jones returned with Seb's phone and a new set of clothes. They were released from the cell without a word from Agent Jones, whom Hudson supposed they'd be seeing more of around Unit Alpha. Seb called a cab, and soon they were outside Seb's front door. This night was so surreal. First that nasty business with Trent, then Seb getting arrested, TIN, and now finding out about Wolf?

As soon as Seb opened the door, Hudson hurried to the kitchen. He opened the end cabinet, grateful Seb still had the electric kettle Hudson had purchased years ago. He filled it with water, aware of Seb hovering quietly beside the island counter. Seb waited patiently as Hudson made some tea. He wasn't about to burn through any more brain cells on this mess until he had a cup of tea in his hands. Once he did, he headed for the living room and sat down on the couch. Seb took a seat beside him.

"Lobito, talk to me."

Hudson sucked in a sharp breath before letting it out slowly. "Wolf's been keeping an eye on me for longer than TIN thought."

Seb blinked at him. "Come again?"

He relayed everything Austen had told him. When he was done, he took a big sip of tea and waited for all that to sink in. Seb reacted as expected. He stood, wincing at the pain in his knee before throwing up his arms.

"Are you fucking kidding me? And they only just found this out *now*?"

Hudson took another sip of tea. Perhaps he should take up yoga or meditation. He had the feeling he was going to need it. Seb continued to pace and rant. Hudson let the poor man vent. He'd been through so much already. When Seb was done, he let out a huff and dropped down onto the couch beside Hudson.

"Tell me what's going through your head." Seb's voice was soft, his fingers gentle against Hudson's jaw.

"Wolf has been watching me, and we work for TIN now. I'm… not sure what else there is to say." He was still attempting to wrap his head around it all. "Are you going to tell Dom?"

Seb ran a hand through his hair and sighed. "I don't know. I mean, if I was an associate like Sparks originally proposed, I wouldn't have hesitated. I would have still been a THIRDS agent first, and TIN associate second. But as a full operative? How could I do that to Dom? We're going to be sent God knows where to do God knows what. If I fuck up, and heaven forbid I'm exposed, everyone I care about will become a target."

Hudson considered this. It was different for him. He had people he cared about, but his family was Nina and Seb's family. Speaking of which…. "Ethan already knows about Dex and Sloane. He's an associate along with Destructive Delta." Seb let out a grunt, and Hudson put a hand to his cheek. "I'm certain he was going to tell you. I imagine he's struggling with the very thing you are at the moment. Between him, Cal, and you, I'm confident our family will be safe."

Seb's smile at the mention of "our family" was breathtaking. He turned his face so he could kiss Hudson's palm. "What do you think I should do?"

"I think whether you tell Dom or not, he could still be in danger because he's your best friend. I believe it's better for him to be prepared than to be caught off guard. He would want to know."

Seb nodded. "You're right. He would. No matter what happens, I know he'd want me to confide in him. The rest of the team... I'll have to think about."

"Fair enough."

Seb took Hudson's hands. "Whatever happens, we won't let that change *us*. Me and you. We're in this together. Always. As long as we're together, I can make it through anything."

Hudson finished his tea and placed the cup on the coffee table before turning to face Seb. There was nothing he could do in regards to Wolf or TIN, but there was certainly a concern he *could* address, and it was sitting beside him, eyes filled with love. "What are we doing?"

"What do you mean?"

"I have no doubt you love me, Sebastian. No one will ever love me the way you do, but that love is dangerous." Hudson brushed his fingers down Seb's stubbly jaw. The love he felt for this man was frightening at times. "You can't go around beating the pulp out of everyone who poses a threat to me. What if Sparks hadn't been there? What if... what if you'd killed Trent?"

Seb straightened. "You make me sound like some kind of monster. I'd never murder anyone."

"When my life is in danger, you lose yourself to your feral half. You allow him to take control. It terrifies me. How far would he go to protect me?" He met Seb's gaze, pleading for him to understand. "Something needs to change, Sebastian. If this is going to work, *we* need to change. I have to learn to lean on you, and you have to learn to take a step back and let me deal with uncomfortable situations."

Seb opened his mouth to reply, but Hudson placed his fingers to Seb's lips.

"I'm not asking you to step away completely. You're my mate, and you need to protect me, I understand, but if you come to my rescue for every little thing, it makes me feel weak, as if I can't take care of myself. All my life, I've been coddled, by my parents, my brothers and sisters. I don't want that from you. I need you to have faith in me."

Seb frowned, taking Hudson's hand and tenderly moving it away from his mouth. "I didn't know I made you feel that way."

"Not you, your actions, and although they come from a good place, it hurts me, hurts us."

"I'm sorry. I'll try harder." Seb lowered his head, but Hudson cupped his face, lifting it so he could place his lips to Seb's.

"*We'll* try harder. We're in this together, remember? I love you."

Seb's smile took Hudson's breath away. "I love you too, Lobito." He drew Hudson into his heavenly embrace, and Hudson closed his eyes, basking in Seb's warmth. He loved Seb's strength, loved how safe it made him feel, how loved and protected, but that didn't mean Hudson couldn't be strong enough for the both of them too. As he snuggled against Seb, inhaling his scent, he tried to think less about the madness around him and concentrated on the one thing that mattered most. He had his Sebastian back. Hudson smiled despite his worries. He'd spent so long living in the past; he couldn't wait to get started on their future.

"YOU'RE SMILING like a loon," Hudson muttered, tapping away at his tablet.

Inside he was as giddy as Nina, but he was hardly about to start giggling like some preteen with their first crush. He was determined to perform his duties as if nothing had changed. Word of his and Seb's reconciliation seemed to have spread through Unit Alpha like wildfire. Hudson was certain a gummy-bear-eating scoundrel was behind it. The man was a worse gossip than the tabloids, especially when he was excited about something. Hudson couldn't be upset, though; Dex had been so ridiculously happy for him. So had the rest of their unit, judging by all the smiles he'd received since arriving at work this morning. And what a morning it had been!

Hudson was still reeling from waking up in Seb's bed. He woke ten minutes before his alarm went off, like he always did, but this time was different. This time, when he turned, a lump formed in his throat at the beautiful sight before him. Seb lay asleep, long lashes against his cheeks, full lips slightly parted. He had one arm thrown over Hudson's waist, holding him close. Hudson studied his face, the barely there freckles sprinkled across his nose and cheeks, the dark stubble on his chiseled jaw. He couldn't keep from reaching out. He ran a thumb across one thick, dark eyebrow, and Seb moaned softly. He opened his eyes slowly, his lips spreading into a beautiful smile.

"Good morning, darling."

Seb pulled him closer and kissed the tip of his nose. "Great morning, Lobito."

That had been followed by Seb pouncing on him, the incredible sex waking him up like no amount of caffeine ever could.

Hudson let out a sigh before he could help himself, and Nina laughed at him, grabbing his arm and shaking him. So much for going on as if nothing had changed.

"Why are you trying to tear my arm off? Honestly, Nina. We're at a crime scene."

Nina rolled her eyes. "Fine. Pretend you're not squealing like a schoolgirl inside. Besides, we're all done here. Vic's on their way to the lab." She released him, and he scrunched up his nose. He was not squealing like a schoolgirl inside. His dreamy sigh was very adultlike.

A lovely breeze washed over Hudson as he stood downwind. It felt good against his face. Then a scent struck him from out of nowhere, sending a jolt of familiarity through him. He reeled back, his heart threatening to beat out of him. Sniffing the air, his lungs filled with the unmistakable scent, but it wasn't possible.

"Hudson?"

Hudson shook his head. It couldn't be. No. Not again.

The first time he'd smelled it, he told himself it was a mistake, a result of stress and sleepless nights. He'd been recovering from several gunshot wounds, followed by nightmares of that evening, and with everything going on with Seb, his mind conjured up the one scent he would have given anything to have again. Only there was no comfort this time, because there was no possible way this could be happening. His feral half woke, its fur bristling and fangs bare. It was confused, frightened, and angry. So much had happened in such a short time, and now this. He was feeling overwhelmed suddenly.

Hudson's vision sharpened, and his breath quickened into harsh pants. *Oh God.*

"Hudson, what's wrong?" Nina tried to get close, but he snarled at her, backing up near the shop door behind him. His body screamed in agony, and he wrapped his arms around himself. He was shivering, and darkness encroached on his vision. This wasn't supposed to happen. Not to him.

Before the darkness claimed him, he heard Nina's panicked voice.

"Seb, Hudson's going feral!"

SEB WAS pretty sure he'd broken every traffic law in existence. He didn't care. The lights on his Suburban flashed, the siren howling his approach as he sped through the city to get to Hudson. He had no idea what the hell was going on, but in all the years he'd known Hudson, his little wolf had never, *ever* lost himself to his feral half. Hell, Hudson might throw a tantrum and get pissy, but he never lost control. Period.

According to Nina's panicked phone call, they'd been out on a routine callout. Nothing to warrant Hudson losing it. To make things worse, Hudson wasn't responding to anyone. Not to Nina, and not to any of the members of Destructive Delta who'd been on scene and about to head back to HQ when Hudson ran into the café and started stripping. The team cleared the area, and after Hudson snarled at Nina and almost bit Ash, Sloane locked him inside the café. It had to be bad when the team remained outside. Seb was grateful Sloane hadn't given the order to tranq Hudson. Not yet, anyway.

Seb pulled the Suburban up near Destructive Delta's BearCat, turned off the engine, and darted from the car. He hurried over to Sloane, and laid a hand on his shoulder when he got there.

"How is he?"

Sloane pointed to the café's glass door. "Have a look."

Seb gave a start when Hudson threw himself against the glass, snarling and baring his fangs. He'd shifted into his feral form, all bristling fur and sharp teeth.

"Shit." Seb turned to Nina. "What the hell happened?"

"I don't know." Nina ran a hand through her hair. "One minute we were talking like normal, and the next he was going feral. Nothing like this has ever happened with him. Is he going to be okay?"

Seb turned to Sloane. "I'm going in."

"Seb, I don't…." Sloane hesitated, and Seb pulled him aside, speaking quietly.

"He's my mate, Sloane. You would do the same for Dex."

Sloane thought about it briefly before nodding. "Okay. But if things go south, I need to know you'll be able to tranq him. We can't let him out on the streets like this."

"You know what you're asking of me?"

Sloane clenched his jaw, his amber eyes intense as he met Seb's gaze. "Yeah, actually I do."

The answer was unexpected, but Seb didn't question him. Clearly Sloane did know what he was asking, and at some point, either he or Dex had been in a similar position. If it meant saving Hudson from hurting himself or someone else, then Seb would do it. It might kill him, but he'd do it.

"You have my word. And thank you"—he patted Sloane's shoulder—"for understanding."

Sloane nodded. He motioned for Ash to open the door, and Seb quickly slipped in the moment it was unlocked. At the far corner of the trendy little café, Hudson was in his wolf form, beautiful and lethal. A sleek, gray wolf with stunning blue eyes. He was also extremely pissed at being locked up in here. His ears were pointed forward, his canines bared, and his fur bristled. He had his neck arched, head up, and tail held high. Hudson was ready to strike.

"Lobito, it's me. It's Seb." Slowly he placed his hands up in front of him and edged closer, taking care not to make any sudden movements. Hudson growled and snapped his jaws, saliva flying as he snarled at Seb. "Come on, baby. Come back to me." Seb stayed exceptionally still. Hudson sniffed the air, and he started pacing. Okay, they were clearly not getting anywhere. He wasn't responding. Maybe if….

Seb slowly edged away, making sure not to give his back to Hudson or move his gaze away. Hudson might not have sharp claws like a Felid, but his jaws were powerful, his teeth capable of shredding through Human flesh.

Gingerly Seb removed one piece of clothing at a time and laid them on a chair beside him. Hudson lowered his head, watching him as he undressed. At least he wasn't snarling at Seb. Once Seb was naked, he breathed in deep through his nose and let it out slowly through his mouth. He gritted his teeth and willed his body to change, inviting his feral half to come out. The first bone popped, and Seb sucked in a sharp breath. Physical pain was a constant in Seb's life, but shifting into his tiger Therian form was a different kind of pain altogether. He grunted as more bones popped out of place, and his muscles pulled and contracted, his mass changing as his body tore itself apart to piece itself back together.

Blackness encroached on his vision, but he remained focused on Hudson, who paced from one end of the café to the other, releasing a small whine.

Soon, baby, soon.

Fur pierced Seb's skin, and the agony in his face as his skull elongated had him screaming. Claws cut through the skin at his fingertips, and his body trembled as he curled in on himself, another cry tearing from his throat as his tail bone sliced open his flesh, growing out. Seb landed on his paws, his vision sharp and his sense of smell picking up the subtlest of scents. His transformation complete, he shook himself from nose to tail. He opened his mouth wide, and stretched his long, muscular body, spreading his toes and twitching his tail. Done stretching, he sat on his haunches and chuffed.

Across from him, his mate paused, flattening his ears back and narrowing his eyes in suspicion. Seb flattened his ears, rotating them back before wrinkling his nose and letting out a long, low roar followed by a series of short, low roars for his mate. Hudson whined, his head perking up and his tail slowly moving. He released a bark-howl, and Seb roared again, calling his mate to him. Hudson bounced over, tail wagging. He stopped in front of Seb and lowered to his front paws, butt in the air as his tail wagged. His Lobito let out a series of howls, and although Seb couldn't understand—what with Hudson being a Canid and not Felid—he knew his Lobito was happy to see him.

Seb mewled at him, and Hudson licked at Seb's muzzle before nuzzling Seb's fur under his chin. Seb lay down, front paws spreading as Hudson lay down against him. Hudson rolled onto his back, paws up in the air, whining and licking up at Seb's chin, pawing at him. His mate had returned to him.

Seb threw one massive paw over Hudson's chest and nuzzled him before grooming him, his broad tongue cleaning Hudson's soft fur. His Lobito made happy noises as he wiggled beneath him, his tail wagging joyously.

"You two are freaking adorable."

Hudson rolled onto his belly, his tail wagging for Dex. Seb pushed his nose against Hudson's cheek, and Hudson jumped to his feet, bounding over to Dex and howling playfully. Dex crouched down, laughing when Hudson licked at his face.

"Yeah, I'm happy to see you too, buddy. You scared us for a second there."

Hudson was so playful and beautiful. Seb pushed up to his paws and trotted over to knock his head against Dex's side.

"Don't be jealous," Dex teased, scratching Seb behind his ear. Seb loved a good ear scratch. "All right, let's get you two in the back of the BearCat before the news crews get wind of this." He held the door open, and Seb dashed outside. Hudson sped out, running circles around him, howling and bouncing. He wanted to play.

Seb chuffed and pounced, swatting at him, his claws sheathed. Hudson ducked and dodged, releasing a series of barking-howls as Seb sat up on his haunches, front paws up in the air. Hudson ran and tackled him. They both fell over, wrestling and nipping playfully.

"All right, you two," Sloane said with a chuckle. "In the truck."

Seb got up as Hudson stilled. He sniffed the air and let out a low, mournful wail of a howl that had Seb moaning from the pain it caused his heart. Everyone stilled, their compassionate gazes on Hudson. Therians might not always be able to understand each other when in their Therian forms, but even in their Human forms they understood the sound of anger, pain, loss…. His Therian friends could feel the heartache in Hudson's howl. When Hudson was done, he hung his head, and Seb quickly joined him, licking his muzzle before rubbing his face against Hudson's fur, offering comfort. His Lobito's soft whines broke Seb's heart.

The doors to the BearCat opened, and Seb nudged Hudson. Reluctantly, Hudson padded over to the truck. He hopped up with ease, and Seb followed, then plopped his huge tiger butt beside the bench where the team sat. Hudson curled up between Seb's front paws, as close to Seb as he could get, his paws covering his head, and his tail hiding what his paws couldn't.

"What's wrong with him?" Dex asked worriedly.

Nina crouched beside Hudson and gently stroked his fur. "I don't know, but I think it has something to do with what made him go feral."

"He was sniffing the air just now," Cael said. "Do you think it's whatever he smelled?"

Hudson lifted his head and howled mournfully.

"I guess that's a yes," Sloane murmured. "But there has to be more to it. We don't go feral just from a scent. Something else happened." He turned to Ethan. "Why don't you help your brother shift back and give him PSTC after Nina helps Hudson."

Hudson stood, turning his head to poke his tongue out and lick Seb's muzzle before he slinked off after Nina. The screen dropped, and Seb raised his head to look at his baby brother. He chuffed, and Ethan smiled. He kneeled in front of Seb before throwing his arms around Seb's neck. His sweet little brother.

Seb closed his eyes, content as Ethan held him and ruffled his fur. He exhaled a purr and was rewarded with a scratch behind the ears. Hudson's painful howl caused Seb's ears to flatten and his tail to twitch. He moaned and groaned, feeling his mate's pain as he shifted back to Human form. When Hudson was done and dressed, Nina helped him around the screen, and he stopped in front of Seb, his touch gentle as he brushed his fingers through Seb's fur. Nina helped him sit, and Seb got up and put his head in Hudson's lap with a chuff. Hudson smiled, but he was sad. It coursed through him, and therefore through Seb. He moaned, and Hudson placed a kiss to the top of Seb's head.

Ethan tapped his leg, and Seb reluctantly left his Lobito. He followed Ethan behind the screen, turning his focus from his mate to shifting his form. He willed his body to change, releasing a roar as the transformation began, bones popping, stretching, muscles contorting under his skin, his fur drawing in along with his claws and fangs. The pain was blinding, and Seb shut his eyes tight, his jaw clenched as his mass morphed from tiger to man. When it was done, he trembled. He was cold and only strong enough to stand with Ethan's help. His brother tapped his shoulder, and Seb gripped him tightly, holding on as Ethan held his boxer briefs out for Seb to step into.

PSTC was generally reserved for partners, family, and lovers, and although most Therians didn't think anything of being naked in front of strangers—considering it was a prerequisite to shifting—Post Shift Trauma Care was different. It was an intimate act, though by no means a sexual one. Shifting to Human form left a Therian at their most vulnerable, a difficult position for any Therian to be in, which was why most Therians preferred someone they trusted to see them this way and to perform PSTC. Ethan helped Seb back into his uniform, doing up his buttons for him, his expression one of concentration. Once Ethan tied Seb's shoelaces, he straightened and smiled that crooked, boyish grin before kissing Seb's cheek. Seb chuckled, throwing his arm around Ethan's shoulders and heading back out to join the others.

They'd need to pick up some meat on their way back to HQ, but for now the Gatorade and protein bars would have to do. His strength slowly returned, and Seb crouched beside Hudson, who sat lost in thought.

"What happened back there, Lobito?"

Hudson looked up at him, blinking as if he'd just woken from a trance. "Seb?"

"Yes, sweetheart." Seb took Hudson's hands, noting how Hudson's whole body was racked with shivers.

"I think… I think I'm losing my mind."

Seb ran a hand over Hudson's hair, brushing his bangs away from his face. It was growing long, the front falling over his brow. "Tell me what happened," he said gently. "Why did you go feral?"

"I swear I thought it was his scent." Hudson's voice broke when he spoke. "And it's not the first time, but it's… not possible. It couldn't be him."

"Who?"

Hudson gazed at him with wide eyes. "Alfie. It was his scent."

The truck fell into silence, broken when Ash spoke up. "Someone wanna tell me who that is?"

Hudson sniffed. "Alfie was my brother."

"Was?" Cael asked softly.

Seb rubbed circles around Hudson's back, wishing he knew what the hell was going on. Hudson was right, this wasn't possible, but his sense of smell was extraordinary and rarely off its mark. Wolf Therians were exceptional trackers, with the ability to sniff out things others might miss. That skill, along with their keen eye for detail, was why so many of them worked in the medical profession. They also made up a good portion of Unit Alpha's Therian Recon agents, along with cheetah Therians.

"He died years ago," Hudson replied with a shuddering sigh. "It's why I was shunned from my pack, my family. They blamed me for his death. It was an accident." Hudson told them the story of his beloved brother's death and how his body had been discovered. Seb had heard it years ago, and it broke his heart hearing it a second time, mostly because of how much it still pained Hudson.

"You sure it was him on the table?" Ash asked. Seb glared at him, and Ash returned his glare. "Hey, I know what it's like to lose a brother, okay, so fuck off. It's a shitty question, but it has to be asked. You gotta admit, when this team is involved, shit has a way of turning all kinds of weird and fucked-up. I swear this team is fucking cursed."

"Speak for yourself," Rosa said. "Milena and I have a very normal life together. She acquires antiques. Can't get any more normal than that."

"Whatever," Ash said, turning his attention back to Hudson. "Come on, Doc. Look at what's happened in the past year alone. Are you sure?"

"Yes, Ash," Hudson replied through his teeth. "It was Alfie on that table, and he was very much dead. Believe me, I wish I had doubts, but I can still see him." Hudson dropped his gaze to the floor.

"Did you…." Ash cleared his throat. "Did you examine him?"

Hudson shook his head. "It may have been possible, with my father's influence, but my family would never have allowed me to lay a hand on him. At one point, I tried to step closer. My father grabbed my arm and pulled me back." He wiped a tear from his cheek and sniffed. "Not that it mattered. All the evidence I needed was in front of me."

Dex looked thoughtful. "Could the scent have been something else masking itself as Hudson's brother? Is that possible?"

"What do you mean?" Sloane asked.

"I'm thinking about the sleeve Sparks gave me to mask the scent of my mark. What if it's possible to mask a scent with another? Therians have a keen sense of smell. One they rely on, especially THIRDS agents. What if someone was trying to fuck with Hudson?"

"Why? Why would someone do such a thing?" Hudson closed his eyes.

Sloane shook his head. "That doesn't answer why you went feral. I can see it being a catalyst, but Therians don't go feral that easily. I know things have been… a little stressful lately. Anything happen that may have pushed you over the edge?"

Seb stroked his hair, and Hudson met his gaze. He gave Hudson a subtle shake of his head. He wasn't quite ready to tell Ethan about TIN yet. The rest of Destructive Delta would find out soon, but the conversation was one he'd have in private with his little brother. He hadn't even decided what to say to his team or Dom. Seb had a lot to think about, like whether to bring his team into this mess or not. The more people he told, the more lives he placed in danger. Dom was his best friend, and Seb didn't keep anything from him, but he had to think about Dom and his family—his parents and four older brothers, two of whom worked for the THIRDS, one in Defense, the other Recon. If something happened to Dom because of Seb's association with TIN, Seb would never forgive himself.

Hudson released a heavy sigh and turned his attention to Sloane with a nod. "I'm not ready to discuss it at the moment, but yes, you're right. I think with everything that's happened recently, the scent was the final straw. It was all too much. I never thought I could lose myself in such a manner."

"Hey, everyone has their limit," Sloane offered gently. "You reached yours. It happens. Trust me."

Hudson nodded. He leaned against Seb, burying his face in Seb's shoulder. "I just want to go home. Take me home, Sebastian."

Seb swallowed hard. He looked over at Nina, who nodded, her big brown eyes filled with worry. Sloane had Ethan stop by a Therian restaurant, and Calvin ordered them some food to go before they dropped Seb and Hudson off at Seb's house. Once he got Hudson settled in the kitchen and eating, he texted Dom and asked him if he wouldn't mind picking up Seb's Suburban, and returning it to HQ. Then Seb texted Sloane to thank him and the team for everything.

That's what family is for.

Seb smiled at Sloane's text. It warmed his heart to know Sloane still considered him part of the Destructive Delta family, even if he was no longer on the team. He returned his phone to his pocket and joined Hudson at the island counter. His Lobito was lost in thought, but at least his appetite remained healthy. Once they'd eaten, they settled on the couch, Hudson lying between Seb's legs, his head on Seb's shoulder as Seb flicked through channels and absently ran his fingers through Hudson's hair, smiling at the soft sigh Hudson let out. It was all so… normal.

"How about a shower?" Seb asked, kissing the top of Hudson's head.

Hudson grunted. "That would require my having to move."

Seb chuckled. "I don't know. Let's see." He sat up, his arm wrapped around Hudson's waist, holding him against Seb as he stood before flopping him over his shoulder.

"This isn't what I had in mind," Hudson grumbled, and Seb smacked his butt for good measure, laughing at his yelp. "You're lucky I'm too tired to do anything about that."

Seb carried him upstairs. "That's a shame." He dropped Hudson onto the bed before pulling his uniform shirt and undershirt up over his head, then dropping them to the floor. "And here I thought you might want to fuck me. But if you're too tired…." Seb shrugged and turned to go, but Hudson launched himself across the bed to snag hold of Seb's hand.

"Wait!" He looked up at Seb, blinking innocently. "Did I say tired? I meant comfortable. Your shoulder was very comfortable."

Seb stretched, arching his back, an arm lifted over his head, drawing Hudson's eyes to his torso. His blue eyes raked over Seb's chest, pupils dilating before he met Seb's gaze, his tongue poking out from between his lips.

"Darling, I would very much like to fuck you."

"Oh, okay, then." Seb turned to face him. "I'm going to go take a shower first."

Hudson scrambled to sit up, and Seb held back a laugh. He took hold of Seb's belt to keep him from moving away. "May I join you?"

"Sure." Seb winked at him, and Hudson let out a huff.

"You enjoy teasing me, don't you?"

Seb lifted Hudson's chin and brushed his lips over Hudson's. "I don't enjoy it. I love it." He kissed Hudson, taking hold of his shoulder, moaning at the taste of him. Hudson's mouth was sweet from the fruit tea he'd had with dinner, and Seb's kisses grew more urgent as he explored Hudson's mouth with his tongue. He pulled Hudson's sweater vest and shirt over his head and dropped them on the floor, a groan escaping him at the feel of Hudson's slender fingers gliding over the muscles of Seb's abdomen to his chest. If he didn't get Hudson naked and in bed, he was going to go crazy. His skin was on fire, his body eager to press against Hudson.

"Come on," Seb growled against Hudson's lips. He took Hudson's wrist and pulled him along into the bathroom. They tore at each other's clothes, mouths sucking, biting, and nipping with every patch of skin exposed. Naked, they stepped into the shower. Normally they would have gotten each other off under the stream of warm water, but Seb was going to lose his shit if he didn't get Hudson inside him. A quick towel dry later, and Seb lay on the bed, his hips lifted so Hudson could place a pillow underneath his stomach. His body was thrumming with anticipation.

The last man to fuck Seb was Hudson. Hudson, of course, had other plans. He wasn't about to dive right in. Nope. His Lobito was going to torture him first. Seb moaned as Hudson sat on his ass and lightly stroked Seb from his shoulders to his lower back. Pushing his hard cock against the pillow, Seb pleaded with Hudson, but Hudson pressed a kiss to his right shoulder, then his left. He planted kisses around Seb's back, alternating with nips to Seb's scorching flesh. Seb grabbed fistfuls of the sheets, rutting against the pillow as his desire threatened to consume him.

The globes of his asscheeks were parted, and Seb bucked his hips, cursing under his breath and gritting his teeth when Hudson licked at his hole. Seb pressed his forehead down against the pillow as Hudson used his tongue to breach Seb's tight entrance.

"Oh fuck." Seb's breath was coming out in pants as Hudson nibbled at him. "Baby, please."

Hudson chuckled, and a rumbling sound rose deep from Seb's chest. Seb heard the lube's cap being opened and the bottle squeezed. Soon after, he shivered at Hudson's cold, lube-slicked finger pushing tenderly into him. The wait was going to drive him nuts. In no apparent rush, Hudson buried his finger down to the knuckle before he pulled out slightly, and a second finger joined in.

"Lobito," Seb growled. "If you don't fuck me, you're going to be the one pounded into the mattress."

"That's not much of a threat, darling." Hudson pulled out his fingers, and when Seb looked over his shoulder to reply, Hudson breached his hole with the tip of his cock. He released a fresh barrage of curses, and Hudson laughed softly. "You were saying?"

Hudson wasn't as big as Seb, but he was hardly small. His cock was thick and long, and Seb was so tight, his muscles fighting the intrusion until they finally accepted and gave way, making him cry out with how damn good it felt to have Hudson inching in until he was balls-deep inside Seb's ass.

"You feel amazing," Hudson breathed. He released a low moan as he started to rock against Seb. The pleasure building inside Seb sent a shiver through him, and he lifted up onto his elbows so he could look back at Hudson, groaning at the sight of Hudson pulling out only to plunge inside Seb, his fingers digging into Seb's hips.

"That's it, baby. Fuck me. God, you're so beautiful."

Hudson closed his eyes and let his head fall back, his lips parted in ecstasy as he picked up his pace, the sound of his skin slapping against Seb's, making Seb whimper. Seb pushed a hand underneath him and took hold of his rock-hard cock.

"Not yet," Hudson warned, lying across Seb's back. He took hold of Seb's hands and laced their fingers together. "Kiss me."

Seb turned his head and sucked on Hudson's tongue before Hudson snapped his hips against Seb's ass, driving his cock in deep.

"Fuck!"

Hudson snapped his hips again. "Like that?" He rotated his hips, pulled out, and then drove in at a different angle, hitting that sweet spot inside Seb.

"Fuck! Baby, yes! Yes, just like that. Fuck me just like that."

Hudson drove himself in deep and hard with each thrust, pounding into Seb until he was seeing stars. The sounds coming from him were unlike anything Seb had ever made. Hudson's moans, his panting breath, and his fingers digging into Seb's hips were going to make him lose his mind. Hudson hit that sweet spot in Seb again, and Seb's muscles tightened. His orgasm threatened to send him spiraling down into the abyss. Hudson lay against his back, one hand on Seb's shoulder holding him in place, while he slipped his fingers into Seb's hair with his other hand, grabbing a fistful of it. He tugged at Seb's hair, pulling his head back so he could lick Seb's neck. He snapped his hips against Seb's ass, his teeth scraping Seb's nape before he bit down gently, suckling Seb's skin and sending him over the edge.

Seb's pleasure tore through him, his orgasm causing his body to tighten, his hole clenching around Hudson's dick. Hudson gasped, throwing his arms around Seb's neck as Seb milked his cock, the heat of Hudson's come coating his insides. Seb rode out his release, his fingers closing around Hudson's arm, his groan deep and long as white heat spread through him. Hudson thrust several more times before stilling, his panting breath hot against Seb's cheek.

"See. Just like… riding a… bike," Seb teased.

"Darling, if my scooter made me come like that, I'd never get off." Hudson kissed his cheek. "Besides, I much prefer riding you."

Seb laughed. He turned his head so Hudson could kiss him, slow and languid this time. Hudson pulled out of him gently before rolling off him and onto the bed. His Lobito was a picture of wanton decadence, his black, tousled hair a contrast against his fair skin now flushed from his exertion. He looked sated and happy. The words left Seb's lips before he could catch himself.

"Let's get married."

Hudson rolled his head to look at Seb. "I beg your pardon?"

"You heard me."

"Are you mad?"

Not the reaction he'd been hoping for.

"We haven't been together a week and look at the mess we made!" Hudson got out of bed, stalked over to the dresser, and pulled out a pair of boxers. "Must be a new bloody record. One week, Sebastian, and you end up in jail, I end up part of a covert organization of Therian spies, and then you go and jump in the fire with me. I lose control to my feral side after having a go at you about that very subject, and I keep catching my dead brother's scent." He pulled out a T-shirt and stilled, his bottom lip quivering. "I'm a jinx."

"Hey, you're not a jinx." And if he was, he was the most adorable jinx Seb had ever known. He got out of bed, stepped up behind Hudson, and wrapped his arms around his waist. "You smelling Alfie, I don't have an answer for, but I'm sure there's a reasonable explanation. We just haven't found it yet. And as far as TIN is concerned, I'm not going to be anywhere you're not. So, are you going to be my husband?"

Hudson worried his bottom lip, and Seb would have given anything to know what was running through his mate's mind. Seb pulled a pair of pajama bottoms from the dresser and quickly slipped into them before taking Hudson's hand and turning him so they faced each other.

"Baby?"

Hudson met his gaze, his blue eyes filled with so much love, and worry. "I love you, Seb, more than anything. I just…. Will you give me some time to think about it?"

Seb nodded. "Of course. Whenever you're ready, I'll be here." A small part of him was disappointed Hudson hadn't said yes, but he couldn't blame him. Everything that had happened between them, plus the events of the last few days, would have broken a less strong man. Hudson needed time, and Seb would give him all the time he needed. He had his mate back, and for that, Seb was grateful. The rest could wait.

CHAPTER 10

"EVERYONE OUT!"

Hudson wondered how everything had gone to hell so quickly. What started as a routine callout in the heart of Wall Street to pick up a DB in one of the flashy corporate buildings suddenly turned into a code red with thousands of lives on the line. The initial victim was believed to have suffered a heart attack, collapsing in the lobby of the seventy-one-story, gilded monstrosity. The moment Hudson and Nina unzipped the dead man's heavy jacket, they'd sprung to action. They had twenty minutes to evacuate the building before the device strapped to the man's chest detonated. Defense agents were on the way, but as Hudson sped through the marble lobby, shouting at Humans and Therians alike to get the hell out of the building, he feared his fellow agents wouldn't make it in time.

Hudson enlisted the help of the building's security team, and emergency evacuation procedures were executed. Citizens flooded out from the emergency exits, from offices, from every floor. The lifts were still working, which was fortunate, considering there were seventy-one floors to evacuate. Nina rushed over to Hudson, her eyes wide and cheeks flushed.

"There are too many floors, too many people, and not enough time."

Hudson had no way to gauge how powerful the blast would be. An idea struck him, and after telling Nina to keep an eye out for their teammates, he ran over to the head security guard.

"Bill, this building used to be a bank, right? Is the vault still here?"

Bill nodded fervently. "Yeah, in the basement. It's a restaurant now."

"Okay. Grab two of your men. You're going to help me." Hudson ran back to the body. Since the man had been moving around before he collapsed and the device had yet to go off, Hudson would hazard a guess it wasn't motion sensitive. Bill and two security guards appeared in seconds. "All right, lads. Help me carry him, and whatever you do, don't touch the device or any of the wires," Hudson instructed. Bill and the guards did as told, and Hudson grabbed under the dead man's arms. They lifted and hurriedly moved toward the emergency exit that would take them downstairs to the basement. The lift was out of the question as people were still flooding in and out.

They carried the body downstairs and through the doors of a posh restaurant with red and gold décor, boasting a "unique dining experience." They had no idea. One side of the restaurant had been a meeting room for the bank's executives and was now an expansive bar, while the other side was the restaurant. It was littered with tables, the exposed steel walls evidence of a time long gone when the room housed the wealth of the city's elite rather than the imported wine and champagne guests now imbibed.

"All the way to the end, fellas," Hudson said. They placed the body at the end of the room and rushed out. "Does this close?" Hudson looked up at the huge steel bank vault door.

Bill shrugged. "It hasn't been moved in years."

"Let's put our backs into it, then." Hudson took position behind the vault door along with the three other men, two of whom were big, strong Felid Therians. "Okay, lads. Push!"

The four of them grunted and groaned as they pushed with all their strength. Since the door was no longer in use, the hinges were a little rusty. There was no electronic switch, but the door had been created with the capability to be shut by hand. Sweat beaded Hudson's brow, and his muscles strained as he gritted his teeth and pushed with all his might. A shrilling squeal resounded before the door inched forward. They continued to push until the blasted thing finally moved. The thunderous bang it made when it closed was terrifying, considering what was on the other side.

"Let's go." They hurried back to the stairs and ran up. "We need to clear the floor over the bank vault," Hudson said and cursed under his breath. The floor in question was in front of the rear exit of the building, toward which dozens of people were running. Hudson took off, waving his arm as he screamed to the panicked citizens. "Get away from the doors! Use the front exit!"

People dispersed, and Hudson turned to Bill and the two security guards just as a deafening boom burst through the floor. Hudson was launched into the smoke-and-fire-filled air. He thought he would never land, and when he did, the impact almost knocked him out. His head hit something soft, but his body was in pain, air rushing from his lungs. He gasped for breath, then coughed when his mouth filled with smoke and ash. It was too dark to see, and he tentatively put a hand down, realizing he was touching a body. He blinked, stunned his glasses were still on his face. Beneath him, he found one of Bill's men, his head twisted at an unnatural angle. Poor fellow.

Carefully, Hudson moved. He was banged up but okay. Miraculously nothing felt broken. Bruised certainly, and he tasted blood on his lip, but he was in one piece. There were groans around him, and he pushed to his feet. Debris surrounded him, and when he threw out a hand, he hit a wall. What the hell? Taking a step back, he came up against another wall. Raising his head, his heart nearly stopped. He'd landed in the lift shaft, and several floors up, the lift made frightful noises. He turned and found the basement's lift doors wedged shut. There had to be a way to get them open.

Another groan caught his attention, and he inspected the small space. Bill lay on his side, his sleeve torn and his arm hanging limply. Hudson's biggest concern was the reinforcement steel rod impaled through Bill's right leg, and the fact it was still attached to a large chunk of concrete that appeared to be pinning his left leg to the floor. Hudson quickly checked his pulse. At least the man was alive.

"Bill, can you hear me?"

Bill's lashes fluttered open, and he blinked up at Hudson. "Dr. Colbourn?"

Hudson smiled warmly. "That's right."

Bill tried to get up, and Hudson put a hand to his shoulder just as Bill cried out. His eyes widened when he saw his leg, and Hudson could see the looming panic.

"Bill, look at me. It's going to be all right. The rod is keeping you from bleeding out, but we're going to need to get you out of here as soon as possible. Until then, I need you to be still, and try to steady your breathing. Can you do that for me?"

Bill nodded, and Hudson turned toward the second groan he'd heard. Beneath a smaller slab of concrete, Hudson discovered a young girl.

"Hi there, I'm Dr. Colbourn. I'm with the THIRDS. I'm going to get this off you, okay?" Hudson kneeled beside the sobbing girl. He gripped the edges of the slab and lifted, able to move it without hurting her. He propped it against the wall and smiled. "It's going to be okay."

Her big brown eyes overflowed with tears. She was covered in scrapes and bruises. The position of her leg told him it was broken. The poor thing. She was fourteen or fifteen years old at most. A slip of a girl, trembling as she sucked in huge gulps of air. He had to calm her. Hudson wrapped an arm around her and ran a hand over her dust-covered curls, subtly checking for any gashes or bumps. Besides her leg, she looked okay. He needed to get them out of here.

Bill groaned as he moved, and Hudson pleaded with him. "Bill, I said don't move."

"I'm sorry," Bill whimpered, holding on to his leg. "It hurts so much."

"I know it does, but it's very important you remain still." Heaven knew what other internal injuries there might be. The girl in Hudson's arm clung to him for dear life. "We're going to get out of here very soon, darling." His phone went off, and Hudson thanked his lucky stars. He quickly answered. "Hello?"

Seb's rough voice came over the line. "Oh thank God. Where are you? Are you okay?"

"I'm fine. I'm down the lift shaft. I'm not sure which. Most likely whichever one was closest to the vault." There was silence. "Seb?"

"Baby, I'm coming to get you. Just stay safe."

"Seb, bring help. I have two civilians with injuries. Hold on." Hudson turned to smile at the young girl clinging to him. "Darling, what's your name?"

"M-Melissa Willis," she said through her tears.

"Well, Melissa, everything's going to be all right. Help is on the way." Hudson turned his attention back to Seb. "Seb, I have Bill, the head of security, down here with me, who has a leg injury I'm going to need a tourniquet for, and Melissa's also going to need medical attention."

"Can they be moved?"

Hudson stood and walked to the farthest end of the shaft so he could speak quietly away from the others. "Melissa can be moved, but Bill's leg was impaled by an exposed steel rod from a piece of concrete wall. I don't know that I'll be able to lift it on my own. There's also the problem of getting the rod out of his leg." A shriek of metal, and a pinging sound caught Hudson's ear, and his head shot up, his eyes going wide. "Seb, you need to hurry."

"What's wrong?"

Hudson didn't want to scare Bill or Melissa any further. "I'm texting you the details and pictures." He hung up and took some quick snapshots of the area around him, managing to get in a shot of Bill's leg without aiming his phone at Bill so as not to upset him. He snapped a picture of the lift hanging above their heads. As soon as he was done, he sent them off to Seb, explaining the state of Bill's leg, his possible injuries, as well as Melissa's injuries, and the noises the lift was making. This whole situation suddenly became so much worse. He returned his phone to his pocket, and looked around. They couldn't simply wait here and do nothing. He spotted a steel rod, but when he tried to move, Melissa cried out.

"Please, don't leave!"

Bill wasn't looking good, and Melissa was on the verge of panicking.

"My leg hurts so bad," Melissa cried.

"I know, sweetheart. Just don't move it. Help is on the way, I promise." Hudson grabbed the steel rod off the ground and moved to the doors. Another groan from the lift above them and Melissa shrieked.

"It's going to fall and crush us!"

"I need you to be a brave girl for me. Can you do that?"

Melissa nodded, and Hudson maneuvered the rod in his hand between the rubber of the lift's steel doors. It was no use. Its rounded tip was too thick to force between them. Hudson shot off a quick text to let Seb know the doors to the lift were wedged tight.

"Hudson?"

Hudson froze. "Dom?"

"They're bringing equipment to open this door," Dom shouted from the other side. Above them, a motor rumbled to life followed by hissing and shouting. The steel doors above them screeched as they were forced open. Seb poked his head in.

"Hudson?"

"Down here!" Hudson waved his arms. The fear and pain in Seb's eyes were unmistakable, even from this distance.

"We're sending a harness down. I'm tossing you the tourniquet." Seb flung the small sealed plastic pouch down. Hudson caught it and stuck it in his back pocket.

Hudson nodded. "I'm sending Melissa up first." The noise increased from the lift doors behind them, and Seb and their fellow agents worked swiftly above them to lower the harness. As soon as it reached Hudson, he helped Melissa strap into it. "It's going to hurt for a little bit as they pull you up, but the paramedics will be waiting for you. You're going to be fine, darling."

Melissa threw her arms around him, hugging him tight before pulling away. Hudson shouted for them to pull her up. The sound of snapping cables resonated around the narrow shaft. Melissa shrieked, and the agents scrambled, moving as fast as they could to pull her up. The lift dropped several feet, and Hudson's heart leaped into his throat. Thankfully, the lift jerked to a stop, but the creaking sound continued.

As they pulled Melissa through the doorway, Seb shouted at the agents around him before Hudson heard Seb growling at Dom. The lift was on the verge of falling, and Dom wasn't sure they'd get the basement doors open in time. The harness was flung down again, and Seb poked his head through the doors. His eyes were glassy, and his face a study in heartache.

"There's a chance we only have enough time to get one of you up here before the elevator falls. The last cable is frayed and about to give way."

Hudson didn't hesitate. He ran over to Bill.

"Hudson," Seb's voice cracked, and Hudson looked up, his heart breaking.

"I love you, Seb." Hudson turned to Bill. "Okay, Bill. There's no way we can get the equipment needed to cut the steel rod out of the concrete fast enough, so we're going to have to pull your leg out. I'll then apply a tourniquet. I won't lie to you. This is going to hurt a hell of a lot. The EMTs are upstairs waiting for you, all right?"

Bill nodded, and Hudson knelt by his foot and took hold of Bill's leg behind his knee and at the ankle in a secure grip.

"Look away and try to occupy your thoughts with something else. Inhale deep through your nose, out through your mouth." Hudson noticed Bill's wedding ring. "Where did you go on your honeymoon, Bill?"

Bill did as Hudson asked, looking away and concentrating on his breathing.

"The Grand Canyon," Bill replied, shutting his eyes tight.

"Oh? I've heard it's magnificent. Tell me about it."

As Bill told Hudson about his honeymoon, Hudson slowly and carefully moved Bill's leg. Thankfully, the rod had pierced Bill's calf muscle, but there would still be a hell of a lot of blood. Hudson encouraged Bill to concentrate on his breathing and talk to him. Bill did his best, relaying a sweet story about his wife, who had been his high school sweetheart.

"You're doing bloody marvelous, Bill," Hudson said, smiling, his pulse racing, and his heart squeezing for the poor man. Bill was in an incredible amount of pain, and in the end, his scream echoed through the shaft. Sweat beaded Hudson's brow. "Just half an inch, Bill. There." The moment he placed Bill's leg on the floor, he tore through Bill's trouser leg all the way up to his thigh. After tearing off a strip, he bandaged the wound as best he could, then swiped the plastic pouch from his back pocket. He unwrapped the tourniquet, then fastened the thick strap around Bill's leg as high up the man's thigh as he could get it.

"I apologize for this, Bill." Hudson applied pressure to the wound, making Bill cry out. Moving swiftly, Hudson tightened the strap, turned the small steel rod, and locked it into place. He checked the time, grabbed one of Bill's pens from his front breast pocket—which miraculously hadn't fallen out—and wrote the time down on the white band so the EMTs would know when it had been applied.

"Hudson?" Seb called down.

"I'm going to try to move the concrete off him." Hudson widened his stance, minded his posture, and gripped the ragged edge of the slab, careful not to slice his hand open on any jagged pieces. "The moment you can move, you do that, Bill."

Bill nodded. He was looking paler with every passing minute.

Hudson gritted his teeth and pulled. Bill screamed, and Hudson quickly stopped.

"It's digging into my leg," Bill said, his voice shaky.

Shit. The lift screeched again, and Bill whimpered. He was panicking, and the look of sheer terror wasn't lost on Hudson. Seb's concerned voice echoed through the shaft.

"Hudson, if you can't—"

"I'm not leaving him," Hudson growled. He tried again, but it was no use. The only thing he was succeeding at was hurting Bill. He couldn't do this alone. Hudson looked up at Seb. "I can't get this off him on my own. It's too heavy, and all I'm doing is causing him injury."

Seb didn't waste any time. He hurriedly pulled the harness back up, strapped in, and was lowered down into the shaft. The second his boots hit the ground, he grabbed Hudson's shoulders. "Baby, there's no time for a second trip, and the harness won't hold three of us. We're going to free Bill, and then I'm going to strap you in, and you take him."

Hudson shook his head. "No, they need you upstairs. Who knows how many more people are trapped. Your team needs you."

"For fuck's sake, Hudson. *I* need you."

Hudson cupped Seb's jaw. "Preserve life, darling. That's our duty, remember?"

Seb opened his mouth to speak, but Bill moaned. With one last squeeze to Hudson's shoulder, they hurried over to Bill. Seb gave him a warm smile.

"We're going to get you out of here, Bill." Seb took position on one side of the large slab, and Hudson took position on the other. "The moment you can slide away from under this, you do that, okay? Can you do that?"

Bill nodded.

"On three," Seb said as he and Hudson readied themselves.

The moment Seb said three, Hudson lifted with all his strength. Between him and Seb, they managed to move the chunk of concrete wall enough for Bill to drag himself out from under it. As soon as he was free, they dropped it with a thud, its heft kicking up dirt and dust at their feet.

Hudson knelt beside Bill. "We're going to lift you up now."

They tried not to jostle the man too much as they lifted him, then secured him to Seb's harness.

"Hudson—"

"Go. *Now*." Hudson pulled on the line. "Get them out of here," Hudson called up. The harness was lifted, and Seb threw out a hand. Hudson caught it. He kissed Seb's palm seconds before Seb's hand was out of reach.

"I love you," Hudson said, loud enough for Seb's ears alone.

"I love you," Seb choked out, doing his best not to give in to his emotions. His jaw clenched, and his eyes never left Hudson's as he was pulled up.

Hudson backed up against the closed doors as the lift dropped several more feet. Urgent shouts filled the doorway above them and behind Hudson. Seb was just about up when the last cable snapped. Hudson gasped, tears blurring his vision as Seb and Bill were snatched up and pulled through the doorway seconds before the lift sped by. Seb's horrified scream pierced Hudson's heart, and he pressed against the doors behind him, his eyes shut tight. Air whooshed around him, and he lurched back, landing with an "oomph." He was pushed onto his stomach, his body shielded as the horrifying sound of crushed metal and snapping wires met his ears, a cloud of dust and spray of debris bursting around him.

When the noise and dust settled, the body moved off him, and Hudson lifted his head. Dom lay on his back catching his breath.

"Fuck."

Hudson blinked at him. "Dom?"

"Don't ever… scare me… like that… again," Dom panted.

Hudson grinned like an idiot before throwing himself at Dom and hugging him tight. Dom laughed, wrapping an arm around him.

"You're welcome," Dom murmured. "Now get off me before the boss man gets any crazy ideas."

Hudson couldn't help but laugh through his tears. He stood and helped Dom to his feet. "Is Nina okay?"

Dom nodded. "Yeah. She was by the front doors when the blast hit."

Seb called out, and Dom shouted back, "He's okay."

Seb came to an abrupt halt at the bottom of the stairs, his stunned, tear-filled gaze on Hudson. As if snapping out of it, he broke into a run, reached Hudson, and threw his arms around him in a crushing hug. He lifted Hudson off his feet, squeezing him again before he put him down. Seb pulled back and cupped Hudson's face.

"I thought I lost you."

Hudson shook his head, unable to speak. He could see how much Seb wanted to kiss him, but they were surrounded by agents and emergency personnel. There was so much still to do, people needing help. Seb swallowed hard.

"Go get yourself checked out. I need to get back."

Hudson nodded, his heart swelling when Seb smiled before running off, shouting orders into his earpiece as he hurried up the stairs.

As expected, it was chaos upstairs, but the explosion had been smaller than Hudson originally believed. It had destroyed the floor above the vault toward the back exit, but other than that, the rest of the building was intact. When he reached one of the EMTs, he smiled at the tall wolf Therian.

"Hi, Mikey."

"Hudson," Mikey greeted, returning his smile. He patted the back of the truck. "Have a seat, and let's get a look at you."

As Mikey inspected him, Hudson asked about the casualties. Dozens were injured, several in critical condition, but so far only a couple of known fatalities.

"You're good to go," Mikey proclaimed. "Maybe now I can tell that guy you're okay and he'll stop calling me."

Hudson frowned. "What guy?"

Mikey shrugged. "Some guy's been calling me like every ten minutes asking about you. Don't know how he got my number." Mikey smiled wide. "Looks like you got yourself an admirer."

"Or a stalker," Hudson mumbled. He thanked Mikey and went in search of Sergeant Maddock, whom he found by Destructive Delta's BearCat.

According to Maddock, Recon agents confirmed that the man who'd collapsed with a bomb strapped to his chest had been trying to send a message. Mr. Pruitt had been arrested previously for vandalism and property damage. The man had a deep loathing for Wall Street and corporate America, which he'd shared with the world through his blog. As of a few months ago, his blog posts had spiraled from rants to unhinged threats. The comments spurred him on, urging someone to do something. Pruitt had decided he'd be that someone.

"Glad you're okay, son." Maddock patted Hudson's shoulder. "Why don't you go home."

Hudson blinked at him. "Home?" He looked around. Did their sergeant not see what was happening around them? As if reading his thoughts, Maddock narrowed his eyes at him.

"Son, what's your badge say?"

Hudson blinked at him, confused. "Um, Chief Medical Examiner?"

"Right. And seeing as how the first dead body we had turned to confetti when the explosive went off and the second was crushed under nearly three thousand pounds of elevator, I suggest you go home, take a shower, and rest. Your team can take it from here."

"But, I can help—"

Maddock planted his hands on his hips. "Boy, you just got blown up and almost had an elevator land on your head. Get your ass home. I will have your skinny British ass dragged away like I did with your partner." Maddock shook his head. "I got boots that weigh more than that woman, but when she puts her foot down, nothing short of a crane is moving her ass."

Hudson chuckled. That sounded like Nina all right.

Maddock's expression softened. "She was worried about you. We called her the second we knew, so she's okay. I imagine she's gonna be giving you an earful soon enough, so good luck with that." Maddock turned and headed toward the building's entrance. "Go home, Colbourn."

"Yes, sir," Hudson promised. He turned to go, but a woman came running, waving her arm and shouting his name. She looked familiar. He recognized the big brown eyes and head full of tight black curls. Hudson braced himself, expecting a verbal thrashing. Instead the woman flung herself into Hudson's arms and hugged him tight. He held on to her trembling frame.

"Thank you so much for saving my little girl, Dr. Colbourn." With a sniff, she pulled away, tears spilling from her eyes. "Thank you."

"It was a team effort, Mrs. Willis."

She shook her head, her curls swishing with her movement. "You were the one down there with her, keeping her from going into shock. I'm grateful to your teammates, but you were there."

"How is she?"

"She's going to be okay, just a few broken bones. I need to go, but I wanted to thank you in person. The city's lucky to have agents like you, Dr. Colbourn." She kissed his cheek before rushing off. Hudson smiled after her. He was glad to hear Melissa would be all right.

Hudson hitched a ride with one of the EMTs heading out. They were carrying two Therians with minor injuries. From the hospital, he took a cab to Seb's house. He sent Seb a text to let him know he was okay and at home. Seconds later his phone rang. Hudson answered with a smile. "Hello, darling."

"You sure you're okay?"

"Promise. Sarge sent me home anyway."

"Good," Seb grunted. Silence came on the line before Seb cleared his throat. "When you say 'home,' do you mean…?"

"Your house." Hudson smiled shyly. "Perhaps when you get home, we can discuss living arrangements."

Seb's sharp intake of breath was not lost on Hudson.

"Really?"

Hudson smiled even though Seb couldn't see him. "Really."

"Okay. You rest up, and I'll see you tonight?"

"I'll be here," Hudson promised. "Stay safe."

"I will. Love you."

"Love you too." Hudson hung up and headed upstairs to take a shower. As he stood under the hot water, washing away the remains of today's ordeal, it struck him how close he'd come to dying. He should have been shaken up, but he wasn't. Seb had listened. He'd been faced with losing Hudson, and although everything in Seb had likely shouted at him to save his mate, he'd listened to Hudson. Together they helped get Bill and Melissa out of there.

Hudson shut off the water and ran a towel over his hair before stepping out. He dried off, his heart pounding fiercely. Perhaps they *could* do this. For the first time in a long time, Hudson felt confident in their bond, in *them*. Dressed in his atom T-shirt and pajama bottoms, he went downstairs and made a cup of tea. Turning on the telly, he curled up on the couch. He released a yawn and placed his mug on the coffee table before sitting back. He hadn't realized he'd fallen asleep until he felt fingers in his hair. Hudson hummed, his head groggy and body heavy with sleep.

"Seb," he murmured, too exhausted to open his eyes.

"Shh. Go back to sleep."

Hudson nodded. He sighed contentedly and sank back into sweet slumber. When he woke, it was to the sound of the front door opening. Yawning, Hudson sat up. He rubbed his eyes with the back of his hands and frowned.

"Seb?"

Seb grinned widely at him as he stepped into the living room. "Hey, sweetheart." He sat down beside Hudson and pulled him onto his lap, inhaling his scent. "God, I missed you."

"Did you just get home?" Hudson blinked at him.

Seb chuckled. "Wow, you really are out of it. Just walked in. You were looking right at me." He placed a kiss on Hudson's temple. "Sleepyhead."

"I could have sworn…." Hudson shook his head. "Must have been dreaming."

"Of me, I hope," Seb said before capturing Hudson's lips in a gentle kiss. Hudson shifted, straddling Seb's lap and slipping his arms around Seb's neck. Seb released a low groan that rose from his chest. He buried his face against Hudson's neck, wrapping his arms tight around Hudson. When he spoke, his words were a whisper. "I was so scared."

"Me too," Hudson admitted, running his fingers through Seb's hair as he held Seb to him. He smelled of shower gel and his own delicious scent. He'd showered and changed at work, dressed in jeans and a long-sleeved T-shirt. His hair was damp, and his jaw clean-shaven. They were quiet, soaking in each other's warmth, holding on as if afraid to let go. Hudson certainly had no intention of letting go, not now, not ever.

Seb was strong and solid beneath Hudson, and he could feel Seb's heart beating. Sebastian Hobbs was a gift, and Hudson would never take him for granted again.

"Darling?" Hudson ran his fingers through Seb's silky hair.

"Hmm?"

Hudson placed his lips to Seb's ear. "Ask me again."

Seb straightened, his brows furrowed together. "Ask you what—" His eyes widened. "You mean…. Um…." He cleared his throat. "Will you marry me?"

Hudson climbed off Seb's lap and peered at him. "That depends."

"On what?" Seb sounded as though he was holding his breath.

"On whether you ask me properly." Hudson sniffed and folded his arms over his chest. "I've been waiting a bloody long time for this."

Seb laughed softly. He got down on one knee, and Hudson's heart was ready to burst from the love he felt for the man in front of him. He smiled down at his beautiful mate.

"Hudson Colbourn, will you do me the honor of being my husband? Marry me?"

Hudson cocked his head in thought. "I suppose someone needs to make an honest man out of you."

"You're killing me here, Lobito." Seb poked Hudson's stomach, making him laugh. "Stop stalling already. I've been waiting a long time for this too. Marry me. Let's be jinxes together."

Hudson laughed. Seb's dazzling green eyes grew glassy, and Hudson nodded. "Yes, Sebastian. I'll marry you."

Seb stood and grabbed Hudson, then lifted him off his feet, sniggering when Hudson flailed before bursting into laughter. Hudson was going to do his damnedest to make Seb happy each and every day. They'd lost so much time. He wasn't going to lose any more. He cupped Seb's face and kissed him, a part of him afraid this was all a wonderful dream. So long he'd been without his mate, without his beautiful, amazing man.

Hudson pulled back, his smile so wide it hurt his face. "Let's not wait."

"Are you serious?" Seb placed Hudson on his feet. "Don't you want a wedding? You've been so excited about Dex and Sloane's, I thought you'd want the same thing."

"I have everything I want right here," Hudson assured him. "Of course Dex is going to have a big wedding. That's his style. I believe his last words to me on the subject were, and I quote, 'If I don't get at least a six-tier wedding cake with enough sugar to power the next shuttle launch, I'mma cut a bitch.'"

Seb laughed at Hudson's impression of Dex. Hudson's American accent was far better than Dex's English one, or what he attempted to pass off as one. If Dex was going to be a spy, he was going to need some lessons.

"Yeah, that sounds like Dex."

"Please, darling. After all these years, after everything we've been through, I don't think I can wait another day."

"Whatever you want, Lobito. Only problem is, it's almost ten in the evening."

Hudson walked to the coffee table to pick up his phone, a wicked smile on his face. "You seem to forget who our friends are." Hudson tapped away at the screen, then placed the phone to his ear. "Dex? I need your help."

CHAPTER 11

"I... I don't know what to say." Hudson couldn't believe it. He had faith Dex would come through for him, but he'd never expected anything like this.

Dekatria's expansive, yet cozy, roof garden had been transformed into something out of a fairy tale. Twinkling fairy lights and strings of tiny white flowers were wrapped around the awning's pillars, with more lights decorating every potted tree and shrub. White gossamer curtains draped from the rectangular steel frame erected around the roof. White lanterns hung from its steel rods, alternating with more fairy lights. The floor was covered in white flower petals, and bouquets of white roses in white vases on white plinths created an aisle running to the end of the roof, where a small white gazebo stood, along with a priest who smiled warmly at Hudson.

To his left, an intricately decorated cake in white, blue, and gold sat in the center of a table sporting a white tablecloth. Gleaming gold dishes held tantalizing appetizers on one end and champagne flutes, bottles of champagne, and a gold bucket with ice on the other. A young Therian in a tuxedo stood in the corner playing a beautiful melody on his violin.

"You... did all this?"

Dex smiled. He shoved his hands into his trouser pockets and shrugged. "I had help."

"But how?" Hudson brushed his fingers over one of the bouquets of white roses.

"Are you kidding? I called Lou, explained it was for you and Seb. The dude let out a war cry, and his army of perky party people laid siege to this place in less than an hour. Scared the shit out of Bradley. I don't think he'd ever seen Lou in crazy Terminator mode. Like he was sent from the future to put on the perfect last-minute wedding. Austen used his superspy voodoo to get you guys the rings you wanted, Father McByrne, and the marriage license. Cal and Hobbs picked up Julia, Thomas, and Darla. The gang's all here. Everything's ready."

Hudson's eyes brimmed with unshed tears, and he brought Dex into a big hug. "Thank you, Dex. You don't know how much this means to me."

"Yeah, I kinda do." Dex wrapped his arms around Hudson, his voice soft. "You deserve it, buddy. You both do."

"Nina's going to be my maid of honor. Would you... would you be my best man?"

Dex went quiet, and for a moment, Hudson worried he might have said something wrong. He pulled back, chuckling at the big sappy grin on Dex's face. "Did I break you?"

"Shut up." Dex sniffed and wiped a tear from his eye. "I'm not crying. You're crying." He grabbed Hudson in a hug that stole the breath from his lungs.

Hudson laughed as Dex released him. "Is that a yes?"

"Yes, dork. Of course it's a yes." Dex stepped away and took hold of Hudson's elbow. "Come on. Seb's going to be up here with the Hobbs brood any minute now."

Hudson paused, turning to Dex. "Could you bring Thomas downstairs? I need to ask him something."

"You got it."

With one last hug, Hudson hurried downstairs to the second floor, which was being used as a sort of prep room. He tried not to pace, but it was impossible. They were actually going to do this. He was about to become Hudson Hobbs. A small part of him was saddened at the thought of his absent family. He wished they could be here to witness the happiest moment of his life. His heart quickly reminded him that his family *was* here. The Hobbs family, Destructive Delta, and their friends were his family, his pack. Hudson smiled.

The sound of Thomas's electric wheelchair caught his attention, and he beamed brightly at Thomas.

"My, but you look dashing," Hudson said, coming to kneel beside Thomas. He looked very handsome in his black tuxedo, a white rosebud pinned to his lapel.

"Not as good as you," Thomas replied, patting Hudson's arm. "That blue suit is stunning. It really brings out your eyes. I can't wait to see Seb's face when he sees you."

Hudson couldn't help his blush. "Thank you, Thomas." He cleared his throat. "I asked you here in the hopes you might... escort me down the aisle."

Thomas's eyes got glassy, his smile wide. "I would be honored, son."

"Thank you. Do you think we're rushing things?"

"How long have you been in love with Sebastian?" Thomas asked gently.

"Forever, it seems." Hudson couldn't help his smile as he looked down at his fingers. "I think I loved him from the moment I saw him."

Thomas sweetly patted his cheek. "Then I think you're good."

The music coming through the speakers faded into silence. That was his cue. He stood and accompanied Thomas to the lift. Inside, Hudson took a deep breath to calm his nerves. Thomas chuckled and gave Hudson's hand a squeeze.

"You're doing much better than Seb." Thomas shook his head and laughed. "You should have seen him. He didn't know what to do with himself. Kept saying he should check up on you to make sure you were okay. He was pacing a hole in the floor. Rafe and Ethan were about ready to tie him to a chair."

"Is he all right?" Hudson asked, his heart swelling. Even at a time like this, Seb's thoughts were on how Hudson was doing, how he was feeling.

"Rafe threatened to tranq him if he didn't sit his butt down, but then Julia told him he'd have to carry Seb to the altar. Rafe said Ethan would carry him, and Ethan smacked Rafe in the back of the head, and the roughhousing started. You know Seb's not one to miss out on a good brawl with his brothers. It settled his nerves, which I'm pretty sure is what the boys intended, but don't worry, they're still presentable. Their mother would have had their hides otherwise."

Hudson laughed. No matter how big the Hobbs boys got, one stern look from Julia was all it took. The lift doors opened, and Hudson smiled. He held out his arm, and Thomas placed his hand on the crook of Hudson's arm. They made their way to the marked spot in front of the aisle, and Hudson felt his cheeks burn as Seb's wide-eyed expression melted into a look of pure adoration, his smile reaching his dazzling tear-filled eyes. Seb stood at the altar with Rafe and Ethan at his side. Across from them, beside a handsome Dex dressed in a tuxedo, Nina looked stunning in her beautiful pale blue dress. A photographer snapped away, unobtrusive, and Pachelbel's Canon in D began to play. Hudson made his way down the aisle with Thomas.

The white chairs to the right of the plinths were filled with his pack. Lou and Bradley sat at the end, most likely so Lou could keep an eye on everything. He dabbed at his eyes with a handkerchief. Hudson was glad to see Austen had granted his request to stay, even if the man was sure to disappear into the night afterward, like the little Felid ninja he was. It was strange seeing Austen in a suit. He looked good. In front of them, Milena sat holding Rosa's hand, and next to Rosa, Letty had her beau's arm around her shoulders. Army-captain-turned-firefighter James Kirk was a sexy white tiger Therian with a charming smile. His name was the source of much entertainment for Dex. Kirk seemed to take it all in stride.

In front of them sat Calvin, dressed handsomely, his smile wide and his bright blue eyes glassy. He winked at Hudson and gave him a thumbs-up, making Hudson chuckle. Beside him, Darla sniffed. She looked beautiful, her dazzling eyes much like her son's, brimming with unshed tears of joy, and her smile lighting up her face. Next to Darla, Julia held tightly to her handkerchief, a tear rolling down her flushed cheek as she waved at him, the love and happiness in her eyes almost too much for Hudson, and Hudson swallowed hard in an attempt to keep his emotions at bay.

In the front row, Dom cut a rugged picture in his suit. He smiled brightly at Hudson. Sloane sat beside him, sleek and debonair in his tuxedo, and next to him, Ash sniffed—very macho-like of course—and wrapped an arm around Cael, who sported a wide, boyish grin. Sergeant Maddock beamed proudly at Hudson from beside Cael. Everyone who meant everything to him was here. His family.

Just before he reached the altar, Hudson caught a whiff of a familiar scent. This time, instead of sending him into a panic, Hudson smiled. His heart swelled, and tears blurred his vision. The thought might seem silly, but it was his wedding day, and if he wanted to believe Alfie was here in spirit, he had the right.

Thomas kissed the back of Hudson's hand before he went off to join Julia, though not before winking at Seb. Hudson let out a dreamy sigh when Seb reached for him, and everyone chuckled. Hudson couldn't help it. Seb looked incredible in his gray three-piece suit and matching tie. It accentuated his broad shoulders and expansive chest. His green eyes sparkled, and that roguish grin Hudson loved so much had the butterflies in his stomach fluttering wildly.

They faced each other, Hudson's hands in Seb's larger, stronger ones. The music softened, and Father McByrne began the ceremony. It was beautiful, unlike anything Hudson could have imagined. The Therian's lyrical voice spoke of undying love, a future of togetherness, friendship, loyalty, and laughter. As Hudson and Seb faced an uncertain future, riddled with challenges, and—unbeknown to Father McByrne—most likely bullets, they gripped each other tight, knowing whatever came their way, they would persevere, together. They came close to giving in to their emotions and tears on more than one occasion, but they laughed softly instead and continued until the rings were exchanged.

Hudson's ring was a simple narrow silver band, but inside the word *Lobito* was engraved in scripted letters. It filled Hudson's heart with joy, and judging by the tear that rolled down Seb's cheek, Hudson would hazard a guess his mate was pleased with the engraved inscription in his own ring. No matter what happened, those two words would never change.

Always yours.

Father McByrne pronounced them married, and everyone cheered as Seb grabbed Hudson and dipped him. Hudson laughed, holding on tight as Seb kissed him. The sweet, tender kiss soon gave way to a heated one, and their family and friends whooped.

Seb chuckled and lifted Hudson back. He kissed Hudson's cheek before murmuring in his ear, "Always yours, Lobito."

"Always," Hudson replied, turning his face to kiss Seb again. He smiled up at Seb and placed a hand to his cheek. "Forever isn't long enough, darling."

Seb took Hudson's hand and placed it to his lips for a kiss. "Guess we'll just have to make the most of every moment."

They were rushed by their friends and family, hugs and kisses all around, before the music picked up, and the roof was transformed into a dance floor before Hudson had a chance to blink. Lou was certainly a force to be reckoned with. Everyone talked and laughed, teased, and ate good food. Hudson and Seb cut the cake, and unsurprisingly Dex ended up with a face full of frosting thanks to Ash. Seb's deep rumble of a laugh was the sweetest sound Hudson had ever heard. He realized he'd never been happier than he was at that moment.

They stuffed themselves full of delicious cake. Lou's catering was exquisite. It was extraordinary how quickly the man was able to pull all this together. Hudson tried his hardest not to laugh when Dex said he wanted a donut wedding cake. He was rather certain Dex was joking, but the look on poor Lou's face said Lou didn't think so.

"I would sooner walk into a bear Therian sex club naked and covered in honey than allow that monstrosity near a wedding."

Dex blinked at him. "First, I had no idea you were so kinky. Second, I'm the groom. It's my wedding. You're supposed to give me what I want."

Lou arched an eyebrow at him. "If you were any other client, yes. As it's you, the answer is a resounding no."

They all laughed, and Dex flipped them off before he was distracted by more food.

"Congratulations, both of you." Maddock gave each of them a fierce hug. "It's time for me to head off and leave the festivities to the youngsters."

"Thank you for coming." Hudson beamed at him before turning to Darla, Julia, and Thomas, who were also getting ready to go. This was more activity than Thomas was used to, and Hudson understood. The fact he'd been here for the ceremony was more than Hudson could have hoped for. Thomas was astounding.

"You call me if you need anything," Hudson told them, and they promised they would. Julia gave a sniff, and Hudson brought her into his embrace, letting his cheek rest against her head.

"My darling," Julia said, squeezing Hudson tight. "I'm so happy you're home."

Hudson closed his eyes, basking in her maternal love before he released her to hug Darla and then Thomas. Rafe was taking them home, his body starting to ache from all the physical exertion. Nina looked torn, and Rafe told her to stay, but Hudson could see she was worried about Rafe, so he kissed her cheek and insisted she accompany her boyfriend.

"He needs you," Hudson whispered in her ear. "I'll always be here for you."

Nina threw her arms around him and hugged him tight. She kissed his cheek, murmuring a sweet thank-you before waving good-bye to everyone.

After eating his weight in flaky minipastries, Dex dragged Hudson and Seb onto the dance floor. As per Dex's request, or most likely sneakiness, they were confronted with every typical wedding party dance, from the hustle to the electric slide, but there was nothing, nothing like seeing Ash trying to dance to something Dex referred to as Gangnam Style. Seb laughed so hard he was crying, and Dex was on the floor gasping for breath. Thankfully, Ash had drunk enough champagne he just flipped them off and called Dex a giant dork.

Hudson's feet hurt from all the dancing, and his face was sore from laughing so much, but he kept going. Everyone was having such a wonderful time. He hadn't seen his friends in such good spirits in a long time. Dom asked Hudson to dance, and Hudson accepted.

"You have a very sappy smile on your face," Hudson commented, laughing when Dom blushed. He wasn't one to get bashful or sentimental.

"I can't help it. My boy's happy, and that's all I wanted for him. For you guys. He's nuts about you."

"I'll tell you a little secret." Hudson leaned in to whisper. "I'm rather fond of him too."

Dom chuckled and shook his head. "You two are such nerds. You belong together."

Hudson thought so too. "Thank you, again, for saving my life."

"Don't mention it," Dom grumbled. Hudson laughed, and Dom shook his head. "No, really, don't mention it. Your husband keeps giving me these funny looks since it happened."

Husband. Hudson certainly liked the sound of that. He glanced over at Seb, who was grinning wide at them.

"See?" Dom turned his gaze back to Hudson. "It's creeping me out, man."

Hudson laughed. "He's just grateful. Don't worry, I'm certain he'll be back to threatening you with imminent demise in no time."

"Good." Dom nodded curtly, as if the matter was settled. Hudson wondered if Dom knew how sweet he and Seb were, always griping and growling at each other, but the moment one of them was hurt or in trouble, they were fussing over each other like a couple of mother hens. It was adorable.

Soon Hudson had danced with almost everyone, and by the end of the evening, only Lou, Bradley, Dex, and Sloane were left. The sun was rising, and they all sat, each huddled with their sweetheart as the sky changed colors. Hudson stroked Seb's nape, his tie a casualty of a conga line gone terribly wrong. It started off well, but ended with everyone on their arses. Unsurprisingly, Dex and Ash were the culprits.

Lou and Bradley excused themselves, going off with the pretense of checking on things downstairs, but Hudson had a feeling they just wanted to get a little frisky now the festivities were over.

Seb stretched. He kissed the top of Hudson's head before getting up, his suit jacket long since removed and lying on the back of his chair. His sleeves were rolled up to his elbows, the top buttons of his white shirt undone. Heavens, but he looked gorgeous. "I need to hit the little tiger's room. I'll be right back."

Hudson chuckled and smacked Seb's arse as he passed in front of him. Seb swatted his hand playfully, his grin wicked.

"Hey now. None of that until the honeymoon."

Hudson scoffed. "Who are you trying to kid, Sebastian? All I have to do is look at you and you'll drop your trousers."

Sloane laughed and jutted a thumb in Dex's direction. "Sounds like someone I know."

"Please," Dex said with a snicker. A mischievous gleam came into his eyes as he tapped the end of Sloane's nose. "You know you love it when I make you *purr*."

Sloane cleared his throat, his cheeks going rosy.

Seb laughed on his way to the stairs, and Dex turned to Hudson. "So where are you guys going on your honeymoon?"

"Hmm, I'm not sure. We haven't really discussed it. Perhaps a lovely cabin up in the mountains, where we could run in our Therian forms and get cozy in front of the fire. What about you two? Have you decided where you're going?"

"Somewhere in Europe," Sloane said before poking Dex playfully in his side, making him squirm. "Dex can't seem to make up his mind."

"Europe is a big place, man. Preferably somewhere we won't freeze our balls off."

Sloane nodded. "I agree."

They chatted about various places in Europe, and Hudson offered his opinion of the many cities he'd visited before moving to the States. Dex and Sloane seemed in agreement over the weather. They wanted to swim together, and Sloane wanted somewhere Therian-friendly.

Hudson glanced over at the door to the stairs. "I wonder what could be taking him so long?"

"He's a big guy," Dex said with a shrug. "And he did eat a whole lot of food. Just saying."

Sloane groaned, and Hudson blinked at him. "I'm... not sure how to respond to that."

"Welcome to my world," Sloane muttered before shaking his head at Dex, his amber eyes lighting up with amusement. "Babe, I don't think you and Hudson have reached that stage in your relationship." That earned him a playful punch in the shoulder. "I keep telling you. No one wants to discuss bowel movements with you."

"Dude, the guy spends most of his days examining corpses. You're telling me he's going to get grossed out by a little poo talk?"

"He's right," Hudson agreed. "Though I have no notion as to why you'd wish to discuss my husband's bowel movements."

"Husband. Aw." Dex put his hand to his heart.

"You're such a softie," Hudson told Dex as he stood. "I'm going to go check on him." He left Dex and Sloane to their debate on how far along in a relationship people had to be before certain bodily functions should be discussed, and headed downstairs. Maybe Seb stopped to chat with Lou and Bradley. When he reached the second floor, his heart plummeted. Seb lay sprawled on his back in the center of the floor, gasping for breath.

"Seb!" Hudson ran over and dropped to his knees, then cupped Seb's reddened face. Seb's lips were turning purple, his eyes wide and filled with fear. "Oh God, Sebastian, please."

Hudson checked Seb's airway, but there was no obstruction. Seb's pupils were blown, and he made horrible wheezing sounds as he tried to breathe. Checking him over, Hudson couldn't find any signs of an abrasion, cut, injection, nothing. Despite the redness in his face, there was no swelling, and Seb didn't have any allergies they knew of. The symptoms were all over the place, and Hudson was having a difficult time figuring out what was causing Seb's rapidly deteriorating condition.

Seb's fingers curled around Hudson's arms, digging into his flesh, his eyes going wider. He was trying to speak, but that was only making things worse. Was it poison? Whatever it was, it was working its way through his system. "Hold on, darling. I'm going to—"

Hudson was jerked to his feet and spun around to face a large lion Therian dressed in a black military uniform, one Hudson was unfamiliar with. He'd opened his mouth to ask the man what the hell he'd done to Seb, when he noticed several other Therians dressed the same enter the room. How did they get into Dekatria? *Oh God, Lou, Bradley.... Please let them be okay.*

"You're coming with us, Dr. Colbourn."

"The hell I am," Hudson spat. He pulled back a fist, only to be spun around, an arm thrown around his neck in a chokehold. He glanced over at Seb, who had been trying to roll over when one of the men kicked him in the stomach. "No! Please. I'll do whatever you want. Just help him!"

"I'm afraid we can't let your husband live. So sorry about the honeymoon."

"You son of a bitch, what did you do to him?" Hudson's fangs elongated as he clawed at the lion Therian's arm. "If he dies, you're going to have to kill me too, because I'm going to tear your throat out!"

"Easy, little wolf. This will be over before you know it. Well, over for him. You're too valuable to our boss. For now," the man sneered. He clamped a hand over Hudson's mouth as one of the other men approached with a syringe. "Nice and quiet now, Doc. Let's not alert your friends, or we're going to have to kill them too."

Hudson bit down on the flesh of the man's gloved hand, earning him a snarl and enough room to thrust his elbow back. With the man's tactical vest, it did little, but Hudson freed his mouth long enough to scream Dex's name. Few knew that Dex's hearing was better than all the Therians in this room. Combined.

"Whatever happens next is on your hands, Doctor. We wanted to do this the easy way."

The door behind the bar slammed open, and a man wearing a black mask and blue suit came out shooting. A bullet hit Hudson's captor in the forehead. The man crumpled, and the uniformed Therians scrambled. Hudson dropped to the floor as bullets tore the room apart. He crawled over to Seb, who lay on his side, his eyes glazing over.

"Please, darling. You can't leave me. Stay with me." Hudson pulled out his phone, but he had no signal. "Bloody wankers!" The bastards surely had something to do with it.

Seb grabbed Hudson's collar and jerked him down just before a uniformed Therian flew over them, smashing through the door leading to the corridor. *Bollocks.* Looking back, Hudson smiled at Dex beating the pulp out of another one of their attackers, Sloane at his back, claws out, and fangs elongated.

Someone grabbed Hudson's wrist, and he found himself staring into piercing blue eyes.

"Here," the man growled, thrusting something into Hudson's hand and tapping Seb's neck. It was a Therian injector. Dozens of questions vied for Hudson's attention, but he didn't waste time on those. Trusting a masked man who could very well be handing him Seb's death sentence was madness, but Seb was already dying. Going with his gut, Hudson pressed the injector to Seb's neck, said a little prayer, and pulled the trigger. Seb arched his back violently, his body going into spasms before his mouth opened and a fierce cry tore from his lips. Hudson tossed the injector aside and cupped Seb's face. The red was subsiding, and he gasped, breathing in deep, air finally making it into his lungs.

The man in the suit hadn't moved from Hudson's side, skillfully and elegantly beating into submission anyone who drew close. His movements were calculated, precise, as if he were simply swatting a pesky fly. More men must have been waiting downstairs, because they flocked up the stairs in droves. Seb groaned, and Hudson put his arm around Seb's back, getting ready to help him up, when half a dozen Therians headed in their direction, ready to take aim. Seb coughed and wheezed as he pushed at Hudson.

"Go, get… out… of here."

"Are you mad? I'm not leaving you."

The man in the suit unbuttoned his jacket and pulled out the two firearms tucked into the double shoulder holster attached to the harness strapped around him. He fired, one bullet per Therian, never hesitating, never missing.

"Go," the man ordered Hudson.

"I'm not leaving him," Hudson spat back. It would be a cold day in hell before he left Seb behind. Dex and Sloane were busy with four Therians they'd unarmed, and Hudson was surprised by the ferocity and skill with which they fended off the intruders. They'd certainly not learned those moves at the THIRDS. The two worked together, Dex using Sloane's bigger, heavier frame to jump off, leaping in the air and coming down with a fist against a larger Therian's head. The man crumbled to the floor with one blow.

"Always so bloody stubborn," the man grumbled under his breath, but Hudson heard him. He was English.

Oh God, is it possible…? "Wolf?"

The man grunted, and Hudson turned to Seb, who was sitting up. "We need to get you away from here." Seb was still weak, but thankfully he was alive. Wolf had saved Seb's life. How? Why? A boom shook the floor, causing dust to come down from the roof and smoke to spread through the room. Hudson fell onto Seb as the men rained down around them. Coughing, and waving the gray smoke from in front of his face, Hudson glared up at Wolf.

"Did you just use an explosive device in here?"

Wolf shrugged, his blue eyes alight with amusement. "Just a little one."

"You're out of your mind." Hudson was hardly about to admit it had been effective. The room was littered with unconscious and dead Therians.

Wolf winked at Hudson before taking off. Only he never made it to the door. Dex slammed a fist into Wolf's face. He staggered back, and before he could get his bearings, Dex tackled him to the floor.

"Dex, wait!" Hudson scrambled to his feet. "He saved Seb's life!"

Dex and Wolf tussled, and Dex snagged a hold of Wolf's mask and tugged it off. He straddled Wolf and raised a fist to punch him, but Hudson caught his arm.

"Hudson, what the hell—"

Hudson imagined it was the look on his face that froze Dex. And that's what Hudson felt was happening to the world around him. In a room strewn with bodies, men who'd come to kidnap him and kill Seb, nothing shook Hudson like the sight before him.

"Alfie?"

The air was sucked out of the room as Alfie smiled warmly at him.

"Hello, little brother."

CHAPTER 12

DEX LOOKED from Hudson to the man they knew as Wolf, then back to Hudson.

"Please tell me I didn't hear what I thought I did." Dex quickly got up and grabbed Hudson's arm. "Hudson, buddy? You gotta say something."

"Lou and Bradley." Hudson was almost afraid to ask.

"Are fine. Taking a little nap in the broom closet. They would have been killed when those Makhai goons showed up." Wolf—Alfie stood and brushed off his suit. He was bigger than Hudson remembered. Stronger. More… muscular. His jaw was still clean-shaven and chiseled, his hair and thick eyebrows as pitch-black as Hudson's. He looked as ruggedly handsome and elegant as always. His suit undoubtedly expensive. Alfie's blue eyes filled with remorse, and Hudson took a tentative step toward him. He hesitantly reached out, unable to believe his brother was there, in front of him, in the flesh. Alive.

"Oh fuck," Dex groaned. "You know what? I see it now. The resemblance. The thought had crossed my mind when you were talking about your brother that night in Dekatria, but you said Alfie was dead."

"He is—*was*," Hudson murmured softly. "How?" He blinked back his tears, his head and heart in turmoil. "You… you're alive."

"I am," Alfie replied quietly.

Disbelief gave way to anger, and it erupted. "You're alive?" Hudson punched his brother across his stupidly square jaw. Dex threw his arms around Hudson before he could hit Alfie again. "You fucking wanker! You've been alive all this time? How could you do this to me? I thought I was losing my bloody mind, catching your scent in Dex's house, then everywhere else, and it's because you were there. You've been there the whole pissing time!"

Alfie rubbed his jaw. "Just, let me explain, little brother."

"Please do, Alfie," Hudson spat out. "Tell me how I saw your corpse on that slab of steel. How you let me mourn your loss for years, let me live with the guilt, let me think I was going crazy."

"First of all," Alfie stated calmly, "don't call me Alfie. It doesn't really strike fear into the hearts of my enemies."

"Piss off!"

Alfie pursed his lips. "Fair enough. Actually, I don't use my name because of you."

"So you could carry on the deception?" Hudson shrugged off Dex's hold and crossed his arms over his chest, his narrowed eyes on his brother. "And if you've been around me as long as TIN says, why could I only smell you some of the time?"

"I needed to protect you. I have many enemies." Alfie cringed. "Perhaps slightly more than many."

Dex let out a snort. "You don't say."

Alfie ignored him. "If they discovered I had a brother, or family, they would have come after you. As for my scent, well, I have this nifty little device that masks my scent with any scent I choose. It's quite extraordinary. The only one of its kind available on the black market. However, it is rather temperamental, and the scent cartridge is not perpetual, at least not yet. Anyway, the blasted thing isn't as stable as it should be. The cartridge has a habit of running dry at the most inopportune moments, which is why you caught my scent. I can hardly stop in the middle of a physical altercation to fiddle with it."

Seb slipped his hand around Hudson's waist, his frown on Alfie, who didn't seem put off by it. He held his hand out to Seb.

"I don't think we've been properly introduced, what with my being dead and all."

Seb looked confused. He hesitantly shook Alfie's hand. "Uh, nice to meet you. I think. I'm not really sure what I'm supposed to feel here."

Alfie patted Seb's hand before releasing him. "Quite all right, mate. Thank you for taking care of my little brother. You're a good man." He turned back to Hudson, his expression softening. "I know this won't help, but you were never supposed to find out I was alive. It was safer for you. You would have gone on grieving the loss of a brother you loved and looked up to."

Hudson didn't know what to say or what to feel, for that matter. How long had he wished for things to be different, for Alfie to be alive, but how much of his brother remained in the man before him? Wolf had done so many terrible things.

"Of course, all my hard work protecting you has been undone," Alfie said, winking at Dex, "thanks to your friend here." He wagged his gloved finger at Dex. "I have half a mind to be cross with you, love, and I would be, if you weren't so blasted pretty."

"I'm going to kill you, you son of a bitch!" Dex launched himself at Alfie, but Hudson caught him. He was sorely tempted to let Dex have at Alfie, but he had too many questions that needed answers. Dex could dismember Alfie some other time.

"Dex, please."

Alfie took a step back and rolled his eyes. "You're not still sore at me, are you?"

"You tortured me!" Dex was practically vibrating with anger, his face crimson. Hudson worried Dex was about to give himself a heart attack.

"In my defense," Alfie stated smoothly, "I was getting paid ridiculous amounts of money for it. Also, I wanted to see if you were as impressive in person. I was not disappointed."

Dex's jaw dropped. "What? That's not—are you insane?"

"Here's a suggestion. How about we kiss and make up. Forget the whole nasty ordeal. I'll forget you hit me with a steel chair, and you forget, you know...." Alfie snapped his fingers as if trying to recall.

"The part where you tortured me?" Dex finished for him.

"Yes, that. It was the Makhai who hired me, by the way. In case you hadn't figured it out yet. What do you say?"

"Um, how about no, and kiss my ass," Dex replied through his teeth.

"I would prefer more private quarters for that."

Dex shook his head in disbelief. "Oh my God, he's like a British Austen."

"I think it's adorable you're comparing me to Sparks's little pet."

"Watch your mouth," Sloane growled.

Sloane's calm surprised Hudson, and he wondered if Sloane was simply biding his time or thinking up one of the many ways in which he could make "Wolf" suffer.

"Ah, so sorry, mate. I forgot you have a soft spot for the little runt." A wicked gleam came onto Alfie's face, one Hudson remembered all too well. He ran his tongue over his bottom lip. "No hard feelings about my kissing your fiancé? I couldn't resist. Those lips are just sinful."

Sloane let out a growl as he made a grab for Alfie, but Seb held him back, a hand to his chest, his green eyes pleading.

"You've got to be kidding me," Sloane hissed, his amber eyes boring into Seb's. "That asshole tortured Dex!"

Seb looked to Hudson for help. He was clearly conflicted. Hudson was too. Instead of talking to Sloane, who was glaring daggers at Alfie, Hudson turned to Dex.

"Please, Dex. I know I have no right to ask this of you, but could I… could I please get some time with him? I'm certain he deserves your wrath, and what he did to you was reprehensible, but he's my brother. I lost him once. I can't lose him again. Not yet."

Dex cursed under his breath before rubbing his hands over his face and letting out a frustrated grunt. "Fine."

"Dex—"

"It's fine, Sloane," Dex assured him, a hand to his cheek. "It's fine. There will be plenty of time to kick his ass later."

"It's not fine, Dex. The man *tortured* you. He was going to kill you." Sloane shook his head. "I'm sorry, Hudson, but I can't just turn the other cheek. Wolf might look like your brother, but whoever your brother was, he obviously died at the bottom of the cliff that day." Sloane's hard gaze moved from him to Alfie, and he spoke through his teeth. "*That* is not Alfie."

Hudson flinched. He swallowed hard and nodded. "You have every right to feel as you do, Sloane. And maybe you're right. Maybe he's not the brother I remember, but he saved Seb's life, and he saved me from Trent." He turned to Alfie. "That was you, wasn't it?" A thought occurred to Hudson, and his blood ran cold. "You sent those texts to my phone knowing Seb would go after Trent. Why would you do such a thing?"

Alfie averted his gaze, as if reluctant to say. Seeming to get his thoughts together, he turned his attention back to Hudson. "TIN and the Makhai want you. As much as I loathe to admit it, TIN can protect you. As an asset, you're far too important to lose. Once you're sworn in, the chances of the Makhai getting their hands on you drops significantly. Your man turned TIN down. That was a mistake."

Seb took a step toward Alfie. "You wanted us to join TIN, so you made sure it happened by using your own brother?"

Alfie's hard gaze was unwavering as he addressed Seb. "Trent provided the perfect opportunity. He had to pay for what he did to Hudson, and who better to serve that justice than you? I knew you wouldn't kill him, but you weren't above causing him pain. I've been watching you for some time,

Sebastian. I know what you're willing to sacrifice for my brother, which is why I didn't use Hudson. I used you. Did you really think TIN wouldn't be watching you? Waiting for the perfect opportunity to bring you in? Why do you think you were picked up by TIN operatives? I set the bait, you took it, and TIN got what they wanted."

"But…." Dex shook his head, confused. "You hate TIN. Why would you want your brother to join them?" He thrust a finger at Hudson. "We are so having a long conversation about that later, by the way."

"My relationship with TIN is… complicated," Alfie said, wrinkling his nose.

"And Trent's friends?" Seb asked. "What did you do with them."

The speed with which the warmth drained from Alfie's eyes, replaced by a dead coldness that made Hudson shiver, was frightening. "They're rapists and abusers. I simply put them where they belong. With the trash. Or rather, six feet beneath it."

"Jesus." Sloane shook his head in disbelief. "You see? The man is a fucking sociopath!"

Alfie let out an indelicate snort. "How very self-righteous. Been there, done that, and all I got was blown up. No thank you. Have fun with TIN. Try not to get stabbed through the heart, or in the back." He put his hand on Hudson's shoulder. "We will talk, little brother. I promise. Right now, I really must dash. The flying monkeys are about to land."

"You're leaving?" Hudson snatched hold of Alfie's sleeve, surprised when Alfie didn't pull away.

"Like hell he is," Sloane growled, reaching out to grab Alfie's arm.

Alfie moved so quick, Hudson barely had a chance to react before Alfie had Sloane's arm pulled up against his back, a knife in his hand against Sloane's throat.

"Stop," Hudson pleaded with Alfie, only to be ignored.

"Manners." Alfie tsked at Sloane. "My little brother was speaking to me. It's been an awfully long time, so I'm sure you can understand how frustrating it is to have you interrupt. You boys really need to polish up that etiquette if you're going to work for TIN. Now, will you be a good little boy if I let you go?"

"Fuck you," Sloane spat out.

Alfie sighed. He moved his gaze to Hudson. "Forgive me, but I really must go. We'll chat. I'm not going anywhere just yet." He moved the knife and pushed Sloane into Dex before making a run for the stairs heading to the roof garden. They took off after him, but by the time they got up there, he was gone.

"I fucking hate it when they do that," Dex shrieked before kicking a chair for good measure. Just as Alfie had warned, TIN arrived within seconds, headed by Sparks.

"Where is he?"

Dex thrust a hand at the sky. "Your guess is as good as mine."

She peered at him, and he scoffed.

"Right, because he was gonna hang around for cake and champagne."

"What did he say to you?" Sparks asked Dex.

Hudson clenched his jaw and averted his gaze. Dex had to hand Alfie over. Who knew what horrid things his brother had done. Hudson couldn't blame Dex. He just wished he had a few minutes with Alfie to understand, to know how he'd become what he was.

"He said those guys were from the Makhai, and that they're the ones who hired him to kidnap and torture me."

"That's it?" Sparks eyed him. "Wolf showed up to save Hudson and get rid of the Makhai out of the kindness of his blackened heart?"

Dex shrugged. "I don't know. The guy does whatever he fucking feels like. You know more about him than we do. I'm sure you've got your theories. Care to share them with us?"

Sparks studied them all before turning on her high heels and heading for the door. "We'll get this place cleaned up. If you see or hear from Wolf again, I expect to be notified."

"Sure thing," Dex said with a salute.

"Oh, and, Hudson, Seb, congratulations on your marriage," she called out over her shoulder. "Take the day off. Put in a request for time off for your honeymoon when you're ready."

Once she was gone, Dex turned to Hudson, speaking quietly. "I'm sorry you're in the middle of this fucked-up situation, and I can't say I'm happy about it, but I understand." He placed a hand on Hudson's shoulder. "I hate the guy. I won't lie. I *really* hate him. But he saved your life, and Seb's. He's done some things that could be perceived as not entirely shitty. I can't guarantee I won't beat the shit out of him or turn him over to the proper authorities, but I promise you, I won't kill him." Sloane huffed, and Dex chuckled. "And neither will Sloane," Dex added.

"What?" Sloane shook his head, and Dex arched an eyebrow at him. Sloane threw his hands up. "Fine. I won't kill him." He narrowed his eyes. "But I reserve the right to cause him some serious pain."

Hudson nodded. "Fair enough." His brother had brought that on himself. All he wanted was a chance, a chance he never thought he'd have. "Thank you. Both of you."

Dex hugged him, and Sloane did the same, patting his back, a soft "I'm sorry" making him feel a little better about what his friends were sacrificing for him. Dex ordered him and Seb to go home, that they'd check on Lou and Bradley and see that the cleaning crew was let in to take care of Dekatria after TIN was gone.

Seb slipped his hand into Hudson's and led him out of Dekatria. A cab was waiting for them, and inside the car, Hudson snuggled close. He didn't even know where to start. How long had his brother really been around, keeping an eye on him, stepping in without him even realizing it?

"I think he saved me twice," Seb murmured.

Hudson held him close. "What do you mean?"

Seb paused, as if uncertain he should say, but a heartbeat later, he sighed. "The night of Dex and Sloane's engagement party, I was so pissed off when I left that I walked out into the middle of the street without realizing. I would have gotten hit by a speeding car if someone hadn't pulled me back. But whoever it was disappeared before I could get a look at them."

Hudson pulled back, his heart squeezing in his chest. "Oh God, what if you'd been hit by that car? It would have been my fault."

"No, baby." Seb cupped his cheek and kissed his brow. "It would have been on me. I let my anger cloud my judgment, and because of it, I put myself in danger. My actions are not your fault. Do you understand?"

Hudson nodded.

"I didn't tell you to upset you. I'm thinking that maybe the guy who pulled me back was Alfie. I think he's been keeping an eye on both of us. Things have happened that at the time I couldn't explain, so I just brushed them off. But now that I know he's been around, it all makes sense."

"So what are you saying?"

Seb was clearly trying to tell him something but appeared hesitant. "Look, I'm not excusing what the guy has done as Wolf or that he's a different person from who he was as Alfie, but maybe… maybe Alfie isn't completely gone. Maybe you're the only thing that's kept him from losing himself completely."

He had so much to think about, and he was far too exhausted for that at the moment, but Seb was right. Hudson had a chance to at least speak with Alfie, or what was left of him, and from what he'd witnessed, perhaps there was some hope for them.

ONCE THEY were in Seb's house, Hudson sat on the couch, with Seb dropping down beside him.

"So… where do you want to go on our honeymoon? Let's make it somewhere far, far away from here."

Hudson stared at Seb. He opened his mouth to speak, then closed it. When he opened his mouth again, only a laugh came out. Oh dear heavens, he'd lost his bloody mind. No matter how hard he tried, he couldn't stop laughing.

Seb pulled him close, his deep laughter warming Hudson's soul.

"Fuck," Seb said through a laugh, letting his head fall back against the couch as he ran a hand up and down Hudson's arm. "You couldn't make this shit up, Lobito."

Hudson straddled Seb's lap and cupped his face. His expression fell, and he stroked Seb's cheeks with his thumb. "We almost lost each other today. Let's not make this a habit, ay?"

Seb wrapped his arms around Hudson's waist, his smile falling away. "I don't think I've ever been so scared. Actually, that's not true. I was fucking beside myself when you were down in that elevator shaft, and in the hospital after you were shot. This time, though, all I kept thinking was that it was too soon. I'd only just gotten you back." Seb took Hudson's hand, the one with his wedding ring, and kissed it. "I wanted more time with my husband. So much more time."

Hudson kissed him, putting his heart and soul into the kiss, letting him know how much he loved him, how happy he was to be here with him, married to him, bonded to him. Their lives had gone from madness to lunacy, but as long as Seb was with him, it would be all right.

"I love you so much," he breathed against Seb's lips. He let his forehead press against Seb's.

"I love you too," Seb replied. "Whatever happens, whatever storms come our way, I will be here, holding your hand, facing it with you. Now let's go upstairs and consummate our marriage, Dr. Hobbs. I'll let you take my temperature with your big, thick thermometer."

Hudson slinked off Seb's lap and crooked his finger at him. "Before we play doctor, we have a couple of stag nights to make up for."

"Is that so?" Seb's smile turned sinful as he stood, his eyes filled with fiery lust. "How about I be the predator, and you be the stag?" With a feral growl, he scooped Hudson up and carried him toward the stairs.

Hudson wrapped his arms around Seb's neck, his heart overflowing with love for his mate, his husband, the man who owned his heart, and everything he was.

Always yours.

CHARLIE COCHET is an author by day and artist by night. Always quick to succumb to the whispers of her wayward muse, no star is out of reach when following her passion. From adventurous agents and sexy shifters to society gentlemen and hardboiled detectives, there's bound to be plenty of mischief for her heroes to find themselves in—and plenty of romance, too!

Currently residing in Central Florida, Charlie is at the beck and call of a rascally Doxiepoo bent on world domination. When she isn't writing, she can usually be found reading, drawing, or watching movies. She runs on coffee, thrives on music, and loves to hear from readers.

Website: www.charliecochet.com
Blog: www.charliecochet.com/blog
E-mail: charlie@charliecochet.com
Facebook: www.facebook.com/charliecochet
Twitter: @charliecochet
Tumblr: www.charliecochet.tumblr.com
Pinterest: www.pinterest.com/charliecochet
Goodreads: www.goodreads.com/CharlieCochet
Instagram: www.instagram.com/charliecochet
THIRDS HQ: www.thirdshq.com

THIRDS

THIRDS

RETRO
RADIO
89.3
FM

HELL
&
HIGH
WATER

CHARLIE
COCHET

THIRDS: Book One

When homicide detective Dexter J. Daley's testimony helps send his partner away for murder, the consequences—and the media frenzy—aren't far behind. He soon finds himself sans boyfriend, sans friends, and, after an unpleasant encounter in a parking garage after the trial, he's lucky he doesn't find himself sans teeth. Dex fears he'll get transferred from the Human Police Force's Sixth Precinct, or worse, get dismissed. Instead, his adoptive father—a sergeant at the Therian-Human Intelligence Recon Defense Squadron otherwise known as the THIRDS—pulls a few strings, and Dex gets recruited as a Defense Agent.

Dex is determined to get his life back on track and eager to get started in his new job. But his first meeting with Team Leader Sloane Brodie, who also happens to be his new jaguar Therian partner, turns disastrous. When the team is called to investigate the murders of three HumaniTherian activists, it soon becomes clear to Dex that getting his partner and the rest of the tightknit team to accept him will be a lot harder than catching the killer—and every bit as dangerous.

www.dreamspinnerpress.com

CHARLIE
COCHET

THIRDS

BLOOD
&
THUNDER

Sequel to *Hell & High Water*
THIRDS: Book Two

When a series of bombs go off in a Therian youth center, injuring members of THIRDS Team Destructive Delta and causing a rift between agents Dexter J. Daley and Sloane Brodie, peace seems unattainable. Especially when a new and frightening group, the Order of Adrasteia, appears to always be a step ahead. With panic and intolerance spreading and streets becoming littered with the Order's propaganda, hostility between Humans and Therians grows daily. Dex and Sloane, along with the rest of the team, are determined to take down the Order and restore peace, not to mention settle a personal score. But the deeper the team investigates the bombings, the more they believe there's a more sinister motive than a desire to shed blood and spread chaos.

Discovering the frightful truth behind the Order's intent forces Sloane to confront secrets from a past he thought he'd left behind for good, a past that could not only destroy him and his career, but also the reputation of the organization that made him all he is today. Now more than ever, Dex and Sloane need each other, and, along with trust, the strength of their bond will mean the difference between justice and all-out war.

www.dreamspinnerpress.com

CHARLIE COCHET

BRODIE

THIRDS

RACK&RUIN

Sequel to *Blood & Thunder*
THIRDS: Book Three

New York City's streets are more dangerous than ever with the leaderless Order of Adrasteia and the Ikelos Coalition, a newly emerged Therian group, at war. Innocent civilians are caught in the crossfire and although the THIRDS round up more and more members of the Order in the hopes of keeping the volatile group from reorganizing, the members of the Coalition continue to escape and wreak havoc in the name of vigilante justice.

Worse yet, someone inside the THIRDS has been feeding the Coalition information. It's up to Destructive Delta to draw out the mole and put an end to the war before anyone else gets hurt. But to get the job done, the team will have to work through the aftereffects of the Therian Youth Center bombing. A skirmish with Coalition members leads Agent Dexter J. Daley to a shocking discovery and suddenly it becomes clear that the random violence isn't so random. There's more going on than Dex and Sloane originally believed, and their fiery partnership is put to the test. As the case takes an explosive turn, Dex and Sloane are in danger of losing more than their relationship.

www.dreamspinnerpress.com

CHARLIE COCHET

RISE&FALL

THIRDS: Book Four

After an attack by the Coalition leaves THIRDS Team Leader Sloane Brodie critically injured, agent Dexter J. Daley swears to make Beck Hogan pay for what he's done. But Dex's plans for retribution are short-lived. With Ash still on leave with his own injuries, Sloane in the hospital, and Destructive Delta in the Coalition's crosshairs, Lieutenant Sparks isn't taking any chances. Dex's team is pulled from the case, with the investigation handed to Team Leader Sebastian Hobbs. Dex refuses to stand by while another team goes after Hogan, and decides to put his old HPF detective skills to work to find Hogan before Theta Destructive, no matter the cost.

With a lengthy and painful recovery ahead of him, the last thing Sloane needs is his partner out scouring the city, especially when the lies—however well-intentioned—begin to spiral out of control. Sloane is all too familiar with the desire to retaliate, but some things are more important, like the man who's pledged to stand beside him. As Dex starts down a dark path, it's up to Sloane to show him what's at stake, and finally put a name to what's in his heart.

www.dreamspinnerpress.com

CHARLIE COCHET

AGAINST THE GRAIN

Sequel to *Rise & Fall*
THIRDS: Book Five

As the fiercest Defense Agent at the THIRDS, Destructive Delta's Ash Keeler is foul-mouthed and foul-tempered. But his hard-lined approach always yields results, evident by his recent infiltration of the Coalition. Thanks to Ash's skills and the help of his team, they finally put an end to the murdering extremist group for good, though not before Ash takes a bullet to save teammate Cael Maddock. As a result, Ash's secrets start to surface, and he can no longer ignore what's in his heart.

Cael Maddock is no stranger to heartache. As a Recon Agent for Destructive Delta, he has successfully maneuvered through the urban jungle that is New York City, picking up his own scars along the way. Yet nothing he's ever faced has been more of a challenge than the heart of Ash Keeler, his supposedly straight teammate. Being in love isn't the only danger he and Ash face as wounds reopen and new secrets emerge, forcing them to question old loyalties.

www.dreamspinnerpress.com